Beauty and the Beast: The Ultimate Collection

Brothers Grimm, Ludwig Bechstein, Joseph Jacobs, Charles Lamb, Carl Colshorn, J. Christian Bay, Otto Sutermeister, Sidney Oldall Addy, Gabrielle-Suzanne Barbot de Villeneuve, Leonard Magnus

CONTENTS

BEAUTY AND THE BEAST

THE ULTIMATE COLLECTION

CUPID AND PSYCHE

BY LUCIUS APULEIUS

FROM THOMAS BULFINCH, *THE AGE OF FABLE; OR, STORIES OF GODS AND HEROES*, 1855

A certain king and queen had three daughters. The charms of the two elder were more than common, but the beauty of the youngest was so wonderful that the poverty of language is unable to express its due praise. The fame of her beauty was so great that strangers from neighboring countries came in crowds to enjoy the sight, and looked on her with amazement, paying her that homage which is due only to Venus herself. In fact Venus found her altars deserted, while men turned their devotion to this young virgin. As she passed along, the people sang her praises, and strewed her way with chaplets and flowers.

This homage to the exaltation of a mortal gave great offense to the real Venus. Shaking her ambrosial locks with indignation, she exclaimed, "Am I then to be eclipsed in my honors by a mortal girl? In vain then did that royal shepherd, whose judgment was approved by Jove himself, give me the palm of beauty over my illustrious rivals, Pallas and Juno. But she shall not so quietly usurp my honors. I will give her cause to repent of so unlawful a beauty."

Thereupon she calls her winged son Cupid, mischievous enough in his own nature, and rouses and provokes him yet more by her complaints. She points out Psyche to him and says, "My dear son, punish that contumacious beauty; give your mother a revenge as sweet as her injuries are great; infuse into the bosom of that haughty girl a passion for some low, mean, unworthy being, so that she may reap a mortification as great as her present exultation and triumph."

Cupid prepared to obey the commands of his mother. There are two fountains in Venus's garden, one of sweet waters, the other of bitter. Cupid filled two amber vases, one from each fountain, and suspending them from the top of his quiver, hastened to the chamber of Psyche, whom he found asleep. He shed a few drops from the bitter fountain over her lips, though the sight of her almost moved him to pity; then touched her side with the point of his arrow. At the touch she awoke, and opened eyes upon Cupid (himself invisible), which so startled him that in his confusion he wounded himself with his own arrow. Heedless of his wound, his whole thought now was to repair the mischief he had done, and he poured the balmy drops of joy over all her silken ringlets.

Psyche, henceforth frowned upon by Venus, derived no benefit from all her

1

charms. True, all eyes were cast eagerly upon her, and every mouth spoke her praises; but neither king, royal youth, nor plebeian presented himself to demand her in marriage. Her two elder sisters of moderate charms had now long been married to two royal princes; but Psyche, in her lonely apartment, deplored her solitude, sick of that beauty which, while it procured abundance of flattery, had failed to awaken love.

Her parents, afraid that they had unwittingly incurred the anger of the gods, consulted the oracle of Apollo, and received this answer, "The virgin is destined for the bride of no mortal lover. Her future husband awaits her on the top of the mountain. He is a monster whom neither gods nor men can resist."

This dreadful decree of the oracle filled all the people with dismay, and her parents abandoned themselves to grief. But Psyche said, "Why, my dear parents, do you now lament me? You should rather have grieved when the people showered upon me undeserved honors, and with one voice called me a Venus. I now perceive that I am a victim to that name. I submit. Lead me to that rock to which my unhappy fate has destined me."

Accordingly, all things being prepared, the royal maid took her place in the procession, which more resembled a funeral than a nuptial pomp, and with her parents, amid the lamentations of the people, ascended the mountain, on the summit of which they left her alone, and with sorrowful hearts returned home.

While Psyche stood on the ridge of the mountain, panting with fear and with eyes full of tears, the gentle Zephyr raised her from the earth and bore her with an easy motion into a flowery dale. By degrees her mind became composed, and she laid herself down on the grassy bank to sleep.

When she awoke refreshed with sleep, she looked round and beheld near a pleasant grove of tall and stately trees. She entered it, and in the midst discovered a fountain, sending forth clear and crystal waters, and fast by, a magnificent palace whose august front impressed the spectator that it was not the work of mortal hands, but the happy retreat of some god. Drawn by admiration and wonder, she approached the building and ventured to enter.

Every object she met filled her with pleasure and amazement. Golden pillars supported the vaulted roof, and the walls were enriched with carvings and paintings representing beasts of the chase and rural scenes, adapted to delight the eye of the beholder. Proceeding onward, she perceived that besides the apartments of state there were others filled with all manner of treasures, and beautiful and precious productions of nature and art.

While her eyes were thus occupied, a voice addressed her, though she saw no one, uttering these words, "Sovereign lady, all that you see is yours. We whose voices you hear are your servants and shall obey all your commands with our utmost care and diligence. Retire, therefore, to your chamber and repose on your bed of down, and when you see fit, repair to the bath. Supper awaits you in the adjoining alcove when it pleases you to take your seat there."

Psyche gave ear to the admonitions of her vocal attendants, and after repose and the refreshment of the bath, seated herself in the alcove, where a table immediately presented itself, without any visible aid from waiters or servants, and covered with the greatest delicacies of food and the most nectareous wines. Her ears too were feasted with music from invisible performers; of whom one sang,

2

another played on the lute, and all closed in the wonderful harmony of a full chorus.

She had not yet seen her destined husband. He came only in the hours of darkness and fled before the dawn of morning, but his accents were full of love, and inspired a like passion in her. She often begged him to stay and let her behold him, but he would not consent. On the contrary he charged her to make no attempt to see him, for it was his pleasure, for the best of reasons, to keep concealed.

"Why should you wish to behold me?" he said. "Have you any doubt of my love? Have you any wish ungratified? If you saw me, perhaps you would fear me, perhaps adore me, but all I ask of you is to love me. I would rather you would love me as an equal than adore me as a god."

This reasoning somewhat quieted Psyche for a time, and while the novelty lasted she felt quite happy. But at length the thought of her parents, left in ignorance of her fate, and of her sisters, precluded from sharing with her the delights of her situation, preyed on her mind and made her begin to feel her palace as but a splendid prison. When her husband came one night, she told him her distress, and at last drew from him an unwilling consent that her sisters should be brought to see her.

So, calling Zephyr, she acquainted him with her husband's commands, and he, promptly obedient, soon brought them across the mountain down to their sister's valley. They embraced her and she returned their caresses.

"Come," said Psyche, "enter with me my house and refresh yourselves with whatever your sister has to offer."

Then taking their hands she led them into her golden palace, and committed them to the care of her numerous train of attendant voices, to refresh them in her baths and at her table, and to show them all her treasures. The view of these celestial delights caused envy to enter their bosoms, at seeing their young sister possessed of such state and splendor, so much exceeding their own.

They asked her numberless questions, among others what sort of a person her husband was. Psyche replied that he was a beautiful youth, who generally spent the daytime in hunting upon the mountains.

The sisters, not satisfied with this reply, soon made her confess that she had never seen him. Then they proceeded to fill her bosom with dark suspicions. "Call to mind," they said, "the Pythian oracle that declared you destined to marry a direful and tremendous monster. The inhabitants of this valley say that your husband is a terrible and monstrous serpent, who nourishes you for a while with dainties that he may by and by devour you. Take our advice. Provide yourself with a lamp and a sharp knife; put them in concealment that your husband may not discover them, and when he is sound asleep, slip out of bed, bring forth your lamp, and see for yourself whether what they say is true or not. If it is, hesitate not to cut off the monster's head, and thereby recover your liberty."

Psyche resisted these persuasions as well as she could, but they did not fail to have their effect on her mind, and when her sisters were gone, their words and her own curiosity were too strong for her to resist. So she prepared her lamp and a sharp knife, and hid them out of sight of her husband. When he had fallen into his first sleep, she silently rose and uncovering her lamp beheld not a hideous monster, but the most beautiful and charming of the gods, with his golden ringlets wandering over his snowy neck and crimson cheek, with two dewy wings on his shoulders, whiter than snow, and with shining feathers like the tender blossoms of spring.

As she leaned the lamp over to have a better view of his face, a drop of burning oil fell on the shoulder of the god. Startled, he opened his eyes and fixed them upon her. Then, without saying a word, he spread his white wings and flew out of the window. Psyche, in vain endeavoring to follow him, fell from the window to the ground.

Cupid, beholding her as she lay in the dust, stopped his flight for an instant and said, "Oh foolish Psyche, is it thus you repay my love? After I disobeyed my mother's commands and made you my wife, will you think me a monster and cut off my head? But go; return to your sisters, whose advice you seem to think preferable to mine. I inflict no other punishment on you than to leave you for ever. Love cannot dwell with suspicion." So saying, he fled away, leaving poor Psyche prostrate on the ground, filling the place with mournful lamentations.

When she had recovered some degree of composure she looked around her, but the palace and gardens had vanished, and she found herself in the open field not far from the city where her sisters dwelt. She repaired thither and told them the whole story of her misfortunes, at which, pretending to grieve, those spiteful creatures inwardly rejoiced.

"For now," said they, "he will perhaps choose one of us." With this idea, without saying a word of her intentions, each of them rose early the next morning and ascended the mountain, and having reached the top, called upon Zephyr to receive her and bear her to his lord; then leaping up, and not being sustained by Zephyr, fell down the precipice and was dashed to pieces.

Psyche meanwhile wandered day and night, without food or repose, in search of her husband. Casting her eyes on a lofty mountain having on its brow a magnificent temple, she sighed and said to herself, "Perhaps my love, my lord, inhabits there," and directed her steps thither.

She had no sooner entered than she saw heaps of corn, some in loose ears and some in sheaves, with mingled ears of barley. Scattered about, lay sickles and rakes, and all the instruments of harvest, without order, as if thrown carelessly out of the weary reapers' hands in the sultry hours of the day.

This unseemly confusion the pious Psyche put an end to, by separating and sorting everything to its proper place and kind, believing that she ought to neglect none of the gods, but endeavor by her piety to engage them all in her behalf. The holy Ceres, whose temple it was, finding her so religiously employed, thus spoke to her, "Oh Psyche, truly worthy of our pity, though I cannot shield you from the frowns of Venus, yet I can teach you how best to allay her displeasure. Go, then, and voluntarily surrender yourself to your lady and sovereign, and try by modesty and submission to win her forgiveness, and perhaps her favor will restore you the husband you have lost."

Psyche obeyed the commands of Ceres and took her way to the temple of Venus, endeavoring to fortify her mind and ruminating on what she should say and how best propitiate the angry goddess, feeling that the issue was doubtful and perhaps fatal.

Venus received her with angry countenance. "Most undutiful and faithless of servants," said she, "do you at last remember that you really have a mistress? Or have you rather come to see your sick husband, yet laid up of the wound given him by his loving wife? You are so ill favored and disagreeable that the only way you can merit your lover must be by dint of industry and diligence. I will make trial of your housewifery." Then she ordered Psyche to be led to the storehouse of her temple, where was laid up a great quantity of wheat, barley, millet, vetches, beans, and lentils prepared for food for her pigeons, and said, "Take and separate all these grains, putting all of the same kind in a parcel by themselves, and see that you get it done before evening." Then Venus departed and left her to her task.

But Psyche, in a perfect consternation at the enormous work, sat stupid and silent, without moving a finger to the inextricable heap.

While she sat despairing, Cupid stirred up the little ant, a native of the fields, to take compassion on her. The leader of the anthill, followed by whole hosts of his six-legged subjects, approached the heap, and with the utmost diligence taking grain by grain, they separated the pile, sorting each kind to its parcel; and when it was all done, they vanished out of sight in a moment.

Venus at the approach of twilight returned from the banquet of the gods, breathing odors and crowned with roses. Seeing the task done, she exclaimed, "This is no work of yours, wicked one, but his, whom to your own and his misfortune you have enticed." So saying, she threw her a piece of black bread for her supper and went away.

Next morning Venus ordered Psyche to be called and said to her, "Behold yonder grove which stretches along the margin of the water. There you will find sheep feeding without a shepherd, with golden-shining fleeces on their backs. Go, fetch me a sample of that precious wool gathered from every one of their fleeces."

Psyche obediently went to the riverside, prepared to do her best to execute the command. But the river god inspired the reeds with harmonious murmurs, which seemed to say, "Oh maiden, severely tried, tempt not the dangerous flood, nor venture among the formidable rams on the other side, for as long as they are under the influence of the rising sun, they burn with a cruel rage to destroy mortals with their sharp horns or rude teeth. But when the noontide sun has driven the cattle to the shade, and the serene spirit of the flood has lulled them to rest, you may then cross in safety, and you will find the woolly gold sticking to the bushes and the trunks of the trees."

Thus the compassionate river god gave Psyche instructions how to accomplish her task, and by observing his directions she soon returned to Venus with her arms full of the golden fleece; but she received not the approbation of her implacable mistress, who said, "I know very well it is by none of your own doings that you have succeeded in this task, and I am not satisfied yet that you have any capacity to make yourself useful. But I have another task for you. Here, take this box and go your way to the infernal shades, and give this box to Proserpine and say, 'My mistress Venus desires you to send her a little of your beauty, for in tending her sick son she has lost some of her own.' Be not too long on your errand, for I must paint myself with it to appear at the circle of the gods and goddesses this evening."

Psyche was now satisfied that her destruction was at hand, being obliged to go with her own feet directly down to Erebus. Wherefore, to make no delay of what was not to be avoided, she goes to the top of a high tower to precipitate herself headlong, thus to descend the shortest way to the shades below. But a voice from the tower said to her, "Why, poor unlucky girl, do you design to put an end to your days in so dreadful a manner? And what cowardice makes you sink under this last danger who have been so miraculously supported in all your former?" Then the voice told her how by a certain cave she might reach the realms of Pluto, and how to avoid all the dangers of the road, to pass by Cerberus, the three-headed dog, and prevail on Charon, the ferryman, to take her across the black river and bring her back again. But the voice added, "When Proserpine has given you the box filled with her beauty, of all things this is chiefly to be observed by you, that you never once open or look into the box nor allow your curiosity to pry into the treasure of the beauty of the goddesses."

Psyche, encouraged by this advice, obeyed it in all things, and taking heed to her ways traveled safely to the kingdom of Pluto. She was admitted to the palace of Proserpine, and without accepting the delicate seat or delicious banquet that was offered her, but contented with coarse bread for her food, she delivered her message from Venus. Presently the box was returned to her, shut and filled with the precious commodity. Then she returned the way she came, and glad was she to come out once more into the light of day.

But having got so far successfully through her dangerous task a longing desire seized her to examine the contents of the box. "What," said she, "shall I, the carrier of this divine beauty, not take the least bit to put on my cheeks to appear to more advantage in the eyes of my beloved husband!" So she carefully opened the box, but found nothing there of any beauty at all, but an infernal and truly Stygian sleep, which being thus set free from its prison, took possession of her, and she fell down in the midst of the road, a sleepy corpse without sense or motion.

But Cupid, being now recovered from his wound, and not able longer to bear the absence of his beloved Psyche, slipping through the smallest crack of the window of his chamber which happened to be left open, flew to the spot where Psyche lay, and gathering up the sleep from her body closed it again in the box, and waked Psyche with a light touch of one of his arrows. "Again," said he, "have you almost perished by the same curiosity. But now perform exactly the task imposed on you by my mother, and I will take care of the rest."

Then Cupid, as swift as lightning penetrating the heights of heaven, presented himself before Jupiter with his supplication. Jupiter lent a favoring ear, and pleaded the cause of the lovers so earnestly with Venus that he won her consent. On this he sent Mercury to bring Psyche up to the heavenly assembly, and when she arrived, handing her a cup of ambrosia, he said, "Drink this, Psyche, and be immortal; nor shall Cupid ever break away from the knot in which he is tied, but these nuptials shall be perpetual."

Thus Psyche became at last united to Cupid, and in due time they had a daughter born to them whose name was Pleasure.

BEAUTY AND THE BEAST

BY

JOSEPH JACOBS

FROM VARIOUS EUROPEAN SOURCES, FIRST PUBLISHED IN
EUROPA'S FAIRY BOOK, 1916

There was once a merchant that had three daughters, and he loved them better than himself. Now it happened that he had to go a long journey to buy some goods, and when he was just starting he said to them, "What shall I bring you back, my dears?"

And the eldest daughter asked to have a necklace; and the second daughter wished to have a gold chain; but the youngest daughter said, "Bring back yourself, papa, and that is what I want the most."

"Nonsense, child," said her father, "you must say something that I may remember to bring back for you."

"So," she said, "then bring me back a rose, father."

Well, the merchant went on his journey and did his business and bought a pearl necklace for his eldest daughter, and a gold chain for his second daughter; but he knew it was no use getting a rose for the youngest while he was so far away because it would fade before he got home. So he made up his mind he would get a rose for her the day he got near his house.

When all his merchanting was done he rode off home and forgot all about the rose till he was near his house; then he suddenly remembered what he had promised his youngest daughter, and looked about to see if he could find a rose. Near where he had stopped he saw a great garden, and getting off his horse he wandered about in it till he found a lovely rosebush; and he plucked the most beautiful rose he could see on it. At that moment he heard a crash like thunder, and looking around he saw a huge monster -- two tusks in his mouth and fiery eyes surrounded by bristles, and horns coming out of its head and spreading over its back.

"Mortal," said the beast, "who told you you might pluck my roses?"

"Please, sir," said the merchant in fear and terror for his life, "I promised my daughter to bring her home a rose and forgot about it till the last moment, and then I saw your beautiful garden and thought you would not miss a single rose, or else I would have asked your permission."

"Thieving is thieving," said the beast, "whether it be a rose or a diamond; your life is forfeit."

The merchant fell on his knees and begged for his life for the sake of his three daughters who had none but him to support them.

"Well, mortal, well," said the beast, "I grant your life on one condition: Seven days from now you must bring this youngest daughter of yours, for whose sake you have broken into my garden, and leave her here in your stead. Otherwise swear that you will return and place yourself at my disposal."

So the merchant swore, and taking his rose mounted his horse and rode home.

As soon as he got into his house his daughters came rushing round him, clapping their hands and showing their joy in every way, and soon he gave the necklace to his eldest daughter, the chain to his second daughter, and then he gave the rose to his youngest, and as he gave it he sighed.

"Oh, thank you, father," they all cried.

But the youngest said, "Why did you sigh so deeply when you gave me my rose?"

"Later on I will tell you," said the merchant.

So for several days they lived happily together, though the merchant wandered about gloomy and sad, and nothing his daughters could do would cheer him up till at last he took his youngest daughter aside and said to her, "Bella, do you love your father?"

"Of course I do, father, of course I do."

"Well, now you have a chance of showing it"; and then he told her of all that had occurred with the beast when he got the rose for her. Bella was very sad, as you can well think, and then she said, "Oh, father, it was all on account of me that you fell into the power of this beast; so I will go with you to him; perhaps he will do me no harm; but even if he does -- better harm to me than evil to my dear father."

So next day the merchant took Bella behind him on his horse, as was the custom in those days, and rode off to the dwelling of the beast. And when he got there and they alighted from his horse the doors of the house opened, and what do you think they saw there! Nothing. So they went up the steps and went through the hall, and went into the dining room, and there they saw a table spread with all manner of beautiful glasses and plates and dishes and napery, with plenty to eat upon it. So they waited and they waited, thinking that the owner of the house would appear, till at last the merchant said, "Let's sit down and see what will happen then." And when they sat down invisible hands passed them things to eat and to drink, and they ate and drank to their heart's content. And when they arose from the table it arose too and disappeared through the door as if it were being carried by invisible servants.

Suddenly there appeared before them the beast who said to the merchant, "Is this your youngest daughter?"

And when he had said that it was, he said, "Is she willing to stop here with me?"

And then he looked at Bella who said, in a trembling voice, "Yes, sir."

"Well, no harm shall befall you." With that he led the merchant down to his horse and told him he might come that day each week to visit his daughter. Then the beast returned to Bella and said to her, "This house with all that therein is yours; if you desire aught, clap your hands and say the word and it shall be brought unto you." And with that he made a sort of bow and went away.

So Bella lived on in the home with the beast and was waited on by invisible servants and had whatever she liked to eat and to drink; but she soon got tired of the solitude and, next day, when the beast came to her, though he looked so terrible, she had been so well treated that she had lost a great deal of her terror of him. So they spoke together about the garden and about the house and about her father's business and about all manner of things, so that Bella lost altogether her fear of the beast. Shortly afterwards her father came to see her and found her quite happy, and he felt much less dread of her fate at the hands of the beast.

So it went on for many days, Bella seeing and talking to the beast every day, till she got quite to like him, until one day the beast did not come at his usual time, just after the midday meal, and Bella quite missed him. So she wandered about the garden trying to find him, calling out his name, but received no reply. At last she came to the rosebush from which her father had plucked the rose, and there, under it, what do you think she saw! There was the beast lying huddled up without any life or motion. Then Bella was sorry indeed and remembered all the kindness that the beast had shown her; and she threw herself down by it and said, "Oh, Beast, Beast, why did you die? I was getting to love you so much."

No sooner had she said this than the hide of the beast split in two and out came the most handsome young prince who told her that he had been enchanted by a magician and that he could not recover his natural form unless a maiden should, of her own accord, declare that she loved him.

Thereupon the prince sent for the merchant and his daughters, and he was married to Bella, and they all lived happy together ever afterwards.

BEAUTY AND THE BEAST

BY

JEANNE-MARIE LE PRINCE DE BEAUMONT

PUBLISHED IN THE *YOUNG MISSES MAGAZINE, CONTAINING DIALOGUES BETWEEN A GOVERNESS AND SEVERAL YOUNG LADIES OF QUALITY HER SCHOLARS,* BY MADAME PRINCE DE BEAUMONT, 4TH ED., V. 1 (LONDON: C. NOURSE, 1783), PP. 45-67. FIRST PUBLISHED IN 1756 IN FRANCE UNDER THE TITLE MAGASIN DES ENFANS, OU DIALOGUES ENTRE UNE SAGE GOUVERNANTE ET PLUSIEURE DE SES ÉLÈVES. THE FIRST ENGLISH TRANSLATION APPEARED IN 1757.

There was once a very rich merchant, who had six children, three sons, and three daughters; being a man of sense, he spared no cost for their education, but gave them all kinds of masters. His daughters were extremely handsome, especially the youngest. When she was little everybody admired her, and called her "The little Beauty;" so that, as she grew up, she still went by the name of Beauty, which made her sisters very jealous.

The youngest, as she was handsomer, was also better than her sisters. The two eldest had a great deal of pride, because they were rich. They gave themselves ridiculous airs, and would not visit other merchants' daughters, nor keep company with any but persons of quality. They went out every day to parties of pleasure, balls, plays, concerts, and so forth, and they laughed at their youngest sister, because she spent the greatest part of her time in reading good books.

As it was known that they were great fortunes, several eminent merchants made their addresses to them; but the two eldest said, they would never marry, unless they could meet with a duke, or an earl at least. Beauty very civilly thanked them that courted her, and told them she was too young yet to marry, but chose to stay with her father a few years longer.

All at once the merchant lost his whole fortune, excepting a small country house at a great distance from town, and told his children with tears in his eyes, they must go there and work for their living. The two eldest answered, that they would not leave the town, for they had several lovers, who they were sure would be glad to have them, though they had no fortune; but the good ladies were mistaken, for their lovers slighted and forsook them in their poverty. As they were not beloved on account of their pride, everybody said; they do not deserve to be pitied, we are very glad to see their pride humbled, let them go and give themselves quality airs in milking the cows and minding their dairy. But, added they, we are extremely concerned for Beauty, she was such a charming, sweet-tempered creature, spoke so

10

kindly to poor people, and was of such an affable, obliging behavior. Nay, several gentlemen would have married her, though they knew she had not a penny; but she told them she could not think of leaving her poor father in his misfortunes, but was determined to go along with him into the country to comfort and attend him. Poor Beauty at first was sadly grieved at the loss of her fortune; "but," said she to herself, "were I to cry ever so much, that would not make things better, I must try to make myself happy without a fortune."

When they came to their country house, the merchant and his three sons applied themselves to husbandry and tillage; and Beauty rose at four in the morning, and made haste to have the house clean, and dinner ready for the family. In the beginning she found it very difficult, for she had not been used to work as a servant, but in less than two months she grew stronger and healthier than ever. After she had done her work, she read, played on the harpsichord, or else sung whilst she spun.

On the contrary, her two sisters did not know how to spend their time; they got up at ten, and did nothing but saunter about the whole day, lamenting the loss of their fine clothes and acquaintance. "Do but see our youngest sister," said they, one to the other, "what a poor, stupid, mean-spirited creature she is, to be contented with such an unhappy dismal situation."

The good merchant was of quite a different opinion; he knew very well that Beauty outshone her sisters, in her person as well as her mind, and admired her humility and industry, but above all her humility and patience; for her sisters not only left her all the work of the house to do, but insulted her every moment.

The family had lived about a year in this retirement, when the merchant received a letter with an account that a vessel, on board of which he had effects, was safely arrived. This news had liked to have turned the heads of the two eldest daughters, who immediately flattered themselves with the hopes of returning to town, for they were quite weary of a country life; and when they saw their father ready to set out, they begged of him to buy them new gowns, headdresses, ribbons, and all manner of trifles; but Beauty asked for nothing for she thought to herself, that all the money her father was going to receive, would scarce be sufficient to purchase everything her sisters wanted.

"What will you have, Beauty?" said her father.

"Since you have the goodness to think of me," answered she, "be so kind to bring me a rose, for as none grows hereabouts, they are a kind of rarity." Not that Beauty cared for a rose, but she asked for something, lest she should seem by her example to condemn her sisters' conduct, who would have said she did it only to look particular.

The good man went on his journey, but when he came there, they went to law with him about the merchandise, and after a great deal of trouble and pains to no purpose, he came back as poor as before.

He was within thirty miles of his own house, thinking on the pleasure he should have in seeing his children again, when going through a large forest he lost himself. It rained and snowed terribly; besides, the wind was so high, that it threw him twice off his horse, and night coming on, he began to apprehend being either starved to death with cold and hunger, or else devoured by the wolves, whom he heard howling all round him, when, on a sudden, looking through a long walk of trees, he saw a light at some distance, and going on a little farther perceived it came from a palace illuminated from top to bottom. The merchant returned God thanks for this happy discovery, and hastened to the place, but was greatly surprised at not meeting with any one in the outer courts. His horse followed him, and seeing a large stable open, went in, and finding both hay and oats, the poor beast, who was almost famished, fell to eating very heartily; the merchant tied him up to the manger, and walking towards the house, where he saw no one, but entering into a large hall, he found a good fire, and a table plentifully set out with but one cover laid. As he was wet quite through with the rain and snow, he drew near the fire to dry himself. "I hope," said he, "the master of the house, or his servants will excuse the liberty I take; I suppose it will not be long before some of them appear."

He waited a considerable time, until it struck eleven, and still nobody came. At last he was so hungry that he could stay no longer, but took a chicken, and ate it in two mouthfuls, trembling all the while. After this he drank a few glasses of wine, and growing more courageous he went out of the hall, and crossed through several grand apartments with magnificent furniture, until he came into a chamber, which had an exceeding good bed in it, and as he was very much fatigued, and it was past midnight, he concluded it was best to shut the door, and go to bed.

It was ten the next morning before the merchant waked, and as he was going to rise he was astonished to see a good suit of clothes in the room of his own, which were quite spoiled; certainly, said he, this palace belongs to some kind fairy, who has seen and pitied my distress. He looked through a window, but instead of snow saw the most delightful arbors, interwoven with the beautifullest flowers that were ever beheld. He then returned to the great hall, where he had supped the night before, and found some chocolate ready made on a little table. "Thank you, good Madam Fairy," said he aloud, "for being so careful, as to provide me a breakfast; I am extremely obliged to you for all your favors."

The good man drank his chocolate, and then went to look for his horse, but passing through an arbor of roses he remembered Beauty's request to him, and gathered a branch on which were several; immediately he heard a great noise, and saw such a frightful Beast coming towards him, that he was ready to faint away.

"You are very ungrateful," said the Beast to him, in a terrible voice; "I have saved your life by receiving you into my castle, and, in return, you steal my roses, which I value beyond any thing in the universe, but you shall die for it; I give you but a quarter of an hour to prepare yourself, and say your prayers."

The merchant fell on his knees, and lifted up both his hands, "My lord," said he, "I beseech you to forgive me, indeed I had no intention to offend in gathering a rose for one of my daughters, who desired me to bring her one."

"My name is not My Lord," replied the monster, "but Beast; I don't love compliments, not I. I like people to speak as they think; and so do not imagine, I am to be moved by any of your flattering speeches. But you say you have got daughters. I will forgive you, on condition that one of them come willingly, and suffer for you. Let me have no words, but go about your business, and swear that if your daughter refuse to die in your stead, you will return within three months."

The merchant had no mind to sacrifice his daughters to the ugly monster, but he thought, in obtaining this respite, he should have the satisfaction of seeing them once more, so he promised, upon oath, he would return, and the Beast told him he might set out when he pleased, "but," added he, "you shall not depart empty handed; go back to the room where you lay, and you will see a great empty chest; fill it with whatever you like best, and I will send it to your home," and at the same time Beast withdrew.

"Well," said the good man to himself, "if I must die, I shall have the comfort, at least, of leaving something to my poor children." He returned to the bedchamber, and finding a great quantity of broad pieces of gold, he filled the great chest the Beast had mentioned, locked it, and afterwards took his horse out of the stable, leaving the palace with as much grief as he had entered it with joy. The horse, of his own accord, took one of the roads of the forest, and in a few hours the good man was at home.

His children came round him, but instead of receiving their embraces with pleasure, he looked on them, and holding up the branch he had in his hands, he burst into tears. "Here, Beauty," said he, "take these roses, but little do you think how dear they are like to cost your unhappy father," and then related his fatal adventure. Immediately the two eldest set up lamentable outcries, and said all manner of ill-natured things to Beauty, who did not cry at all.

"Do but see the pride of that little wretch," said they; "she would not ask for fine clothes, as we did; but no truly, Miss wanted to distinguish herself, so now she will be the death of our poor father, and yet she does not so much as shed a tear."

"Why should I," answered Beauty, "it would be very needless, for my father shall not suffer upon my account, since the monster will accept of one of his daughters, I will deliver myself up to all his fury, and I am very happy in thinking that my death will save my father's life, and be a proof of my tender love for him."

"No, sister," said her three brothers, "that shall not be, we will go find the monster, and either kill him, or perish in the attempt."

"Do not imagine any such thing, my sons," said the merchant, "Beast's power is so great, that I have no hopes of your overcoming him. I am charmed with Beauty's kind and generous offer, but I cannot yield to it. I am old, and have not long to live, so can only loose a few years, which I regret for your sakes alone, my dear children."

"Indeed father," said Beauty, "you shall not go to the palace without me, you cannot hinder me from following you." It was to no purpose all they could say. Beauty still insisted on setting out for the fine palace, and her sisters were delighted at it, for her virtue and amiable qualities made them envious and jealous.

The merchant was so afflicted at the thoughts of losing his daughter, that he had quite forgot the chest full of gold, but at night when he retired to rest, no sooner had he shut his chamber door, than, to his great astonishment, he found it by his bedside; he was determined, however, not to tell his children, that he was grown rich, because they would have wanted to return to town, and he was resolved not to leave the country; but he trusted Beauty with the secret, who informed him, that two gentlemen came in his absence, and courted her sisters; she begged her father to consent to their marriage, and give them fortunes, for she was so good, that she loved them and forgave heartily all their ill usage. These wicked creatures rubbed their eyes with an onion to force some tears when they parted with their sister, but her brothers were really concerned. Beauty was the only one who did not shed tears at parting, because she would not increase their uneasiness.

The horse took the direct road to the palace, and towards evening they perceived it illuminated as at first. The horse went of himself into the stable, and the good man and his daughter came into the great hall, where they found a table splendidly served up, and two covers. The merchant had no heart to eat, but Beauty, endeavoring to appear cheerful, sat down to table, and helped him. "Afterwards," thought she to herself, "Beast surely has a mind to fatten me before he eats me, since he provides such plentiful entertainment." When they had supped they heard a great noise, and the merchant, all in tears, bid his poor child, farewell, for he thought Beast was coming. Beauty was sadly terrified at his horrid form, but she took courage as well as she could, and the monster having asked her if she came willingly; "ye -- e -- es," said she, trembling.

The beast responded, "You are very good, and I am greatly obliged to you; honest man, go your ways tomorrow morning, but never think of coming here again."

"Farewell Beauty, farewell Beast," answered he, and immediately the monster withdrew. "Oh, daughter," said the merchant, embracing Beauty, "I am almost frightened to death, believe me, you had better go back, and let me stay here."

"No, father," said Beauty, in a resolute tone, "you shall set out tomorrow morning, and leave me to the care and protection of providence." They went to bed, and thought they should not close their eyes all night; but scarce were they laid down, than they fell fast asleep, and Beauty dreamed, a fine lady came, and said to her, "I am content, Beauty, with your good will, this good action of yours in giving up your own life to save your father's shall not go unrewarded." Beauty waked, and told her father her dream, and though it helped to comfort him a little, yet he could not help crying bitterly, when he took leave of his dear child.

As soon as he was gone, Beauty sat down in the great hall, and fell a crying likewise; but as she was mistress of a great deal of resolution, she recommended herself to God, and resolved not to be uneasy the little time she had to live; for she firmly believed Beast would eat her up that night.

However, she thought she might as well walk about until then, and view this fine castle, which she could not help admiring; it was a delightful pleasant place, and she was extremely surprised at seeing a door, over which was written, "Beauty's Apartment." She opened it hastily, and was quite dazzled with the magnificence that reigned throughout; but what chiefly took up her attention, was a large library, a harpsichord, and several music books. "Well," said she to herself, "I see they will not let my time hang heavy upon my hands for want of amusement." Then she reflected, "Were I but to stay here a day, there would not have been all these preparations." This consideration inspired her with fresh courage; and opening the library she took a book, and read these words, in letters of gold:

Welcome Beauty, banish fear,

You are queen and mistress here.

Speak your wishes, speak your will,

Swift obedience meets them still.

"Alas," said she, with a sigh, "there is nothing I desire so much as to see my poor father, and know what he is doing." She had no sooner said this, when casting her eyes on a great looking glass, to her great amazement, she saw her own home, where her father arrived with a very dejected countenance. Her sisters went to meet him, and notwithstanding their endeavors to appear sorrowful, their joy, felt for having got rid of their sister, was visible in every feature. A moment after, everything disappeared, and Beauty's apprehensions at this proof of Beast's complaisance.

At noon she found dinner ready, and while at table, was entertained with an excellent concert of music, though without seeing anybody. But at night, as she was going to sit down to supper, she heard the noise Beast made, and could not help being sadly terrified. "Beauty," said the monster, "will you give me leave to see you sup?"

"That is as you please," answered Beauty trembling.

"No," replied the Beast, "you alone are mistress here; you need only bid me gone, if my presence is troublesome, and I will immediately withdraw. But, tell me, do not you think me very ugly?"

"That is true," said Beauty, "for I cannot tell a lie, but I believe you are very good natured."

"So I am," said the monster, "but then, besides my ugliness, I have no sense; I know very well, that I am a poor, silly, stupid creature."

"'Tis no sign of folly to think so," replied Beauty, "for never did fool know this, or had so humble a conceit of his own understanding."

"Eat then, Beauty," said the monster, "and endeavor to amuse yourself in your palace, for everything here is yours, and I should be very uneasy, if you were not happy."

"You are very obliging," answered Beauty, "I own I am pleased with your kindness, and when I consider that, your deformity scarce appears."

"Yes, yes," said the Beast, "my heart is good, but still I am a monster."

"Among mankind," says Beauty, "there are many that deserve that name more than you, and I prefer you, just as you are, to those, who, under a human form, hide a treacherous, corrupt, and ungrateful heart."

"If I had sense enough," replied the Beast, "I would make a fine compliment to thank you, but I am so dull, that I can only say, I am greatly obliged to you."

Beauty ate a hearty supper, and had almost conquered her dread of the monster; but she had like to have fainted away, when he said to her, "Beauty, will you be my wife?"

She was some time before she dared answer, for she was afraid of making him angry, if she refused. At last, however, she said trembling, "no Beast." Immediately the poor monster went to sigh, and hissed so frightfully, that the whole palace echoed. But Beauty soon recovered her fright, for Beast having said, in a mournful voice, "then farewell, Beauty," left the room; and only turned back, now and then, to look at her as he went out.

When Beauty was alone, she felt a great deal of compassion for poor Beast. "Alas," said she, "'tis thousand pities, anything so good natured should be so ugly."

Beauty spent three months very contentedly in the palace. Every evening Beast paid her a visit, and talked to her, during supper, very rationally, with plain good common sense, but never with what the world calls wit; and Beauty daily discovered some valuable qualifications in the monster, and seeing him often had so accustomed her to his deformity, that, far from dreading the time of his visit, she would often look on her watch to see when it would be nine, for the Beast never missed coming at that hour. There was but one thing that gave Beauty any concern, which was, that every night, before she went to bed, the monster always asked her, if she would be his wife. One day she said to him, "Beast, you make me very uneasy, I wish I could consent to marry you, but I am too sincere to make you believe that will ever happen; I shall always esteem you as a friend, endeavor to be satisfied with this."

"I must," said the Beast, "for, alas! I know too well my own misfortune, but then I love you with the tenderest affection. However, I ought to think myself happy, that you will stay here; promise me never to leave me."

Beauty blushed at these words; she had seen in her glass, that her father had pined himself sick for the loss of her, and she longed to see him again. "I could," answered she, "indeed, promise never to leave you entirely, but I have so great a desire to see my father, that I shall fret to death, if you refuse me that satisfaction."

"I had rather die myself," said the monster, "than give you the least uneasiness. I will send you to your father, you shall remain with him, and poor Beast will die with grief."

"No," said Beauty, weeping, "I love you too well to be the cause of your death. I give you my promise to return in a week. You have shown me that my sisters are married, and my brothers gone to the army; only let me stay a week with my father, as he is alone."

"You shall be there tomorrow morning," said the Beast, "but remember your promise. You need only lay your ring on a table before you go to bed, when you have a mind to come back. Farewell Beauty." Beast sighed, as usual, bidding her good night, and Beauty went to bed very sad at seeing him so afflicted. When she waked the next morning, she found herself at her father's, and having rung a little bell, that was by her bedside, she saw the maid come, who, the moment she saw her, gave a loud shriek, at which the good man ran up stairs, and thought he should have died with joy to see his dear daughter again. He held her fast locked in his arms above a quarter of an hour. As soon as the first transports were over, Beauty began to think of rising, and was afraid she had no clothes to put on; but the maid told her, that she had just found, in the next room, a large trunk full of gowns, covered with gold and diamonds. Beauty thanked good Beast for his kind care, and taking one of the plainest of them, she intended to make a present of the others to her sisters. She scarce had said so when the trunk disappeared. Her father told her, that Beast insisted on her keeping them herself, and immediately both gowns and trunk came back again.

Beauty dressed herself, and in the meantime they sent to her sisters who hastened thither with their husbands. They were both of them very unhappy. The eldest had married a gentleman, extremely handsome indeed, but so fond of his own person, that he was full of nothing but his own dear self, and neglected his wife. The second had married a man of wit, but he only made use of it to plague and torment everybody, and his wife most of all. Beauty's sisters sickened with envy, when they saw her dressed like a princess, and more beautiful than ever, nor could all her obliging affectionate behavior stifle their jealousy, which was ready to burst when she told them how happy she was. They went down into the garden to vent it in tears; and said one to the other, in what way is this little creature better than us, that she should be so much happier? "Sister," said the oldest, "a thought just strikes my mind; let us endeavor to detain her above a week, and perhaps the silly monster will be so enraged at her for breaking her word, that he will devour her."

"Right, sister," answered the other, "therefore we must show her as much kindness as possible." After they had taken this resolution, they went up, and behaved so affectionately to their sister, that poor Beauty wept for joy. When the week was expired, they cried and tore their hair, and seemed so sorry to part with her, that she promised to stay a week longer.

In the meantime, Beauty could not help reflecting on herself, for the uneasiness she was likely to cause poor Beast, whom she sincerely loved, and really longed to see again. The tenth night she spent at her father's, she dreamed she was in the palace garden, and that she saw Beast extended on the grass plat, who seemed just expiring, and, in a dying voice, reproached her with her ingratitude. Beauty started out of her sleep, and bursting into tears. "Am I not very wicked," said she, "to act so unkindly to Beast, that has studied so much, to please me in everything? Is it his fault if he is so ugly, and has so little sense? He is kind and good, and that is sufficient. Why did I refuse to marry him? I should be happier with the monster than my sisters are with their husbands; it is neither wit, nor a fine person, in a husband, that makes a woman happy, but virtue, sweetness of temper, and complaisance, and Beast has all these valuable qualifications. It is true, I do not feel the tenderness of affection for him, but I find I have the highest gratitude, esteem, and friendship; I will not make him miserable, were I to be so ungrateful I should never forgive myself." Beauty having said this, rose, put her ring on the table, and then laid down again; scarce was she in bed before she fell asleep, and when she waked the next morning, she was overjoyed to find herself in the Beast's palace.

She put on one of her richest suits to please him, and waited for evening with the utmost impatience, at last the wished-for hour came, the clock struck nine, yet no Beast appeared. Beauty then feared she had been the cause of his death; she ran crying and wringing her hands all about the palace, like one in despair; after having sought for him everywhere, she recollected her dream, and flew to the canal in the garden, where she dreamed she saw him. There she found poor Beast stretched out, quite senseless, and, as she imagined, dead. She threw herself upon him without any dread, and finding his heart beat still, she fetched some water from the canal, and poured it on his head. Beast opened his eyes, and said to Beauty, "You forgot your promise, and I was so afflicted for having lost you, that I resolved to starve myself, but since I have the happiness of seeing you once more, I die satisfied."

"No, dear Beast," said Beauty, "you must not die. Live to be my husband; from this moment I give you my hand, and swear to be none but yours. Alas! I thought I had only a friendship for you, but the grief I now feel convinces me, that I cannot live without you." Beauty scarce had pronounced these words, when she saw the palace sparkle with light; and fireworks, instruments of music, everything seemed to give notice of some great event. But nothing could fix her attention; she turned to her dear Beast, for whom she trembled with fear; but how great was her surprise! Beast was disappeared, and she saw, at her feet, one of the loveliest princes that eye ever beheld; who returned her thanks for having put an end to the charm, under which he had so long resembled a Beast. Though this prince was worthy of all her attention, she could not forbear asking where Beast was.

"You see him at your feet, said the prince. A wicked fairy had condemned me to remain under that shape until a beautiful virgin should consent to marry me. The fairy likewise enjoined me to conceal my understanding. There was only you in the world generous enough to be won by the goodness of my temper, and in offering you my crown I can't discharge the obligations I have to you."

Beauty, agreeably surprised, gave the charming prince her hand to rise; they went together into the castle, and Beauty was overjoyed to find, in the great hall, her father and his whole family, whom the beautiful lady, that appeared to her in her dream, had conveyed thither.

"Beauty," said this lady, "come and receive the reward of your judicious choice; you have preferred virtue before either wit or beauty, and deserve to find a person in whom all these qualifications are united. You are going to be a great queen. I hope the throne will not lessen your virtue, or make you forget yourself. As to you, ladies," said the fairy to Beauty's two sisters, "I know your hearts, and all the malice they contain. Become two statues, but, under this transformation, still retain your reason. You shall stand before your sister's palace gate, and be it your punishment to behold her happiness; and it will not be in your power to return to your former state, until you own your faults, but I am very much afraid that you will always remain statues. Pride, anger, gluttony, and idleness are sometimes conquered, but the conversion of a malicious and envious mind is a kind of miracle."

Immediately the fairy gave a stroke with her wand, and in a moment all that were in the hall were transported into the prince's dominions. His subjects received him with joy. He married Beauty, and lived with her many years, and their happiness -- as it was founded on virtue -- was complete.

THE SINGING, SPRINGING LARK

BY

JACOB AND WILHELM GRIMM

GERMANY, 1857

Once upon a time there was a man who was about to set forth on a long journey. At his departure he asked his three daughters what he should bring for them when he returned.

The oldest one wanted pearls, the second one wanted diamonds, but the third one said, "Father dear, I would like a singing, springing lark."

The father said, "Yes, if I can get it, you shall have it." Then kissing all three, he set forth.

Now when the time had come for him to return home, he had bought pearls and diamonds for the two oldest ones, but he had searched everywhere in vain for a singing, springing lark for the youngest one. This made him very sad, for she was his favorite child.

His path led him through a forest, in the middle of which there was a splendid castle. Near the castle there stood a tree, and at the very top of the tree he saw a singing, springing lark.

"Aha, you are just what I have been looking for," he said happily, then told his servant to climb up and catch the little creature.

But as he approached the tree, a lion jumped up from beneath it, shook himself, and roared until the leaves on the trees trembled. "I will eat up anyone who tries to steal my singing, springing lark!" he cried.

The man said, "I did not know that the bird belongs to you. I will make amends for my wrong and ransom myself with a large sum of money. Just spare my life."

The lion said, "Nothing can save you unless you will promise to give me that which first meets you upon your arrival at home. If you will do that, I will grant you your life, and you shall have the bird for your daughter as well."

The man hesitated, saying, "That could be my youngest daughter. She loves me the most, and always runs to meet me when I return home."

The servant, however, was frightened and said, "Why must it be your daughter that meets you? It could also be a cat or a dog."

Then the man let himself be persuaded, took the singing, springing lark, and promised to give the lion whatever should first meet him at home.

When he reached home and entered his house, the first one who met him was none other than his youngest and dearest daughter. She came running up, kissed and hugged him, and when she saw that he had brought with him a singing, springing lark, she was beside herself with joy.

The father, however, could not be glad, but instead began to cry, saying, "My dearest child, I paid dearly for that little bird. To get it I had to promise you to a wild lion, and when he has you he will tear you to pieces and eat you up." Then he told her everything that had happened, and begged her not to go there, come what may.

But she consoled him, saying, "Dearest father, your promise must be kept. I will go there and appease the lion, so that I can return safely to you."

The next morning she had the way pointed out to her, took leave, and in good spirits walked into the woods.

Now the lion was an enchanted prince. By day he was a lion, and all his people became lions with him, but by night they had their natural human form.

On her arrival she was kindly received and led into the castle. When night came, the lion was a handsome man, and their wedding was celebrated with splendor. They lived happily together, remaining awake by night, and sleeping by day.

One day he came and said, "Tomorrow there will be a feast at your father's house, because your oldest sister is getting married. If you would like to go, my lions will take you."

She said yes, that she would like to see her father again, and she went there, accompanied by the lions.

There was great joy when she arrived, for they all believed that she had been torn to pieces by the lion, and was no longer alive. But she told them what a handsome husband she had, and how well off she was. She stayed until the wedding was over, and then went back into the woods.

When the second daughter got married, and she was again invited to the wedding, she said to the lion, "This time I do not want to be alone. You must come with me."

The lion, however, said that that would be too dangerous for him, for if a ray from a burning light were to fall on him there, he would be transformed into a dove, and would have to fly with doves for seven years.

"Oh," she said, "do come with me. I will protect you, and guard you from all light."

So they went together, taking their little child with them as well.

She had a room built there, so strong and thick that no ray of light could penetrate it. He was to sit inside it when the wedding lights were lit. However, the door was made of green wood which split, leaving a little crack that no one noticed.

The wedding was celebrated with splendor, but when the procession returning from the church with all its torches and lights passed by this room, a ray of light no wider than a hair touched the prince, and he was transformed in an instant. And when she came in looking for him, she did not see him, but a white dove was sitting there.

The dove said to her, "For seven years I must fly about into the world. Every seven steps I will let fall a drop of red blood and a white feather. These will show you the way, and if you follow this trail you can redeem me."

Then the dove flew out the door, and she followed him, and every seven steps a drop of red blood and a little white feather fell down showing her the way.

Thus she went further and further into the wide world. She neither looked aside nor rested. When the seven years were almost past, she rejoiced, thinking that they would soon be redeemed, but they were far from it.

One day when she was thus walking onward, no little feather and no drop of red blood fell, and when she raised her eyes the dove had disappeared.

Then she thought, "Humans cannot help you now," so she climbed up to the sun, and said, "You shine into every crack, and over every peak. Have you not seen a little white dove flying?"

"No," said the sun, "I have not seen it, but I will give you a little chest. Open it if you are in great need."

Then she thanked the sun and went on until evening came and the moon was shining. She then asked the moon, "You shine all night, across all the fields and woods. Have you not seen a little white dove flying?"

"No," said the moon, I have not seen it, but I will give you an egg. Break it open if you are in great need."

Then she thanked the moon and went on until the night wind came up and blew against her. She said to it, "You blow over all the trees and under all the leaves. Have you not seen a little white dove flying."

"No," said the night wind, "I have not seen it, but I will ask the three other winds. Perhaps they have seen it."

The east wind and the west wind came, and had seen nothing, but the south wind said, "I have seen the white dove. It has flown to the Red Sea. There it has become a lion again, for the seven years are over, and the lion is fighting there with a serpent. However, the serpent is an enchanted princess."

Then the night wind said to her, "I will give you some advice. Go to the Red Sea. On the right bank are some tall reeds. Count them, cut off the eleventh one, and strike the serpent with it. Then the lion will be able to subdue it, and both will then regain their human bodies. After that look around and you will see the griffin which lives near the Red Sea. Climb onto its back with your beloved, and the bird will carry you home across the sea. Here is a nut for you. When you are above the middle of the sea, drop the nut. It will immediately sprout upward, and a tall nut tree will grow out of the water, upon which the griffin can rest. If it were not able to rest, it would not be strong enough to carry you across. If you forget to drop the nut, it will let the two of you fall into the sea."

Then she went there, and found everything just as the night wind had said. She counted the reeds by the sea, cut off the eleventh one, struck the serpent with it, and the lion subdued it. Immediately they both regained their human bodies. However, when the princess who had been a serpent was free from the enchantment, she took the youth by the arm, mounted the griffin, and carried him away with her.

There stood the poor girl who had wandered so far and was forsaken again. She sat down and cried. At last, however, she took courage and said, "I will continue on as far as the wind blows and as long as the cock crows, until I find him." And she went on a long, long way, until at last she came to the castle where both of them were living together. There she heard that a feast was to be held soon, at which they were to be married.

She said, "God will still help me," and opened the little chest that the sun had given her. Inside was a dress that glistened like the sun itself. She took it out and put it on, then went up into the castle, where everyone, even the bride herself, looked at her with astonishment.

The bride liked the dress so well that she thought it could be her wedding dress, and she asked if it was for sale.

"Not for money or property," answered the girl, "but for flesh and blood."

The bride asked what she meant by that. She said, "Let me sleep one night in the room where the bridegroom sleeps."

The bride did not want to allow this, but she wanted very much to have the dress, so at last she consented. However, she ordered a servant to give the prince a sleeping-potion.

That night after the youth was already asleep she was led into his room. She sat down on the bed and said, "I have followed you for seven years. I have been to the sun and the moon and the four winds and have asked about you, and I have helped you against the serpent. Will you, then, forget me entirely?"

However, the prince was so sound asleep that it only seemed to him like the wind was rustling outside in the fir trees.

When morning broke she was led out again, and she had to give up the golden dress.

She grew sad because even that had not helped, and she went out into a meadow, and sat down and cried. While she was sitting there she thought of the egg which the moon had given her. She broke it open, and out came a mother hen with twelve little chicks, all of gold. They ran about peeping, then crept back under the old hen's wings. It was the most beautiful thing to be seen in all the world. Then she got up, and drove them across the meadow before her, until the bride looked out of the window. She liked the little chicks so much that she immediately came down and asked if they were for sale.

"Not for money or property, but for flesh and blood. Let me sleep one more night in the room where the bridegroom sleeps."

The bride said yes, intending to cheat her as she had done the previous evening

However, when the prince went to bed he asked his servant what the murmuring and rustling in the night had been. Then the servant told him everything -- that he had been forced to give him a sleeping-potion because a poor girl secretly had slept in his room, and that he was supposed to give him another sleeping-potion tonight.

The prince said, "Pour the drink out next to the bed."

That night she was again led in, and when she began to relate how sadly she had fared, he immediately recognized his dear wife by her voice, jumped up and cried, "Now I am redeemed for sure. It is as if I had been in a dream, for the strange princess has bewitched me, causing me to forget you. But God has removed the spell from me just in time."

Then they both left the castle secretly in the night, for they feared the princess's father, who was a sorcerer. They mounted the griffin, which carried them across the Red Sea, and when they were half way, she dropped the nut. Immediately a tall nut tree grew up, and the bird rested on it, and then carried them home, where they found their child, who had grown tall and handsome, and from that time they lived happily until they died.

EAST OF THE SUN AND WEST OF THE MOON

BY

PETER CHRISTEN ASBJØRNSEN
AND JØRGEN MOE

TRANSLATED FROM NORWEGIAN
BY
GEORGE WEBB DASENT, 1859

Once upon a time there was a poor peasant who had so many children that he did not have enough of either food or clothing to give them. Pretty children they all were, but the prettiest was the youngest daughter, who was so lovely there was no end to her loveliness.

One day -- it was on a Thursday evening late in the fall -- the weather was wild and rough outside, and it was cruelly dark. The rain was falling and the wind blowing, until the walls of the cottage shook. They were all sitting around the fire busy with this thing and that. Then all at once something gave three taps on the window. The father went out to see what was the matter. Outside, what should he see but a great big white bear.

"Good evening to you," said the white bear.

"The same to you," said the man.

"Will you give me your youngest daughter? If you will, I'll make you as rich as you are now poor," said the bear.

Well, the man would not be at all sorry to be so rich; but still he thought he must have a bit of a talk with his daughter first; so he went in and told them how there was a great white bear waiting outside, who had given his word to make them so rich if he could only have the youngest daughter.

The girl said "No!" outright. Nothing could get her to say anything else; so the man went out and settled it with the white bear, that he should come again the next Thursday evening and get an answer. Meantime he talked to his daughter, and kept on telling her of all the riches they would get, and how well off she herself would be. At last she agreed to it, so she washed and mended her rags, and made herself as smart as she could. Soon she was ready for the trip, for she didn't have much to take along.

The next Thursday evening came the white bear to fetch her. She got on his back with her bundle, and off they went. After they had gone a good way, the white bear said, "Are you afraid?"

No, she wasn't.

"Just hold tight to my shaggy coat, and there's nothing to be afraid of," said the bear.

She rode a long, long way, until they came to a large steep cliff. The white bear knocked on it. A door opened, and they came into a castle, where there were many rooms all lit up; rooms gleaming with silver and gold. Further, there was a table set there, and it was all as grand as grand could be. Then the white bear gave her a silver bell; and when she wanted anything, she only had to ring it, and she would get it at once.

Well, after she had eaten, and it became evening, she felt sleepy from her journey, and thought she would like to go to bed, so she rang the bell. She had barely rung it before she found herself in a room, where there was a bed made as fair and white as anyone would wish to sleep in, with silken pillows and curtains, and gold fringe. All that was in the room was gold or silver. After she had gone to bed, and put out the light, a man came and laid himself alongside her. It was the white bear, who cast off his pelt at night; but she never saw him, for he always came after she had put out the light. Before the day dawned he was up and off again. Things went on happily for a while, but at last she became quiet and sad. She was alone all day long, and she became very homesick to see her father and mother and brothers and sisters. So one day, when the white bear asked what was wrong with her, she said it was so lonely there, and how she longed to go home to see her father and mother and brothers and sisters, and that was why she was so sad, because she couldn't get to them.

"Well," said the bear, "that can happen all right, but you must promise me, not to talk alone with your mother, but only when the others are around to hear. She will want to take you by the hand and lead you into a room to talk alone with her. But you must not do that, or else you'll bring bad luck on both of us."

So one Sunday the white bear came and said they could now set off to see her father and mother. Off they went, she sitting on his back; and they went far and long. At last they came to a grand house. Her brothers and sisters were outside running about and playing. Everything was so pretty, it was a joy to see.

"This is where your father and mother live now," said the white bear. "Now don't forget what I told you, else you'll make us both unhappy."

No, heaven forbid, she'd not forget. When they reached the house, the white bear turned around and left her.

She went in to see her father and mother, and there was such joy, that there was no end to it. None of them could thank her enough for all she had done for them. They now had everything they could wish for, as good as good could be. Then they wanted to know how she was.

Well, she said, it was very good to live where she did; she had all she wished. I don't know what else she said, but I don't think she told any of them the whole story. That afternoon, after they had eaten dinner, everything happened as the white bear had said it would. Her mother wanted to talk with her alone in her bedroom; but she remembered what the white bear had said, and wouldn't go with her.

"What we have to talk about we can talk about any time," she said, and put her mother off. But somehow or other, her mother got to her at last, and she had to tell her the whole story. She told her, how every night, after she had gone to bed, a man came and lay down beside her as soon as she had put out the light, and how

24

she never saw him, because he was always up and away before the morning dawned; and how she was terribly sad, for she wanted so much to see him, and how she was by herself all day long, and how dreary, and lonesome it was.

"Oh dear," said her mother; "it may well be a troll you are sleeping with! But now I'll give you some good advice how to see him. I'll give you a candle stub, which you can carry home in your bosom; just light it while he is asleep, but be careful not to drop any tallow on him."

Yes, she took the candle, and hid it in her bosom, and that evening the white bear came and took her away.

But when they had gone a piece, the white bear asked if all hadn't happened as he had said.

She couldn't deny that it had.

"Take care," said he, "if you have listened to your mother's advice, you will bring bad luck on us both, and it will be finished with the two of us."

No, by no means!

So when she reached home, and had gone to bed, it was the same as before. A man came and lay down beside her; but in the middle of the night, when she heard that he was fast asleep, she got up and lit the candle. She let the light shine on him, and saw that he was the most handsome prince one ever set eyes on. She fell so deeply in love with him, that she thought she couldn't live if she didn't give him a kiss at once. And so she did, but as she kissed him she let three drops of hot tallow drip onto his shirt, and he woke up.

"What have you done?" he cried; "now you have made us both unlucky, for had you held out only this one year, I would have been free! I have a stepmother who has bewitched me, so that I am a white bear by day, and a man by night. But now all ties are broken between us. Now I must leave you for her. She lives in a castle east of the sun and west of the moon, and there, too, is a princess, one with a nose three yards long, and now I will have to marry her."

She cried and grieved, but there was no help for it; he had to go.

Then she asked if she could go with him.

No, she could not.

"Tell me the way, then" she said, "so I can look for you; surely I may do that."

Yes, she could do that, but there was no way leading to the place. It lay east of the sun and west of the moon, and she'd never find her way there.

The next morning, when she woke up, both the prince and the castle were gone, and she was lying on a little green patch, in the midst of the thick, dark forest, and by her side lay the same bundle of rags she had brought with her from her old home.

When she had rubbed the sleep out of her eyes, and cried until she was tired, she set out on her way, and walked many, many days, until she came to a high cliff. An old woman sat under it, and played with a golden apple which she tossed about. The girl asked her if she knew the way to the prince, who lived with his stepmother in the castle east of the sun and west of the moon, and who was to marry the princess with a nose three yards long.

"How did you come to know about him?" asked the old woman. "Maybe you are the girl who should have had him?"

Yes, she was.

"So, so; it's you, is it?" said the old woman. "Well, all I know about him is, that he lives in the castle east of the sun and west of the moon, and that you'll get there too late or never; but still you may borrow my horse, and you can ride him to my next neighbor. Maybe she'll be able to tell you; and when you get there just give the horse a switch under the left ear, and beg him to be off home. And you can take this golden apple along with you."

So she got on the horse, and rode a long, long time, until she came to another cliff, under which sat another old woman, with a golden carding comb. The girl asked her if she knew the way to the castle that lay east of the sun and west of the moon, and she answered, like the first old woman, that she knew nothing about it, except that it was east of the sun and west of the moon.

"And you'll get there too late or never; but you can borrow my horse to my next neighbor; maybe she'll tell you all about it; and when you get there, just switch the horse under the left ear, and beg him to be off for home."

This old woman gave her the golden carding comb; she might find some use for it, she said. So the girl got up on the horse, and again rode a long, long way. At last she came to another great cliff, under which sat another old woman, spinning with a golden spinning wheel. She asked her, as well, if she knew the way to the prince, and where the castle was that lay east of the sun and west of the moon. But it was the same thing over again.

"Perhaps you are the one who should have had the prince?" said the old woman.

Yes, that she was.

But she didn't know the way any better than the other two. She knew it was east of the sun and west of the moon, but that was all.

"And you'll get there too late or never; but I'll lend you my horse, and then I think you'd best ride to the east wind and ask him; maybe he knows his way around those parts, and can blow you there. When you get to him, just give the horse a switch under the left ear, and he'll trot home by himself."

She too gave her her golden spinning wheel. "Maybe you'll find a use for it," said the old woman.

She rode many weary days, before she got to the east wind's house, but at last she did reach it, and she asked the east wind if he could tell her the way to the prince who lived east of the sun and west of the moon. Yes, the east wind had often heard tell of it, the prince and the castle, but he didn't know the way there, for he had never blown so far.

"But, if you want, I'll go with you to my brother the west wind. Maybe he knows, for he's much stronger. If you will just get on my back I'll carry you there."

Yes, she got on his back, and off they went in a rush.

When they arrived at the west wind's house, the east wind said the girl he had brought was the one who was supposed to have had the prince who lived in the castle east of the sun and west of the moon. She had set out to find him, and he had brought her here, and would be glad to know if the west wind knew how to get to the castle.

"No," said the west wind, "I've never blown so far; but if you want, I'll go with you to our brother the south wind, for he's much stronger than either of us, and he has flown far and wide. Maybe he'll tell you. Get on my back, and I'll carry you to him."

Yes, she got on his back, and so they traveled to the south wind, and I think it didn't take long at all.

When they got there, the west wind asked him if he could tell her the way to the castle that lay east of the sun and west of the moon, for she was the one who was supposed to have had the prince who lived there.

"Is that so?" said the south wind. "Is she the one? Well, I have visited a lot of places in my time, but I have not yet blown there. If you want, I'll take you to my brother the north wind; he is the oldest and strongest of us all, and if he doesn't know where it is, you'll never find anyone in the world to tell you. Get on my back, and I'll carry you there."

Yes, she got on his back, and away he left his house at a good clip. They were not long underway. When they reached the north wind's house he was so wild and cross, that he blew cold gusts at them from a long way off. "Blast you both, what do you want?" he roared at them from afar, so that it struck them with an icy shiver.

"Well," said the south wind, "you don't need to bluster so, for here I am, your brother, the south wind, and here is the girl who was supposed to have had the prince who lives in the castle that lies east of the sun and west of the moon, and now she wants to ask you if you ever were there, and can show her the way, for she wants so much to find him again."

"Yes, I know where it is," said the north wind; "a single time I blew an aspen leaf there, but afterward I was so tired that I couldn't blow a puff for many days. But if you really wish to go there, and aren't afraid to come along with me, I'll take you on my back and see if I can blow you there."

Yes, with all her heart; she wanted to and had to get there if it were at all possible; and she wouldn't be afraid, however madly he went.

"Very well, then," said the north wind, "but you must sleep here tonight, for we must have the whole day before us, if we're to get there at all."

Early next morning the north wind woke her, and puffed himself up, and blew himself out, and made himself so stout and big. that he was gruesome to look at. Off they went high up through the air, as if they would not stop until they reached the end of the world.

Here on earth there was a terrible storm; acres of forest and many houses were blown down, and when it swept over the sea, ships wrecked by the hundred.

They tore on and on -- no one can believe how far they went -- and all the while they still went over the sea, and the north wind got more and more weary, and so out of breath he could barely bring out a puff, and his wings drooped and drooped, until at last he sunk so low that the tops of the waves splashed over his heels.

"Are you afraid?" said the north wind.

No, she wasn't.

They weren't very far from land by now, and the north wind had enough strength left that he managed to throw her up on the shore under the windows of the castle which lay east of the sun and west of the moon. But then he was so weak and worn out, that he had to stay there and rest many days before he could go home again.

The next morning the girl sat down under the castle window, and began to play with the golden apple. The first person she saw was the long-nosed princess who was to have the prince.

"What do you want for your golden apple, you girl?" said the long-nosed one, as she opened the window.

"It's not for sale, for gold or money," said the girl.

"If it's not for sale for gold or money, what is it that you will sell it for? You may name your own price," said the princess.

"Well, you can have it, if I may get to the prince, who lives here, and be with him tonight," said the girl whom the north wind had brought.

Yes, that could be done. So the princess took the golden apple; but when the girl came up to the prince's bedroom that night, he was fast asleep. She called him and shook him, and cried and grieved, but she could not wake him up. The next morning. as soon as day broke, the princess with the long nose came and drove her out.

That day she sat down under the castle windows and began to card with her golden carding comb, and the same thing happened. The princess asked what she wanted for it. She said it wasn't for sale for gold or money, but if she could have permission to go to the prince and be with him that night, the princess could have it. But when she went to his room she found him fast asleep again, and however much she called, and shook, and cried, and prayed, she couldn't get life into him. As soon as the first gray peep of day came, the princess with the long nose came, and chased her out again.

That day the girl sat down outside under the castle window and began to spin with her golden spinning wheel, and the princess with the long nose wanted to have it as well. She opened the window and asked what she wanted for it. The girl said, as she had said twice before, that it wasn't for sale for gold or money, but if she could go to the prince who was there, and be alone with him that night she could have it.

Yes, she would be welcome to do that. But now you must know that there were some Christians who had been taken there, and while they were sitting in their room, which was next to the prince's, they had heard how a woman had been in there, crying, praying, and calling to him for two nights in a row, and they told this to the prince.

That evening, when the princess came with a sleeping potion, the prince pretended to drink it, but threw it over his shoulder, for he could guess it was a sleeping potion. So, when the girl came in, she found the prince wide awake, and then she told him the whole story of how she had come there.

"Ah," said the prince, "you've come in the very nick of time, for tomorrow is to be our wedding day. But now I won't have the long-nose, and you are the only woman in the world who can set me free. I'll say that I want to see what my wife is fit for, and beg her to wash the shirt which has the three spots of tallow on it. She'll agree, for she doesn't know that you are the one who put them there. Only Christians, and not such a pack of trolls, can wash them out again. I'll say that I will marry only the woman who can wash them out, and ask you to try it."

So there was great joy and love between them all the night. But next day, when the wedding was planned, the prince said, "First of all, I'd like to see what my bride is fit for."

"Yes!" said the stepmother, with all her heart.

"Well," said the prince, "I've got a fine shirt which I'd like for my wedding shirt, but somehow or other it got three spots of tallow on it, which I must have washed out. I have sworn to marry only the woman who is able to do that. If she can't, then she's not worth having."

Well, that was no big thing they said, so they agreed, and the one with the long nose began to wash away as hard as she could, but the more she rubbed and scrubbed, the bigger the spots grew.

"Ah!" said the old troll woman, her mother, "you can't wash. Let me try."

But she had hardly touched the shirt, before it got far worse than before, and with all her rubbing, and wringing, and scrubbing, the spots grew bigger and blacker, and the shirt got ever darker and uglier.

Then all the other trolls began to wash, but the longer it lasted, the blacker and uglier the shirt grew, until at last it was as black all over as if it been up the chimney.

"Ah!" said the prince, "none of you is worth a straw; you can't wash. Why there, outside, sits a beggar girl, I'll bet she knows how to wash better than the whole lot of you. Come in, girl!" he shouted.

She came in.

"Can you wash this shirt clean, girl, you?" he said.

"I don't know," she said, "but I think I can."

And almost before she had taken it and dipped it into the water, it was as white as driven snow, and whiter still.

"Yes, you are the girl for me," said the prince.

At that the old troll woman flew into such a rage, she exploded on the spot, and the princess with the long nose after her, and the whole pack of trolls after her -- at least I've never heard a word about them since.

As for the prince and princess, they set free all the poor Christians who had been captured and shut up there; and they took with them all the silver and gold, and flew away as far as they could from the castle that lay east of the sun and west of the moon.

BEAUTY AND THE BEAST

BY
WENTWORTH WEBSTER

FIRST PUBLISHED IN *BASQUE LEGENDS* (1879)

As there are many in the world in its state now, there was a king who had three daughters. He used continually to bring handsome presents to his two elder daughters, but did not pay any attention at all to his youngest daughter, and yet she was the prettiest and most amiable.

The king kept going from fair to fair, and from feast to feast, and from everywhere he used to bring something for the two eldest daughters. One day, when he was going to a feast, he said to his youngest daughter, "I never bring anything home for you; tell me then what you want and you shall have it."

She said to her father, "And I do not want anything."

"Yes, yes, I am going to bring you something."

"Very well then, bring me a flower."

He goes off, and is busy buying and buying; for one a hat, for the other a beautiful piece of stuff for a dress, and for the first again a shawl; and he was returning home, when in passing before a beautiful castle, he sees a garden quite full of flowers, and he says to himself, "What! I was going home without a flower for my daughter; here I shall have plenty of them."

He takes some then, and as soon, as he has done so, a voice says to him, "Who gave you permission to take that flower? As you have three daughters, if you do not bring me one of them before the year be finished, you shall be burnt wherever you are -- you, and your whole kingdom."

The king goes off home. He gives his elder daughters their presents, and her nosegay to the youngest. She thanks her father. After a certain time this king became sad. His eldest daughter said to him, "What is the matter with you ?"

He says to her, "If one of my daughters will not go to such a spot before the end of the year, I shall be burned."

His eldest daughter answers him, "Be burned if you like; as for me, I shall not go. I have no wish at all to go there. Settle it with the others."

The second also asks him, "You seem very sad, papa; what is the matter with you?"

He told her how he is bound to send one of his daughters to such a place before the end of the year, otherwise he should be burned.

This one too says to him, "Manage your own business as you like, but do not reckon upon me."

The youngest, after some days, said to him, "What is the matter with you, my father, that you are so sad? Has someone done you some hurt?"

He said to her, "When I went to get your nosegay, a voice said to me, 'I must have one of your daughters before the year be completed,' and now I do not knew what I must do. It told me that I shall be burned."

This daughter said to him, "My father, do not be troubled about it. I will go."

And she sets out immediately in a carriage. She arrives at the castle and goes in, and she hears music and sounds of rejoicing everywhere, and yet she did not see anyone. She finds her chocolate ready (in the morning), and her dinner the same. She goes to bed, and still she does not see anyone.

The next morning a voice says to her, "Shut your eyes; I wish to place my head on your knees for a moment."

"Come, come; I am not afraid."

There appears then an enormous serpent. Without intending it, the young lady could not help giving a little shudder. An instant after the serpent went away; and the young lady lived very happily, without lacking anything. One day the voice asked her if she did not wish to go home.

She answers, "I am very happy here. I have no longing for it."

"Yes, if you like, you may go for three days."

He gives her a ring, and says to her, "If that changes colour, I shall be ill, and if it turns to blood, I shall be in great misery."

The young lady sets out for her father's house. Her father was very glad (to see her). Her sisters said to her, "You must be happy there. You are prettier than you were before. With whom do you live there?"

She told them, "With a serpent."

They would not believe her. The three days flew by like a dream, and she forgot her serpent. The fourth day she looked at her ring, and she saw that it was changed. She rubs it with her finger, and it begins to bleed. Seeing that she goes running to her father, and says to him that she is going. She arrives at the castle, and finds everything sad. The music will not play -- everything was shut up. She called the serpent (his name was Azor, and hers Fifine). She kept on calling and crying out to him, but Azor appeared nowhere. After having searched the whole house, after having taken off her shoes, she goes to the garden, and there too she cries out.

She finds a corner of the earth in the garden quite frozen, and immediately she makes a great fire over this spot, and there Azor comes out, and he says to her, "You had forgotten me, then. If you had not made this fire, it would have been all up with me."

Fifine said to him, "Yes, I had forgotten you, but the ring made me think of you."

Azor said to her, "I knew what was going to happen; that is why I gave you the ring."

And coming into the house, she finds it as before, all full of rejoicings -- the music was playing on all sides.

Some days after that Azor said to her, "You must marry me."

Fifine gives no answer. He asks her again like that three times, and still she remained silent, silent. The whole house becomes sad again. She has no more her meals ready. Again Azor asks her if she will marry him. Still she does not answer, and she remains like that in darkness several days without eating anything, and she said to herself, "Whatever it shall cost me I must say yes."

When the serpent asks her again, "Will you marry me?" she answers, "Not with the serpent, but with the man."

As soon as she had said that the music begins as before. Azor says to her that she must go to her father's house and get all things ready that are necessary, and they will marry the next day. The young lady goes as he had told her. She says to her father that she is going to be married to the serpent tomorrow, (and asks him) if he will prepare everything for that. The father consents, but he is vexed. Her sisters, too, ask her whom she is going to marry, and they are astounded at hearing that it is with a serpent.

Fifine goes back again, and Azor says to her, "Which would you prefer, from the house to the church, serpent, or from the church to the house, serpent?"

Fifine says to him, "From the house to the church, serpent."

Azor says to her, "I, too."

A beautiful carriage comes to the door. The serpent gets in, and Fifine places herself at his side, and when they arrive at the king's house the serpent says to her, "Shut the doors and the curtains, that nobody may see."

Fifine says to him, "But they will see you as you get down."

"No matter; shut them all the same."

She goes to her father. Her father comes with all his court to fetch the serpent. He opens the door, and who is astonished ? Why, everybody. Instead of a serpent there is a charming young man; and they all go to the church.

When they come out there is a grand dinner at the king's, but the bridegroom says to his wife, "Today we must not make a feast at all. We have a great business to do in the house; we will come another day for the feast."

She told that to her father, and they go on to their house. When they are come there her husband brings her in a large basket a serpent's skin, and says to her, "You will make a great fire, and when you hear the first stroke of midnight you will throw this serpent's skin into the fire. That must be burnt up, and you must throw the ashes out of window before the last stroke of twelve has ceased striking. If you do not do that I shall be wretched forever."

The lady says to him, "Certainly; I will do everything that I can to succeed."

She begins before midnight to make the fire. As soon as she heard the first stroke she throws the serpent's skin on the fire, and takes two spits and stirs the fire, and moves about the skin and burns it, till ten strokes have gone. Then she takes a shovel, and throws the ashes outside as the last twelfth stroke is ending.

Then a terrible voice says, "I curse your cleverness, and what you have just done."

At the same time her husband comes in. He did not know where he was for joy. He kisses her, and does not know how to tell his wife what great good she has done him.

"Now I do not fear anything. If you had not done as I told you, I should have been enchanted for twenty-one years more. Now it is all over, and we will go at our ease tomorrow to your father's house for the wedding feast."

They go the next day and enjoy themselves very much. They return to their palace to take away the handsomest things, because they did not wish to stop any more in that corner of the mountain. They load all their valuable things in carts and waggons, and go to live with the king. This young lady has four children, two boys and two girls, and as her sisters were very jealous of her, their father sent them out of the house. The king gave his crown to his son-in-law, who was already a son of a king. As they had lived well, they died well too.

THE SUMMER AND WINTER GARDEN

BY

JACOB AND WILHELM GRIMM

GERMANY, 1812

A merchant was planning to go to a fair, so he asked his three daughters what he should bring back for them.

The oldest one said, "A beautiful dress."

The second, "A pair of pretty shoes."

The third, "A rose."

To find a rose would be difficult, for it was the middle of winter, but because the youngest daughter was the most beautiful, and because she took great pleasure in flowers, the father said that he would do his best to find her one.

The merchant was now on his homeward trip. He had a splendid dress for the oldest daughter, a pair of beautiful shoes for the second one, but he had not been able to get a rose for the third one. Whenever he had entered a garden looking for roses, the people just laughed at him, asking him if he believed that roses grew in the snow. He was very sad about this, and as he was thinking about what he might bring his dearest child, he came to a castle. It had an adjoining garden where it was half summer and half winter. On the one side the most beautiful flowers were blossoming -- large and small. On the other side everything was bare and covered with deep snow.

The man climbed from his horse. He was overjoyed to see an entire hedge full of roses on the summer side. He approached it, picked one of them, and then rode off.

He had already ridden some distance when he heard something running and panting behind him. Turning around, he saw a large black beast, that called out, "Give me back my rose, or I'll kill you! Give me back my rose, or I'll kill you!"

The man said, "Please let me have the rose. I am supposed to bring one home for my daughter, the most beautiful daughter in the world."

"For all I care, but then give me your beautiful daughter for a wife!"

In order to get rid of the beast, the man said yes, thinking that he would not come to claim her.

However, the beast shouted back to him, "In eight days I will come and get my bride."

So the merchant brought each daughter what she had wanted, and each one was delighted, especially the youngest with her rose.

Eight days later the three sisters were sitting together at the table when something came stepping heavily up the stairs to the door. "Open up! Open up!" it shouted.

They opened the door, and were terrified when a large black beast stepped inside. "Because my bride did not come to me, and the time is up, I will fetch her myself." With that he went to the youngest daughter and grabbed hold of her. She began to scream, but it did not help. She had to go away with him. And when the father came home, his dearest child had been taken away.

The black beast carried the beautiful maiden to his castle where everything was beautiful and wonderful. Musicians were playing there, and below there was the garden, half summer and half winter, and the beast did everything to make her happy, fulfilling even her unspoken desires. They ate together, and she had to scoop up his food for him, for otherwise he would not have eaten. She was dear to the beast, and finally she grew very fond of him.

One day she said to him, "I am afraid, and don't know why. It seems to me that my father or one of my sisters is sick. Couldn't I see them just once?"

So the beast led her to a mirror and said, "Look inside."

She looked into the mirror, and it was as though she were at home. She saw her living room and her father. He really was sick, from a broken heart, because he held himself guilty that his dearest child had been taken away by a wild beast and surely had been eaten up. If he could know how well off she was, then he would not be so sad. She also saw her two sisters sitting on the bed and crying.

Her heart was heavy because of all this, and she asked the beast to allow her to go home for a few days. The beast refused for a long time, but she grieved so much that he finally had pity on her and said, "Go to your father, but promise me that you will be back here in eight days."

She promised, and as she was leaving, he called out again, "Do not stay longer than eight days."

When she arrived home her father was overjoyed to see her once again, but sickness and grief had already eaten away at his heart so much that he could not regain his health, and within a few days he died.

Because of her sadness, she could think of nothing else. Her father was buried, and she went to the funeral. The sisters cried together, and consoled one another, and when her thoughts finally turned to her dear beast, the eight days were long past.

She became frightened, and it seemed to her that he too was sick. She set forth immediately and returned to his castle. When she arrived there everything was still and sad inside. The musicians were not playing. Black cloth hung everywhere. The garden was entirely in winter and covered with snow. She looked for the beast, but he was not there. She looked everywhere, but could not find him.

Then she was doubly sad, and did not know how to console herself. She sadly went into the garden where she saw a pile of cabbage heads. They were old and rotten, and she pushed them aside. After turning over a few of them she saw her dear beast. He was lying beneath them and was dead.

She quickly fetched some water and poured it over him without stopping.

Then he jumped up and was instantly transformed into a handsome prince. They got married, and the musicians began to play again, and the summer side of the garden appeared in its splendor, and the black cloth was all ripped down, and together they lived happily ever after.

THE CLINKING CLANKING LOWESLEAF

BY
CARL AND THEODOR COLSHORN

GERMANY, 1854

Once upon a time there was a king who had three daughters. The youngest was his pride and joy. One day he wanted to go to the fair to buy something, and he asked his three daughters what he should bring home for them. The first one asked for a golden spinning wheel. The second one a golden yarn reel, and the third one a clinking clanking lowesleaf. The king promised to bring these things and rode away. At the fair he bought the golden spinning wheel and the golden yarn reel, but no one had a clinking clanking lowesleaf for sale. He looked everywhere, but could not find one. This saddened him, because the youngest daughter was the joy of his life, and he wanted to please her ever so much.

As he sorrowfully made his way homeward, he came to a great, great forest and to a large birch tree. Under the birch tree there lay a large black poodle dog. Because the king looked so sad, the dog asked him what was the matter. "Oh," answered the king, "I was supposed to bring a clinking clanking lowesleaf to my youngest daughter, whom I love above anything else, but I cannot find one anywhere, and that is why I am so sad."

"I can help you," said the poodle. "The clinking clanking lowesleaf grows in this tree. If a year and a day from now you will give me that which first greets you upon your arrival home today, then you can have it."

At first the king did not want to agree, but he thought about it long and hard, then said to himself, "What could it be but our dog? Go ahead and make the promise." And he made the promise.

The poodle wagged his tail, climbed up into the birch, broke off the leaf with his frizzy-haired paw, and gave it to the king, saying, "You had better keep your word, or you will wish that you had!" The king repeated his promise, took the leaf, and rode on joyfully.

As he approached home, his youngest daughter jumped out with joy to greet him. The king was horrified. His heart was so filled with grief that he pushed her aside. She started to cry, thinking, "What does this mean, that father is pushing me away?" and she went inside and complained to her mother. Soon the king came in. He gave the oldest girl the golden spinning wheel, the middle one the golden yarn reel, and the youngest one the clinking clanking lowesleaf, and he was quiet and sad. Then the queen asked him was wrong with him, and why he had pushed the youngest daughter away; but he said nothing.

He grieved the entire year. He lamented and mourned and became thin and pale, so concerned was he. Whenever the queen asked him what was wrong, he only shook his head or walked away. Finally, when the year was nearly at its end, he could not longer keep still, and he told her about his misfortune, and thought that his wife would die of shock. She too was horrified, but she soon took hold of herself and said, "You men don't think of anything! After all, don't we have the goose herder's daughter? Let's dress her up and give her to the poodle. A stupid poodle will never know the difference."

The day arrived, and they dressed up the goose girl in their youngest daughter's clothes until she looked just perfect. They had scarcely finished when they heard a bark outside, and a scratching sound at the gate. They looked out, and sure enough, it was the large black poodle dog. They wondered who had taught him to count. After all, a year has more than three hundred days, and even a human can lose count, to say nothing of a dog! But he had not lost count. He had come to take away the princess.

The king and queen greeted him in a friendly manner, then led him outside to the goose girl. He wagged his tail and pawed at her, then he lay down on his belly and said,

Sit upon my tail,

And I'll take you away!

She sat down on him, and he took off across the heath. Soon they came to a great, great forest. When they came to the large birch tree, the poodle stopped to rest a while, for it was a hot day, and it was cool and shady here. Around and about there were many daisies poking up their white heads from the beautiful grass, and the girl thought about her parents, and sighed, "Oh, if only my father were here. He could graze the geese so nicely here in this beautiful, lush meadow."

The poodle stood up, shook himself, and said, "Just what kind of a girl are you?"

"I am a goose girl, and my father tends geese," she answered. She would have liked to say what the queen had told her to say, but it was impossible for anyone to tell a lie under this tree. She could not, and she could not.

He jumped up abruptly, looked at her threateningly, and said, "You are not the right one. I have no use for you:"

Sit upon my tail,

And I'll take you away!

They were not far from the king's house, when the queen saw them and realized which way the wind was blowing. Therefore she took the broom binder's daughter, dressed her up in even more beautiful clothes. When the poodle arrived and made nasty threats, she brought the broom girl out to him, saying, "This is the right girl!"

"We shall see," responded the poodle dog. The queen became very uneasy, and the king's throat tightened, but the poodle wagged his tail and scratched, then lay down on his belly, saying, "Sit upon my tail, And I'll take you away!"

The broom girl sat down on him, and he took off across the heath. Soon they too came to the great forest and to the large birch tree. As they sat there resting, the girl thought about her parents, and sighed, "Oh, if only my father were here. He could make brooms so easily, for here there are masses of thin twigs!"

The poodle stood up, shook himself, and said, "Just what kind of a girl are you?"

She wanted to lie, for the queen had ordered her to, and she was a very strict mistress, but she could not, because she was under this tree, and she answered, "I am a broom girl, and my father makes brooms."

He jumped up as though he were mad, looked at her threateningly, and said, "You are not the right one. I have no use for you:"

"Sit upon my tail, And I'll take you away!"

They approached the king's house, and the king and queen, who had been steadily looking out the window, began to moan and cry, especially the king, for the youngest daughter was the apple of his eye. The court officials cried and sobbed as well, and there was nothing but mourning everywhere. But it was to no avail. The poodle arrived and said, "This time give me the right girl, or you will wish that you had!" He spoke with such a frightful voice and made such angry gestures, that everyone's heart stood still, and their skin shuddered. Then they led out the youngest daughter, dressed in white, and as pale as snow. It was as though the moon had just come out from behind dark clouds. The poodle knew that she was the right one, and said with a caressing voice,

"Sit upon my tail, And I'll take you away!"

He ran much more gently this time, and did not stop in the great forest under the birch tree, but hurried deeper and deeper into the woods until they finally reached a small house, where he quietly lay the princess, who had fallen asleep, onto a soft bed. She slumbered on and dreamed about her parents, and about the strange ride, and she laughed and cried in her sleep. The poodle lay down in his hut and kept watch over the little house and the princess.

When she awoke the next morning and found herself soul alone, she cried and grieved and wanted to run away, but she could not, because the house was enchanted. It let people enter, but no one could leave. There was plenty there to eat and drink, everything that even a princess could desire, but she did not want anything and did not take a single bite. She could neither see nor hear the poodle, but the birds sang wonderfully. There were deer grazing around and about, and they looked at the princess with their large eyes. The morning wind curled her golden locks and poured fresh color over her face. The princess sighed and said, "Oh, if only someone were here, even if it were the most miserable, dirty beggar woman. I would kiss her and hug her and love her and honor her!"

"Is that true?" screeched a harsh voice close behind her, startling the princess. She looked around, and there stood a bleary-eyed woman as old as the hills. She glared at the princess and said, "You called for a beggar woman, and a beggar woman is here! In the future do not despise beggar women. Now listen well! The poodle dog is an enchanted prince, this hut an enchanted castle, the forest an enchanted city, and all the animals enchanted people. If you are a genuine princess and are also kind to poor people, then you can redeem them all and become rich and happy. The poodle goes away every morning, because he has to, and every evening he returns home, because he wants to. At midnight he pulls off his rough hide and becomes an ordinary man. If he knocks on your bedroom door, do not let him in, however much he asks and begs, not the first night, not the second night, and especially not the third night. During the third night, after he has tired himself out talking and has fallen asleep, take the hide, make a large fire, and burn it. But first lock your bedroom door securely, so that he cannot get in, and do not open it when he scratches on the door, if you cherish your life. And on your wedding day say three times, don't forget it now, say three times:

"Old tongues, Old lungs! and I will see you again." The princess took very careful notice of everything, and the old woman disappeared.

The first night the prince asked and begged her to open her door, but she answered, "No, I'll not do it," and she did not do it. The second night he asked her even more sweetly, but she did not answer at all. She buried her head in her pillow, and she did not open the door. The third night he asked her so touchingly and sang such beautiful melodies to her, that she wanted to jump up and open the door for him, but fortunately she remembered the old woman and her mother and father. She pulled the bedcovers over her head, and did not open the door. Complaining, the prince walked away, but she did not hear him leave. While he slept she built up the fire, crept out on tiptoe, picked up the rough hide from the corner where the poodle always put it, barred the bedroom door, and threw it into the flames. The poodle jumped up howling, gnawed and clawed at the door, threatened, begged, growled, and howled again. But she did not open the door, and he could not open the door, however fiercely he threw himself against it.

The fire flamed up brightly one last time, and there was an enormous bang, as if heaven and hell had exploded. Standing before her was the most handsome prince in the world. The hut was now a magnificent castle, the forest a great city full of palaces, and the animals were all kinds of people.

At their wedding ceremony, the prince and the princess were seated at the table with the old king and the old queen and the two sisters and many rich and important people, when the bride called out three times,

Old tongues,

Old lungs!

and the tattered old woman came in. The old queen scolded, and the two princesses scolded, and they wanted to chase her away, but the young queen stood up and let the old woman sit down at her place, eat from her plate, and drink from her goblet. When the old woman had eaten and drunk her fill, she looked at the old queen and the evil daughters, and they became crooked and lame. But she blessed the young queen, and she became seven times more beautiful, and no one ever saw or heard from the old woman again.

THE LITTLE NUT TWIG

BY

LUDWIG BECHSTEIN

GERMANY, 1847

Once upon a time there was a wealthy merchant whose business required him to travel abroad. Taking leave, he said to his three daughters, "Dear daughters, I would like to have something nice for you when I return. What should I bring home for you?"

The eldest daughter said, "Father dear, a beautiful pearl necklace for me!"

The second one said, "I would like a finger ring with a diamond stone."

The youngest one cuddled up to her father and whispered, "Daddy, a pretty green nut twig for me."

"Good, my dear daughters," said the merchant, "I will remember. Farewell."

The merchant traveled far and purchased many goods, but he also faithfully remembered his daughters' wishes. To please his eldest he had packed a costly pearl necklace into his baggage, and he had also purchased an equally valuable diamond ring for the middle daughter. But, however much he tried, he could not find a green nut twig. For this reason he went on foot a good distance on his homeward journey. His way led him in large part through the woods, and he hoped thus finally to find a nut twig. However, he did not succeed, and the good father became very depressed that he had not been able to fulfill the harmless request of his youngest and dearest child.

Finally, as he was sadly making his way down a path that led through a dark forest and next to a dense thicket, his hat rubbed against a twig, and it made a sound like hailstones falling on it. Looking up he saw that it was a pretty green nut twig, from which was hanging a cluster of golden nuts. The man was delighted. He reached his hand up and plucked the magnificent twig. But in that same instant, a wild bear shot out from the thicket and stood up on his back paws, growling fiercely, as though he were about to tear the merchant to pieces.

With a terrible voice he bellowed, "Why did you pick my nut twig, you? Why? I will eat you up!"

Shaking and trembling with fear the merchant said, "Dear bear, don't eat me. Let me go on my way with the little nut twig. I'll give you a large ham and many sausages for it!"

But the bear bellowed again, "Keep your ham and your sausages! I will not eat you, only if you will promise to give me the first thing that meets you upon your arrival home."

The merchant gladly agreed to this, for he recalled how his poodle usually ran out to greet him, and he would gladly sacrifice the poodle in order to save his own life.

Following a crude handshake the bear lumbered back into the thicket. The merchant, breathing a sigh of relief, went hurriedly and happily on his way.

The golden nut twig decorated the merchant's had splendidly as he hurried homeward. Filled with joy, the youngest girl ran to greet her dear father. The poodle followed her with bold leaps. The oldest daughters and the mother were not quite so fast to step out the door and greet home-comer.

The merchant was horrified to see that the first one to greet him was his youngest daughter. Concerned and saddened, he withdrew from the happy child's embrace, and -- following the initial greetings -- told them all that had happened with the nut twig.

They all cried and were very sad, but the youngest daughter showed the most courage, and she resolved to fulfill her father's promise.

The mother soon thought up a good plan. She said, "Dear ones, let's not be afraid. If the bear should come to hold you to your promise, dear husband, instead of giving him our youngest daughter, let's give him the herdsman's daughter. He will be satisfied with her."

This proposal was accepted. The daughters were happy once again, and they were very pleased with their beautiful presents. The youngest one always kept her nut twig with her, and she soon forgot the bear and her father's promise.

But one day a dark carriage rattled through the street and up to the front of the merchant's house. The ugly bear climbed out and walked into the house growling. He went up to the startled man and asked that his promise be fulfilled. Quickly and secretly they fetched the herdsman's daughter, who was very ugly, dressed her in good clothes, and put her in the bear's carriage.

The journey began. Once outside the town, the bear laid his wild shaggy head in the shepherd girl's lap and growled,

Tussle me, scuffle me
Soft and gentle, behind my ears,
Or I will eat you, skin and bone

The girl began to do so, but she did not do it the way the bear wanted her to, and he realized that he had been deceived. He was about to eat the disguised shepherd girl, but in her fright she quickly fled from the carriage.

Then the bear rode back to the merchant's house and, with terrible threats, demanded the right bride. So the dear maiden had to come forward, and -- following a bitterly sorrowful farewell -- she rode away with the ugly bridegroom.

Once outside the town, he laid his coarse head in the girl's lap and growled again,

Tussle me, scuffle me
Soft and gentle, behind my ears,
Or I will eat you, skin and bone

And the girl did just that, and she did it so softly that it pacified him, and his terrible bearish expression became friendly. Gradually the bear's poor bride began to gain some trust toward him. The journey did not last long, for the carriage traveled extremely fast, like a windstorm through the air. They soon came to a very dark forest, and the carriage suddenly stopped in front of a dark and yawning cave. This was where the bear lived. Oh, how the girl trembled!

The bear embraced her with his claw-arms and said to her with a friendly growl, "This is where you will live, my little bride; and you will be happy, as long as you behave yourself here, otherwise my wild animals will tear you apart."

As soon as they had gone a few steps inside the dark cave, he unlocked an iron door and stepped with his bride into a room that was filled with poisonous worms. They hissed at them rapaciously. The bear growled into his little bride's ear,

Do not look around!
Neither right nor left,
Straight ahead, and you'll be safe!

Then the girl did indeed walk through the room without looking around, and all the while not a single worm stirred or moved. And in this manner they went through ten more rooms, and the last one was filled with the most terrible creatures: dragons and snakes, toads swollen with poison, basilisks and lindorms. And in each room the bear growled,

Do not look around!
Neither right nor left,
Straight ahead, and you'll be safe!

The girl trembled and quaked with fear, like the leaves of an aspen, but she remained steadfast and did not look around, neither right nor left. When the door to the twelfth room opened up, a glistening stream of light shone toward the two of them. The most beautiful music sounded from within, and everywhere there were cries of joy.

Before the bride could comprehend this -- she was still trembling from seeing such horrible things, and now this surprising loveliness -- there was a terrible clap of thunder, and she thought that earth and heaven were breaking apart.

It was soon quiet once again. The forest, the cave, the poisonous animals, and the bear had all disappeared. In their place stood a splendid castle with rooms decorated in gold and with beautifully dressed servants. And the bear had been transformed into a handsome young man. He was the prince of this magnificent castle, and he pressed his little bride to his heart, thanking her a thousand times that she had redeemed him and his servants -- the wild animals -- from their enchantment.

She was now a high and wealthy princess, but she always wore the beautiful nut twig on her breast. It never wilted, and she especially liked to wear it, because it had been the key to her good fortune.

Her parents and sisters were soon informed of this happy turn of events. The bear prince had them brought to the castle, where they lived in splendid happiness forever after.

LITTLE BROOMSTICK

BY
LUDWIG BECHSTEIN

GERMANY, 1847

There was once a merchant who had three daughters. The two older ones were proud and haughty. The younger one, however, was well behaved and modest, although her beauty greatly surpassed that of her sisters. She dressed simply, and thus unconsciously enhanced her beauty more than her sisters were able to do with the most expensive clothing and jewelry.

Nettchen, that was the name of the merchant's youngest daughter, had a dear girlfriend who was very poor, but equally beautiful and virtuous. She was a broom binder's daughter, and was for this reason was called Little Broomstick by young and old alike. Both girls were of one heart and one soul. They entrusted one another with their little secrets, and between them all class distinctions fell by the wayside. This angered the older sisters greatly, but Nettchen let them scold, and loved her Little Broomstick nonetheless.

Once the merchant was planning a long journey, although the season was already very advanced. He asked his daughters if they had a wish as to what he should bring home to them.

The oldest one said, "Bring me a golden necklace!"

The second, "Bring me a pair of earrings that are so beautiful that all women be envious of me because of them!"

The youngest said that she had no wish, because her father, in his goodness, had already given her everything. But the merchant insisted, so she answered with a smile, "Then bring me three roses growing on one stem."

She was convinced that her father would not be able to find such a present in the middle of winter. He kissed her for her modesty and set forth on his journey.

He was on his way home when he remembered the presents that he was supposed to get for his daughters. He soon found a golden necklace and a pair of splendid earrings, but not so the three roses for Nettchen. The father had just decided to buy some other valuable present for his darling, when suddenly -- to his surprise -- he came upon a green area. He stepped through a wide gateway and found himself in a large, blossoming garden adjacent to a splendid castle. Outside everything was covered with snow, but in the garden the trees were in blossom, nightingales were singing in the bushes, and finally he even saw a blossoming rosebush, and on one of its branches were three of the most beautiful half-open buds. Elated, he thought that now he would be able to fulfill Nettchen's wish, and he broke off the branch.

He had scarcely done so when an enormous beast with a long ugly snout, ears hanging down, and a shaggy coat and tail appeared before him and laid his long sharp claws on his shoulder. The merchant was deathly frightened, and even worse when the beast began to speak, threatening him with death for his misdeed.

The merchant begged, telling him why he wanted the roses, whereupon the beast answered, "Your youngest daughter must be a true pearl of her sex. Very well, if you will promise to give her to me as a wife in seven months, then you shall live and return to your people."

As terrified as the merchant was at this proposal, his fear nevertheless led him to make the promise, thinking that he would be able to trick the monster.

The merchant returned to his people and distributed the presents. However, he was sad and melancholy, and they noticed that he was carrying a great burden in his heart. Nettchen asked him to tell her what was troubling him, but he only gave her excuses. He told the secret only to the two older daughters, who wickedly took pleasure in the situation.

So that the father could keep his eyes on her, Nettchen was almost never allowed to leave the house. Only Little Broomstick came to visit her from time to time.

One day -- the seventh month had just passed -- she and Little Broomstick were again together when a carriage stopped before the house. A servant, gesturing silently, handed a note to the merchant. On it were written the words, "Fulfill your promise!"

The merchant was terrified, but he collected himself and asked Little Broomstick to come to him. The girl came, expecting nothing bad. The merchant pointed at her. She was lifted into the carriage, and away they went in a thundering gallop.

However, the beast recognized the deception as soon as Little Broomstick was brought before him, and he ordered the girl to go home immediately and bring back the right one. The carriage stopped again before the merchant's house, and when Little Broomstick stepped out, Nettchen fell around her neck with friendly greetings. But then she was picked up and shoved into the carriage, which drove away with its booty as fast as an arrow.

Nettchen was very frightened, but she soon collected herself. Inside the strange, beautiful castle she was received with honor, although with silent gestures, and she no longer felt concerned. Silent servants brought her the most delicious things to eat and showed her to a bedroom, where a blinding white canopy bed invited her to rest. After saying her prayers, she surrendered to the arms of sleep.

When she awoke she saw to her fright that a disgusting shaggy monster lay next to her. But it was lying there still and quiet, so she left it alone. Then it left, and she had time to think about her adventure.

The ugly beast gradually became her sleeping companion, and she grew less and less afraid of him. He cuddled up to her, and she stroked his shaggy coat and even allowed him to touch her lips with his long, cold snout. This had gone on for four weeks when one night the beast did not come to her. Nettchen could not sleep for worry and concern about what might have happened to the beast, whom she had become quite fond of.

The next morning she was walking in the garden when she saw the beast lying all stretched out on the bank of a pond that served as a bath. He did not move a limb and showed every sign of being dead. A bitter pain penetrated her breast, and she cried over the death of the poor beast. But her tears had scarcely started to flow when the monster was transformed into a handsome youth.

He stood up before her, pressed her hand to his breast, and said, "You have redeemed me from a terrible curse. My father wanted me to marry a woman whom I did not love. I refused steadfastly, and in his anger, my father had a sorceress transform me into a monster. The transformation was to last until an innocent virgin would fall in love with me in spite of my ugly form, and would cry tears on my behalf. You with your heart of an angel have done just that, and I cannot thank you enough. If you will become my wife, I will repay with love what you have done for me."

Nettchen extended him her hand, and they were married. Then the deathly quiet castle awoke in a hustle and bustle. Joy ruled everywhere, and the newlyweds lived in bliss.

Now the young wife had been given the requirement that she not return to her father's house for one year. However, she obtained a mirror in which she could see everything that was happening in her family circle. Nettchen looked into the mirror often, and she saw her father in his sorrow, although her sisters were cheerful and gay. She observed Little Broomstick as well, and how she mourned for her lost girlfriend. She did not look into the mirror for some time, and when she returned to it, she saw her father on his deathbed and her sisters in the next room making merry with their friends.

This saddened the good sister, and she confided her sorrow with her husband. He comforted her, saying, "Your father will not die. In my garden there is a plant whose sap can call back the fleeing life-spirits. The year is nearly over. Then we will fetch your father, and you will not have to be separated from him any longer."

Nettchen was pleased with this, and as soon as the year had passed, the husband and wife and their magnificent entourage journeyed to Nettchen's home city. The two older sisters nearly burst with envy and anger, while the father's joy brought back his health, so that evil turned to good. The sap restored his full strength and wellbeing. Little Broomstick too was overjoyed, and Nettchen was her old girlfriend once again. She and the merchant accompanied them back to the prince's castle.

Nettchen had a forgiving heart, and however much she had been hurt by her sisters, she wanted to share her good fortune with them. Therefore she invited them to visit her, and showed them all her wealth. However, the splendor angered the sisters, and they resolved to kill their happy sister. Once when they were in the bath, they forced Nettchen under the water, and she drowned.

They had scarcely done this when a tall female figure rose up before them and glared at them with angry eyes. She touched the dead woman with a wand, and she came back to life. "I am the sorceress who once transformed the prince," said the tall figure. I have noted your good heart and taken you under my protection. These miserable ones killed you. Now I leave their fate in your hands!"

Nettchen begged for mercy for them, but the sorceress shook her head and said, "They must die, for you will never be safe from their malice, and as soon as they have been punished, my power will cease."

"Then do with them what you will!" sobbed Nettchen.

"Let them be transformed into columns and remain such until a man falls in love with them, and that will never happen."

She touched the sisters with her hand, and they were immediately transformed into two stone columns, which to this day are still standing in the garden of the splendid castle, for it has not yet occurred to any man that he should fall in love with cold, heartless stones.

The good Little Broomstick remained Nettchen's most faithful girlfriend. She still shares her good fortune with her, if in the meantime the two of them have not died.

BEAUTY AND THE HORSE

BY
J. CHRISTIAN BAY

FROM *DANISH FAIRY AND FOLK TALES*, 1899

There was once a merchant whose business was so immense that he was the wealthiest tradesman known. He had three daughters, one of whom was named Beauty. One day the merchant received word from friends far away, informing him of the failure of one of his connections, and he at once prepared himself for a journey to that place. The two older daughters asked him to buy all sorts of finery and dresses for them, but Beauty asked for nothing at all. When the merchant left, these two girls had rubbed their eyes with onions in order to look as if they were sorry to bid him good-bye; but Beauty needed no such artifice; her tears were quite natural.

So the merchant went away, and in due time arrived at the place where the tradesman of whom he had heard the bad news was living. But instead of obtaining money, as he hoped, he was kicked and beaten so violently that it seems a great wonder he came away without losing his life. Of course he had now nothing to do but return, so he mounted his horse and turned homeward. Towards evening he unfortunately lost his way, and when it became quite dark he knew no better than to ride in the direction of a light which was shining from a distance. At length he reached a beautiful little palace, but although it was lighted, there seemed to be no one at home.

After a while he found a shelter and food for his horse -- pure oats, and nothing else. The animal might well dance for joy, for both man and beast were well-nigh exhausted from the long ride. When the horse had been provided for, the master stepped into the palace. There a light was burning, and a table was laid for one person, but no one was to be seen. As the merchant was tired, he sat down without invitation, and ate a hearty supper. A fine bed was there, too, and when he had eaten enough he stretched himself among the pillows and enjoyed a good night's rest.

The next morning everything appeared as on the evening before. The horse was well supplied, and as breakfast was ready on the table, the merchant seated himself, doing justice to the good meal. At he was now ready to leave, he thought it might be well to look over the premises, and glancing into the garden he perceived some exquisite flowers. He went down, intending to carry some of them home with him as a present for Beauty; but no sooner had he touched them than a horse came running towards him as fast as it could trot, saying, "You thoughtless man; I was good to you last night, I gave you shelter and provisions, and now you would even take with you the most beautiful flowers in my garden."

The merchant immediately begged pardon, saying that he had intended the flowers as a gift for Beauty, his daughter.

"Have you several daughters?" asked the horse.

"Yes, I have three, and Beauty is the youngest one," he replied.

"Now you must promise me," said the horse, "that you will give me the daughter whose name is Beauty; if you refuse, I will take your life."

Well, the merchant did not wish to lose his life, so he promised to bring his daughter to the palace, whereupon the horse disappeared among the trees, and the man rode home.

As soon as he reached his house, the two older daughters came out and asked him for the fine things which they were expecting. But Beauty came and bid him welcome. He produced the flowers and gave them to her, saying, "These are for you, but they cost your life," and he then told her how he had been obliged to make the fatal promise to the horse, in order to save his life.

Beauty at once said, "I am willing to follow you, father, and am always glad to help you." They started on their journey, and soon arrived at the palace.

As before, no one was to be seen, but the merchant found food for his horses and a good stable The table was also laid for two persons, and there were two beds. Having done justice to the supper, father and daughter retired and slept soundly. When they awoke the next morning, they found breakfast ready for both, ate heartily, and having exchanged many loving and tender words, they separated, the father riding away. We will let him proceed, and see what occurred at the palace.

Shortly before dinnertime the horse arrived. He came into the room and said, "Welcome, Beauty!" She did not feel very glad, and had all she could do in keeping her tears back. "You shall do nothing but walk around in these rooms and in the garden," continued the horse. "Your meals are provided for. I shall come home every day at noon; at other times you must not expect me."

Time passed, and Beauty felt so lonely that she often longed for noon, when the horse came home, and she could talk with him. She gradually came to look at him more and more kindly; but one thing caused her great distress, namely, that she had no news from her father. One day she mentioned this to the horse.

"Yes," said he, "I understand that very well. In the large room you will find a mirror in which you can see all that you are thinking of."

She was happy to learn this, and went straight into the room where the mirror was hanging. As soon as she thought of her father, her old home was visible in the glass, and she noticed how he was sitting in his chair with a sorrowful expression upon his countenance, while his two daughters were singing and dancing. Beauty felt sorry over this state of affairs, and the next day she told the horse what she had seen.

"Your father is sorry, I suppose," said the horse, "because he has lost you. He will soon feel better, however."

But on the next day, when Beauty consulted the mirror, her father looked pale and ill, like one who is deadly sick; both of her sisters were dressed for a ball, and neither of them seemed to care for the weak man. Beauty burst into tears, and when the horse came home, asking what ailed her, she told him of the bad state of affairs, wishing that he would allow her to return and nurse her poor father during his illness.

"If you will promise to come back," said the horse, "you may return and stay for three days; but under no condition must you break your word."

Beauty told him she would come back in three days.

"Tonight," resumed the horse, "before going to bed, you must place the mirror under your pillow, saying, 'I wish to be home tomorrow.' Then your wish will be fulfilled. When you desire to return, you must do likewise."

The next morning, when Beauty awoke, she was at her old home. Her father became so glad to see her again that he at once felt a great deal better. She cared so well for him that the next day he was able to be up, and on the third day he was almost well. As he wished her to stay with him a few days longer, she complied, thinking that no harm would come from it. On the third day after, however, when she looked into the mirror, she saw the horse stretched on the ground in front of the bench which was her favorite seat in the garden. She now felt that it would be impossible for her to remain longer, hence in the evening, before going to bed, she placed the mirror under her pillow, saying: "I wish to be at the palace tomorrow morning."

She promptly awoke in the palace the following morning, and hurrying into the garden she found the horse so very sick that he could not stand on his legs. Beauty knelt down and asked him to forgive her for staying away longer than she had promised. The horse asked her if she could not persuade herself to stay with him all her life, but she answered that it would seem very singular to live with a horse all her lifetime. The poor animal now sighed so deeply that she took pity on him and said, fearing that he might die then and there, that she would always stay with him and never leave him.

As soon as she had made this promise, the horse vanished, and a beautiful young prince stood before her. He seized her hand and asked whether she was not sorry for the promise she had made. No, she said, she would rather stay with him now than when he was in the shape of a horse. He now told her that both he and the whole land had been enchanted by his wicked stepmother, who had converted him into a horse, and told him that only when a beautiful young girl would promise to stay with him, in his altered shape, would the enchantment be over. He wanted to marry Beauty, and live in the palace which belonged to him.

So they sent for her father to take up his residence with them, and now the marriage was performed and celebrated in a splendid manner. They lived long and happily together, the prince and his Beauty.

THE SINGING ROSE

BY
IGNAZ AND JOSEPH ZINGERELE

AUSTRIA, 1852

A king had three daughters. They were more beautiful than the young women of today, and each had passed her sixteenth year of life. The king thought about making one of his daughters queen, but he did not know which one he should select over the other two.

One day he summoned all three and said to them, "My dear children, I am now old and frail, and every day is a gift. Before I die, I would like to bring everything in my realm into order and name one of you as the heir to my kingdom. Now go out into the wide world, and the one of you who brings back a singing rose shall inherit my throne, and she shall be queen over the entire land."

When the three daughters had heard this, they tearfully took leave of their old father, then -- trusting their luck -- set forth for foreign lands, each taking a different path.

It happened that the youngest and most beautiful of them had to go through a dark pine forest. All kinds of birds were singing at the same time. It was wonderful to listen to them. It began to get dark, the birds flew to their nests, and after a while it became quiet as a mouse. Then suddenly a bright, beautiful, loud tone sounded forth, such as the princess had never heard before, neither from birds nor from humans, and she immediately thought, "That can only be the singing rose."

She hurried on in the direction that the marvelous sounds seemed to be coming from. She had not walked long before she saw a large, old-fashioned castle on a cliff. She eagerly climbed up to the castle and pulled several times on the latch. Finally the gate opened with a creaking sound, and an old man with a long, ice-gray beard looked out.

"What is your wish?" he grumpily asked the startled maiden.

"I would like a singing rose," she answered. "Do you have such a thing in your garden?"

"Yes indeed," answered the old man.

"What will you take for it, if I could get it from you?"

"You need give me nothing for the singing rose. You can have it today, but as payment, I will come to you in seven years and bring you back with me to this, my castle."

"Just bring me quickly the valuable flower," shouted the maiden joyfully, for she was thinking only about the singing rose and the kingdom, but not about what would happen after seven years.

The old man went back into the castle, and returned soon with a full, glowing rose. It was singing so beautifully that the maiden's heart jumped for joy. She eagerly reached out her hand for it, and as soon as she had the flower in her hands she ran down the mountain like a deer.

The old man called after her with a serious voice, "I will see you in seven years!"

The maiden wandered the entire night through the dark woods with her rose. Her pleasure in the singing flower and the inherited kingdom caused her to forget all fear. The rose sang without pause the entire way; and the louder and more beautifully it sang, the faster the princess hurried on toward her homeland.

She arrived home and told her father everything that had happened to her, and the rose sang beautifully. Immeasurable joy ruled in the castle, and the king gave one celebration after the other. Soon the two older sisters returned. They had found nothing, and had had to return home empty handed. And now the youngest daughter, who had brought back the rose, became queen, although the old father continued to rule. The royal family lived beautiful, joyful days. Day after day and year after year slipped by.

Finally the seventh year came to an end, and on the first day of the eighth year the old man from the castle appeared before the king and demanded from him the one of his daughter who had brought home the singing rose. The king presented to him his oldest daughter, but the old man rejected her, shaking his head and growling, "She is not the right one."

When the king saw that he could not get away with deception, he -- with a bleeding heart -- turned over the youngest and dearest of his children.

The princess now had to go with the grumbling graybeard to his castle, from which she had once obtained the singing rose. The beautiful maiden was very sad, for she had no one there except for her old master. Day after day she sorrowfully thought about her father and her sisters.

In the castle there were other pleasures in abundance, but they did not comfort her, for she did not have the company of her loved ones. Her thoughts were always in her homeland. Further, all the doors and chests in the castle were locked, and the old man did not let her have access to a single key.

One day she learned -- God knows from where! -- that her oldest sister was to marry a neighboring prince, and that the wedding would take place in a few days. Disquieted, she went to the old man and asked him for permission to attend her sister's wedding.

"Just go!" growled the old man. "But I am telling you in advance, do not laugh once during the entire wedding day. If you disobey my order, I will tear you into a thousand pieces. I myself will continually be by your side, and if you as much as open your mouth to laugh, it will be over with you. Take notice!"

The princess thought that this would be easy to follow, and on the announced day she appeared with the old graybeard at her sister's wedding. Joy ruled in the king's castle when they saw the long missing queen returning. She was very happy and took advantage of the day, but she did not forget the old man's order, and she did not once open her mouth to laugh. That evening she had to take leave from her loved ones, and she sadly returned to the lonely castle with her companion. Her time of monotony began once again, and the poor princess was always glad when a day finally ended.

Then the rumor came to her ears that the other sister would marry soon. This disquieted her again, and she asked the old man if she could not attend her second sister's wedding.

"Just go!" growled the old man." But this time you are not allowed to speak a single word the entire day. I will go with you again and observe you vigilantly.

The princess thought that this would be easy to follow, and on the announced day she appeared with the old graybeard at her sister's wedding. Joy ruled in the king's castle when they saw the long missing queen returning. Everyone ran out to meet her. They greeted her and welcomed her and asked her about everything. But she pretended that she could not talk, and did not allow a single sound to escape from her beautiful lips. But this time she did not keep up her courage as well as she had the last time, and that evening when everyone was talking together until it was humming like a beehive, a little word slipped out. The old man quickly jumped up, took her by the hand, and led her out of the hall and back to his lonely castle.

Here the princess had other things in great abundance, but she greatly missed the company of her loved ones, and everything seemed terribly monotonous to her.

One day when she was sadly walking through the garden where the rose had previously blossomed and sung, the old man came to her and said with a serious expression, "Your majesty, if tomorrow while it is striking twelve you will cut off my head in three blows, then everything that you find in the castle will be yours, and you will be free forever!"

The princess took heart from the old man's speech and decided to attempt the risky deed.

The next day -- it was Saturday -- the old man appeared a little before twelve o'clock and uncovered his neck. She drew the sword that she had hung about her waist, and as the castle clock struck one she swung the sword once, then quickly again two more times. The old man's head rolled away on the floor. But behold! Instead of blood, a key fell from the head. It opened all the chests and doors in the entire castle. There the princess found many, many precious things, and she was rich and free forever.

THE BEAR PRINCE

BY
OTTO SUTERMEISTER

SWITZERLAND, 1873

A merchant once wanted to go to market. He asked his three daughters what he should bring home for them.

The oldest one said, "I would like pearls and precious stones."

"You can buy a sky-blue dress for me," said the middle one.

But the youngest one said, "Nothing in the world would be dearer to me than a grape."

Once at the market, the merchant saw as many pearls and precious stones as he could possibly want. And he soon purchased a sky-blue dress as well. But as for a grape, he could not find one anywhere at the market. This saddened him greatly, because he loved his youngest daughter most of all.

Buried thus in his thoughts, he was making his way toward home when a little dwarf stepped before him. He asked, "Why are you so sad?"

"Oh," answered the merchant, "I was supposed to bring home a grape for my youngest daughter, but I was not able to find one anywhere at the market."

The dwarf said, "Just take a few steps into that meadow down there, and you will come to a large vineyard. A white bear will be there. He will growl fiercely when you approach, but don't let that frighten you. You'll get a grape after all."

So the merchant went down into the meadow, and it happened just as the dwarf had said. A white bear was keeping guard at the vineyard, and he growled at the merchant when he was still a long way off.

"What do you want here?"

"Be so good," said the merchant, "and let me take a grape for my youngest daughter, just a single one."

"You cannot have one," said the bear, "unless you promise to give me that which will first greet you upon your arrival home."

The merchant did not think long about this before accepting the bear's terms. Then he was permitted to take a grape, and he happily made his way toward home.

Upon his arrival home, the youngest daughter ran out to meet him, for she -- more than anyone else -- had missed him, and she could hardly wait to see him. Seeing the grape in his hand, she threw her arms around his neck and could scarcely contain herself for joy.

But the father was overcome with sorrow, and he could not tell anyone why. Every day he expected the white bear to come and demand from him his dearest child.

When exactly one year had passed since he taken the grape from the vineyard, the bear did indeed trot up, confronted the merchant, and said, "Now give me that which first greeted you upon your arrival home, or I'll eat you."

The merchant had not lost all of his senses, and he said, "Take my dog. He jumped right out the door when he saw me coming."

But the bear began to growl loudly and said, "He is not the right one. If you don't keep your promise, I'll eat you."

Then the merchant said, "So just take the apple tree in front of the house. That was the first thing that I met."

But the bear growled even stronger and said, "That is not the right one. If you don't keep your promise immediately, I'll eat you."

Nothing more would help. The merchant had to surrender his youngest daughter. When she came out, a coach drove up. The bear led her inside, sat down next to her, and away they went.

After a while the coach stopped in the courtyard of a castle, and the bear led the daughter into the castle and welcomed her. This was his home, he said, and from now on she would be his wife. He gave her everything that her heart could desire, so that with time it no longer occurred to her that her husband was a bear. There were just two things that seemed strange to her: Why did the bear insist on having no lights at nighttime, and why did he always feel so cold?

After she had been with him for some time he asked her, "Do you know how long you have been here?"

"No," she said, "I haven't been thinking about time at all."

"All the better," said the bear. "It's been exactly one year. Get ready for a journey, for we must visit your father once again."

She did so with great joy, and after arriving at her father's she told him all about her life in the castle. Afterward, when she was taking leave from him, he secretly gave her some matches that the bear was not supposed to see. But the bear did see them, and he growled angrily, "Stop that, or I'll eat you."

Then he took his wife back to the castle, and they lived there together as before.

Some time later the bear said, "Do you know how long you have been here?"

"No," she said, "I don't notice the time."

"All the better," said the bear. "You have been here exactly two years. Get ready for a journey. It is time for us to visit your father once again."

She did it once again, and everything happened as the first time. But when she visited her father the third time, the bear failed to see that her father secretly gave her some matches. After arriving back at the castle, she could hardly wait for night to come when the bear was sleeping next to her in bed. Silently she struck a light and was startled with amazement and joy, for next to her was lying a handsome youth with a golden crown on his head.

He smiled at her and said, "Many thanks for redeeming me. You were the wife of an enchanted prince. Now we can celebrate our wedding properly, for now I am the king of this land." With that the entire castle came alive. Servants and attendants came from all sides, wishing good luck to the king and the queen.

ZELINDA AND THE MONSTER

BY
THOMAS FREDERICK CRANE

FROM *ITALIAN POPULAR TALES* (1885)

There was once a poor man who had three daughters; and as the youngest was the fairest and most civil, and had the best disposition, her other two sisters envied her with a deadly envy, although her father, on the contrary, loved her dearly. It happened that in a neighboring town, in the month of January, there was a great fair, and that poor man was obliged to go there to lay in the provisions necessary for the support of his family; and before departing he asked his three daughters if they would like some small presents in proportion, you understand, to his means. Rosina wished a dress, Marietta asked him for a shawl, but Zelinda was satisfied with a handsome rose.

The poor man set out on his journey early the next day, and when he arrived at the fair quickly bought what he needed, and afterward easily found Rosina's dress and Marietta's shawl; but at that season he could not find a rose for his Zelinda, although he took great pains in looking everywhere for one. However, anxious to please his dear Zelinda, he took the first road he came to, and after journeying a while arrived at a handsome garden enclosed by high walls; but as the gate was partly open he entered softly. He found the garden filled with every kind of flowers and plants, and in a corner was a tall rosebush full of beautiful rosebuds. Wherever he looked no living soul appeared from whom he might ask a rose as a gift or for money, so the poor man, without thinking, stretched out his hand, and picked a rose for his Zelinda.

Mercy! Scarcely had he pulled the flower from the stalk when there arose a great noise, and flames darted from the earth, and all at once there appeared a terrible monster with the figure of a dragon, and hissed with all his might, and cried out, enraged at that poor Christian, "Rash man! what have you done? Now you must die at once, for you have had the audacity to touch and destroy my rosebush."

The poor man, more than half dead with terror, began to weep and beg for mercy on his knees, asking pardon for the fault he had committed, and told why he had picked the rose; and then he added, "Let me depart; I have a family, and if I am killed they will go to destruction"

But the monster, more wicked than ever, responded, "Listen; one must die. Either bring me the girl that asked for the rose or I will kill you this very moment." It was impossible to move him by prayers or lamentations; the monster persisted in his decision, and did not let the poor man go until he had sworn to bring him there in the garden his daughter Zelinda.

Imagine how downhearted that poor man returned home! He gave his oldest daughters their presents and Zelinda her rose; but his face was distorted and as

54

white as though he had arisen from the dead; so that the girls, in terror, asked him what had happened and whether he had met with any misfortune. They were urgent, and at last the poor man, weeping bitterly, related the misfortunes of that unhappy journey and on what condition he had been able finally to return home. "In short," he exclaimed, "either Zelinda or I must be eaten alive by the monster."

Then the two sisters emptied the vials of their wrath on Zelinda. "Just see," they said, "that affected, capricious girl! She shall go to the monster! She who wanted roses at this season. No, indeed! Papa must stay with us. The stupid creature!"

At all these taunts Zelinda, without growing angry, simply said, "It is right that the one who has caused the misfortune should pay for it. I will go to the monster's. Yes, Papa, take me to the garden, and the Lord's will be done."

The next day Zelinda and her sorrowful father began their journey and at nightfall arrived at the garden gate. When they entered they saw as usual no one, but they beheld a lordly palace all lighted and the doors wide open. When the two travelers entered the vestibule, suddenly four marble statues, with lighted torches in their hands, descended from their pedestals, and accompanied them up the stairs to a large hall where a table was lavishly spread. The travelers, who were very hungry, sat down and began to eat without ceremony; and when they had finished, the same statues conducted them to two handsome chambers for the night. Zelinda and her father were so weary that they slept like dormice all night.

At daybreak Zelinda and her father arose, and were served with everything for breakfast by invisible hands. Then they descended to the garden, and began to seek the monster. When they came to the rosebush he appeared in all his frightful ugliness. Zelinda, on seeing him, became pale with fear, and her limbs trembled, but the monster regarded her attentively with his great fiery eyes, and afterward said to the poor man, "Very well; you have kept your word, and I am satisfied. Now depart and leave me alone here with the young girl."

At this command the old man thought he should die; and Zelinda, too, stood there half stupefied and her eyes full of tears; but entreaties were of no avail; the monster remained as obdurate as a stone, and the poor man was obliged to depart, leaving his dear Zelinda in the monster's power.

When the monster was alone with Zelinda he began to caress her, and make loving speeches to her, and managed to appear quite civil. There was no danger of his forgetting her, and he saw that she wanted nothing, and every day, talking with her in the garden, he asked her, "Do you love me, Zelinda? Will you be my wife?"

The young girl always answered him in the same way, "I like you, sir, but I will never be your wife."

Then the monster appeared very sorrowful, and redoubled his caresses and attentions, and, sighing deeply, said, "But you see, Zelinda, if you should marry me wonderful things would happen. What they are I cannot tell you until you will be my wife."

Zelinda, although in her heart not dissatisfied with that beautiful place and with being treated like a queen, still did not feel at all like marrying the monster, because he was too ugly and looked like a beast, and always answered his requests in the same manner.

One day, however, the monster called Zelinda in haste, and said, "Listen,

Zelinda; if you do not consent to marry me it is fated that your father must die. He is ill and near the end of his life, and you will not be able even to see him again. See whether I am telling you the truth." And, drawing out an enchanted mirror, the monster showed Zelinda her father on his deathbed.

At that spectacle Zelinda, in despair and half mad with grief, cried, "Oh, save my father, for mercy's sake! Let me be able to embrace him once more before he dies. Yes, yes, I promise you I will be your faithful and constant wife, and that without delay. But save my father from death."

Scarcely had Zelinda uttered these words when suddenly the monster was transformed into a very handsome youth. Zelinda was astounded by this unexpected change, and the young man took her by the hand, and said, "Know, dear Zelinda, that I am the son of the King of the Oranges. An old witch, touching me, changed me into the terrible monster I was, and condemned me to be hidden in this rosebush until a beautiful girl consented to become my wife."

THE SMALL-TOOTH DOG

BY

SIDNEY OLDALL ADDY

FROM
HOUSEHOLD TALES AND OTHER TRADITIONAL REMAINS, (1895)

Once upon a time there was a merchant who traveled about the world a great deal. On one of his journeys thieves attacked him, and they would have taken both his life and his money if a large dog had not come to his rescue and driven the thieves away. When the dog had driven the thieves away he took the merchant to his house, which was a very handsome one, and dressed his wounds and nursed him till he was well.

As soon as he was able to travel the merchant began his journey home, but before starting he told the dog how grateful he was for his kindness, and asked him what reward he could offer in return, and he said he would not refuse to give the most precious thing he had.

And so the merchant said to the dog, "Will you accept a fish I have that can speak twelve languages?"

"No," said the dog, "I will not."

"Or a goose that lays golden eggs?"

"No," said the dog, "I will not."

"Or a mirror in which you can see what anybody is thinking about?"

"No," said the dog, "I will not."

"Then what will you have?" said the merchant.

"I will have none of such presents," said the dog; "but let me fetch your daughter, and bring her to my house."

When the merchant heard this he was grieved, but what he had promised had to be done, so he said to the dog, "You can come and fetch my daughter after I have been home for a week."

So at the end of the week, the dog came to the merchant's house to fetch his daughter, but when he got there he stayed outside the door, and would not go in.

But the merchant's daughter did as her father told her, and came out of the house dressed for a journey and ready to go with the dog.

When the dog saw her he looked pleased, and said, "Jump on my back, and I will take you away to my house."

So she mounted on the dog's back, and away they went at a great pace, until they reached the dog's house, which was many miles off.

But after she had been a month at the dog's house she began to mope and cry.

"What are you crying for?" said the dog.

"Because I want to go back to my father," she said.

57

The dog said, "If you will promise me that you will not stay there more than three days I will take you there. But first of all," said he, "what do you call me?"

"A great, foul, small-tooth dog," said she.

"Then," said he, "I will not let you go."

But she cried so pitifully that he promised again to take her home.

"But before we start," he said, "tell me what you call me."

"Oh," she said, "your name is Sweet-as-a-Honeycomb."

"Jump on my back," said he, "and I'll take you home."

So he trotted away with her on his back for forty miles, when they came to a stile.

"And what do you call me?" said he, before they got over the stile.

Thinking she was safe on her way, the girl said, "A great, foul, small-tooth dog."

But when she said this, he did not jump over the stile, but turned right round again at once, and galloped back to his own house with the girl on his back.

Another week went by, and again the girl wept so bitterly that the dog promised to take her to her father's house.

So the girl got on the dog's back again, and they reached the first stile, as before, and the dog stopped and said, "And what do you call me?"

"Sweet-as-a-Honeycomb," she replied.

So the dog leaped over the stile, and they went on for twenty miles until they came to another stile.

"And what do you call me?" said the dog with a wag of his tail.

She was thinking more of her father and her own house than of the dog, so she answered, "A great, foul, small-tooth dog."

Then the dog was in a great rage, and he turned right round about, and galloped back to his own house as before.

After she had cried for another week, the dog promised again to take her back to her father's house. So she mounted upon his back once more, and when they got to the first stile, the dog said, "And what do you call me?"

"Sweet-as-a-Honeycomb," she said.

So the dog jumped over the stile, and away they went -- for now the girl made up her mind to say the most loving things she could think of -- until they reached her father's house.

When they got to the door of the merchant's house, the dog said, "And what do you call me?"

Just at that moment the girl forgot the loving things she meant to say and began, "A great --," but the dog began to turn, and she got fast hold of the door latch, and was going to say "foul," when she saw how grieved the dog looked and remembered how good and patient he had been with her, so she said, "Sweeter-than-a-Honeycomb."

When she had said this she thought the dog would have been content and have galloped away, but instead of that he suddenly stood upon his hind legs, and with his forelegs he pulled off his dog's head and tossed it high in the air. His hairy coat dropped off, and there stood the handsomest young man in the world, with the finest and smallest teeth you ever saw.

Of course they were married, and lived together happily.

THE ENCHANTED TSARÉVICH

BY

LEONARD MAGNUS

FROM *RUSSIAN FOLK TALES*, 1916

Once upon a time there was a merchant who had three daughters. It so happened he had one day to go to strange countries to buy wares, and so he asked his daughters, "What shall I bring you from beyond the seas?"

The eldest asked for a new coat, and the next one also asked for a new coat; but the youngest one only took a sheet of paper and sketched a flower on it. "Bring me, bátyushka [father], a flower like this!"

So the merchant went and made a long journey to foreign kingdoms, but he could never see such a flower. So he came back home, and he saw on his way a splendid lofty palace with watchtowers, turrets, and a garden. He went a walk in the garden, and you cannot imagine how many trees he saw and flowers, every flower fairer than the other flowers. And then he looked and he saw a single one like the one which his daughter had sketched.

"Oh," he said, "I will tear off and bring this to my beloved daughter; evidently there is nobody here to watch me."

So he ran up and broke it off, and as soon as he had done it, in that very instant a boisterous wind arose and thunder thundered, and a fearful monster stood in front of him, a formless, winged snake with three heads. "How dared you play the master in my garden!" cried the snake to the merchant. "Why have you broken off a blossom?"

The merchant was frightened, fell on his knees and besought pardon.

"Very well," said the snake, "I will forgive you, but on condition that whoever meets you first, when you reach home, you must give me for all eternity; and, if you deceive me, do not forget, nobody can ever hide himself from me. I shall find you wherever you are."

The merchant agreed to the condition and came back home. And the youngest daughter saw him from the window and ran out to meet him. Then the merchant hung his head, looked at his beloved daughter, and began to shed bitter tears.

"What is the matter with you? Why are you weeping, bátyushka?"

He gave her the blossom and told what had befallen him.

"Do not grieve, bátyushka ," said the youngest daughter. "It is God's gift. Perhaps I shall fare well. Take me to the snake."

So the father took her away, set her in the palace, bade farewell, and set out home. Then the fair maiden, the daughter of the merchant, went in the different rooms, and beheld everywhere gold and velvet; but no one was there to be seen,

59

not a single human soul.

Time went by and went by, and the fair damsel became hungry and thought, "Oh, if I could only have something to eat!" But before ever she had thought, in front of her stood a table, and on the table were dishes and drinks and refreshments. The only thing that was not there was birds' milk. Then she sat down to the table, drank and ate, got up, and it had all vanished.

Darkness now came on, and the merchant's daughter went into the bedroom, wishing to lie down and sleep. Then a boisterous wind rustled round and the three-headed snake appeared in front of her.

"Hail, fair maiden! Put my bed outside this door!"

So the fair maiden put the bed outside the door and herself lay on the bedstead.

She awoke in the morning, and again in the entire house there was not a single soul to be seen. And it all went well with her. Whatever she wished for appeared on the spot.

In the evening the snake flew to her and ordered, "Now, fair maiden, put my bed next to your bedstead."

She then laid it next to her bedstead, and the night went by, and the maiden awoke, and again there was never a soul in the palace.

And for the third time the snake came in the evening and said, "Now, fair maiden, I am going to lie with you in the bedstead."

The merchant's daughter was fearfully afraid of lying on a single bed with such a formless monster. But she could not help herself, so she strengthened her heart and lay down with him.

In the morning the serpent said to her, "If you are now weary, fair maiden, go to your father and your sisters. Spend a day with them, and in the evening come back to me. But see to it that you are not late. If you are one single minute late I shall die of grief."

"No, I shall not be late," said the maiden, the merchant's daughter, and descended the steps; there was a barouche ready for her, and she sat down. That very instant she arrived at her father's courtyard.

Then the father saw, welcomed, kissed her, and asked her, "How has God been dealing with you, my beloved daughter ? Has it been well with you?"

"Very well, father!" And she started telling of all the wealth there was in the palace, how the snake loved her, how whatever she only thought of was in that instant fulfilled.

The sisters heard, and did not know what to do out of sheer envy.

Now the day was ebbing away, and the fair maiden made ready to go back, and was bidding farewell to her father and her sisters, saying, "This is the time I must go back. I was bidden keep to my term."

But the envious sisters rubbed onions on their eyes and made as though they were weeping: "Do not go away, sister; stay until tomorrow."

She was very sorry for her sisters, and stayed one day more.

In the morning she bade farewell to them all and went to the palace. When she arrived it was as empty as before. She went into the garden, and she saw the serpent lying dead in the pond! He had thrown himself for sheer grief into the water.

"Oh, my God, what have I done!" cried out the fair maiden, and she wept bitter tears, ran. up to the pond, hauled the snake out of the water, embraced one head and kissed it with all her might. And the snake trembled, and in a minute turned into a good youth.

"I thank you, fair maiden," he said. "You have saved me from the greatest misfortune. I am no snake, but an enchanted prince."

Then they went back to the merchant's house, were betrothed, lived long, and lived for good and happy things.

THE STORY OF BEAUTY & THE BEAST

BY

GABRIELLE-SUZANNE BARBOT DE VILLENEUVE

TRANSLATED FROM THE FRENCH BY J. R. PLANCHÉ IN *FOUR AND TWENTY FAIRY TALES* (1858)

IN a country very far from this is to be seen a great city wherein trade flourishes abundantly. It numbered amongst its citizens a merchant, who succeeded in all his speculations, and upon whom Fortune, responding to his wishes, had always showered her fairest favours. But if he had immense wealth, he had also a great many children, his family consisting of six boys and six girls. None of them were settled in life: the boys were too young to think of it; the girls, too proud of their fortunes, upon which they had every reason to count, could not easily determine upon the choice they should make. Their vanity was flattered by the attentions of the handsomest young gentlemen. But a reverse of fortune which they did not at all expect, came to trouble their felicity. Their house took fire; the splendid furniture with which it was filled, the account books, the notes, gold, silver, and all the valuable stores which formed the merchant's principal wealth, were enveloped in this fatal conflagration, which was so violent that very few of the things could be saved.

This first misfortune was but the forerunner of others. The father, with whom hitherto everything had prospered, lost at the same time, either by shipwreck or by pirates, all the ships he had at sea; his correspondents made him a bankrupt, his foreign agents were treacherous; in short, from the greatest opulence, he suddenly fell into the most abject poverty. He had nothing left but a small country house, situated in a lonely place, more than a hundred leagues from the city in which he usually resided. Impelled to seek a place of refuge from noise and tumult, he took his family to this retired spot, who were in despair at such a revolution. The daughters of this unfortunate merchant were especially horrified at the prospect of the life they should have to lead in this dull solitude. For some time they flattered themselves that, when their father's intention became known, their lovers, who had hitherto sued in vain, would be only too happy to find they were inclined to listen to them. They imagined that the many admirers of each would be all striving to obtain the preference. They thought if they wished only for a husband they would obtain one; but they did not remain very long in such a delightful illusion. They had lost their greatest attractions when, like a flash of lightning, their father's splendid fortune had disappeared, and their time for choosing had departed with it. Their crowd of admirers vanished at the moment of their downfall; their beauty was not sufficiently powerful to retain one of them. Their friends were not more generous than their lovers. From the hour they became poor, every one, without exception, ceased to know them. Some were even cruel enough to impute their misfortunes to their own acts. Those whom the father had most obliged were his most vehement calumniators: they reported that all his calamities were brought on by his own bad conduct, his prodigality, and the foolish extravagance of himself and his children.

This wretched family, therefore, could not do better than depart from a city wherein everybody took a pleasure in insulting them in their misfortunes. Having no resource whatever, they shut themselves up in their country house, situated in the middle of an almost impenetrable forest, and which might well be considered the saddest abode in the world. What misery they had to endure in this frightful solitude! They were forced to do the hardest work. Not being able to have any one to wait upon them, this unfortunate merchant's sons were compelled to divide the servant's duties amongst them, as well as to exert themselves in every way that people must do who have to earn their livelihood in the country. The daughters, on their part, had sufficient employment.

Like the poor peasant girls, they found themselves obliged to employ their delicate hands in all the labours of a rural life. Wearing nothing but woollen dresses, having nothing to gratify their vanity, existing upon what the land could give them, limited to common necessaries, but still retaining a refined and dainty taste, these girls incessantly regretted the city and its attractions. The recollection even of their younger days passed so rapidly in a round of mirth and pleasure was their greatest torment. The youngest girl, however, displayed greater perseverance and firmness in their common misfortune. She bore her lot cheerfully, and with a strength of mind much beyond her years: not but what, at first, she was truly melancholy. Alas! who would not have felt such misfortunes. But, after deploring her father's ruin, could she do better than resume her former gaiety, make up her mind to the position she was placed in, and forget a world which she and her family had found so ungrateful, and the friendship of which she was so fully persuaded was not to be relied upon in the time of adversity?

Anxious to console herself and her brothers, by her amiable disposition and sprightliness, there was nothing she did not do to amuse them. The merchant had spared no cost in her education, nor in that of her sisters. At this sad period she derived all the advantage from it she desired. As she could play exceedingly well upon various instruments, and sing to them charmingly, she asked her sisters to follow her example, but her cheerfulness and patience only made them more miserable. These girls, who were so inconsolable in their ill fortune, thought their youngest sister showed a poor and mean spirit, and even silliness, to be so merry in the state it had pleased Providence to reduce them to. "How happy she is," said the eldest; "she was intended for such coarse occupations. With such low notions, what would she have done in the world?" Such remarks were unjust. This young person was much more fitted to shine in society than either of them. She was a perfectly beautiful young creature, her good temper rendered her adorable. A generous and tender heart was visible in all her words and actions. Quite as much alive to the reverses that had just overwhelmed her family as either of her sisters, by a strength of mind which is not common in her sex, she concealed her sorrow, and rose superior to her misfortunes. So much firmness was considered to be insensibility. But one can easily appeal from a judgment pronounced by jealousy.

Every intelligent person, who saw her in her true light, was eager to give her the preference over her sisters. In the midst of her greatest splendour, although distinguished by her merit, she was so handsome that she was called "The Beauty." Known by this name only, what more was required to increase the jealousy and hatred of her sisters? Her charms, and the general esteem in which she was held, might have induced her to hope for a much more advantageous establishment than her sisters; but feeling only for her father's misfortunes, far from retarding his departure from a city in which she had enjoyed so much pleasure, she did all she could to expedite it. This young girl was as contented in their solitude as she had been in the midst of the world. To amuse herself in her hours of relaxation, she would dress her hair with flowers, and, like the shepherdesses of former times, forgetting in a rural life all that had most gratified her in the height of opulence, every day brought to her some new innocent pleasure.

Two years had already passed, and the family began to be accustomed to a country life, when a hope of returning prosperity arrived to discompose their tranquillity. The father received news that one of his vessels, that he thought was lost, had safely arrived in port, richly laden. His informants added, they feared the factors would take advantage of his absence, and sell the cargo at a low price, and by this fraud make a great profit at his expense. He imparted these tidings to his children, who did not doubt for an instant but that they should soon be enabled to return from exile. The girls, much more impatient than the boys, thinking it was unnecessary to wait for more certain proof, were anxious to set out instantly, and to leave everything behind them. But the father, who was more prudent, begged them to moderate their delight. However important he was to his family at a time when the labours of the field could not be interrupted without great loss, he determined to leave his sons to get in the harvest, and that he would set out upon this long journey. His daughters, with the exception of the youngest, expected they would soon be restored to their former opulence. They fancied that, even if their father's property would not be considerable enough to settle them in the great metropolis, their native place, he would at least have sufficient for them to live in a less expensive city. They trusted they should find good society there, attract admirers, and profit by the first offer that might be made to them. Scarcely remembering the troubles they had undergone for the last two years, believing themselves to be already, as by a miracle, removed from poverty into the lap of plenty, they ventured (for retirement had not cured them of the taste for luxury and display) to overwhelm their father with foolish commissions. They requested him to make purchases of jewelry, attire, and head-dresses. Each endeavoured to outvie the other in her demands, so that the sum total of their father's supposed fortune would not have been sufficient to satisfy them.

"Beauty", who was not the slave of ambition, and who always acted with prudence, saw directly that if he executed her sisters' commissions, it would be useless for her to ask for anything. But the father, astonished at her silence, said, interrupting his insatiable daughters, "Well, Beauty, dost thou not desire anything? What shall I bring thee? what dost thou wish for? Speak freely."

"My dear papa," replied the amiable girl, embracing him affectionately, "I wish for one thing more precious than all the ornaments my sisters have asked you for; I have limited my desires to it, and shall be only too happy if they can be fulfilled. It is the gratification of seeing you return in perfect health."

This answer was so unmistakeably disinterested, that it covered the others with shame and confusion. They were so angry, that one of them, answering for the rest, said with bitterness, "This child gives herself great airs, and fancies that she will distinguish herself by these affected heroics. Surely nothing can be more ridiculous."

But the father, touched by her expressions, could not help showing his delight at them; appreciating, too, the feeling which induced her to ask nothing for herself, he begged she would choose something; and to allay the ill-will that his other daughters had towards her, he observed to her that such indifference to dress was not natural at her age—that there was a time for everything. "Very well, my dear father," said she, "since you desire me to make some request, I beg you will bring me a rose; I love that flower passionately, and since I have lived in this desert I have not had the pleasure of seeing one." This was to obey her father, and at the same time to avoid putting him to any expense for her.

At length the day arrived, that this good old man was compelled to leave his family. He travelled as fast as he could to the great city to which the prospect of a new fortune recalled him. But he did not meet with the benefits he had hoped for. His vessel had certainly arrived; but his partners, believing him to be dead, had taken possession of it, and all the cargo had been disposed of. Thus, instead of entering into the full and peaceable possession of that which belonged to him, he was compelled to encounter all sorts of chicanery in the pursuit of his rights. He overcame them, but after more than six months of trouble and expense, he was not any richer than he was before. His debtors had become insolvent, and he could hardly defray his own costs. Thus terminated this dream of riches.

To add to his disagreeables, he was obliged, on the score of economy, to start on his homeward journey at the most inconvenient time, and in the most frightful weather. Exposed on the road to the piercing blasts, he thought he should die with fatigue; but when he found himself within a few miles of his house (which he did not reckon upon leaving for such false hopes, and which Beauty had shown her sense in mistrusting) his strength returned to him. It would be some hours before he could cross the forest; it was late, but he wished to continue his journey. He was benighted, suffering from intense cold, buried, one might say, in the snow, with his horse; not knowing which way to bend his steps, he thought his last hour had come: no hut in his road, although the forest was filled with them. A tree, hollowed by age, was the best shelter he could find, and only too happy was he to hide himself in it. This tree protecting him from the cold, was the means of saving his life; and the horse, a little distance from his master, perceiving another hollow tree, was led by instinct to take shelter in that.

The night, in such a situation, appeared to him to be never-ending; furthermore, he was famished, frightened at the roaring of the wild beasts, that were constantly passing by him. Could he be at peace for an instant? His trouble and anxiety did not end with the night. He had no sooner the pleasure of seeing daylight than his distress was greater. The ground appeared so extraordinarily covered with snow, no road could he find—no track was to be seen. It was only after great fatigue and frequent falls, that he succeeded in discovering something like a path upon which he could keep his footing.

Proceeding without knowing in which direction, chance led him into the avenue of a beautiful castle, which the snow seemed to have respected. It consisted of four rows of orange-trees, laden with flowers and fruit. Statues were seen here and there, regardless of order or symmetry—some were in the middle of the road, others among the trees — all after the strangest fashion; they were of the size of life, and had the colour of human beings, in different attitudes, and in various dresses, the greatest number representing warriors. Arriving at the first court-yard, he perceived a great many more statues. He was suffering so much from cold that he could not stop to examine them. An agate staircase, with balusters of chased gold, first presented itself to his sight: he passed through several magnificently furnished rooms; a gentle warmth which he breathed in them renovated him. He needed food; but to whom could he apply? This large and magnificent edifice appeared to be inhabited only by statues. A profound silence reigned throughout it; nevertheless it had not the air of an old palace that had been deserted. The halls, the rooms, the galleries were all open; no living thing appeared to be in this charming place.

Weary of wandering over this vast dwelling, he stopped in a saloon, wherein was a large fire. Presuming that it was prepared for some one, who would not be long in appearing, he drew near the fireplace to warm himself; but no one came. Seated on a sofa near the fire, a sweet sleep closed his eyelids, and left him no longer in a condition to observe the entrance of any one. Fatigue induced him to sleep; hunger awoke him; he had been suffering from it for the last twenty-four hours. The exercise that he had taken ever since he had been in this palace increased his appetite. When he awoke and opened his eyes, he was astonished to see a table elegantly laid. A light repast would not have satisfied him; but the viands, magnificently dressed, invited him to eat of everything.

His first care was to utter in a loud voice his thanks to those from whom he had received so much kindness, and he then resolved to wait quietly till it pleased his host to make himself known to him. As fatigue caused him to sleep before his repast, so did the food produce the same effect, and his repose was longer and more powerful; in fact, this second time he slept for at least four hours. Upon awaking, in the place of the first table he saw another of porphyry, upon which some kind hand had set out a collation consisting of cakes, preserved fruits, and liqueurs. This was likewise for his use. Profiting, therefore, by the kindness shown him, he partook of everything that suited his appetite, his taste, and his fancy.

Finding at length no one to speak to, or to inform him whether this palace was inhabited by a man or by a God, fear began to take possession of him, for he was naturally timid. He resolved, therefore, to repass through all the apartments, and overwhelm with thanks the Genius to whom he was indebted for so much kindness, and in the most respectful manner solicit him to appear. All his attentions were useless: no appearance of servants, no result by which he could ascertain that the palace was inhabited. Thinking seriously of what he should do, he began to fancy, for what reason he could not imagine, that some good spirit had made this mansion a present to him, with all the riches that it contained. This idea seemed like inspiration, and without further delay, making a new inspection of it, he took possession of all the treasures he could find. More than this, he settled in his own mind what share of it he should allow to each of his children, and selected the apartments which would particularly suit them, enjoying the delight beforehand which his journey would afford them. He entered the garden, where, in spite of the severity of the winter, the rarest flowers were exhaling the most delicious perfume in the mildest and purest air. Birds of all kinds blending their songs with the confused noise of the waters, made an agreeable harmony.

The old man, in ecstasies at such wonders, said to himself, "My daughters will not, I think, find it very difficult to accustom themselves to this delicious abode. I cannot believe that they will regret, or that they will prefer the city to this mansion. Let me set out directly," cried he, in a transport of joy rather uncommon for him; "I shall increase my happiness in witnessing theirs: I will take possession at once."

Upon entering this charming castle he had taken care, notwithstanding he was nearly perished, to unbridle his horse and let him wend his way to a stable which he had observed in the fore-court. An alley, ornamented by palisades, formed by rose-bushes in full bloom, led to it. He had never seen such lovely roses. Their perfume reminded him that he had promised to give Beauty a rose. He picked one, and was about to gather enough to make half-a-dozen bouquets, when a most frightful noise made him turn round. He was terribly alarmed upon perceiving at his side a horrible beast, which, with an air of fury, laid upon his neck a kind of trunk, resembling an elephant's, and said, with a terrific voice, "Who gave thee permission to gather my roses? Is it not enough that I kindly allowed thee to remain in my palace. Instead of feeling grateful, rash man, I find thee stealing my flowers! Thy insolence shall not remain unpunished."

The good man, already too much overpowered by the unexpected appearance of this monster, thought he should die of fright at these words, and quickly throwing away the fatal rose. "Ah! my Lord," said he, prostrating himself before him, "have mercy on me! I am not ungrateful! Penetrated by all your kindness, I did not imagine that so slight a liberty could possibly have offended you."

The monster very angrily replied, "Hold thy tongue, thou foolish talker. I care not for thy flattery, nor for the titles thou bestowest on me. I am not my Lord; I am The Beast; and thou shalt not escape the death thou deservest."

The merchant, dismayed at so cruel a sentence, and thinking that submission was the only means to preserve his life, said, in a truly affecting manner, that the rose he had dared to take was for one of his daughters, called Beauty. Then, whether he hoped to escape from death, or to induce his enemy to feel for him, he related to him all his misfortunes; he told him the object of his journey, and did not omit to dwell on the little present he was bound to give Beauty; adding, that was the only thing she had asked for, while the riches of a king would hardly have sufficed to satisfy the wishes of his other daughters ; and so came to the opportunity which had offered itself to satisfy the modest desire of Beauty, and his belief that he could have done so without any unpleasant consequences ; asking pardon, moreover, for his involuntary fault. The Beast considered for a moment, then, speaking in a milder tone, he said to him, "I will pardon thee, but upon condition that thou wilt give me one of thy daughters—I require some one to repair this fault."

"Just Heaven!" replied the merchant; "how can I keep my word? Could I be so inhuman as to save my own life at the expense of one of my children's; under what pretext could I bring her here?"

"There must be no pretext," interrupted the Beast. "I expect that whichever daughter you bring here she will come willingly, or I will not have either of them.

Go; see if there be not one amongst them sufficiently courageous, and loving thee enough, to sacrifice herself to save thy life. Thou appearest to be an honest man. Give me thy word of honour to return in a month. If thou canst decide to bring one of them back with thee, she will remain here and thou wilt return home. If thou canst not do so, promise me to return hither alone, after bidding them farewell for ever, for thou wilt belong to me. Do not fancy," continued the Monster, grinding his teeth, "that by merely agreeing to my proposition thou wilt be saved. I warn thee, if thou thinkest so to escape me, I will seek for thee, and destroy thee and thy race, although a hundred thousand men appear to defend thee."

The good man, although quite convinced that he should vainly put to the proof the devotion of his daughters, accepted, nevertheless, the Monster's proposition. He promised to return to him at the time named, and give himself up to his sad fate, without rendering it necessary for the Beast to seek for him. After this assurance he thought himself at liberty to retire and take leave of the Beast, whose presence was most distressing to him. The respite was but brief, yet he feared he might revoke it. He expressed his anxiety to depart; but the Beast told him he should riot do so till the following day. "Thou wilt find," said he, a horse ready at break of day. He will carry thee home quickly. Adieu—go to supper, and wait my orders."

The poor man, more dead than alive, returned to the saloon in which he had feasted so heartily. Before a large fire his supper, already laid, invited him to sit and enjoy it. The delicacy and richness of the dishes had no longer, however, any temptation for him. Overwhelmed by his grief, he would not have seated himself at the table, but that he feared that the Beast was concealed somewhere, and observing him, and that he would excite his anger by any slight of his bounty. To avoid further disaster, he made a momentary truce with his grief, and, as well as his afflicted heart would permit, he tasted, in turn, the various dishes. At the end of the repast a great noise was heard in the adjoining apartment, and he did not doubt that it was his formidable host. As he could not manage to avoid his presence, he tried to recover from the alarm which this sudden noise had caused him. At the same moment, the Beast, who appeared, asked him abruptly if he had made a good supper. The good man replied, in a modest and timid tone, that he had, thanks to his attention, eaten heartily.

"Promise me," replied the Monster, "to remember your word to me, and to keep it as a man of honour, in bringing me one of your daughters."

The old man, who was not much entertained with this conversation, swore to him that he would fulfil what he had promised, and return in a month alone or with one of his daughters, if he should find one who loved him sufficiently to follow him on the conditions he must propose to her.

"I warn thee again," said the Beast, "to take care not to deceive her as to the sacrifice which thou must exact from her, or the danger she will incur. Paint to her my face such as it is. Let her know what she is about to do: above all, let her be firm in her resolution. There will be no time for reflection when thou shalt have brought her hither. There must be no drawing back: thou wilt be equally lost, without obtaining for her the liberty to return." The merchant, who was overcome at this discourse, reiterated his promise to conform to all that was prescribed to him. The Monster, satisfied with his answer, ordered him to retire to rest, and not to rise till he should see the sun, and hear a golden bell.

"Thou wilt breakfast before setting out," said he again; "and thou mayest take a rose with thee for Beauty. The horse which shall bear thee will be ready in the court-yard. I reckon on seeing thee again in a month, if thou art an honest man. If thou failest in thy word, I shall pay thee a visit." The good man, for fear of prolonging a conversation already too painful to him, made a profound reverence to the Beast, who told him again not to be anxious respecting the road by which he should return; as at the time appointed the same horse which he would mount the next morning would be found at his gate, and would suffice for his daughter and himself.

However little disposition the old man felt for sleep, he dared not disobey the orders he had received. Obliged to lie down, he did not rise till the sun began to illumine the chamber. His breakfast was soon despatched, and he then descended into the garden to gather the rose which the Beast had ordered him to take to Beauty. How many tears this flower caused him to shed. But the fear of drawing on himself new disasters made him constrain his feelings, and he went, without further delay, in search of the horse which had been promised him. He found on the saddle a light but warm cloak. As soon as the horse felt him on his back, he set off with incredible speed. The merchant, who in a moment lost sight of this fatal palace, experienced as great a sensation of joy as he had on the previous evening felt in perceiving it, with this difference, that the delight of leaving it was embittered by the cruel necessity of returning to it.

"To what have I pledged myself?" said he, whilst his courser carried him with a velocity and a lightness which is only known in fairy land. "Would it not be better that I should become at once the victim of this monster who thirsts for the blood of my family? By a promise I have made, as unnatural as it is indiscreet, I have prolonged my life. Is it possible that I could think of extending my days at the expense of those of my daughters? Can I have the barbarity to lead one to him, to see him, no doubt, devour her before my eyes?" But all at once, interrupting himself, he cried, "Miserable wretch that I am, what have I to fear? If I could find it in my heart to silence the voice of nature, would it depend on me to commit this cowardly act? She must know her fate and consent to it. I see no chance that she will be inclined to sacrifice herself for an inhuman father, and I ought not to make such a proposition to her. It is unjust. But even if the affection which they all entertain for me should induce one to devote herself, would not a single glance at the Beast destroy her constancy, and I could not complain. Ah! too imperious Beast," exclaimed he, "thou hast done this expressly! By putting an impossible condition to the means thou offerest me to escape thy fury, and obtain the pardon of a trifling fault, thou hast added insult to injury! But," continued he, "I cannot bear to think of it. I hesitate no longer; and I would rather expose myself without turning away from thy rage, than attempt a useless mode of escape, which my paternal love trembles to employ. Let me retrace," said he, "the road to this frightful palace, and without deigning to purchase so dearly the remnant of a life which can never be but miserable—without waiting for the month which is accorded me to expire,—return and terminate this day my miserable existence!"

At these words he endeavoured to retrace his steps, but he found it impossible to turn the bridle of his horse. Allowing himself, therefore, against his will, to be carried forward, he resolved at least to propose nothing to his daughters. Already he saw his house in the distance, and strengthening himself more and more in his resolution, "I will not speak to them," he said, "of the danger which threatens me: I shall have the pleasure of embracing them once more; I shall give them my last advice; I will beg them to live on good terms with their brothers, whom I shall also implore not to abandon them."

In the midst of this reverie, he reached his door. His own horse, which had found its way home the previous evening, had alarmed his family. His sons, dispersed in the forest, had sought him in every direction; and his daughters, in their impatience to hear some tidings of him, were at the door, in order to obtain the earliest intelligence. As he was mounted on a magnificent steed, and wrapt in a rich cloak, they could not recognise him, but took him at first for a messenger sent by him, and the rose which they perceived attached to the pummel of the saddle made them perfectly easy on his account.

When this afflicted father, however, approached nearer, they recognised him, and thought only of evincing their satisfaction at seeing him return in good health. But the sadness depicted in his face, and his eyes filled with tears, which he vainly endeavoured to restrain, changed their joy into anxiety. All hastened to inquire the cause of his trouble. He made no reply but by saying to Beauty, as he presented her with the rose. There is what thou hast demanded of me, but thou wilt pay dearly for it, as well as the others."

"I was certain," exclaimed the eldest, "and I was saying, this very moment, that she would be the only one whose commission you would execute. At this time of the year, a rose must have cost more than you would have had to pay for us all five together; and, judging from appearances, the rose will be faded before the day is ended: never mind, however, you were determined to gratify the fortunate Beauty at any price."

"It is true," replied the father, mournfully, "that this rose has cost me dear, and more dear than all the ornaments which you wished for would have done. It is not in money, however; and would to Heaven that I might have purchased it with all I am yet worth in the world."

These words excited the curiosity of his children, and dispelled the resolution which he had taken not to reveal his adventure. He informed them of the ill-success of his journey, the trouble which he had undergone in running after a chimerical fortune, and all that had taken place in the palace of the Monster. After this explanation, despair took the place of hope and of joy.

The daughters seeing all their projects annihilated by this thunderbolt, uttered fearful cries; the brothers, more courageous, said resolutely that they would not suffer their father to return to this frightful castle; that they were bold enough to deliver the earth from this horrible Beast, even supposing he should have the temerity to come in search of him. The good man, although moved at their affliction, forbad them to commit violence, telling them, that as he had given his word, he would kill himself rather than fail to keep it.

Notwithstanding this, they sought for expedients to save his life; the young men, full of courage and filial affection, proposed that one of them should go and offer himself as a victim to the wrath of the Beast; but the monster had said positively and explicitly that he would have one of the daughters, and not one of the sons. The brave brothers grieved that their good intentions could not be acted upon, then did what they could to inspire their sisters with the same sentiments. But their jealousy of Beauty was sufficient to raise an invincible obstacle to such heroic action.

"It is not just," said they, "that we should perish in so frightful a manner for a fault of which we are not guilty. It would be to render us victims to Beauty, to whom they would be very glad to sacrifice us; but duty does not require such a sacrifice. Here is the fruit of the moderation and perpetual preaching of this unhappy girl! Why did she not ask, like us, for a good stock of clothes and jewels. If we have not had them, it has at all events cost nothing for asking, and we have no cause to reproach ourselves for having exposed the life of our father by indiscreet demands. If, by an affected disinterestedness, she had not sought to distinguish herself, as she is in all things more favoured than we, he would have, no doubt, found enough money to content her. But she must needs, by her singular caprice, bring on us all this misfortune. It is she who has caused it, and they wish us to pay the penalty. We will not be her dupe. She has brought it on herself, and she must find the remedy."

Beauty, whose grief had almost deprived her of consciousness, suppressing her sobs and sighs, said to her sisters, "I am the cause of this misfortune; it is I alone who must repair it. I confess it would be unjust to allow you to suffer for my fault. Alas! it was, notwithstanding, an innocent wish. Could I foresee that the desire to have a rose when we were in the middle of summer would be punished so cruelly? The fault is committed, however; whether I am innocent or guilty, it is just that I should expiate it. It cannot be imputed to any one else. I will risk my life," pursued she, in a firm tone, "to release my father from his fatal engagement. I will go to find the Beast; too happy in being able to die in order to preserve the life of him from whom I received mine, and to silence your murmurs. Do not fear that anything can turn me from my purpose; but I pray you during this month to do me the favour to spare me your reproaches."

So much firmness in a girl of her age surprised them all much; and the brothers, who loved her tenderly, were moved at her resolution. They paid her infinite attention, and felt the loss they were about to sustain. But it was requisite to save the life of a father; this pious motive closed their mouths; and well persuaded that it was a thing decided on, far from thinking of combating so generous a purpose, they contented themselves by shedding tears, and giving their sister all the praise which her noble resolution merited, all the more from her being only sixteen years of age, and having the right to regret a life which she was about to sacrifice in so cruel a manner. The father alone would not consent to the design of his youngest daughter; but the others reproached him insolently with the charge that Beauty alone was cared for by him, in spite of the misfortune which she had caused, and that he was sorry that it was not one of the elders who should pay for her imprudence.

This unjust language forced him to desist; besides, Beauty assured him that if he would not accept the exchange, she would make it in spite of him, for she would go alone to seek the Beast, and so perish without saving him. "How do we know," said she, forcing herself to assume more tranquillity than she really felt; "perhaps the dreadful fate which appears to await me conceals another as happy as this seems terrible?"

Her sisters, hearing her speak thus, smiled maliciously at the wild idea; they were enchanted at the delusion in which they believed her to be indulging. But the old man, conquered by all her reasons, and remembering an ancient prediction, by which he had learnt that this daughter should save his life, and that she should be a source of happiness to all her family, ceased to oppose the will of Beauty. Insensibly they began to speak of their departure as a thing almost indifferent. It was she who gave the tone to the conversation, and in their presence she appeared to consider it as a happy event; it was only, however, to console her father and brothers, and not to alarm them more than necessary. Although discontented with the conduct of her sisters towards her, who appeared even impatient to see her depart, and thought the month passed too slowly, she had the generosity to divide all her little property and the jewels which she had at her own disposal amongst them.

They received with pleasure this new proof of her generosity, but without abating their hatred of her. An extreme joy took possession of their hearts when they heard the horse neigh which was sent to canter away a sister whose amiability their jealous natures would not allow them to perceive. The father and the sons alone were so afflicted that they could not contain themselves at this fatal moment. They proposed to strangle the horse. Beauty, however, preserving all her tranquillity, showed them again on this occasion the absurdity of such a design, and the impossibility executing it. After having taken leave of her brothers, she embraced her hardhearted sisters, taking such a tender farewell of them that she drew from them some tears, and they believed, for the space of a few minutes, that they were almost as much afflicted as their brothers.

During these brief, yet lingering leave-takings, the good man, hurried by his daughter, had mounted his horse. She placed herself behind him with as much alacrity as though she were going to make an agreeable journey. The animal rather flew than walked. But this extreme speed did not inconvenience her in the least; the paces of this singular horse were so gentle that Beauty felt no more shaken by him than she would have been by the breath of a zephyr.

In vain, during the journey, did her father offer a hundred times to allow her to dismount, and to go himself alone to find the Beast. "Consider, my dear child," said he; "there is still time. This Monster is more terrible than thou canst imagine. However firm thy resolution may be, I cannot but fear it will fail on beholding him; then it will be too late; thou wilt be lost, and we shall both perish together."

"If I went," replied Beauty, "to seek this terrible Beast with the hope of being happy, it is not impossible that that hope would fail me at the sight of him; but as I reckon on a speedy death, and believe it to be unavoidable, what does it signify whether he who shall destroy me be agreeable or hideous."

Conversing thus, night closed around them, but the horse went quite as fast in the darkness. It was, however, suddenly dissipated by a most unexpected spectacle. This was caused by the discharge of all kinds of beautiful fireworks—flowerpots, catherine-wheels, suns, bouquets,—which dazzled the eyes of our travellers. This agreeable and unlooked-for illumination lighted up the entire forest, and diffused a gentle heat through the air, which was become desirable, for the cold in this country was more keenly felt in the night than by day.

By this charming light the father and daughter found themselves in an avenue of orange-trees. At the moment that they entered it the fireworks ceased. The illumination was, however, continued by all the statues having in their hands lighted torches. Besides these, lamps without number covered the front of the palace, symmetrically arranged in forms of true-lover's knots and crowned cyphers, consisting of double LL's and double BB's. On entering the court they were received by a salute of artillery, which, added to the sound of a thousand instruments of various kinds, some soft some warlike, had a fine effect.

"The Beast must be very hungry indeed," said Beauty, half-jestingly, "to make such grand rejoicings at the arrival of his prey." However, in spite of her agitation at the approach of an event which, according to all appearance, was about to be fatal to her, she could not avoid paying attention to the magnificent objects which succeeded each other, and presented to her view the most beautiful spectacle she had ever seen, nor help saying to her father that the preparations for her death were more brilliant than the bridal pomp of the greatest king in the world.

The horse stopped at the foot of the flight of steps. She alighted quickly, and her father, as soon as he had put foot to the ground, conducted her by a vestibule to the saloon in which he had been so well entertained. They found there a large fire, lighted candles which emitted an exquisite perfume, and, above all, a table splendidly served. The good man, accustomed to the manner in which the Beast regaled his guests, told his daughter that this repast was intended for them, and that they were at liberty to avail themselves of it. Beauty made no difficulty, well-persuaded that it would not hasten her death. On the contrary, she imagined that it would make known to the Beast the little repugnance she had felt in coming to see him. She hoped that her frankness might be capable of softening him, and even that her adventure might be less sad than she had at first apprehended. The formidable Monster with which she had been menaced did not show himself, and the whole palace spoke of joy and magnificence. It appeared that her arrival had caused these demonstrations, and it did not seem probable that they could have been designed for a funeral ceremony.

Her hope did not last long, however. The Monster made himself heard. A frightful noise, caused by the enormous weight of his body, by the terrible clank of his scales, and an awful roaring, announced his arrival. Terror took possession

"I have not thought it necessary to alter these initials, signifying those of La Belle of Beauty. " The old man, embracing his daughter, uttered piercing cries. But recovering herself in a moment, she suppressed her agitation. Seeing the Beast approach, whom she could not behold without a shudder, she advanced with a firm step, and with a modest air saluted him very respectfully. This behaviour pleased the Monster. After having contemplated her, he said to the old man, in a tone which, without being one of anger, might, however, fill with terror the boldest heart, "Good evening, my good friend," and turning to Beauty, he said also to her, "Good evening, Beauty." The old man, fearing every instant that something awful would happen to his daughter, had not the strength to reply. But Beauty, without agitation and in a sweet and firm voice, said, "Good evening, Beast."

"Do you come here voluntarily?" inquired the Beast; "and will you consent to let your father depart without following him?" Beauty replied that she had no other intention. "Ah! and what do you think will become of you after his departure?"

"What it may please you," said she; "my life is at your disposal, and I submit blindly to the fate which you may doom me to."

"I am satisfied with your submission," replied the Beast; "and as it appears that they have not brought you here by force, you shall remain with me. As for thee, good man," said he to the merchant, "thou shalt depart to-morrow, at daybreak; the bell will warn you; delay not after thy breakfast; the same horse will reconduct thee. But," added he, "when thou shalt be in the midst of thy family, dream not of revisiting my palace, and remember it is forbidden thee for ever. You, Beauty," continued the Monster, addressing her, "conduct your father into the adjoining wardrobe, and choose anything which both of you think will give pleasure to your brothers and sisters. You will find two trunks; fill them. It is right that you should send them something of sufficient value to oblige them to remember you."

In spite of the liberality of the Monster, the approaching departure of her father sensibly affected Beauty, and caused her extreme grief; however, she determined to obey the Beast, who quitted them, after having said, as he had done on entering, "Good-night, Beauty; good-night, good man." When they were alone, the good man, embracing his daughter, wept without ceasing. The idea of leaving her with the Monster was a most cruel trial to him. He repented having brought her into that place. The gates were open; he wished to lead her away again, but Beauty impressed upon him the danger and consequences of such a proceeding.

They entered the wardrobe which had been indicated to them; they were surprised at the treasures it contained. It was filled with apparel so superb that a Queen could not wish for anything more beautiful, or in better taste. Never was warehouse better filled.

When Beauty had chosen the dresses she thought the most suitable, not to the present situation of the family, but proportioned to the riches and liberality of the Beast, who was the donor, she opened a press, the door of which was of rock crystal, mounted in gold. Although such a magnificent exterior prepared her to find it contain some rare and precious treasures, she saw such a mass of jewels of all kinds, that her eyes could hardly support the brilliancy of them. Beauty, from a feeling of obedience, took without hesitation, a prodigious quantity, which she divided as well as she could amongst the lots she had already made.

On opening the last cabinet, which was no less than a cabinet filled with pieces of gold, she changed her mind. "I think," said she to her father, "that it will be better to empty these trunks, and to fill them with coin, which you can give to your children according to your pleasure. By this means you will not be obliged to confide your secret to any one, and your riches will be possessed by you without danger. The advantage that you would derive from the possession of these jewels, although their value might be more considerable, would be attended by inconvenience. In order to profit by them you would be forced to sell them, and to trust them to persons who would only look on you with envious eyes. Your confidence in them might even prove fatal to you, whilst gold pieces of current coin will place you," continued she, "beyond the reach of any misfortune, by giving you the means of acquiring land and houses, and purchasing rich furniture, ornaments, and precious stones."

The father approved her forethought. But wishing to take for his daughters some dresses and ornaments, in order to make room for them as well as the gold, he took out of the trunks what he had selected for his own use. The great quantity of coin which he put in did not fill them, however. They were composed of folds which stretched at pleasure. He found room for the jewels which he had displaced, and, in fact, these trunks contained more than he could even wish for.

"So much money," said he to his daughter, "will place me in a position to sell my jewels at my own convenience. Following thy counsel, I will hide my wealth from the world, and even from my children. If they knew me to be as rich as I shall be, they would torment me to abandon my country life, which, however, is the sole one wherein I have found happiness, and not experienced the perfidy of false friends, with whom the world is filled." But the trunks were so immensely heavy, that an elephant would have sunk under their weight, and the hope which he had begun to cherish appeared to him a dream, and nothing more. "The Beast mocks us," said he, "and feigns to give me wealth, which he makes it impossible for me to carry away."

"Suspend your judgment," replied Beauty; "you have not provoked his liberality by any indiscreet request nor by any greedy or interested looks. Raillery would be without point. I think, as the Monster has bestowed it on you, that he will certainly find the means of allowing you to enjoy it. We have only to close the trunks, and leave them here. No doubt he knows by what coach to send them."

Nothing could be more prudent than this advice. The good man, conformably to it, re-entered the saloon with his daughter. Seated together on the sofa, they saw the breakfast instantly served. The father ate with more appetite than he had done the preceding night. That which had come to pass had diminished his despair and revived his confidence. He would have departed without concern if the Beast had not had the cruelty to make him understand that he must not dream of seeing his palace again, and that he must wish his daughter an eternal farewell. There is no evil but death without remedy. The good man was not completely stunned by this order. He flattered himself that it would not be irrevocable, and this hope prepared him to quit his host with tolerable satisfaction. Beauty was not so well satisfied. Little persuaded that a happy future was prepared for her, she feared that the rich presents with which the Monster loaded her family was but the price of her life, and that he would devour her immediately that he should be alone with her, or at least that a perpetual prison would be her fate, and that her only companion would be this frightful Monster.

This reflection plunged her into a profound reverie, but a second stroke of the bell warned them that it was time to separate. They descended into the court, where the father found two horses, the one loaded with the two trunks, and the other destined for himself. The latter, covered with a good cloak, and the saddle having two bags attached to it full of refreshments, was the same which he had ridden before. So much attention on the part of the Beast again supplied them with subject of conversation; but the horses, neighing and stamping with their hoofs, made known to them that it was time to part.

The merchant, afraid of irritating the Beast by his delay, bade his daughter an eternal farewell. The two horses set off faster than the wind, and Beauty instantly lost sight of them. She mounted in tears to the chamber which was appropriated to her, where for some time she was lost in sad reflections.

At length, being overcome with sleep, she felt a wish to seek repose, which, during a month past, she had not enjoyed. Having nothing better to do, she was about to go to bed, when she perceived on the table a service of chocolate prepared. She took it, half asleep, and her eyes almost immediately closed. She fell into a quiet slumber, which since the moment she had received the fatal rose had been unknown to her.

During her sleep, she dreamt that she was on the bank of a canal, a long way off, the two sides of which were ornamented with two rows of orange trees and flowering myrtles of immense size, where, engrossed with her sad situation, she lamented the misfortune which condemned her to pass her days in this place without hope of ever leaving it.

A young man, beautiful as Cupid is painted, in a voice which touched her heart, then said— "Do not, Beauty, believe thou wilt be as unhappy as it now appears to thee. It is in this place that thou wilt receive the recompence which they have elsewhere unjustly denied thee. Let thy penetration assist thee to extricate me from the appearance which disguises me. Judge in seeing me if my company is contemptible, and ought not to be preferred to a family unworthy of thee. Wish, and all thy desires shall be fulfilled. I love thee tenderly; thou alone canst bestow happiness on me by being happy thyself. Never deny me this. Excelling all other women as far in the qualities of thy mind as thou excellest them in beauty, we shall be perfectly happy together."

This charming apparition then kneeling at her feet, made her the most flattering promises in the most tender language. He pressed her in the warmest terms to consent to his happiness, and assured her that she should be entirely her own mistress.

"What can I do?" said she to him with eagerness.

"Follow the first impulse of gratitude," said he. "Judge not by thine eyes, and, above all, abandon me not, but release me from the terrible torment which I endure."

After this first dream, she fancied she was in a magnificent cabinet with a lady^ whose majestic mien and surprising beauty created in her heart a feeling of profound respect. This lady said to her in an affectionate tone—" Charming Beauty, regret not that thou hast left; a more illustrious fate awaits thee; but if thou wouldst deserve it, beware of allowing thyself to be prejudiced by appearances." Her sleep lasted more than five hours, during which time she saw the young man in a hundred different places, and under a hundred different circumstances.

Sometimes he offered her a fine entertainment; sometimes he made the most tender protestations to her. How pleasant her sleep was! She would have wished to prolong it, but her eyes, open to the light, could not be induced to close again, and Beauty believed she had only had an agreeable dream.

A clock struck twelve, repeating twelve times her own name, which obliged her to rise. She then saw a toilet-table covered with everything necessary for a lady. After having dressed herself with a feeling of pleasure of which she did not imagine the cause, she passed into the saloon, where her dinner was served.

When one eats alone, a repast is very soon over. On returning to her chamber, she threw herself on the sofa; the young man of whom she had dreamt again presented himself to her thoughts. "'I can make thy happiness,' were his words.

Probably this horrible Beast, who appears to command all here, keeps him in prison. How can he be extricated? They repeated to me that I was not to be deceived by appearances. I understand nothing; but how foolish I am! I amuse myself by seeking for reasons to explain an illusion formed by sleep, and which my waking has destroyed. I ought not to pay attention to it. I must only occupy myself with my present fate, and seek such amusements as will prevent my being overcome by melancholy."

Shortly afterwards she began to wander through the numerous apartments of the palace. She was enchanted with them, having never seen anything so beautiful. The first that she entered was a large cabinet of mirrors. She saw herself reflected on all sides. At length a bracelet, suspended to a girandole, caught her sight. She found on it the portrait of the handsome Cavalier, just as she had seen him in her sleep. How was it she recognised him immediately? His features were already too deeply impressed on her mind, and. perhaps, in her heart. With joyful haste she placed the bracelet on her arm, without reflecting whether this action was correct. From this cabinet, having passed into a gallery full of pictures, she there found the same portrait the size of life, which appeared to regard her with such tender attention, that she coloured, as if this picture had been the person himself; or that she had had witnesses of her thoughts.

Continuing her walk, she found herself in a saloon filled with different kinds of instruments. Knowing how to play on almost all, she tried several, preferring the harpsichord to the others, because it was a better accompaniment for the voice. From this saloon, she entered another gallery, corresponding to that in which were the paintings. It contained an immense library. She liked reading, and since her sojourn in the country she had been deprived of this pleasure. Her father, by the confusion of his affairs, had found himself obliged to sell his books. Her great taste for study could easily be satisfied in this place, and would guarantee her against the dullness consequent on solitude. The day passed before she could see everything. At the approach of night, all the apartments were illuminated by perfumed wax-lights, placed in lustres either transparent or of different colours, and not of crystal, but made of diamonds and rubies.

At the usual hour, Beauty found her supper served, with the same delicacy and neatness as before. No human figure presented itself to her view; her father had told her she would be alone. This solitude began no longer to trouble her, when the Beast made himself heard. Never having yet found herself alone with him, ignorant how this interview would pass off, fearing even that he only came to devour her, is it any wonder that she trembled? But on the arrival of the Beast, whose approach was by no means furious, her fears were dissipated.

This monstrous giant said, roughly, "Good evening, Beauty." She returned his salutation in the same terms, with a calm air, but a little tremulously. Amongst the different questions which the monster put to her, he asked how she amused herself? Beauty replied, "I have passed the day in inspecting your palace, but it is so vast that I have not had time to see all the apartments, and the beauties which it contains." The Beast asked her, "Do you think you can get accustomed to living here?"

The girl replied, politely, that she could live without trouble in so beautiful an abode. After an hour's conversation, Beauty discovered that the terrible tone of his voice was attributable only to the nature of the organ; and that the Beast was more inclined to stupidity than to ferocity. At length he asked her bluntly if she would marry him. At this unexpected demand, her fears were renewed, and uttering a terrible shriek, she could not help exclaiming, "Oh! Heavens, I am lost!"

"Not at all," replied the Beast, quietly; "but without frightening yourself, reply properly. Say precisely 'yes' or 'no.'"

Beauty replied, trembling, "No, Beast."

"Well, as you object, I will leave you," replied the docile Monster. "Good evening, Beauty."

"Good evening, Beast," said the frightened girl, with much satisfaction. Extremely relieved by finding that she had no violence to fear, she lay quietly down and went to sleep. Immediately her dear unknown returned to her mind. He appeared to say to her, tenderly, "How overjoyed I am to see you once more, dear Beauty, but what pain has your severity caused me? I know that I must expect to be unhappy for a long time." Her ideas as rain changed, the young man appeared to offer her a crown, and sleep presented him to her in a hundred different manners. Sometimes he seemed to be at her feet, sometimes abandoning himself to the most excessive delight, at others shedding u torrent of tears, which touched the depths of her soul. This mixture of joy and sadness lasted all the night. On waking, having her imagination full of this dear object, she sought for his portrait, to compare it once more with her recollections, and to see if she were not deceived. She ran to the picture gallery, where she recognised him still more perfectly. How long she was admiring him! but feeling ashamed of her weakness, she contented herself at length by looking at the miniature on her arm.

At length, to put an end to these tender reflections, she descended into the garden, the fine weather seeming to invite her to a stroll. Her eyes were enchanted; they had never seen anything in nature so beautiful. The groves were ornamented with admirable statues and numberless fountains, which cooled the air, and shot up to such a height that the eye could scarcely follow them.

What surprised her most was, that she recognised the places wherein she had dreamt she had seen the unknown. Especially at the sight of the grand cansil, bordered with orange and myrtle trees, she could not but think of her vision, which appeared no longer a fiction. She thought to explain the mystery by imagining that the Beast kept some one shut up in his palace. She resolved to be enlightened on the subject that same evening, and to question the Monster, from whom she expected a visit at the usual hour. She walked for the rest of the day, as long as her strength permitted, without being able to see all.

The apartments which she had not been able to inspect the evening before, were no less worthy of her admiration than the others. Besides the instruments and curiosities with which she was surrounded, she found in another cabinet plenty to occupy her. It was tilled with purses, and shuttles for knotting, scissors for cutting out, and fitted up for all sorts of ladies' work; in fact, everything was to be found there.

In this gallery care had been taken to place a cage filled with rare birds, all of which, on the arrival of Beauty, formed an admirable concert. They came also and perched on her shoulders, and these loving little creatures vied with each other as to which should nestle closest to her. "Amiable prisoners," said she, "I think you charming, and I am vexed that you should be so far from my apartment, I should often like the pleasure of hearing you sing."

What was her surprise, when as she said these words, she opened a door and found herself in her own chamber, which she believed was very distant from this gallery, having only arrived in it after turning and threading a labyrinth of apartments which composed this pavilion. A panel which had concealed from her the neighbourhood of the birds, opened into the gallery, and was very convenient, as it completely shut out the noise of them when quiet was desirable.

Beauty, continuing her route, perceived another feathered group; these were parrots of all kinds and of all colours. All at her approach began to chatter. One said, "Good day" to her; the other asked her for some breakfast; one more gallant begged a kiss; several sang opera airs, others declaimed verses composed by the best authors; and all exerted themselves to entertain her. They were as gentle and as affectionate as the inhabitants of the aviary. Their presence was a real pleasure to her. She was delighted to find something she could talk with, for silence was not agreeable to her. She put several questions to some of them, who answered her like very intelligent creatures. She selected one from amongst them as the most amusing. The others, jealous of this preference, complained sadly. She consoled them by some caresses, and the permission to pay her a visit whenever they pleased.

Not far from this spot she saw a numerous troop of monkeys of all sizes, great and small, sapajous(1), some with human faces, others with beards, blue, green, black, and crimson. They advanced to meet her at the door of their apartment, which she had by chance arrived at. They made her low bows, accompanied by countless capers, and testified, by action, how highly sensible they were of the honour she had done them. To celebrate her visit, they -

(1) A South American tribe (genus Erbus), distinguished from all other monkeys for their gentleness and intelligence. There are many varieties, — the white-fronted, the horned, the large-headed, the golden-footed.

- danced upon the tight-rope, and bounded about with a skill and an agility beyond example. Beauty was much pleased with the monkeys, but she was disappointed at not finding anything which could enlighten her respecting the handsome unknown. Losing all hope of doing so, and looking upon her dream as altogether an illusion, she did her best to drive the recollection of it from her mind; but her efforts were vain. She praised the monkeys, and, caressing them, said she should like some of them to follow her and keep her company. Instantly two tall young apes, in court dresses, who appeared to have been only waiting for her orders, advanced and placed themselves with great gravity beside her.

Two sprightly little monkeys took up her train as her pages. A facetious baboon, dressed as a Spanish gentleman of the chamber, presented his paw to her, very neatly gloved, and accompanied by this singular cortege, Beauty proceeded to the supper table. During her meal the smaller birds whistled, in perfect tune, an accompaniment to the voices of the parrots, who sang the finest and most fashionable airs.

During the concert, the monkeys, who had taken upon themselves the right of attending upon Beauty, having in an instant settled their several ranks and duties, commenced their service, and waited on her in full state, with all the attention and respect that officers of a royal household are accustomed to pay to queens.

On rising from table, another troop proceeded to entertain her with a novel spectacle. They were a sort of company of actors, who played a tragedy in the most extraordinary fashion. These Signor Monkeys and Signora Apes, in stage dresses covered with embroidery, pearls, and diamonds, executed all the actions suitable to the words of their parts, which were spoken with great distinctness and proper emphasis by the parrots; so cleverly, indeed, that it was necessary to be assured that these birds were concealed in the wig of one actor or under the mantle of another, not to believe that these new-fashioned tragedians were speaking themselves. The drama appeared to have been written expressly for the actors, and Beauty was enchanted. At the end of the tragedy, one of the performers advanced and paid Beauty a very well-turned compliment, and thanked her for the indulgence with which she had listened to them. All then departed, except the monkeys of her household, and those selected to keep her company.

After supper, the Beast paid her his usual visit, and after the same questions and the same answers, the conversation ended with a "Good night, Beauty." The Lady-Apes of the bedchamber undressed their mistress, put her to bed, and took care to open the window of the aviary, that the birds, by a warbling much softer than their songs by day, might induce slumber, and afford her the pleasure of again beholding her lover. Several days passed without her experiencing any feeling of dullness. Every moment brought with it fresh pleasures. The monkeys, in three or four lessons, succeeded each one in teaching a parrot, who, acting as an interpreter, replied to Beauty's questions with as much promptitude and accuracy as the monkeys themselves had done by gestures. In fine, Beauty found nothing to complain of but the obligation of enduring every evening the presence of the Beast; but his visits were short, and it was undoubtedly to him that she was indebted for the enjoyment of all imaginable amusements.

The gentleness of the monster occasionally inspired Beauty with the idea of asking some explanation respecting the person she saw in her dreams; but sufficiently aware that he was in love with her, and fearing by such questioning to awaken his jealousy, she had the prudence to remain silent, and did not venture to satisfy her curiosity.

By degrees she had visited every apartment in this enchanted palace: but one willingly returns to the inspection of things which are rare, singular, and costly. Beauty turned her steps towards a great saloon, which she had only seen once before. This room had four windows in it on each side. Two only were open, and admitted a glimmering light. Beauty wished for more light, but in lieu of obtaining any by opening another window, she found it only looked into some enclosed space, which, although large, was obscure, and her eyes could distinguish nothing but a distant gleam, which appeared to reach them through the medium of a very thick crape. Whilst pondering for what purpose this place could have been designed, she was suddenly dazzled by a brilliant illumination. The curtain rose and discovered to Beauty a theatre, exceedingly well lighted. On the benches and in the boxes she beheld all that was most handsome and well-made of either sex.

A sweet symphony, which instantly commenced, terminated only to permit other actors than monkey and parrot performers to represent a very fine tragedy, which was followed by a little piece, quite equal in its own style to that which had preceded it.

Beauty was fond of plays. It was the only pleasure she had regretted when she left the city. Desiring to ascertain what sort of material the hangings of the box next to her were made of, she found herself prevented doing so by a glass which separated them, and thereby discovered that what she had seen were not the actual objects, but a reflection of them by means of this crystal mirror, which thus conveyed to her sight all that was passing on the stage of the finest city in the world, it is a master-stroke in optics to be able to reflect from such a distance. She remained in her box some time after the play was over, in order to see the fine company go out. The darkness that gradually ensued compelled her to think of other matters. Satisfied with this discovery, of which she promised to avail herself often, she descended into the gardens. Prodigies were becoming familiar to her. She rejoiced to find they were all performed for her advantage and amusement.

After supper, the Beast came, as usual, to ask her what she had been doing during the day. Beauty gave him an exact account of all her amusements, and told him she had been to the play. "Do you like it?" inquired the dull creature. "Wish for whatever you please, you shall have it. You are very handsome." Beauty smiled to herself at the coarse manner in which he paid her compliments; but what she did not smile at was the usual question, and the words, "Will you marry me?" put an end to her good humour. She had only to answer "I will" but, nevertheless, his docility during this last interview did not reassure her. Beauty was alarmed at it. "What is to be the end of all this?" she said to herself. "The question he puts to me every time, 'Will I marry him' proves that he persists in loving me his bounty to me confirms it. But though he does not insist on my compliance -

(1) Perhaps an allusion to the New Theatre in the Rue des Fosses, St. Germaine. Vide page 272, note.

- nor show any signs of resentment at my refusal, who will be answerable to me that he do not eventually lose his patience, and that my death will not be the consequence?"

These reflections rendered her so thoughtful that it was almost day-light before she went to bed. The unknown, who but awaited that moment to appear, reproached her tenderly for her delay He found her melancholy, lost in thought, and inquired what could have displeased her in such a place. She answered that nothing displeased her, except the Monster whom she saw every evening. She should have become accustomed to him, but he was in love with her, and this love made her apprehensive of some violence.

"By the foolish compliments he pays me," said Beauty to her lover, "I find he desires to marry me. Would you advise me to consent? Alas! were he as charming as he is frightful, you have rendered my heart inaccessible to him and to all others; and I do not blush to own that I can love no one but you." So sweet a confession could but flatter the unknown, yet he replied to her only by saying, "Love him who loves you. Do not be misled by appearances, and release me from prison."

These words, continually repeated without any explanation, caused Beauty infinite distress. "What would you that I should do?" said she to him. " I would restore you to liberty at any price; but my desire is vain while you abstain from furnishing me with the means to put it in practice."

The unknown made her some answer, but of so confused a nature that she could not comprehend it. A thousand extravagant fancies passed before her eyes. She saw the Monster on a throne all blazing with jewels; he called to her and invited her to sit beside him. A moment afterwards, the unknown compelled him precipitately to descend, and seated himself in his place. The Beast regaining the advantage, the unknown disappeared in his turn, lie spoke to her from behind a black veil, which changed his voice, and rendered it horrible.

All her sleep passed in this manner, and yet, notwithstanding the agitation it caused her, she felt it was too soon over, as her awakening deprived her of the sight of the object of her affections. After she had finished dressing, various sorts of work, books, and animals occupied her attention until the hour when the play began. She arrived just in time, but she was not at the same theatre. It was the opera, and the performance commenced as soon as she was seated. The spectacle was magnificent, and the spectators were not less so. The mirrors represented to her distinctly the most minute details of the dresses even of the people in the pit. Delighted to behold human forms and faces, many of which she recognised as those of persons she knew, it would have been a still greater pleasure to her could she have spoken to them, so that they could have heard her.

More gratified with this day's entertainment than with that of the preceding, the rest of it passed in the same way that each had done since she had been in that palace. The Beast came in the evening, and after his visit she retired, as usual. The night resembled former nights,—that is, it was passed in agreeable dreams. "When she awoke, she found the same number of domestics to wait upon her; but after dinner her occupations were different. The day before, on opening another of the windows, she had found herself at the opera.

To diversify her amusements, she now opened a third window, which displayed to her all the pleasures of the Fair of St. Germain, much more brilliant then than it is at the present clay. But as the hour had not quite arrived when the best company resorted to it, she had leisure to observe and examine everything. She saw the rarest curiosities, the most extraordinary productions of nature and works of art. The minutest trifles were visible to her. The puppet-show was not unworthy her attention, whilst waiting for more refined entertainments. The comic opera was in its splendour. Beauty was very much delighted. At the termination of the performances, she saw all the well-dressed people visiting the tradesmen's shops. She recognised amongst the crowd several -

(1) At this period, the Grand Opera, or "Academic Royal de Musique," under the direction of the celebrated Lulli, was located at the Theatre du Palais Royal, which had been occupied by Moliere from 1660 to his death in 1673. It was opened in 1674, with the opera of Alceste, and destroyed by fire on the 6th of April, 1763.

(2) Of this celebrated Fair a notice will be found in the notes to the Fairy Tales of Madame d'Aulnoy, page 65. It was visited by the royal family, and may be said to

have been the birthplace of the opera comique and the vaudeville of France. It was suppressed in 1789.

(3) The most celebrated was that of Brioche, who is said to have been the inventor of that species of entertainment.

(4) Le Sage and other equally celebrated authors wrote for this theatre.

- professional gamesters, who flocked to this place as their workshop. She observed persons who, having lost their money by the cleverness of those they played with, went out with less joyous countenances than they exhibited as they entered. The prudent gamblers, who did not stake their whole fortunes on the hazard of a card, and who played to profit by their skill, could not conceal from Beauty their sleight of hand.

She longed to warn the victims of the tricks they were plundered by; but at a distance from them of more than a thousand leagues it was not in her power to do so. She heard and saw everything distinctly, without its being possible for her to make herself heard or seen by others. The reflections and echoes which conveyed to her all these sights and sounds had no returning power. Placed above the air and wind, everything came to her like a thought. The consideration of this fact deterred her from making vain attempts.

It was past midnight before she thought it was time to retire. The need of some refreshment might have hinted to her the lateness of the hour; but she had found in her box liqueurs and baskets filled with everything requisite for a collation. Her supper was light and of short duration; she was in a hurry to go to bed. The Beast observed her impatience, and came merely to say good-night, that she might have more time to sleep and the Unknown liberty to reappear. The following days resembled each other. She found in her windows an inexhaustible source of fresh entertainments. The first of the other three afforded her the pleasure of witnessing Italian comedy in the second, a sight of the Tuileries, the resort of all the most distinguished and handsome of both sexes. The last window was very far from being the least agreeable. It enabled her to see everything of consequence that -

(1) The Italian company invited to France by Cardinal Mazarin, from 1645 to 1680, performed at the Hotel du Petit Bourbon, the Theatre du Palais Royal, and the Hotel de Bourgogne, alternately with the French comedians. On the removal of the latter company to the Rue Que'negaud, the Italians remained in possession of the Hotel de Bourgogne until the performance of the False Prude, in 1597, gave offence to Madame de Maintenon, and excited the anger of Louis XIV, who suppressed the Italian troop, and ordered seals to be placed on the doors of their theatre. Having obtained an audience to remonstrate, the King refused to listen to them, saying, "You have no reason to regret that Cardinal Manzarin induced you to quit your country. You came to France on foot, and have gained enough to return in a carriage." They returned to Paris in 1716, at the invitation of the Duke of Orleans, and took the title of Comediens du Regent.

- was going on in the world. The scene was amusing and interesting in all sorts of ways. Sometimes it was the reception of a grand embassy, at others the marriage of some illustrious personages, and occasionally some exciting revolutions. She was at this window during the last revolt of the Janizaries, and witnessed the whole of it to the very end.

At all times she was certain to find something here to entertain her. The weariness she had felt at first in listening to the Beast had entirely departed. Her eyes had become accustomed to his ugliness. She was prepared for his foolish questions, and if their conversations had lasted longer, perchance she would have not been displeased; but four or five sentences, always the same, uttered in a coarse manner, and productive only of a "Yes" or "No," were not much to her taste.

As the slightest desires of Beauty appeared to be anticipated, she bestowed more care upon her toilet, although certain that no one could see her. But she owed this attention to herself, and it was a pleasure to her to dress herself in the habits of all the various nations on the face of the earth. She could do this the more easily, as her wardrobe furnished her with everything she chose, and presented her every day with some novelty. Contemplating her mirror in these various dresses, it revealed to her that she was to be admired in all lands; and her attendant animals, each according to their talent, repeated to her unceasingly the same fact—the monkeys by their actions, the parrots by their language, and the other birds by their songs.

So delightful a life ought to have perfectly contented her, but we weary of everything. The greatest happiness fades when it is continual, derived always from the same source, and we find ourselves exempted from fear and from hope. Beauty had experienced this. The remembrance of her family arose to trouble her in the midst of her prosperity. Her happiness could not be perfect as long as she was denied the pleasure of informing her relations of it.

As she had become more familiar with the Beast, either from the habit of seeing him or from the gentleness which she had discovered in his nature, she thought she might venture to ask him a question. She did not take this liberty, however, until she had obtained from him a promise that he would not be angry. The question she put to him was, "Were they the only two persons in that castle?"

"Yes, I protest to you," replied the Beast, in a rather excited tone; "and I assure you that you and I, the monkeys, and the other animals, are the only breathing creatures in this place." The Beast said no more, and departed more abruptly than usual.

Beauty had asked this question only with a view of ascertaining whether her lover was not confined in the palace. She would have wished to see and speak with him. It was a happiness she would have purchased at the price of her own liberty and of all the pleasures by which she was surrounded. That charming youth existing only in her imagination, she now looked upon this palace as a prison which would be one day her tomb.

These melancholy ideas crowded also upon her mind at night. She dreamed she was on the banks of a great canal; she was weeping, when her dear Unknown, alarmed at her sad state, said to her, pressing her hand tenderly between his own, "What is the matter, my beloved Beauty? Who can have offended you, and what can possibly have disturbed your tranquillity? By the love I bear you, I conjure you to explain the cause of your distress. Nothing shall be refused to you. You are sole sovereign here—everything is at your command. Whence arises the sorrow that overpowers you? Is it the sight of the Beast that afflicts you? You must be relieved from it!"

At these words Beauty imagined she saw the Unknown draw a dagger, and prepare to plunge it in the throat of the Monster, who made no attempt to defend himself, but, on the contrary, offered his neck to the blow with a submission and a calmness which caused the beautiful dreamer to fear the Unknown would accomplish his purpose before she could endeavour to prevent him, notwithstanding she had instantly risen to protect the Beast.

The instant she saw her efforts likely to be anticipated, she exclaimed, with all her might, "Hold, barbarian! Harm not my benefactor, or else kill me!" The Unknown, who continued striking at the Beast, notwithstanding the shrieks of Beauty, said to her, angrily, " You love me, then, no longer, since you take the part of this Monster, who is an obstacle to my happiness!"

"You are ungrateful," she replied, still struggling with him; "I love you more than my life, and I would lose it sooner than cease to love you. You are all the world to me, and I would not do you the injustice to compare you with any other treasure it possesses. I would, without a sigh, abandon all it could offer me, to follow you into the wildest desert. But this tender affection does not stifle my gratitude. I owe everything to the Beast. He anticipates all my wishes: it is to him I am indebted for the joy of knowing you, and I would die sooner than endure seeing you do him the slightest injury."

After several similar struggles the objects vanished, and Beauty fancied she saw the lady who had appeared to her some nights before, and who said to her, "Courage, Beauty; be a model of female generosity; show thyself to be as wise as thou art charming; do not hesitate to sacrifice thy inclination to thy duty. Thou takest the true path to happiness. Thou wilt be blest, provided thou art not misled by deceitful appearances."

When Beauty awoke she pondered on this mysterious vision, but it still remained an enigma to her. Her desire to see her father superseded, during the day, the anxiety caused by these dreams of the Monster and the Unknown. Thus, neither tranquil at night nor contented by day, although surrounded by the greatest luxuries, the only distraction she could find was in the theatre. She went to the Italians, but after the first scene she quitted that performance for the Opera, which she left almost as quickly. Her melancholy followed her everywhere. She frequently opened each of the six windows as many times without finding one minute's respite from her cares. Days and nights of equal and unceasing agitation began seriously to affect her appearance and her health.

She took great pains to conceal from the Beast the sorrow which preyed upon her; and the Monster, who had frequently surprised her with the tears in her eyes, upon hearing her say that she was only suffering from a headache, pressed his inquiries no further. One evening, however, her sobs having betrayed her, and feeling it impossible longer to dissimulate, she acknowledged to the Beast, who begged to know what had caused her afflictions, that she was yearning to see her family. At this declaration the Beast sank down without power to sustain himself, and heaving a deep sigh, or rather uttering a howl that might have frightened any one to death, he replied, "How, Beauty! would you, then, abandon an unfortunate Beast? Could I have imagined you possessed so little gratitude? What have I left undone to make you happy? Should not the attentions I have paid you preserve me from your hatred ? Unjust as you are, you prefer the house of your father and the jealousy of your sisters to my palace and my affections. You would rather tend the flocks with them than enjoy with me all the pleasures of existence. It is not love for your family, but antipathy to me, that makes you anxious to depart."

"No, Beast," replied Beauty, timidly and soothingly; "I do not hate you, and should regret to lose the hope of seeing you again; but I cannot overcome the desire I feel to embrace my relations. Permit me to go away for two months, and I promise you that I will return with pleasure to pass the rest of my days with you, and never ask you another favour."

While she spoke the Beast stretched on the ground, his head thrown back, only evinced that he still breathed by his sorrowful sighs. He answered her in these words: "I can refuse you nothing ; but it will perhaps cost me my life. No matter. In the cabinet nearest to your apartment you will find four chests. Fill them with anything you like for yourself or for your family. If you break your word you will repent it, and regret the death of your poor Beast when it will be too late. Return at the end of two months, and you will still see me alive. For your journey back to me you will need no equipage. Merely take leave of your family the previous night before you retire to rest, and when you are in bed turn your ring, the stone inside your hand, and say, with a firm voice, ' I desire to return to my palace, and behold my Beast again.' Good-night; fear nothing; sleep in peace. You will see your father early to-morrow morning. Adieu, Beauty."

As soon as she was alone she hastened to fill the chests with all the treasures and beautiful things imaginable. They only appeared to be full when she was tired of putting things into them. After these preparations, she went to bed. The thoughts of seeing her family so soon kept her awake great part of the night, and sleep only stole upon her towards the hour when she should have been stirring. She saw in her dreams her amiable Unknown, but not as formerly. Stretched upon a bed of turf, he appeared a prey to the keenest sorrow. Beauty, touched at seeing him in such a state, nattered herself she could alleviate his profound affliction by requesting to know the cause of it; but her lover, casting on her a look full of despair, said, "Can you ask me such a question, inhuman girl? Are you not aware that your departure dooms me to death?"

"Abandon not yourself to sorrow, dear Unknown," replied she, "my absence will be brief. I wish but to undeceive my family respecting the cruel fate they imagine has befallen me. I return immediately afterwards to this palace. I shall leave you no more. Ah! could I abandon a residence in which I so delight! Besides, I have pledged my word to the Beast, that I will return. I cannot fail to keep it; and why must this journey separate us? Be my escort. I will defer my departure another day in order to obtain the Beast's permission. I am sure he will not refuse me. Agree to my proposal, and we shall not part. We will return together; my family will be delighted to see you, and I will answer for their showing you all the attention you deserve."

"I cannot accede to your wishes," replied the Unknown, "unless you determine never to return hither. It is the only means of enabling me to quit this spot. How will you decide? The inhabitants of this palace have no power to compel you to return. Nothing can happen to you beyond the knowledge that you have grieved the Beast."

"You do not consider," rejoined Beauty, quickly, "that he assured me he should die if I broke my word to him."

"What matters it to you?" retorted the lover; "is it to be counted a misfortune that your happiness should cost only the life of a monster? Of what use is he to the world? Will any one be a loser by the destruction of a being who appears upon earth only to be the horror of all nature."

"Ha!" exclaimed Beauty, almost angrily, "know that I would lay down my life to save his, and that this Monster, who is only one in form, has a heart so humane, that he should not be persecuted for a deformity which he refrains from rendering more hideous by his actions. I will not repay his kindness with such black ingratitude."

The Unknown, interrupting her, inquired what she would do if the Monster endeavoured to kill him; and, if it were decreed that one of them must slay the other, to which would she afford assistance?

"I love you only," she replied; "but extreme as is my affection for you, it cannot weaken my gratitude to the Beast, and if I found myself placed in so fatal a position, I would escape the misery which the result of such a combat would inflict on me, by dying by my own hand. But why indulge in such dreadful suppositions ? However chimerical, the idea freezes my blood. Let us change the conversation."

She set him the example, by saying all that an affectionate girl could say, most flattering to her lover. She was not restrained by the rigid customs of society, and slumber left her free to act naturally. She acknowledged to him her love with a frankness which she would have shrunk from when in full possession of her reason. Her sleep was of long duration, and when she awoke she feared the Beast had failed in his promise to her. She was in this uncertainty when she heard the sound of a human voice which she recognised. Undrawing her curtains precipitately, what was her surprise when she found herself in a strange apartment, the furniture of which was not near so superb as that in the Palace of the Beast. This prodigy induced her to rise hastily, and open the door of her chamber. The next room was equally strange to her; but what astonished her still more, was to find in it the four chests she had filled the previous evening. The transport of herself and her treasures was a proof of the power and bounty of the Beast; but where was she?

She could not imagine; when at length she heard the voice of her father, and rushing out, she flung her arms round his neck. Her appearance astounded her brothers and sisters. They stared at her as at one come from the other world. All her family embraced her with the greatest demonstrations of delight; but her sisters, in their hearts, were vexed at beholding her. Their jealousy was not extinguished. After many caresses on both sides, the good man desired to speak with her privately, to learn from her own lips all the circumstances of so extraordinary a journey, and to inform her of the state of his own fortune, of which he had set apart a large share for herself. He told her that on the evening of the same day that he had left the Palace of the Beast, he had reached his own house without the least fatigue. That on the road he had cogitated how he could best manage to conceal his trunks from the sight of his children, and wished that they could be carried without their knowledge into a little cabinet adjoining his bed-chamber, of which he alone had the key: that he had looked upon this as an impossibility; but that, on dismounting at his door, he found the horse on which his trunks had been placed had run away, and therefore saw himself suddenly spared the trouble of hiding his treasures.

"I assure thee," said the old man to his daughter, "that the loss of these riches did not distress me. I had not possessed them long enough to regret them greatly; but the adventure appeared to me a gloomy prognostic of my fate. I did not hesitate to believe that the perfidious Beast would act in the same manner by thee. I feared that the favours he conferred upon thee would not be more durable. This idea caused me great anxiety. To conceal it, I feigned to be in need of rest,—it was only to abandon myself without restraint to my grief. I looked upon thy destruction as certain, but my sorrow as soon dissipated. The sight of the trunks I thought I had lost renewed my hopes of thy happiness. I found them placed in my little cabinet, precisely where I had wished them to be. The keys of them, which I had forgotten and left behind me on the table in the salon wherein we had passed the night, were in the locks. This circumstance, which afforded me a new proof of the kindness of the Beast, and his constant attention, overwhelmed me with joy. It was then that, no longer doubting the advantageous result of thy adventure, I reproached myself for entertaining such unjust suspicions of the honour of that generous Monster, and craved his pardon a hundred times for the abuse which, in my distress, had mentally lavished upon him.

"Without informing my children of the extent of my wealth, I contented myself with distributing amongst them the presents thou hadst sent them, and showing them some jewels of moderate value. I afterwards pretended to have sold them, and have employed the money in various ways for the improvement of our income. I have bought this house; I have slaves, who relieve us from the labours to which necessity had subjected us. My children lead an easy life,— that is all I care for. Ostentation and luxury drew upon me, in other clay, the hatred of the envious; I should incur it again did I live in the style of a very wealthy man. Many offers have been made to thy sisters, Beauty; I am about to marry them off immediately, and thy fortunate arrival decides me. Having given to them such portions of the wealth thou hast brought to me, as thou shall think fit, and relieved of all care for their establishment, we will live, my daughter, with thy brothers, whom thy presents were not able to console for thy loss; or, if thou prefer it, we two will live together independently of them."

Beauty, affected by the kindness of her father, and the assurance he gave her of the love of her brothers, thanked him tenderly for all his offers, and thought it would be wrong to conceal from him the fact that she had not come to stay with him. The good man, distressed to learn that he should not have the support of his child in his declining years, did not, however, attempt to dissuade her from the fulfilment of a duty which he acknowledged indispensable.

Beauty, in her turn, related to him all that had happened to her since they parted. She described to him the pleasant life she led. The good man, enraptured at the charming account of his daughter's adventures, heaped blessings on the head of the Beast. His delight was much greater still when Beauty, opening the chests, displayed to him the immense treasures they contained, and satisfied him that he was at liberty to dispose of those which he had brought himself, in favour of his daughters, as he would possess, in these last proofs of the Beast's generosity, ample means to live merrily with his sons. Discovering in this Monster too noble a mind to be lodged in so hideous a body, he deemed it his duty to advise his daughter to marry him, notwithstanding his ugliness. He employed even the strongest arguments to induce her to take that step.

"Thou shouldst not take counsel from thine eyes alone," said he to her. "Thou hast been unceasingly exhorted to let thyself be guided by gratitude. By following her inspirations thou art assured thou wilt be happy. It is true these warnings are only given thee in dreams; but these dreams are too significant and too frequent to be attributed to chance. They promise thee great advantages, enough to conquer thy repugnance. Therefore, the next time that the Beast asks thee if thou wilt marry him, I advise thee not to refuse him. Thou hast admitted to me that he loves thee tenderly: take the proper means to make thy union with him indissoluble. It is much better to have an amiable husband than one whose only recommendation is a handsome person. How many girls are compelled to marry rich brutes, much more brutish than the Beast, who is only one in form, and not in his feelings or his actions."

Beauty admitted the reason of all these arguments; but to resolve to marry a monster so horrible in person and who seemed as stupid as he was gigantic, appeared to her an impossibility. "How can I determine," replied she to her father, "to take a husband with whom I can have no sympathy, and whose hideousness is not compensated for by the charms of his conversation? no other object to distract my attention, and relieve that wearisome companionship; not to have the pleasure of being sometimes absent from him; to hear nothing beyond five or six questions respecting my health or my appetite, followed by a 'Good-night, Beauty,' a chorus which my parrots know by heart, and repeat a hundred times a day. It is not in my power to endure such a union, and I would rather perish at once than be dying every day of fright, sorrow, disgust, and weariness. There is nothing to plead in his favour, except the consideration he evinces in paying me very short visits, and presenting himself before me but once in four-and-twenty hours. Is that enough to inspire one with affection?"

The father admitted that his daughter had reason on her side, but observing so much civility in the Beast, he could not believe him to be as stupid as she represented him. The order, the abundance, the good taste that was discernible through his palace, were not, according to his thinking, the work of a fool. In fact, he found him worthy of the consideration of his daughter, and Beauty might have felt more inclined to listen to the Monster, had not her nocturnal lover's appearance thrown an obstacle in the way. The comparison she drew between these two admirers could not be favourable to the Beast. The old man himself was fully aware of the great distinction which must be made between them. Notwithstanding, he tried by all manner of means to overcome her repugnance. He recalled to her the advice of the lady who had warned her not to be prejudiced by appearances, and whose language seemed to imply that this youth would only make her miserable.

It is easier to reason with love than to conquer it. Beauty had not the power to yield to the reiterated requests of her father. He left her without having been able to persuade her. Night, already far advanced, invited her to repose, and the daughter, although delighted to see her father once more, was not sorry that he left her at liberty to retire to rest. She was glad to be alone. Her heavy eyelids inspired her with the hope that in slumber she would soon again behold her beloved Unknown. She was eager to enjoy this innocent pleasure. A quickened pulsation evinced the joy with which her gentle heart would greet that pleasant vision; but her excited imagination, while representing to her the scenes in which she had usually held sweet converse with that dear Unknown, had not sufficient power to conjure up his form to her as she so ardently desired.

She awoke several times, but on falling asleep again no cupids fluttered round her couch. In a word, instead of a night full of sweet thoughts and innocent pleasures, which she had counted on passing in the arms of sleep, it was to her one of interminable length and endless anxiety. She had never known any like it in the Palace of the Beast, and the day, which she at last saw break with a mingled feeling of satisfaction and impatience, came opportunely to relieve her from this weariness.

Her father, enriched by the liberality of the Beast, had quitted his country house, and in order to facilitate the establishment of his daughters, resided in a very large city, where his new fortune obtained for him new friends, or rather new acquaintances. Amidst the circle who visited him the tidings soon spread that his youngest daughter had returned. Everybody evinced an equal impatience to see her, and were each as much charmed with her intellect as with her beauty. The peaceful days she had passed in her desert palace, the innocent pleasures which a gentle slumber had invariably procured her, the thousand amusements which succeeded, so that dulness could never take possession of her spirit,—in brief, all the attentions of the Monster had combined to render her still more beautiful and more charming than she was when her father first parted from her.

She was the admiration of all who saw her. The suitors to her sisters, without condescending to excuse their infidelity by the slightest pretext, fell in love with her, and attracted by the power of her charms, deserted, without a blush, their former mistresses. Insensible to the marked attentions of a crowd of adorers, she neglected nothing that could discourage them and induce them to return to the previous objects of their affection; but, notwithstanding all her care, she could not escape the jealousy of her sisters.

The inconstant lovers, far from concealing their new passion, invented every day some fresh entertainment, with the view of paying their court to her. They entreated her even to bestow the prize in the games which took place in her honour ; but Beauty, who could not be blind to the mortification she was causing her sisters, and yet was unwilling to refuse utterly the favour they implored so ardently, and in so flattering a manner, found means to satisfy them all, by declaring that she would, alternately with her sisters, present the prize to the victor. What she selected was a flower, or some equally simple guerdon. She left to her elder sisters the honour of giving, in their turn, jewels, crowns of diamonds, costly weapons, or superb bracelets, presents which her liberal hand supplied them with, but for which she would not take the slightest credit. The treasures lavished on her by the Monster left her in want of nothing. She divided between her sisters everything she had brought that was most rare and elegant. Bestowing nothing but trifles herself, and leaving them the pleasure of giving largely, she counted on securing for them the love as well as the gratitude of the youthful combatants. But these lovers sought only to gain her heart, and the simplest gift from her hand was more precious to them than all the treasures that were prodigally heaped upon them by the others.

The amusements she partook of amongst her family, though vastly inferior to those she enjoyed in the Palace of the Beast, entertained her sufficiently to prevent the time hanging heavily on her hands. At the same time, neither the gratification of seeing her father, whom she tenderly loved, nor the pleasure of being with her brothers, who in a hundred ways studied to prove to her the extent of their affection, nor the delight of conversing with her sisters, of whom she was very fond, though they were not so of her, could prevent her regretting her agreeable dreams. Her Unknown (greatly to her sorrow) came not, when she slumbered under her lather's roof, to address her in the tenderest language; and the court paid to her by those who had been the admirers of her sisters, did not compensate for the loss of that pleasing illusion. Had she even been of a nature to feel nattered by such conquests, she would still have distinguished an immense difference between their attentions, or those of the Beast, and the devotion of her charming Unknown.

Their assiduities were received by her with the greatest indifference; but Beauty perceiving that, notwithstanding her coolness, they were obstinately bent on rivalling each other in the task of proving to her the intensity of their passion, thought it her duty to make them clearly understand they were losing their time. The first she endeavoured to undeceive was one who had courted her eldest sister. She told him that she had only returned for the purpose of being present at the marriage of her sisters, particularly that of her eldest sister, and that she was about to press her father to settle it immediately. Beauty found that she had to deal with a man who saw no longer any charms in her sister. He sighed alone for her, and coldness, disdain, the threat to depart before the expiration of the two months—nothing, in short, could discourage him. Much vexed at having failed in her object, she held a similar conversation with the others, whom she had the mortification to find equally infatuated.

To complete her distress, her unjust sisters, who looked upon her as a rival, conceived a hatred to her which they could not dissemble; and whilst Beauty was deploring the too great power of her charms, she had the misery of learning that her new adorers, believing each to be the cause of the other's rejection, were bent, in the maddest way, on fighting it out amongst themselves. All these annoyances induced her to determine upon returning sooner than she had contemplated.

Her father and brothers did all they could to detain her; but the slave of her word, and firm in resolution, neither the tears of the one nor the prayers of the others could prevail upon her. All that they could extort from her was, that she would defer her departure as long as she could. The two months had nearly expired, and every morning she determined to bid adieu to her family, without having the heart when night arrived to say farewell. In the combat between her affection and her gratitude, she could not lean to the one without doing injustice to the other. In the midst of her embarrassment, it needed nothing less than a dream to decide her. She fancied she was at the Palace of the Beast, and walking in a retired avenue, terminated by a thicket full of brambles, concealing the entrance to a cavern, out of which issued horrible groans. She recognised the voice of the Beast, and ran to his assistance.

The Monster, who, in her dream, appeared stretched upon the ground and dying, reproached her with being the cause of his death, and having repaid his affection with the blackest ingratitude. She then saw the lady who had before appeared to her in her sleep, and who said to her in a severe tone, that it would be her destruction if she hesitated any longer to fulfil her engagements; that she had given her word to the Beast that she would return in two months that the time had expired; that the delay of another day would be fatal to the Beast; that the trouble she was creating in her father's house, and the hatred of her sisters, ought to increase her desire to return to the Palace of the Beast, where everything combined to delight her. Beauty, terrified by this dream, and fearing to be the cause of the death of the Beast, awoke with a start, and went immediately to inform her family that she could no longer delay her departure.

This intelligence produced various effects. Her father's tears spoke for him; her brothers protested that they would not allow her to leave them; and her lovers, in despair, swore they would not suffer the house to be robbed of its brightest ornament. Her sisters alone, far from appearing distressed at her departure, were loud in praise of her sense of honour; and affecting to possess the same virtue themselves, had the audacity to assure her that if they had pledged their words to the Beast as she had done, they should not have suffered his ugliness to have interfered with their feelings of duty, and that they should have long ere that time been on their road back to the marvellous palace. It was thus they endeavoured to disguise the cruel jealousy that rankled in their hearts. Beauty, however, charmed by their apparent generosity, thought only of convincing her brothers and her lovers of the obligation she was under to leave them; but her brothers loved her too much to consent to her going, and her lovers were too infatuated to listen to reason. All of them being ignorant of the mode in which Beauty had arrived at her father's house, and never doubting but that the horse which first conveyed her to the Palace of the Beast would be sent to take her back again, resolved amongst themselves to prevent it.

Her sisters, who only concealed their delight by the affectation of a sentiment of horror, as they perceived the hour approach for Beauty's departure, were frightened to death lest anything should occur to delay her; but Beauty, firm in her resolution, knowing whither duty called her, and having no more time to lose, if she would prolong the existence of the Beast, her benefactor, at nightfall took leave of her family, and of all those who were interested in her destiny.

She assured them that whatever steps they took to prevent her departure, she should, nevertheless, be in the Palace of the Beast the next morning before they were stirring; that all their schemes would be fruitless; and that she had determined to return to the Enchanted Palace. She did not forget, on going to bed, to turn her ring. She slept very soundly, and did not awake until the clock in her chamber, striking noon, chimed her name to music. By that sound she knew that her wishes were accomplished. As soon as she evinced a disposition to rise, her couch was surrounded by all the animals who had been so eager to serve her, and who unanimously testified their gratification at her return, and expressed the sorrow they had felt at her long absence.

The day seemed to her longer than any she had previously passed in that Palace, not so much from regret for those she had quitted as from her impatience again to behold the Beast, and to say everything she could to him in the way of excuse for her conduct. She was also animated by another desire,— that of again holding in slumber one of those sweet conversations with her dear Unknown, a pleasure she had been deprived of during the two months she had passed with her family, and which she could not enjoy anywhere but in that Palace. The Beast and the Unknown were, in short, alternately the subjects of her reflections. One moment she reproached herself for not returning the affection of a lover who, under the form of a monster, displayed so noble a mind; the next she deplored having set her heart upon a visionary object, who had no existence except in her dreams. She began to doubt whether she ought to prefer the imaginary devotion of a phantom to the real affection of the Beast. The very dream in which the Unknown appeared to her was invariably accompanied by warnings not to trust to sight. She feared it was but an idle illusion, born of the vapours of the brain, and destroyed by light of day.

Thus undecided, loving the Unknown, yet not wishing to displease the Beast, and seeking repose from her thoughts in some entertainment, she went to the French Comedy, which she found exceedingly poor. Shutting the window abruptly, she hoped to be better pleased at the Opera. She thought the music miserable. The Italians were equally unable to amuse her. Their comedy appeared to her to want smartness, wit and action. Weariness and distaste accompanied her everywhere, and prevented her taking pleasure in anything.

The gardens had no attractions for her. Her Court endeavoured to entertain her, but the monkeys lost their labour in frisking, and the parrots and other birds in chattering and singing. She was impatient for the visit of the Beast, the noise of whose approach she expected to hear every instant. But the hour so much desired came without the appearance of the Monster. Alarmed, and almost angry at his delay, she tried in vain to account for his absence. Divided through hope and fear, her mind agitated, her heart a prey to melancholy, she descended into the gardens, determined not to re-enter the Palace till she had found the Beast. No trace of him could she discover anywhere. She called him. Echo alone answered her. Having passed more than three hours in this disagreeable exercise, overcome by fatigue, she sank upon a garden seat. She imagined the Beast was either dead or had abandoned the place. She saw herself alone in that -

(1) After the death of Moliere, in 1673, transferred to the Rue Quene'gaud. In 1680, the King gave the company the title of "Comertiens du Hoy," and granted them a pension of 12,000 livres; but at the period at which this story was written, they had established themselves, by an Order in Council, in a tennis-court in the Rue des Fosses, St. Germain, where they created a theatre after the designs of D'Orbay which remained till 1770.

- Palace, without the hope of ever leaving it. She regretted her conversations with the Beast, unentertaining as they had been to her, and what appeared to her extraordinary, even to discover she had so much feeling for him. She blamed herself for not having married him, and considering she had been the cause of his death (for she feared her too long absence had occasioned it), heaped upon herself the keenest and most bitter reproaches. In the midst of her miserable reflections she perceived that she was seated in that very avenue in which, during the last night she had passed under her father's roof, she had dreamed she saw the Beast expiring in some strange cavern.

Convinced that chance had not conducted her to this spot, she rose and hurried towards the thicket, which she found was not impenetrable. She discovered another hollow, which appeared to be that she had seen in her dream. As the moon gave but a feeble light, the monkey pages immediately appeared with a sufficient number of torches to illuminate the chasm, and to reveal to her the Beast stretched upon the earth, as she thought, asleep. Far from being alarmed at his sight, Beauty was delighted, and, approaching him boldly, placed her hand upon his head, and called to him several times ; but finding him cold and motionless, she no longer doubted he was dead, and consequently gave utterance to the most mournful shrieks and the most affecting exclamations.

The assurance of his death, however, did not prevent her from making every effort to recall him to life. On placing her hand on his heart she felt, to her great joy, that it still beat. Without further delay, Beauty ran out of the cave to the basin of a fountain, where, taking up some water in her joined hands, she hastened back with it, and sprinkled it upon him; but as she could bring very little at a time, and spilt some of it before she could return to the Beast, her assistance had been but meagre if the monkey courtiers had not flown to the Palace, and returned with such speed that in a moment she was furnished with a vase for water, as well as with proper restoratives. She caused him to smell them and swallow them, and they produced so excellent an effect that he soon began to move and show some kind of consciousness. She cheered him with her voice arid caressed him as he recovered.

"What anxiety have you caused me?" said she to him, kindly; "I knew not how much I loved you. The fear of losing you has proved to me that I was attached to you by stronger ties than those of gratitude. I vow to you that I had determined to die if I had failed in restoring you to life." At these tender words the Beast, feeling perfectly revived, replied, in a voice which was still feeble, "It is very kind of you, Beauty, to love so ugly a monster, but you do well. I love you better than my life. I thought you would never return: it would have killed me. Since you love me I will live. Retire to rest, and assure yourself that you will be as happy as your good heart renders you worthy to be."

Beauty had never before heard so long a speech from the Beast. It was not very eloquent, but it pleased, from its gentleness and the sincerity observable in it. She had expected to be scolded, or at least to have been reproached. She had from this moment a better opinion of his disposition. No longer thinking him so stupid, she even considered his short answers a proof of his prudence, and, more and more prepossessed in his favour, she retired to her apartment, her mind occupied with the most flattering ideas. Extremely fatigued, she found there all the refreshments she needed. Her heavy eyelids promised her a sweet slumber. Asleep almost as soon as her head was on her pillow, her dear Unknown failed not to present himself immediately.

What tender words did he not utter to express the pleasure he experienced at seeing her again? He assured her that she would be happy ; that it only remained to her to follow the impulse of her good heart. Beauty asked him if her happiness was to arise from her marriage with the Beast. The Unknown replied that it was the only means of securing it. She felt somewhat annoyed at this. She thought it even extraordinary that her lover should advise her to make her rival happy. After this first dream, she thought she saw the Beast dead at her feet. An instant afterwards the Unknown re-appeared, and disappeared again as instantly, to give place to the Beast. But what she observed most distinctly was the Lady, who seemed to say to her, "I am pleased with thee. Continue to follow the dictates of reason, and trouble thyself about naught. I undertake the task of rendering thee happy." Beauty, although asleep, appeared to acknowledge her partiality to the Unknown and her repugnance to the Monster, whom she could not consider loveable. The Lady smiled at her objections, and advised her not to make herself uneasy about her affection for the Unknown, for that the emotions she felt were not incompatible with the resolution she had formed to do her duty; that she might follow her inclinations without resistance, and that her happiness would be perfected by espousing the Beast.

This dream, which only ended with her sleep, furnished her with an inexhaustible source of reflection. In this vision, as in those which had preceded it, she found more coherence than is usually displayed in dreams, and she therefore determined to consent to this strange union. But the image of the Unknown rose unceasingly to trouble her. It was the sole obstacle, but not a slight one. Still uncertain as to the course she ought to take, she went to the Opera, but without terminating her embarrassment. At the end of the performance she sat down to supper. The arrival of the Beast was alone capable of deciding her.

Far from reproaching her for her long absence, the Monster, as if the pleasure of seeing her had made him forget his past distresses, appeared, on entering Beauty's apartment, to have no other anxiety but that of ascertaining if she had been much amused, if she had been well received, and if her health had been good. She answered these questions, and added politely that she had paid dearly for all the pleasures his care had enabled her to enjoy, by the cruel pain she had endured on finding him in so sad a state on her return.

The Beast briefly thanked her, and then being about to take his leave, asked her, as usual, if she would marry him. Beauty was silent for a short time, but at last making up her mind, she said to him, trembling, "Yes, Beast, I am willing, if you will pledge me your faith, to give you mine."

"I do," replied the Beast, "and I promise you never to have any wife but you."

"Then," rejoined Beauty, "I accept you for my husband, and swear to be a fond and faithful wife to you."

She had scarcely uttered these words when a discharge of artillery was heard, and that she might not doubt it being a signal of rejoicing, she saw from her windows the sky all in a blaze with the light of twenty thousand fireworks, which continued rising for three hours. They formed true-lovers' knots, while on elegant escutcheons appeared Beauty's initials, and beneath them, in well-defined letters, "Long live Beauty and her Husband."

After this display had terminated, the Beast took his departure, and Beauty retired to rest. No sooner was she asleep than her dear Unknown paid her his usual visit. He was more richly attired than she had ever seen him. "How deeply am I obliged to you, charming Beauty," said he. You have released me from the frightful prison in which I have groaned for so long a time. Your marriage with the Beast will restore a king to his subjects, a son to his mother, and life to a whole kingdom. We shall all be happy."

Beauty, at these words, felt bitterly annoyed, perceiving that the Unknown, far from evincing the despair such an engagement as she had entered into should have caused him, gazed on her with eyes sparkling with extreme delight. She was about to express her discontent to him, when the Lady, in her turn, appeared in her dream.

"Behold thee victorious," said she. "We owe everything to thee, Beauty. Thou hast suffered gratitude to triumph over every other feeling. None but thou would have had the courage to keep their word at the expense of their inclination, nor to have periled their life to have saved that of their father. In return for this, there are none who can ever hope to enjoy such happiness as thy virtue has won for thee. Thou knowest at present little, but the rising sun shall tell thee more."

When the Lady had disappeared, Beauty again saw the unknown youth, but stretched on the earth as dead. All the night passed in such dreams; but they had become familiar to her, and did not prevent her from sleeping long and soundly. It was broad daylight when she awoke. The sun streamed into her apartment with more brilliancy than usual: her monkeys had not closed the shutters. Believing the sight that met her eyes but a continuation of her dreams, and that she was sleeping still, her joy and surprise were extreme at discovering that it was a reality, and that on a couch beside her lay, in a profound slumber, her beloved Unknown, looking a thousand times more handsome than he had done in her vision. To assure herself of the fact, she arose hastily and took from off her toilet-table the miniature she usually wore on her arm; but she could not have been mistaken. She spoke to him, in the hope of awaking him from the trance into which he seemed to have been thrown by some wonderful power. Not stirring at her voice, she shook him by the arm.

This effort was equally ineffectual, and only served to convince her that he was under the influence of enchantment, and that she must await the end of the charm, which it was reasonable to suppose had an appointed period.

How delighted was she to find herself betrothed to him who alone had caused her to hesitate, and to find that she had done from duty that which she would have done from inclination. She no longer doubted the promise of happiness which had been made to her in her dreams. She now knew that the Lady had truly assured her that her love for the Unknown was not incompatible with the affection she entertained for the Beast, seeing that they were one and the same person. In the meanwhile, however, her husband never woke. After a slight meal she endeavoured to pass away the time in her usual occupations, but they appeared to her insipid. As she could not resolve to leave her apartments, nor bear to sit idle, she took up some music, and began to sing. Her birds hearing her, joined their voices to hers, and made a concert, the more charming to her as she expected every moment it would be interrupted by the awakening of her husband, for she flattered herself she could dissolve the spell by the harmony of her voice. The spell was soon broken, but not by the means she imagined. She heard the sound of a chariot rolling beneath the windows of her apartment, and the voices of several persons approaching. At the same moment the monkey Captain of the Guard, by the beak of his parrot Interpreter, announced the visit of some ladies. Beauty, from her windows, beheld the chariot that brought them. It was of an entirely novel description, and of matchless beauty. Four white stags, with horns and hoofs of gold, superbly caparisoned, drew this equipage, the singularity of which increased Beauty's desire to know who were the owners of it.

By the noise, which became louder, she was aware that the ladies had nearly reached the ante-chamber. She considered it right to advance and receive them. She recognised in one of them the Lady she had been accustomed to behold in her dreams. The other was not less beautiful. Her high and distinguished bearing sufficiently indicated that she was an illustrious personage. She was no longer in the bloom of youth, but her air was so majestic that Beauty was uncertain to which of the two strangers she ought first to address herself. She was still under this embarrassment, when the one with whose features she was already familiar, and who appeared to exercise some sort of superiority over the other, turning to her companion, said, " Well, Queen, what think you of this beautiful girl? You owe to her the restoration of your son to life, for you must admit that the miserable circumstances under which he existed could not be called living. Without her, you would never again have beheld this Prince. He must have remained in the horrible shape to which he had been transformed, had he not found in the world one only person who possessed virtue and courage equal to her beauty. I think you will behold with pleasure the son she has restored to you become her husband. They love each other, and nothing is wanting to their perfect happiness but your consent. Will you refuse to bestow it on them?'

The Queen, at these words, embracing Beauty affectionately, exclaimed, " Far from refusing my consent, their union will afford me the greatest felicity ! Charming and virtuous child, to whom I am under so many obligations, tell me who you are, and the names of the sovereigns who are so happy as to have given birth to so perfect a Princess?"

"Madam," replied Beauty, modestly, "it is long since I had a mother; my father is a merchant more distinguished in the world for his probity and his misfortunes than for his birth."

At this frank declaration, the astonished Queen recoiled a pace or two, and said, "What! you are only a merchant's daughter? Ah, great Fairy!" she added, casting a mortified look on her companion, and then remained silent; but her manner sufficiently expressed her thoughts, and her disappointment was legible in her eyes.

"It appears to me," said the Fairy, haughtily, "that you are discontented with my choice. You regard with contempt the condition of this young person, and yet she was the only being in the world who was capable of executing my project, and who could make your son happy."

"I am very grateful to her for what she has done," replied the Queen; "but, powerful spirit," she continued, "I cannot refrain from pointing out to you the incongruous mixture of that noblest blood in all the world which runs in my son's veins with that of the obscure race from which the person has sprung to whom you would unite him. I confess I am little gratified by the supposed happiness of the Prince, if it must be purchased by an alliance so degrading to us, and so unworthy of him. Is it impossible to find in the world a maiden whose birth is equal to her virtue? I know many excellent princesses by name; why am I not permitted to hope that I may see him the possessor of one of those?"

At this moment the handsome Unknown appeared. The arrival of his mother and the Fairy had aroused him, and the noise they had made was more effective than all the efforts of Beauty ; such being the nature of the spell. The Queen held him a long time in her arms, without speaking a word. She found again a son whose fine qualities rendered him worthy of all her affection. What joy for the Prince to see himself released from a horrible form, and a stupidity more painful to him because it was affected and had not obscured his reason. He had recovered the liberty to appear in his natural form by means of the object of his love, and that reflection made it still more precious to him.

After the first transports which nature inspired him with at the sight of his mother, the Prince hastened to pay those thanks to the Fairy which duty and gratitude prompted. He did so in the most respectful terms, but as briefly as possible, in order to be at liberty to turn his attentions towards Beauty.

He had already, by tender glances, expressed to her his feelings, and was about to confirm with his lips, in the most touching language, what his eyes had spoken, when the Fairy stopped him, and bade him be the judge between her and his mother. " Your mother," said she, "condemns the engagement you have entered into with Beauty. She considers that her birth is too much beneath ours. For my part, I think that her virtues make up for that inequality. It is for you, Prince, to say with which of us your own feelings coincide; and that you may be under no restraint in declaring to us your real sentiments, I announce to you that you have full liberty of choice. Although you have pledged your word to this amiable person, you are free to withdraw it. I will answer for her, that Beauty will release you from your promise without the least hesitation, although, through her kindness, you have regained your natural form ; and I assure you also that her generosity will cause her to carry disinterestedness to the extent of leaving you at liberty to dispose of your hand in favour of any person on whom the Queen may advise you to bestow it.— What say you, Beauty?" pursued the Fairy, turning towards her; "have I been mistaken in thus interpreting your sentiments? Would you desire a husband who would become so with regret?"

"Assuredly not, Madam," replied Beauty." The Prince is free. I renounce the honour of being his wife. When I accepted him, I believed I was taking pity on something below humanity. I engaged myself to him only with the object of conferring on him the most signal favour. Ambition had no place in my thoughts. Therefore, great Fairy, I implore you to exact no sacrifice from the Queen, whom I cannot blame for the scruples she entertains under such circumstances."

"Well, Queen, what say you to that?" inquired the Fairy, in a disdainful and displeased tone. "Do you consider that princesses, who are so by the caprice of fortune, better deserve the high rank in which it has placed them than this young maiden? For my part, I think she should not be prejudiced by an origin from which she has elevated herself by her conduct."

The Queen replied with some embarrassment, "Beauty is incomparable! Her merit is infinite; nothing can surpass it; but, madam, can we not find some other mode of rewarding her? Is it not to be effected without sacrificing to her the hand of my son?" Then turning to Beauty, she continued, "Yes, I owe you more than I can pay. I put, therefore, no limit to your desires. Ask boldly, I will grant you everything, with that sole exception ; but the difference will not be great to you.

Choose a husband from amongst the nobles of my Court. However high in rank, he will have cause to bless his good fortune, and for your sake I will place him so near the throne that your position will be scarcely less enviable."

"I thank you, Madam," replied Beauty; "but I ask no reward from you. I am more than repaid by the pleasure of having broken the spell which had deprived a great prince of his mother and of his kingdom. My happiness would have been perfect if I had rendered this service to my own sovereign. All I desire is that the Fairy will deign to restore me to my father."

The Prince, who, by order of the Fairy, had been silent throughout this conversation, was no longer master of himself, and his respect for the commands he had received, failed to restrain him. He flung himself at the feet of the Fairy and of his mother, and implored them, in the strongest terms, not to make him more miserable than he had been, by sending away Beauty, and depriving him of the happiness of being her husband.

At these words, Beauty, gazing on him with an air full of tenderness, but mingled with a noble pride, said, "Prince, I cannot conceal from you my affection. Your disenchantment is a proof of it, and I should in vain endeavour to disguise my feelings. I confess without a blush, that I love you better than myself. Why should I dissimulate? We may disavow evil impulses; but mine are perfectly innocent, and are authorised by the generous Fairy to whom we are both so much indebted. But if I could resolve to sacrifice my feelings when I thought it my duty to do so for the Beast, you must feel assured that I shall not falter on this occasion when it is no longer the interest of the Monster that is at stake, but your own. It is enough for me to know who you are, and that I am to renounce the glory of being your wife. I will even venture to say, that if, yielding to your entreaties, the Queen should grant the consent you ask, it would not alter the case, for in my own reason, and even in my love, you would meet with an insurmountable obstacle. I repeat that I ask no favour but that of being allowed to return to the bosom of my family, where I shall for ever cherish the remembrance of your bounty and your affection."

"Generous Fairy!" exclaimed the Prince, clasping her hands in supplication, "for mercy's sake, do not allow Beauty to depart! Make me, rather, again the Monster that I was, for then I shall be her husband. She pledged her word to the Beast, and I prefer that happiness to all those she has restored me to, if I must purchase them so dearly!"

The Fairy made no answer; she but looked steadily at the Queen, who was moved by so much true affection, but whose pride remained unshaken. The despair of her son affected her, yet she could not forget that Beauty was the daughter of a merchant, and nothing more. She, notwithstanding, feared the anger of the Fairy, whose manner and silence sufficiently evinced her indignation. Her confusion was extreme. Not having power to utter a word, she feared to see a fatal termination to a conference which had offended the protecting spirit.

No one spoke for some minutes, but the Fairy at length broke the silence, and casting an affectionate look upon the lovers, she said to them, "I find you worthy of each other. It would be a crime to part two such excellent persons. You shall not be separated, I promise you; and I have sufficient power to fulfil my promise." The Queen shuddered at these words, and would have made some remonstrance, but the Fairy anticipated her by saying, " For you, Queen, the little value you set upon virtue, unadorned by the vain titles which alone you respect, would justify me in heaping on you the bitterest reproaches. But I excuse your fault, arising from pride of birth, and I will take no other vengeance beyond doing this little violence to your prejudices, and for which you will not be long without thanking me."

Beauty, at these words, embraced the knees of the. Fairy, and exclaimed, "Ah, do not expose me to the misery of being told all my life that I am unworthy of the rank to which your bounty would elevate me. Reflect that this Prince, who now believes that his happiness consists in the possession of my hand may very shortly perhaps be of the same opinion as the Queen."

"No, no, Beauty, fear nothing," rejoined the Fairy. " The evils you anticipate cannot come to pass. I know a sure way of protecting you from them, and should the Prince be capable of despising you after marriage, he must seek some other reason than the inequality of your condition. Your birth is not inferior to his own. Nay, the advantage is even considerably on your side, for the truth is," said she, sternly, to the Queen, "that you behold your niece; and what must render her still more worthy of your respect is, that she is mine also, being the daughter of my sister, who was not, like you, a slave to rank which is lustreless without virtue.

"That Fairy, knowing how to estimate true worth, did your brother, the King of the Happy Island, the honour to marry him. I preserved this fair fruit of their union from the fury of a Fairy who desired to be her step-mother. From the moment of her birth I destined her to be the wife of your son. I desired, by concealing from you the result of my good service, to give you an opportunity of showing your confidence in me. I had some reason to believe that it was greater than it appears to have been. You might have relied upon me for watching over the destiny of the Prince. I had given you proofs enough of the interest I took in it, and you needed not to have been under any apprehension that I should expose him to anything that would be disgraceful to himself or to you. I feel persuaded, Madam," continued she, with a smile which had still something of bitterness in it, "that you will not object to honour us with your alliance."

The Queen, astonished and embarrassed, knew not what to answer. The only way to atone for her fault was to confess it frankly, and evince a sincere repentance. "I am guilty, generous Fairy," said she. "Your bounties should have satisfied me that you would not suffer my son to have formed an alliance unworthy of him. But pardon, I beseech you, the prejudices of my rank, which urged that royal blood could not marry one of humbler birth without degradation. I acknowledge that I deserve you should punish me by giving to Beauty a mother-in-law more worthy of her; but you take too kind an interest in my son to render him the victim of my error. As to you, dear Beauty," she continued, embracing her tenderly, "you must not resent my resistance. It was caused by my desire to marry my son to my niece, whom the Fairy had often assured me was living, notwithstanding all appearances to the contrary. She had drawn so charming a portrait of her, that without knowing you, I loved you dearly enough to risk offending the Fairy, in order to preserve to you the throne and the heart of my son." So saying, she recommended her caresses, which Beauty received with respect.

The Prince, on his part, enraptured at this agreeable intelligence, expressed his delight in looks alone.

"Behold us all satisfied," said the Fairy; "and now, to terminate this happy adventure, we only need the consent of the royal father of the Princess; but we shall shortly see him here." Beauty requested her to permit the person who had brought her up, and whom she had hitherto looked upon as her father, to witness her felicity. "I admire such consideration," said the Fairy; "it is worthy a noble mind, and as you desire it, I undertake to inform him." Then taking the Queen by the hand, she led her away, under the pretext of showing her over the enchanted Palace. It was to give the newly-betrothed pair the liberty of conversing with each other for the first time without restraint or the aid of illusion. They would have followed, but she forbade them. The happiness in store for them inspired each with equal delight. They could not entertain the least doubt of their mutual affection.

Their conversation, confused and unconnected, their protestations a hundred times repeated, were to them more convincing proofs of love than the most eloquent language could have afforded. After having exhausted all the expressions that passion suggests under such circumstances to those that are truly in love, Beauty inquired of her lover by what misfortune he had been so cruelly transformed into a beast. She requested him also to relate to her all the events of his life preceding that shocking metamorphosis.

The Prince, whose recovery of his natural form had not lessened his anxiety to obey her, without more ado commenced his narrative in the following words:—

The King, my father, died before I was born. The Queen would never have been consoled for his loss if her interest for the child she bore had not struggled with her sorrow. My birth caused her extreme delight. The sweet task of rearing the fruit of the affection of so dearly-beloved a husband was destined to dissipate her affliction. The care of my education and the fear of losing me occupied her entirely. She was assisted in her object by a Fairy of her acquaintance, who showed the greatest anxiety to preserve me from all kinds of accidents. The Queen felt greatly obliged to her, but she was not pleased when the Fairy asked her to place me entirely in her hands. The Fairy had not the best of reputations— she was said to be capricious in her favours. People feared more than they loved her; and even had my mother been perfectly convinced of the goodness of her nature, she could not have resolved to lose sight of me.

By the advice, however, of prudent persons, and for fear of suffering from the fatal effects of the resentment of this vindictive Fairy, she did not flatly refuse her. If voluntarily confided to her care there was no reason to suppose she would do me any injury. Experience had proved that she took pleasure in hurting those only by whom she considered herself offended. The Queen admitted this, and was only reluctant to forego the pleasure of gazing on me continually with a mother's eyes, which enabled her to discover charms in me I owed solely to her partiality.

She was still irresolute as to the course she should adopt, when a powerful neighbour imagined it would be an easy matter for him to seize upon the dominions of an infant governed by a woman. He invaded my kingdom with a formidable army. The Queen hastily raised one to oppose him, and, with a courage beyond that of her sex, placed herself at the head of her troops, and marched to defend our frontiers. It was then that, being compelled to leave me, she could not avoid confiding to the Fairy the care of my education.

I was placed in her hands after she had sworn by all she held most sacred that she would, without the least hesitation, bring me back to the Court as soon as the war was over, which my mother calculated would not last more than a year at the utmost. Notwithstanding, however, all the advantages she gained over the enemy, she found it impossible to return to the capital so soon as she expected. To profit by her victory, after having driven the foe out of our dominions, she pursued him in his own.

She took entire provinces, gained battle after battle, and finally reduced the vanquished to sue for a degrading peace, which he obtained only on the hardest conditions. After this glorious success, the Queen returned triumphantly, and enjoyed in anticipation the pleasure of beholding me once more ; but having learned upon her march that her base foe, in violation of the treaty, had surprised and massacred our garrisons, and repossessed himself of nearly all the places he had been compelled to cede to us, she was obliged to retrace her steps. Honour prevailed over the affection which drew her towards me, and she resolved never to sheathe the sword till she had put it out of her enemy's power to perpetrate more treachery. The time employed in this second expedition was very considerable. She had flattered herself that two or three campaigns would suffice; but she had to contend with an adversary as cunning as he was false. He contrived to excite rebellion in some of our own provinces, and to corrupt entire battalions, which forced the Queen to remain in arms for fifteen years. She never thought of sending for me. She was always flattering herself that each month would be the last she should be absent, and that she was on the point of seeing me again.

In the meanwhile, the Fairy, in accordance with her promise, had paid every attention to my education. From the day she had taken me out of my kingdom, she had never left me, nor ceased to give me proof of the interest she felt in all that concerned my health and amusement. I evinced by my respect for her how sensible I was of her kindness. I showed her the same deference, the same attention that I should have shown to my mother, and gratitude inspired me with as much affection for her.

For some time she appeared satisfied with my behaviour; but one day, without imparting to me the motive, she set out on a journey, from which she did not return for some years, and when she did return, struck with the effect of her care of me, she conceived for me an affection differing from that of a mother. She had previously permitted me to call her by that name, but now she forbade me. I obeyed her without inquiring what were her reasons, or suspecting what she was about to exact from me.

I saw clearly that she was dissatisfied; but could I imagine why she continually complained of my ingratitude? I was the more surprised at her reproaches as I did not feel I deserved them. They were always followed or preceded by the tenderest caresses. I was not old enough to comprehend her. She was compelled to explain herself. She did so one day when I evinced some sorrow, mingled with impatience, respecting the continued absence of the Queen. She reproached me for this, and on my assuring her that my affection for my mother in nowise interfered with that I owed to herself, she replied that she was not jealous, although she had done so much for me, and had resolved to do still more; but that, to enable her to carry out her designs in my favour with greater freedom, it was requisite, she added, that I should marry her; that she did not desire to be loved by me as a mother, but as an admirer; that she had no doubt of my gratitude to her for making this proposal, or of the great joy with which I should accept it, and that, consequently, I had only to abandon myself to the delight with which the certainty of becoming the husband of a powerful fairy, who could protect me from all dangers, assure me an existence full of happiness, and cover me with glory, must naturally awaken.

I was sadly embarrassed by this proposition. I knew enough of the world in my own country, to be aware that amongst the wedded portion of the community the happiest were those whose ages and characters assimilated, and that many were much to be pitied who, marrying under opposite circumstances, had found antipathies existing between them which were the source of constant misery.

The Fairy being old and of a haughty disposition, I could not flatter myself that my lot would be so agreeable as she predicted. I was far from entertaining for her such feelings as one should for the woman with whom we intend to pass our days; and besides, I was not inclined to enter into any such engagement at so early an age. My only desire was to see the Queen again, and to signalize myself at the head of her forces. I sighed for liberty; that was the sole boon that would have gratified me, and the only one the Fairy would not grant.

I had often implored her to allow me to share the perils to which I knew the Queen exposed herself for the protection of my interests, but my prayers had hitherto been fruitless. Pressed to reply to the astounding declaration she had made to me, I. in some confusion, recalled to her that she had often told me that I had no right to dispose of my hand without the commands of my mother, and in her absence. "That is exactly my opinion," she replied; "I do not wish you to do otherwise; I am satisfied that you should refer the matter to the Queen."

I have already informed you, beautiful Princess, that I had been unable to obtain from the Fairy permission to seek the Queen, my mother. The desire she now had to receive her sanction, which she never doubted she should obtain, obliged her to grant, even without my asking, that which she had always denied me; but it was on the condition, by no means agreeable to me, that she should accompany me. I did what I could to dissuade her, but found it impossible, and we set out together with a numerous escort. We arrived upon the eve of a decisive action. The Queen had maneuvered with such skill that the next day was certain to decide the fate of the enemy, who would have no resource if he lost the battle.

My presence created great pleasure in the camp, and gave additional courage to our troops, who drew a favourable augury from my arrival. The Queen was ready to die with joy; but this first transport of delight was succeeded by the greatest alarm. Whilst I exulted in the hope of acquiring glory, the Queen trembled at the danger to which I was about to expose myself. Too generous to endeavour to prevent me. she implored me by all her affection, to take as much care of myself as honour would permit, and entreated the Fairy not to abandon me on that occasion. Her solicitations were unnecessary. The too susceptible Fairy was as much alarmed as the Queen, for she possessed no spell which could protect me from the chances of war. However, by instantly inspiring me with the art of commanding an army, and the prudence requisite for so important an office, she achieved much. The most experienced captains were surprised at me. I remained master of the field. The victory was complete. I had the happiness of saving the Queen's life, and of preventing her from being made prisoner of war. The enemy was pursued with such vigour that he abandoned his camp, lost his baggage, and more than three-fourths of his army, while the loss on our side was inconsiderable. A slight wound which I had received was the only advantage the foe could boast of; but the Queen, fearing that if the war continued some more serious mischief might befall me, in opposition to the desire of the whole army, to which my presence had imparted fresh spirit, made peace on more advantageous terms than the vanquished had ventured to hope for.

A short time afterwards we returned to our capital, which we entered in triumph. My occupation during the war, and the continual presence of my ancient adorer, had prevented me from informing the Queen of what had occurred. She was, therefore, completely taken by surprise when the Fairy told her, in so many words, that she had determined to marry me immediately. This declaration was made in this very Palace, but which was at that time not so superb as it is at present. It had been a country residence of the late King, which a thousand occupations had prevented his embellishing. My mother, who cherished everything that he had loved, had selected it in preference to any other as a place of retirement after the fatigues of the war. At the avowal of the Fairy, unable to control her first feelings, and unused to dissemble, she exclaimed, "Have you reflected, Madam, on the absurdity of the arrangement you propose to me!" In truth it was impossible to conceive one more ridiculous. In addition to the almost decrepit old age of the Fairy, she was horribly ugly. Nor was this the effect of time. If she had been handsome in her youth, she might have preserved some portion of her beauty by the aid of her art; but naturally hideous, her power could only invest her with the appearance of beauty for one day in each year, and that day ended, she returned to her former state.

The Fairy was surprised at the exclamation of the Queen. Her self-love concealed from her all that was actually horrible in her person, and she calculated that her power sufficiently compensated for the loss of a few charms of her youth. "What do you mean," said she to the Queen, "by an absurd arrangement! Consider, that it is imprudent in you to make me remember what I have condescended to forget. You ought only to congratulate yourself on possessing a son so amiable that his merit induces me to prefer him to the most powerful Genii in all the elements; and as I have deigned to descend to him, accept with respect the honour I am good enough to confer on you, and do not give me time to change my mind."

The Queen, as proud as the Fairy, had never conceived that there was a rank on earth higher than the throne. She valued little the pretended honour which the Fairy offered her. Having always commanded every one who approached her, she by no means desired to have a daughter-in-law to whom she must herself pay homage. Therefore, far from replying to her, she remained motionless, and contented herself with fixing her eyes upon me. I was as much astounded as she was, and fixing my eyes on her in the same manner, it was easy for the Fairy to perceive that our silence expressed sentiments very opposite to the joy with which she would have inspired us.

"What is the meaning of this?" said she, sharply. "How comes it that mother and son are both silent? Has this agreeable surprise deprived you of the power of speech ? or are you blind and rash enough to reject my offer? Say, Prince," said she to me, are you so ungrateful and so imprudent as to despise my kindness? Do you not consent to give me your hand this moment?"

"No, Madam, I assure you," replied I, quickly. "Although I am sincerely grateful to you for past favours, I cannot agree to discharge my debt to you by such means; and, with the Queen's permission, I decline to part so soon with my liberty. Name any other mode of acknowledging your favours, and I will not consider it impossible; but as to that you have proposed, excuse me if you please, for "

"How! insignificant creature!" interrupted the Fairy, furiously. "Thou darest to resist me! And you, foolish Queen! you see, without anger, this conduct—What do I say? without anger! It is you who authorize it! For it is your own insolent looks that have inspired him with the audacity to refuse me!"

The Queen, already stung by the contemptuous language of the Fairy, was no longer mistress of herself, and accidentally casting her eyes on a looking-glass, before which we happened to be standing at the moment, the wicked Fairy thus provoked her: "What answer can I make you," said she, "that you ought not to make to yourself ? Deign to contemplate, without prejudice, the object this glass presents to you, and let it reply for me."

The Fairy easily comprehended the Queen's insinuation. "It is the beauty, then, of this precious son of yours that renders you so vain," said she to her, "and has exposed me to so degrading a refusal! I appear to you unworthy of him. Well," she continued, raising her voice furiously, "having taken so much pains to make him charming, it is fit that I should complete my work, and that I should give you both a cause, as novel as remarkable, to make you remember what you owe to me. Go, wretch!" said she to me; "boast that thou hast refused me thy heart and thy hand. Give them to her thou findest more worthy of them than I am." So saying, my terrible lover struck me a blow on the head. It was so heavy that I was dashed to the ground on my face, and felt as though I were crushed by the fall of a mountain. Irritated by this insult, I struggled to rise, but found it impossible. The weight of my body had become so great that I could not lift myself; all that I could do was to sustain myself on my hands, which had in an instant become two horrible paws, and the sight of them apprised me of the change I had undergone. My form was that in which you found me. I cast my eyes for an instant on that fatal glass, and could no longer doubt my cruel and sudden transformation.

My despair rendered me motionless. The Queen at this dreadful sight was almost out of her mind. To put the last seal upon her barbarity, the furious Fairy said to me, in an ironical tone, "Go make illustrious conquests, more worthy of thee than an august Fairy. And as sense is not required when one is so handsome, I command thee to appear as stupid as thou art horrible, and to remain in this state until a young and beautiful girl shall, of her own accord, come to seek thee, although fully persuaded thou wilt devour her. She must also," continued the Fairy, "after discovering that her life is not in danger, conceive for thee a sufficiently tender affection to induce her to marry thee. Until thou canst meet with this rare maiden it is my pleasure that thou remain an object of horror to thyself and to all who behold thee. As for you, too happy mother of so lovely a child," said she to the Queen, "I warn you that if you acknowledge to any one that this monster is your son, he shall never recover his natural shape. Neither interest, nor ambition, nor the charms of his conversation, must assist to restore him to it. Adieu! Do not be impatient; you will not have long to wait. Such a darling will soon find a remedy for his misfortune."

"Ah, cruel one!" exclaimed the Queen, "if my refusal has offended you, let your vengeance light on me. Take my life, but do not, I conjure you, destroy your own work."

"You forget yourself, great Princess," replied the Fairy, in an ironical tone, "you demean yourself too much. I am not handsome enough for you to condescend to entreat me; but I am firm in my resolutions. Adieu, powerful Queen; adieu, beautiful Prince; it is not fair that I should longer annoy you with my hateful presence. I withdraw; but I have still charity enough to warn thee," addressing herself to me, "that thou must forget who thou art. If thou sufferest thyself to be flattered by vain respects or by pompous titles, thou art lost irretrievably! And thou art equally lost if thou shouldst dare to avail thyself of the intellect I leave thee possessed of, to shine in conversation."

With these words she disappeared, and left the Queen and me in a state which can neither be described nor imagined.

Lamentations are the consolation of the unhappy; but our misery was too great to seek relief in them. My mother determined to stab herself, and I to fling myself in the adjacent canal. Without communicating our intentions to each other, we were on the point of executing these fatal designs, when a female of majestic mien, and whose manner inspired us with profound respect, appeared, and bade us remember that it was cowardice to succumb to the greatest misfortunes, and that with time and courage there was no evil that could not be remedied. The Queen, however, was inconsolable; tears streamed from her eyes, and not knowing how to inform her subjects that their sovereign was transformed into a horrible monster, she abandoned herself to the most fearful despair. The Fairy (for she was one, and the same whom you have seen here), knowing both her misery and her embarrassment, recalled to her the indispensable obligation she was under to conceal from her people this dreadful adventure, and that in lieu of yielding to despair, it would be better to seek some remedy for the mischief.

"Is there one to be found," exclaimed the Queen, "which is powerful enough to prevent the fulfilment of a Fairy's sentence?"

"Yes, Madam," replied the Fairy, "there is a remedy for everything. I am a Fairy as well as she whose fury you have just felt the effects of, and my power is equal to hers. It is true that I cannot immediately repair the injury she has done you, for we are not permitted to act directly in opposition to each other. She who has caused your misfortune is older than I am, and age has amongst us a particular title to respect. But as she could not avoid attaching a condition upon which the spell might be broken, I will assist you to break it. I grant that it will be a difficult task to terminate this enchantment; but it does not appear to me to be impossible. Let me see what I can do for you by the exertion of all the means in my power."

Upon this she drew a book from under her robe, and after taking a few mysterious steps, she seated herself at a table, and read for a considerable time with such intense application that large drops of perspiration stood on her forehead. At length she closed the book and meditated profoundly. The expression of her countenance was so serious that for some time we were led to believe that she considered my misfortune irreparable; but recovering from a sort of trance, and her features resuming their natural beauty, she informed us that she had discovered a remedy for our disasters. "It will be slow," said she, "but it will be sure. Keep your secret; let it not transpire, so that any one can suspect you are concealed beneath this horrible disguise, for in that case you will deprive me of the power of delivering you from it. Your enemy flatters herself you will divulge it; it is for that reason she did not take from you the power of speech."

The Queen declared that the condition was an impossible one, as two of her women had been present at the fatal transformation, and had rushed out of the apartment in great terror, which must have excited the curiosity of the guards and the courtiers. She imagined that the whole Court was by this time aware of it, and that all the kingdom, and even all the world, would speedily receive the intelligence; but the Fairy knew a way to prevent the disclosure of the secret. She made several circles, now solemnly, now rapidly, uttering words of which we could not comprehend the meaning, and finished by raising her hand in the air in the style of one who is pronouncing an imperative order. This gesture, added to the words she had uttered, was so powerful, that every breathing creature in the Palace became motionless, and was changed into a statue. They are all still in the same state. They are the figures you behold in various directions and in the very attitudes they had assumed at the instant the Fairy's potent spell surprised them.

The Queen, who at that moment cast her eyes upon the great court-yard, observed this change taking place in a prodigious number of persons. The silence which suddenly succeeded to the stir of a multitude, awoke a feeling of compassion in her heart for the man}'- innocent beings who were deprived of life for my sake; but the Fairy comforted her by saying that she would only retain her subjects in that condition as long as their discretion was necessary. It was a precaution she was compelled to take, but she promised she would make up to them for it, and that the period they passed in that state would not be added to the years allotted to their existence.

"They will be so much the younger," said the Fairy to the Queen; "so cease to deplore them, and leave them here with your son. He will be quite safe, for I have raised such thick fogs around this Castle, that it will be impossible for any one to enter it but when we think fit. I will convey you," she continued, "where your presence is necessary. Your enemies are plotting against you. Be careful to proclaim to your people that the Fairy who educated your son retains him near her for an important purpose, and keeps with her also all the persons who were in attendance on you."

It was not without shedding a flood of tears that my mother could force herself to leave me. The Fairy renewed her assurances to her that she would always watch over me, and protested that I had only to wish, and to see the accomplishment of my desires. She added that my misfortunes would shortly end, provided neither the Queen nor I raised up an obstacle by some act of imprudence. All these promises could not console ray mother. She wished to remain with me, and to leave the Fairy, or any one she might consider the most proper person, to govern the kingdom; but fairies are imperious, and will be obeyed. My mother, fearing by a refusal to increase my miseries and deprive me of the aid of this beneficent spirit, consented to all she insisted on. She saw a beautiful car approach ; it was drawn by the same white stags that brought her here to day. The Fairy made the Queen mount by her side. She had scarcely time to embrace me, her affairs demanded her presence elsewhere, and she was warned that a longer sojourn in this place would be prejudicial to me. She was transported with extraordinary velocity to the spot where her army was encamped. They were not surprised to see her arrive with this equipage. Everybody believed her to be accompanied by the old Fairy, for the one who was with her kept herself unseen, and departed again immediately to return to this place, which, in an instant, she embellished with everything that her imagination could suggest and her art supply.

This good-natured Fairy permitted me also to add whatever I fancied would please me, and after having done for me all she could, she left me with exhortations to take courage, and promising to come occasionally and impart to me such hopes as she might entertain of a favourable issue to my adventure.

I seemed to be alone in the Palace. I was only so to sight. I was served as if I were in the midst of my courtiers, and my occupations were nearly the same as those which were afterwards yours. I read, I went to the play, I cultivated a garden which I had made to amuse me, and found something agreeable in everything I undertook. What I planted arrived at perfection in the same day. It took no more time to produce the bower of roses to which I am indebted for the happiness of beholding you here.

My benefactress came very often to see me. Her presence and her promises alleviated my distresses. Through her, the Queen received news of me, and I news of the Queen. One day I saw the Fairy arrive with joy sparkling in her eyes. "Dear Prince," said she to me, "the moment of your happiness approaches!" She then informed me that he whom you believed to be your father had passed a very uncomfortable night in the forest. She related to me, in a few words, the adventure which had caused him to undertake the journey, without revealing to me your real parentage. She apprized me that the worthy man was compelled to seek an asylum from the misery he had endured during four-and-twenty hours.

"I go," said she, "to give orders for his reception. It must be an agreeable one. He has a charming daughter. I propose that she shall release you. I have examined the conditions which my cruel companion has attached to your disenchantment. It is fortunate that she did not ordain that your deliverer should come hither out of love for you. On the contrary, she insisted that the young maiden should expect no less than death, and yet expose herself to it voluntarily. I have thought of a scheme to oblige her to take that step. It is to make her believe the life of her father is in danger, and that she has no other means of saving him. I know that in order to spare her father any expense on her account, she has asked him only to bring her a rose, whilst her sisters have overwhelmed him with extravagant commissions. He will naturally avail himself of the first favourable opportunity. Hide yourself in this arbour, and seizing him the instant he attempts to gather your roses, threaten him that death will be the punishment of his audacity, unless he give you one of his daughters; or, rather, unless she sacrifice herself, according to the decree of our enemy. This man has five daughters besides the one I have destined for you; but not one of them is sufficiently magnanimous to purchase the life of their father at the price of their own. Beauty is alone capable of so grand an action."

I executed exactly the Fairy's commands. You know, lovely Princess, with what success. The merchant, to save his life, promised what I demanded. I saw him depart without being able to persuade myself that he would return with you. I could not flatter myself that my desire would be fulfilled. What torment did I not suffer during the month he had requested me to allow him. I longed for its termination only to be certain of my disappointment. I could not imagine that a young, lovely, and amiable girl would have the courage to seek a monster, of whom she believed she was doomed to be the prey. Even supposing her to have sufficient fortitude to devote herself, she would have to remain with me without repenting the step she had taken, and that appeared to me an invincible obstacle.

Besides, how could she behold me without dying with affright? I passed my miserable existence in these melancholy reflections, and never was I more to be pitied. The month, however, elapsed, and my protectress announced to me your arrival. You remember, no doubt, the pomp with which you were received. Not daring to express my delight in words, I endeavoured to prove it to you by the most magnificent signs of rejoicing. The Fairy, ceaseless in her attentions to me, prohibited me from making myself known to you. Whatever terror I might inspire you with, or whatever kindness you might show me, I was not permitted to seek to please you, nor to express any love for you, nor to discover to you in any way who I was. I could have recourse, however, to excessive good-nature, as, fortunately, the malignant Fairy had forgotten to forbid my giving you proof of that.

These regulations seemed hard to me, but I was compelled to subscribe to them, and I resolved to present myself before you only for a few moments every day, and to avoid long conversations, in which my heart might betray its tenderness. You came, charming Princess, and the first sight of you produced upon me a diametrically opposite effect to that which my monstrous appearance must have done upon you. To see you was instantly to love you. Entering your apartment, tremblingly, my joy was excessive to find that you could behold me with greater intrepidity than I could behold myself. You delighted me infinitely when you declared that you would remain with me. An impulse of self-love, which I retained even under that most horrible of forms, led me to believe that you had not found me so hideous as you anticipated.

Your father departed satisfied. But my sorrow increased as I reflected that I was not allowed to win your favour in any way except by indulging the caprices of your taste. Your demeanour, your conversation, as sensible as it was unpretending, everything in you convinced me that you acted solely on the principles dictated to you by reason and virtue, and that consequently I had nothing to hope for from a fortunate caprice. I was in despair at being forbidden to address you in any other language than that which the Fairy had dictated, and which she had expressly chosen as coarse and stupid.

In vain did I represent to her it was unnatural to expect you would accept my proposition to marry you. Her answer was always, "Patience, perseverance, or all is lost." To recompense you for my silly conversation, she assured me she would surround you with all sorts of pleasures, and give me the advantage of seeing you continually, without alarming you, or being compelled to say rude and impertinent things to you. She rendered me invisible, and I had the gratification of seeing you waited on by spirits who were also invisible, or who presented themselves to you in the shapes of various animals.

More than this, the Fairy caused you to behold my natural form in your nightly slumbers, and in portraits by day, and made it speak to you in your dreams as I should have spoken to you myself. You obtained a confused idea of my secret and my hopes, which she urged you to realize, and by the means of a starry mirror I witnessed all your interviews, and read in it either all you imagined you uttered or all that you actually thought. This position, however, did not suffice to render me happy. I was only so in a dream, and my sufferings were real. The intense affection with which you had inspired me obliged me to complain of the restraint under which I lived; but my state was much more wretched when I perceived that these beautiful scenes had no longer any charms for you. I saw you shed tears, which pierced my heart, and would have destroyed me. You asked me if I was alone here, and I was on the verge of discarding my feigned stupidity, and assuring you by the most passionate vows of the fact. They would have been uttered in terms that would have surprised you, and caused you to suspect that I was not so coarse a brute as I pretended to be. I was on the point even of declaring myself, when the Fairy, invisible to you, appeared before me. By a threatening gesture, which terrified me, she found a way to close my lips. O, heavens! by what means did she impose silence upon me? She approached you with a poniard in her hand, and made signs to me that the first word I uttered would cost you your life. I was so frightened that I naturally relapsed into the stupidity she had ordered me to affect.

My sufferings were not yet at an end. You expressed a desire to visit your father. I gave you permission without hesitation. Could I have refused you anything? But I regarded your departure as my death-blow, and without the assistance of the Fairy I must have sunk under it. During your absence that generous being never quitted me. She saved me from destroying myself, which I should have done in my despair, not daring to hope that you would return. The time you had passed in this Palace rendered my condition more insupportable than it had been previously, because I felt I was the most miserable of all men, without the hope of making it known to you.

My most agreeable occupation was to wander through the scenes which you had frequented, but my grief was increased by no longer seeing you there. The evenings and hours when I used to have the pleasure of conversing with you for a moment, redoubled my afflictions, and were still more painful to me. Those two months, the longest I had ever known, ended at last, and you did not return. It was then my misery reached its climax, and that the Fairy's power was too weak to prevent my sinking under my despair. The precautions she took to prevent my attempting my life were useless. I had a sure way which eluded her power. It was to refrain from food. By the potency of her spells she contrived to sustain me for some time, but having exhausted all her secrets, I grew weaker and weaker, and finally had but a few moments to breathe, when you arrived to snatch me from the tomb.

Your precious tears, more efficacious than all the cordials of the disguised Genii who attended on me, delayed my soul upon the point of flight. In learning from your lamentations that I was clear to you, I enjoyed perfect felicity, and that felicity was at its height when you accepted me for your husband. Still I was not permitted to divulge to you my secret, and the Beast was compelled to leave you without daring to disclose to you the Prince. You know the lethargy into which I fell, and which ended only with the arrival of the Fairy and the Queen. On awaking I found myself as you behold me, without being aware of how the change took place.

You have witnessed what followed, but you could only imperfectly judge of the pain which the obstinacy of my mother caused me in opposing a marriage so suitable and so glorious for me. I had determined, Princess, rather to be a monster again than to abandon the hope of being the husband of so virtuous and charming a maiden. Had the secret of your birth remained for ever a mystery to me, love and gratitude would not less have assured me that in possessing you I was the most fortunate of men!

The Prince thus ended his narration, and Beauty was about to speak, when she was prevented by a burst of loud voices and warlike instruments, which, however, did not appear to announce anything alarming. The Prince and Princess looked out of the window, as did also the Fairy and the Queen who returned from their promenade. The noise was occasioned by the arrival of a personage who, according to all appearances, could be no less than a king. His escort was obviously a royal one, and there was an air of majesty in his demeanour which accorded with the state that accompanied him. The fine form of this sovereign, although of a certain age, testified that there had been few who could have equalled him in appearance when in the flower of his youth. He was followed by twelve of his body-guard, and some courtiers in hunting-dresses, who appeared as much astonished as their master to find themselves in a castle till now quite unknown to them. He was received with the same honours that would have been paid to him in his own dominions, and all by invisible beings. Shouts of joy and flourishes of trumpets were heard, but no one was to be seen.

The Fairy, immediately on beholding him, said to the Queen, "Here is the King your brother, and the father of Beauty. He little expects the pleasure of seeing you both here. He will be so much the more gratified, as you know he believes that his daughter has been long dead. He mourns her still, as he also does his wife, of whom he retains an affectionate remembrance." These words increased the impatience of the Queen and the young Princess to embrace this monarch. They reached the court-yard just as he dismounted. He saw, but could not recognize them ; not doubting, however, that they were advancing to receive him, he was considering how and in what terms he should pay his compliments to them, when Beauty, flinging herself at his feet, embraced his knees, and called him "Father!"

The King raised her and pressed her tenderly in his arms, without comprehending why. she addressed him by that title. He imagined she must be some orphan Princess, who sought his protection from some oppressor, and who made use of the most touching expression in order to obtain her request. He was about to assure her that he would do all that lay in his power to assist her, when he recognized the Queen his sister, who, embracing him in her turn, presented her son to him. She then informed him of some of the obligations they were under to Beauty, and especially of the frightful enchantment that had just been terminated. The King praised the young Princess, and desired to know her name, when the Fairy, interrupting him, asked if it was necessary to name her parents, and if he had never known any one whom she resembled sufficiently to enable him to guess them.

"If I judged only from her features," said he, gazing upon her earnestly, and not being able to restrain a few tears, "the title she has given to me is legitimately my due; but notwithstanding that evidence, and the emotion which her presence occasions me, I dare not flatter myself that she is the daughter whose loss I have deplored; for I had the most positive proof that she had been devoured by wild beasts. Yet," he continued, still examining her countenance, " she resembles perfectly the tender and incomparable wife whom death has deprived me of. Oh, that I could but venture to indulge in the delightful hope of beholding again in her the fruit of a happy union, the bonds of which were too soon broken!"

"You may, my liege," replied the Fairy; "Beauty is your daughter. Her birth is no longer a secret here. The Queen and Prince know who she is. I caused you to direct your steps this way on purpose to inform you; but this is not a fitting place for me to enter into the details of this adventure. Let us enter the Palace. After you have rested yourself there a short time I will relate to you all you desire to know. When you have indulged in the delight which you must feel at finding a daughter so beautiful and so virtuous I will communicate to you another piece of intelligence, which will afford you equal gratification."

The King, accompanied by his daughter and the Prince, was ushered by the monkey officers into the apartment destined for him by the Fairy, who took this opportunity of restoring to the statues the liberty of relating what they had witnessed. As their fate had excited the compassion of the Queen, it was from her hands that the Fairy desired they should receive the benefit of re-animation. She placed her wand in the Queen's hand, who, by her instructions, described with it seven circles in the air, and then pronounced these words: "Be re-animated. Your King is restored to you." All the statues immediately began to move, walk, and act as formerly, retaining only a confused idea of what had happened to them.

After this ceremony the Fairy and the Queen returned to the King, whom they found in conversation with Beauty and the Prince, caressing each in turn, and most fondly his daughter, of whom he inquired a hundred times how she had been preserved from the wild beasts who had carried her off, without remembering that she had answered him from the first that she knew nothing about it, and had been ignorant even of the secret of her birth.

The Prince also talked without being attended to, repeating a hundred times the obligations he was under to Princess Beauty. He desired to acquaint the King with the promises which the Fairy had made him, that he should marry the Princess, and to beg he would not refuse his cheerful consent to the alliance. This conversation and these caresses were interrupted by the entrance of the Queen and the Fairy. The King, who had recovered his daughter, fully appreciated his happiness, but was as yet ignorant to whom he was indebted for this precious gift.

"It is to me," said the Fairy; "and I alone can explain to you the adventure. I shall not limit my benefits to the recital of that alone. I have other tidings in store for you, not less agreeable. Therefore, great King, you may note this day as one of the happiest of your life." The company, perceiving that the Fairy was about to commence her narration, evinced by their silence the great attention they were anxious to pay to it. To satisfy their curiosity the Fairy thus addressed the King:—

"Beauty, my liege, and perhaps the Prince, are the only persons present who are not acquainted with the laws of the Fortunate Island. It is necessary I should explain those laws to them. The inhabitants of that island, and even the King himself, are allowed perfect liberty to marry according to their inclinations, in order that there may be no obstacle whatever to their happiness. It was in virtue of this privilege that you, Sire, selected for your wife a young shepherdess whom you met one day when you were hunting. Her beauty and her good conduct were considered by you deserving of that honour. You raised her to the throne, and placed her in a rank from which the lowliness of her birth seemed to have excluded her, but of which she was worthy, by the nobleness of her character and the purity of her mind. You know that you had continual reasons to rejoice in the selection you had made. Her gentleness, her obliging disposition, and her affection for you, equalled the charms of her person. But you did not long enjoy the happiness of beholding her. After she had made you the father of Beauty you were under the necessity of travelling to the frontiers of your kingdom, to suppress some revolutionary demonstrations of which you had received intimation. During this period you lost your dear wife, an affliction which you felt the more sensibly because, in addition to the love with which her beauty had inspired you, you had the greatest respect for the many rare qualities that adorned her mind. Despite her youth and the little education she had received, you found her naturally endowed with profound judgment, and your wisest ministers were astonished at the excellent advice she gave you, and the policy by which she enabled you to succeed in all your undertakings."

The King, who still brooded over his affliction, and to whose imagination the death of that dear wife was ever present, could not listen to this account without being sensibly affected, and the Fairy, who observed his emotion, said, "Your feelings prove that you deserved that happiness. I will no longer dwell on a subject that is so painful to you, but I must reveal to you that the supposed shepherdess was a Fairy, and my sister, who, having heard that the Fortunate Island was a charming country, and also much praise of its laws and of the gentle nature of your government, was particularly anxious to visit it. The dress of a shepherdess was the only disguise she assumed, intending to enjoy for a short time a pastoral life. You encountered her in her new abode. Her youth and beauty touched your heart. She yielded to a desire to discover whether the qualities of your mind equalled those she found in your person. She trusted to her condition and power as a Fairy, which could place her at a wish beyond the reach of your assiduities if they became too importunate, or if you should presume to take advantage of the humble position in which you found her. She was not alarmed at the sentiments with which you might inspire her, and persuaded that her virtue was sufficient to guarantee her against the snares of love, she attributed her sensations to a simple curiosity to ascertain if there were still upon the earth men capable of loving virtue unembellished by exterior ornaments, which render it more brilliant and respectable to vulgar souls than its own intrinsic merit, and frequently, by their fatal attractions, obtain the reputation of virtue for the most abominable vices.

"Under this illusion, far from retreating to our common asylum, as she had at first proposed, she chose to inhabit a little cottage she had raised for herself in the solitude in which you met her, accompanied by a phantom, representing her mother. These two persons appeared to live there upon the produce of a pretended flock that had no fear of the wolves, being, in fact, genii in that form. It was in that cottage she received your attentions, which produced all the effect you could desire. She could not resist the offer you made her of your crown. You now know the extent of the obligations you were under to her at a time when you imagined she owed everything to you, and were satisfied to remain in that error.

"What I now tell you is a positive proof that ambition had no share in the consent she accorded to your wishes. You are aware that we look upon the greatest kingdoms but as gifts which we can bestow on any one at our pleasure. But she appreciated your generous behaviour, and esteeming herself happy in uniting herself to so excellent a man, she rashly entered into that engagement without reflecting on the danger which she thereby incurred. For our laws expressly forbid union with those who have not as much power as ourselves, more especially when we have not arrived at that age when we are privileged to exercise our authority over others, and enjoy the right of presiding in our turn. Previous to that time we are subordinate to our elders, and that we may not abuse our power, we have only the liberty of disposing of our hands in favour of some spirit or sage whose knowledge is at least equal to our own. It is true that after that period we are free to form what alliance we please; but it is seldom that we avail ourselves of that right, and never without scandal to our order. Those who do are generally old fairies, who almost always pay dearly for their folly; for they marry young men, who despise them, and, although they are not punished as criminals, they are sufficiently punished by the bad conduct of their husbands, on whom they are not permitted to avenge themselves.

"It is the only penalty imposed upon them. The disagreements which almost invariably follow the indiscretion they have committed takes from them the desire of revealing to those profane persons from whom they expected respect and attention the great secrets of art. My sister, however, was not placed in either of these positions. Endowed with every charm that could inspire affection, she was not of the required age; but she consulted only her love. She flattered herself she could keep her marriage a secret. She succeeded in so doing for a short time. We rarely make inquiries about those who are absent. Each is occupied with her own affairs, and we fly through the world, doing good or ill, according to our inclinations, without being obliged at our return to account for our actions, unless we have been guilty of some act which causes us to be talked about, or that some beneficent fairy, moved by the unjust persecution of some unfortunate mortal, lays a complaint against the offender. In short, there must arise some unforeseen event to occasion us to consult the general book in which all we do is written at the same instant without the aid of hands. Saving these occasions, we have only to appear in the general assembly three times in the year; and, as we travel very swiftly, the affair does not occupy more than a couple of hours.

"My sister was obliged to give light to the throne (such is our phrase for the performance of that duty). On such occasions, she arranged for you a hunting party at some distance, or a journey of pleasure, and after your departure she feigned some indisposition, to remain alone in her cabinet, or that she had letters to write, or that she wished to repose. Neither in the palace nor amongst us was there any suspicion of that which it was so much her interest to conceal. This mystery, however, was not one for me. The consequences were dangerous, and I warned her of them ; but she loved you too much to repent the step she had taken. Desiring even to justify it in my eyes, she insisted that I should pay you a visit.

"Without flattering you, I confess that, if the sight of you did not compel me entirely to excuse her weakness, it at least diminished considerably my surprise at it, and increased the zeal with which I laboured to keep it a secret. Her dissimulation was successful for two years; but at length she betrayed herself. We are obliged to confer a certain number of favours on the world generally, and to return an account of them. When my sister gave in hers, it appeared that she had limited her excursions and her benefits to the confines of the Fortunate Island.

"Several of our ill-natured fairies blamed this conduct, and our Queen, in consequence, demanded of her why she had restricted her benevolence to this small corner of the earth, when she could not be ignorant that a young fairy was bound to travel far and wide, and manifest to the universe at large our pleasure and our power.

"As this was no new regulation, my sister could not murmur at the enforcement of it, nor find a pretext for objecting to obey it. She promised, therefore, to do so; but her impatience to see you again, the fear of her absence being discovered at the Palace, the impossibility of acting secretly on a throne, did not permit her to absent herself long enough and often enough to fulfil her promise; and at the next assembly she could hardly prove that she had been out of the Fortunate Island for a quarter of an hour.

"Our Queen, greatly displeased with her, threatened to destroy that island, and so prevent her continuing to violate our laws. This threat agitated her so greatly that the least sharp-sighted fairy could see to what a point she carried her interest for that fatal island, and the wicked fairy who turned the Prince here present into a frightful monster, was convinced by her confusion that, on opening the great book, she should find in it an important entry which would afford some exercise to her propensities for mischief. ' It is there,' she exclaimed, 'that the truth will appear, and that we shall learn what has really been her occupation!' and with these words, she opened the volume before the whole assembly, and read the details of all that had taken place during the last two years in a loud and distinct voice.

"All the fairies made an extraordinary uproar on hearing of this degrading alliance, and overwhelmed my wretched sister with the most cruel reproaches. She was degraded from our order, and condemned to remain a prisoner amongst us. If her punishment had consisted of the first penalty only, she would have consoled herself; but the second sentence, far more terrible, made her feel all the rigour of both. The loss of her dignity little affected her; but, loving you fondly, she begged, with tears in her eyes, that they would be satisfied with degrading her, and not deprive her of the pleasure of living as a simple mortal with her husband and her dear daughter.

"Her tears and supplications touched the hearts of the younger judges, and I felt, from the murmur that arose, that if the votes had been collected at that instant, she would certainly have escaped with a reprimand. But one of the eldest, who, from her extreme decrepitude had obtained amongst us the name of 'the Mother of the Seasons,' did not give the Queen time to speak and admit that pity had touched her heart as well as the others'.

"'There is no excuse for this crime,' cried the detestable old creature, in her cracked voice. 'If it is permitted to go unpunished, we shall be daily exposed to similar insults. The honour of our order is absolutely involved in it. This miserable being, attached to earth, does not regret the loss of a rank which elevated her a hundred degrees higher above monarchs than they are above their subjects. She tells us that her affections, her fears, and her wishes, all turn upon her unworthy family. It is through them we must punish her. Let her husband deplore her! Let her daughter, the shameful fruit of her illegal marriage, become the bride of a monster, to expiate the folly of a mother who could allow herself to be captivated by the frail and contemptible beauty of a mortal!'

"This cruel speech revived the severity of many who had been previously inclined to mercy. Those who continued to pity her being too few to offer any opposition, the sentence was approved of in its integrity; and our Queen herself, whose features had indicated a feeling of compassion, resuming their severity, confirmed the majority of votes in favour of the motion of the ill-natured old Fairy. My sister, however, in her endeavours to obtain a revocation of this cruel decree, to propitiate her judges, and to excuse her marriage, had drawn so charming a portrait of you, that it inflamed the heart of the fairy Governess of the Prince (she who had opened the great volume); but this dawning passion only served to increase the hatred which that wicked Fairy already bore to your unfortunate wife.

"Unable to resist her desire to see you, she concealed her passion under the colour of a pretext that she was anxious to ascertain if you deserved that a fairy should make such a sacrifice for you as my sister had done. As she had obtained the sanction of the assembly to her guardianship of the Prince, she could not have ventured to quit him for any length of time if the ingenuity of love had not inspired her with the idea of placing a protecting genius and two inferior and invisible fairies to watch over him in her absence. After taking this precaution, there was nothing to prevent her following her inclination, which speedily carried her to the Fortunate Island. In the meanwhile, the women and officers of the imprisoned Queen, surprised that she did not come out of her private cabinet, became alarmed. The express orders she had given them not to disturb her, induced them to pass the night without knocking at the door; but impatience at last taking place of all other considerations, they knocked loudly, and no one answering, they forced the doors, under the impression that some accident

had happened to her. Although they had prepared themselves for the worst, they were not the less astonished at perceiving no trace of her. They called her, they hunted for her in vain. They could discover nothing to appease the despair into which her disappearance had plunged them. They imagined a thousand reasons for it, each more absurd than the other. They could not suspect her evasion to be voluntary. She was all-powerful in your kingdom. The sovereign jurisdiction you had confided to her was not disputed by any one. Everybody obeyed her cheerfully. The affection you had for each other, that which she entertained for her daughter and for her subjects, who adored her, prevented them from supposing she had fled. Where could she go to be more happy? On the other hand, what man would have dared to carry off a queen from the midst of her own guards, and the centre of her own palace? Such a ravisher must have left some indications of the road he had taken.

"The disaster was certain, although the causes of it were unknown. There was another evil to dread; namely, the feelings with which you would receive this fatal news. The innocence of those who were responsible for the safety of the Queen's person by no means satisfied them that they should not feel the effects of your wrath. They felt they must either fly the kingdom, and thereby appear guilty of a crime they had not committed, or they must find some means of hiding this misfortune from you.

"After long deliberation, they could imagine no other than that of persuading you the Queen was dead, and this plan they put instantly into execution. They sent off a courier to inform you that she had been suddenly taken ill; a second followed a few hours afterwards, bearing the news of her death, in order to prevent your love inducing you to return post-haste to Court. Your appearance would have deranged all the measures they had taken for general security. They paid to the supposed defunct all the funeral honours due to her rank, to your affection, and the sorrow of a people who adored her, and who wept her loss as sincerely as yourself.

"This cruel adventure was always kept a profound secret from you, although it was known to every other inhabitant of the Fortunate Island. The first astonishment had given publicity to the whole affair. The affliction you felt at this loss was proportionate to your love; you found no consolation except in the innocent caresses of your infant daughter, whom you sent for to be with you. You determined never again to be separated from her; she was charming, and presented you continually with a living portrait of the Queen, her mother. The hostile Fairy, who had been the original cause of all this trouble by opening the great book in which she discovered my sister's marriage, had not come to see you without paying the price of her curiosity. Your appearance had produced the same effect upon her heart as it had previously done on that of your wife, and instead of this experience inducing her to excuse my sister, she ardently desired to commit the same fault. Hovering about you invisibly, she could not resolve to quit you. Beholding you inconsolable, she had no hope of success, and fearing to add the shame of your refusal to the pain of disappointment, she did not dare make herself known to you; on the other hand, supposing she did appear, she imagined that by skilful manoeuvring, she might accustom you to see her, and perhaps in time induce you to love her. But to effect this, she must be introduced to you ; and after much pondering to find some decorous way of presenting herself, she hit on one. There was a neighbouring Queen who had been driven out of her dominions by a usurper, who had murdered her husband. This unhappy Princess was ranging the world to find an asylum and an avenger. The Fairy carried her off, and having deposited her in a safe place, put her to sleep, and assumed her form. You beheld, Sire, that disguised Fairy fling herself at your feet, and implore your protection and assistance to punish the assassin of a husband whom she professed she regretted as deeply as you did your Queen. She protested that her love for him alone impelled her to this course, and that she renounced, with all her heart, a crown which she offered to him who should avenge her dear husband.

"The unhappy pity each other. You interested yourself in her misfortunes the more readily for that she wept the loss of a beloved spouse, and that mingling her tears with yours, she talked to you incessantly of the Queen. You gave her your protection, and lost no time in re-establishing her authority in the kingdom she pretended to, by punishing the rebels and the usurper she seemed to desire; but she would neither return to it nor quit you. She implored you, for her own security, to govern the kingdom in her name, as you were too generous to accept it as a gift from her, and to permit her to reside at your Court. You could not refuse her this new favour. She appeared to be necessary to you for the education of your daughter, for the cunning Fairy knew well enough that child was the sole object of your affection. She feigned an exceeding fondness for her, and had her continually in her arms. Anticipating the request you were about to make to her, she earnestly begged to be permitted to take charge of her education, saying that she would have no heir but that dear child, whom she looked on as her own, and who was the only being she loved in the world; because she said she reminded her of a daughter she had had by her husband, and who perished along with him.

"The proposal appeared to you so advantageous that you did not hesitate to entrust the Princess to her care, and to give her full authority over her. She acquitted herself of her duties to perfection, and by her talent and her affection obtained your implicit confidence and your love as for a tender sister. This was not sufficient for her: all her anxiety was but to become your wife. She neglected nothing to gain this end; but even had you never been the husband of the most beautiful of fairies, she was not formed to inspire you with love. The shape she had assumed could not bear comparison with hers into whose place she would have stolen. It was extremely ugly, and being naturally so herself, she had only the power of appearing beautiful one day in the year.

"The knowledge of this discouraging fact convinced her that to succeed she must have recourse to other charms than those of beauty. She intrigued secretly to oblige the people and the nobility to petition you to take another wife, and to point her out to you as the desirable person; but certain ambiguous conversations she had held with you, in order to sound your inclinations, enabled you easily to discover the origin of the pressing solicitations with which you were importuned. You declared positively that you would not hear of giving a step-mother to your daughter, nor lower her position, by making her subordinate to a queen, from that which she held as the highest person next to yourself in the kingdom, and the acknowledged heir to your throne. You also gave the false Queen to understand that you should feel obliged by her returning to her own dominions immediately, and without ado, and promised her that when she was settled there you would render her all the services she could expect from a faithful friend and a generous neighbour; but you did not conceal from her that if she did not take this course willingly, she ran the risk of being compelled to do so.

"The invincible obstacle you then opposed to her love threw her into a terrific rage, but she affected so much indifference about the matter that she succeeded in persuading you that her attempt was caused by ambition, and the fear that eventually you might take possession of her dominions, preferring, notwithstanding the earnestness with which she had appeared to offer them to you, to let you believe she was insincere in that case, rather than you should suspect her real sentiments. Her fury was not less violent because it was suppressed. Not doubting that it was Beauty who, more powerful in your heart than policy, caused you to reject the opportunity of increasing your empire in so glorious a manner, she conceived for her a hatred as violent as that which she felt for your wife, and resolved to get rid of her, fully believing that if she were dead, your subjects, renewing their remonstrances, would compel you to change your state, in order to leave a successor to the throne. The good soul was anything but of an age to present you with one; but that she cared little about. The Queen, whose resemblance she had assumed, was still young enough to have many children, and her ugliness was no obstacle to a royal and political alliance.

"Notwithstanding the official declaration you had made, it was thought that if your daughter died you would yield to the continual representations of your council. It was believed, also, that your choice would fall upon this pretended Queen; and that idea surrounded her with numberless parasites. It was her design, therefore, by the aid of one of her flatterers, whose wife was as base as her husband, and as wicked as she was herself, to make away with your daughter. She had appointed this woman governess to the little Princess. These wretches settled between them that they would smother her, and report that she had died suddenly; but for more security they decided to commit this murder in the neighbouring forest, so that nobody could surprise them in the execution of this barbarous deed. They counted on no one having the slightest knowledge of it, and that it would be impossible to blame them for not having sought for assistance before she expired, having the legitimate excuse that they were too far away from any. The husband of the governess proposed to go in search of aid as soon as the child was dead; and that no suspicion might be awakened, he was to appear surprised at finding it too late when he returned to the spot where he had left this tender victim of their fury, and he also rehearsed the sorrow and consternation he was to affect.

"When my wretched sister saw herself deprived of her power and condemned to a cruel imprisonment, she requested me to console you and to watch over the safety of her child. It was unnecessary for her to take that precaution. The tie which unites us, and the pity I felt for her, would have sufficed to ensure you my protection, and her entreaties could not increase the zeal with which I hastened to fulfil her decrees.

"I saw you as often as I could, and as much as prudence permitted me, without incurring the risk of arousing the suspicions of our enemy, who would have denounced me as a Fairy in whom sisterly affection prevailed over the honour of her order, and who protected a guilty race. I neglected nothing to convince all the Fairies that I had abandoned my sister to her unhappy fate, and, by so doing, trusted to be more at liberty to serve her. As I watched every movement of your perfidious admirer, not only with my own eyes, but those of the Genii, who were my servants, her horrible intentions were not unknown to me. I could not oppose her by open force; and though it would have been easy for me to annihilate those into whose hands she had delivered the little innocent, prudence restrained me; for, had I carried off your daughter, the malignant Fairy would have retaken her from me, without its being possible for me to defend her.

"It is a law amongst us that we must be a thousand years old before we can dispute the power of the ancient fairies, or at any rate we must have become serpents. The perils which accompany the latter condition cause us to call it the Terrible Act. The bravest amongst us shudder at the thought of undertaking it. We hesitate a long time before we can resolve to expose ourselves to its consequences; and without the urgent motive of hatred, love, or vengeance, there are few who do not prefer waiting for time to make them Elders than to acquire their privilege by that dangerous transformation, in which the greater number are destroyed. I was in this position. I wanted ten years of the thousand, and I had no resource but in artifice. I employed it successfully. I took the form of a monstrous she-bear, and, hiding myself in the forest selected for the execution of this detestable deed, when the wretches arrived to fulfil the barbarous order they had received, I flung myself upon the woman who had the child in her arms, and who had already placed her hand on its mouth. Her fright made her drop the precious burden, but she was not allowed to escape so easily; the horror I felt at her unnatural conduct inspired me with the ferocity of the brute I had assumed the form of. I strangled her, as well as the traitor who accompanied her, and I carried off Beauty, after having rapidly stripped off her clothes and dyed them with the blood of her enemies. I scattered them also about the forest, taking the precaution to tear them in several places, so that they should not suspect the Princess had escaped; and I withdrew, delighted at having succeeded so completely.

"The Fairy believed her object had been attained. The death of her two accomplices was an advantage to her. She was mistress of her secret, and the fate they had met with was but what she had herself destined them to, in recompence of their guilty services. Another circumstance was also favourable to her. Some shepherds who had seen this affair from a distance ran for assistance, which arrived just in time to see the infamous wretches expire, and prevent the possibility of suspicion that she had any part in it.

"The same circumstances were equally favourable to my enterprise. The wicked Fairy was as fully convinced as the people by them. The event was so natural, that she never doubted it. She did not even condescend to exert her skill to satisfy herself of the fact. I was delighted at her fancied security. I should not have been the strongest had she attempted to recover little Beauty, because, in addition to the reasons which made her my superior, and which I have explained to you, she possessed the advantage of having received that child from you. You had deputed to her your authority, which you alone could re-assume, and short of your wresting her yourself out of her hands, nothing could interfere with the control she had a right to exercise over the Princess till she was married.

"Preserved from this anxiety, I found myself overwhelmed by another, on recollecting that the Mother of the Seasons had condemned my niece to marry a monster; but she was then not three years old, and I flattered myself I should be able, by study, to discover some expedient to prevent this curse being fulfilled to the letter, and to evade it by some equivocation. I had plenty of time to ponder on it, and my first care was, therefore, only to find some spot where I could place my precious charge in safety.

"Profound secresy was absolutely necessary to me. I dared not place her in a castle, nor exercise for her benefit any of the magnificent wonders of our art. Our enemy would have noticed it. It would have awakened an anxiety, the consequences of which would have been fatal to us. I thought it better to assume an humble garb, and confide the infant to the care of the first person I met with, who appeared to me to be an honest man, and under whose roof I could promise myself she would enjoy the comforts of life.

"Chance soon favoured my intentions. I found what suited me exactly. It was a small house in a village, the door of which was open. I entered this cottage, which appeared to me that of a peasant in easy circumstances. I saw by the light of a lamp three country women asleep beside a cradle, which I concluded contained a baby. The cradle did not at all correspond with the general simplicity of the apartment.

Everything about it was sumptuous. I imagined that its little occupant was ill, and that the deep sleep into which its nurses had fallen was the consequence of long watching over it. I approached silently, with the intention of curing the infant, and anticipated with pleasure the surprise of these women, on awaking, to find their invalid restored to health, without knowing what to attribute it to. I was about to take the child out of the cradle in order to breathe health into it; but my good intentions were vain: it expired at the instant I touched it.

"I immediately conceived the idea of taking advantage of this melancholy event, and substituting my niece for the dead child, which, by good fortune, was also a girl. I lost no time in making the exchange, and bearing away the lifeless infant, buried it carefully. I then returned to the house, at the door of which I knocked long and loudly, to awaken them.

"I told them, feigning a provincial dialect, that I was a stranger to those parts, who was in want of a night's lodging. They good-naturedly offered me one, and then went to look at their nursling, whom they found quietly asleep, with all the appearance of being in perfect health. They were astonished and delighted, not dreaming of the deception I had practised upon them. They informed me that the child was the daughter of a rich merchant; that one of their party had been her nurse, and after having weaned her had restored her to her parents, but that the child, having fallen ill in her father's house, had been sent back to the country, in hope that the change of air would be of service to her. They added, with satisfied countenances, that the experiment had succeeded, and produced a better effect than all the remedies which had been resorted to previous to its adoption. They determined to carry her back to her father as soon as it was daylight, in order to afford him, as early as possible, the gratification he would derive from her restoration, for conducing to which, also, they expected to receive a liberal reward, as the child was his particular favourite, although the youngest of eleven.

"At sunrise they set out, and I feigned to continue my journey, congratulating myself on having so well provided for my niece's safety. To insure this object more completely, and induce the supposed father still more to attach himself to the little girl, I assumed the form of one of those women who go about telling fortunes, and arriving at the merchant's door just as the nurses reached it with the child, I followed them into the house. He received them with delight, and taking the little girl in his arms, became the dupe of his paternal affection, and fancied that the emotions simply caused by his kindly disposition were the mysterious workings of nature at the sight of his offspring. I seized this opportunity of increasing the interest he believed he had in the child.

"'Look well upon this little one, my good gentleman,' said I, in the usual language of the class to which by my dress I appeared to belong. 'She will be a great honour to thy family, she will bring thee immense wealth, and save thy life and that of all thy children. She will be so beautiful—so beautiful, that she will be called Beauty by all who behold her.' As a reward for my prediction, he gave me a piece of gold, and I withdrew, perfectly satisfied. I had no longer any reason for residing with the race of Adam. To profit by my leisure, I returned to Fairyland, resolving to remain in it some time. I passed my days there quietly in consoling my sister, in giving her news of her dear daughter, and in assuring her that, far from forgetting her, you cherished her memory as fondly as you had formerly herself.

"Such, great King, was our situation whilst you were suffering under the fresh calamity which had deprived you of your child, and renewed all the affliction you had felt at the loss of her mother. Although you could not positively accuse the person to whom you had confided the infant of being the wilful cause of the accident, it was still impossible for you not to look upon her with an evil eye; for though it did not appear that she was guilty of intentional mischief, it was certainly through her neglecting to see that the young Princess was properly attended and protected that the event had proved fatal.

"After the first paroxysms of your grief had subsided, she flattered herself that no obstacle would arise to prevent your espousing her. She caused her emissaries to renew the proposal to you; but she was undeceived, and her mortification was excessive, when you declared that not only were your intentions unchanged respecting a second marriage, but that even, could anything alter your determination, it would never be in her favour. To this declaration you added a positive order for her to quit the kingdom immediately. Her presence continually reminded you of your child, and renewed your affliction. Such was the reason you adduced for this step; but your principal object was to put an end to the intrigues she was constantly carrying on in order to gain her end.

"She was furious; but she was obliged to obey without being able to avenge herself. I had persuaded one of our ancient fairies to protect you. Her power was considerable, for she joined to her age the advantage of having been four times a serpent. In proportion to the excessive peril incurred by that process, are the honours and powers attached to it. This Fairy, out of consideration for me, took you under her protection, and put it out of the power of your indignant lover to do you any mischief.

"This disappointment was fortunate for the Queen, whose form she had assumed. She awoke her from her magic slumber, and concealing from her the criminal use she had made of her features, placed her conduct in the best light before her.

"She expatiated on the value of her intercession with the King, and on the trouble she had saved her, and gave her the best advice she could how to maintain herself for the future in her proper person. It was then that, to console herself for your indifference, the Fairy returned to the young Prince and resumed her care of him. She became too fond of him, and not being able to make herself beloved, she caused him to suffer that terrible effect of her fury.

"In the meanwhile, I had insensibly arrived at the privileged age, and my power was increased, but my desire to serve my sister and yourself induced me to feel that still I had not sufficient. My sincere friendship blinding me to the perils of "the Terrible Act," I resolved to undertake it.

"I became a serpent, and passed fortunately through the ordeal. I was then in a position to act openly in favour of those who were persecuted by my malicious companions. If I cannot at all times entirely dissolve their fatal spells, I can at least counteract them by my skill and by my counsels.

"My niece was amongst the number of those whom I could not completely favour. Not daring to discover all the interest I took in her, it appeared to me that the best thing I could do was to allow her still to pass as the merchant's daughter. I visited her under various forms, and always returned satisfied. Her virtue and beauty equalled her good sense. At the age of fourteen she had already given proof of great fortitude during the changes of fortune which had befallen her supposed father.

"I was delighted to find that the most cruel reverses had not been able to affect her tranquillity. On the contrary, by her cheerfulness, by the charm of her conversation, she had succeeded in restoring it to the hearts of her father and her brothers; and I rejoiced to observe also that her sentiments were worthy of her birth. These pleasant reflections were, however, mingled with much bitterness, when I remembered that, with so many perfections, she was destined to be the wife of a monster. I toiled, I studied night and day to find some means of saving her from so great a misfortune, and was in despair at finding none.

"This anxiety did not prevent me, however, from paying occasional visits to you. Your wife, who was deprived of that liberty, implored me incessantly to go and see you; and, notwithstanding the protection of our friend, her affectionate heart was continually alarmed about you, and persuaded her that the instant I lost sight of you would be the last of your life, and in which you would be sacrificed to the fury of our enemy. This fear possessed her so strongly, that she scarcely gave me a moment's rest. No sooner did I bring her news of you than she supplicated me so earnestly to return to you, that it was impossible to refuse her.

"Compassionating her anxiety, and more desirous to end it than to save myself the trouble it gave me, I employed against my cruel companion the same weapons she had made use of against you. I proceeded to open the great book. By good fortune, it was at the very moment she was holding that conversation with the Queen and Prince which terminated in his transformation. I lost not a word of it, and my rapture was extreme at finding that, in seeking to assure her vengeance, she neutralized, without knowing it, the mischief which the Mother of the Seasons had done us in dooming Beauty to be the bride of a monster.

"To crown our happiness, she added conditions so advantageous, that it almost seemed as if she made them on purpose to oblige me, for she thereby furnished my sister's daughter with an opportunity of proving that she was worthy of being the issue of the purest of fairy-blood.

"The slightest sign or gesture expresses amongst us as much as it would take an ordinary mortal three days to explain. I uttered but one contemptuous word. It was enough to inform the assembly that our enemy had pronounced her own sentence in that which she had caused ten years before to be passed upon your wife. At the age of the latter, the weakness of love was more natural than at the advanced period of existence of a fairy of the highest order. I spoke of the base and wicked actions which had accompanied that superannuated passion. I urged that if so many infamous acts were allowed to pass unpunished, mortals would be justified in saying that fairies existed in the world but to dishonour nature and afflict the human race. Presenting the book to them, I condensed this abrupt oration in the single word "Behold!" It was not the less powerful in its effect.

"There were present also friends of mine, both young and old, who treated the amorous fury as she deserved. She had not succeeded in becoming your wife, and to that disgrace was now added degradation from her order, and imprisonment, as in the case of the Queen of the Happy Island.

"This council was held whilst she was with you, Madam, and your son. As soon as she appeared amongst us, the result was communicated to her. I had the pleasure to be present, after which, closing the book, I descended rapidly from the middle region of air in which our empire is situated, to combat the effect of the despair to which you were ready to abandon yourselves. I performed my journey in as short a space of time as I had occupied with my laconical address. I arrived soon enough to promise you my assistance. All sorts of reasons combined to invite me. Your virtues, your misfortunes, (said the Fairy, turning to the Prince), the advantages they offered to Beauty made me see in you the Monster that suited me. You appeared to me worthy of each other, and I felt convinced that when you became acquainted, your hearts would do each other mutual justice.

"You know," she continued, addressing the Queen, " what I have since done to attain my object, and by what means I obliged Beauty to come to this Palace, where the sight of the Prince, and her interviews with him, in the dreams I conjured up for her, had the effect I desired. They kindled love in her heart without diminishing her virtue or weakening the sense of duty arid gratitude which attached her to the Monster. In short, I have happily brought my scheme to perfection. Yes, Prince," pursued the Fairy, "you have no longer anything to fear from your enemy. She is stripped of her power, and will never again be able to injure you by other spells. You have exactly fulfilled the conditions she imposed on you. Had you not done so, you would have been still bound by them, notwithstanding her eternal degradation. You have made yourself beloved without the aid of your rank or your intelligence; and you, Beauty, are equally relieved from the curse pronounced upon you by the Mother of the Seasons. You cheerfully accepted a monster for your husband. She has nothing more to exact. All now tends to your happiness."

The Fairy ceased speaking, and the King threw himself at her feet. "Great Fairy," he exclaimed, "how can I thank you for all the favours you have heaped on my family? My gratitude for the benefits you have bestowed on us far exceeds my power of expression; but, my august sister," added he, "that title encourages me to ask more favours; for, despite the obligations I am already under to you, I cannot avoid confessing to you that I shall never be truly happy so long as I am deprived of the presence of my beloved Fairy Queen. This account of what she has done and what she has suffered for me would increase my love and my affliction, were either of them capable of being augmented. Ah, Madam," he added, "can you not crown all your benefactions by enabling me to behold her?"

The question was useless. If the Fairy had had the power to have afforded him that gratification, she was too willing to have waited for the request: but she could not alter what the Council of the Fairies had decreed. The young Queen being a prisoner in the middle regions of air, there was not the shadow of a chance of his being enabled to see her; and the Fairy was about to explain this to him kindly, and to exhort him to await patiently some unforeseen events, of which she might take advantage, when an enchanting melody stole upon their ears and interrupted her. The King, his daughter, the Queen, and the Prince, were in ecstasies, but the Fairy experienced another sort of surprise. Such music indicated the triumph of some Fairy. She could not imagine what Fairy had achieved a victory. Her fears suggested that it was the old one, or the Mother of the Seasons, who in her absence had obtained, the former her liberty, or the latter permission to persecute the lovers afresh.

She was in this perplexity when it was agreeably ended by the presence of her Fairy-sister, the Queen of the Happy Island, who suddenly appeared in the centre of that charming group. She was no less lovely than when the King, her husband, lost her. The monarch, who instantly recognised her, making the respect he owed her yield to the love he had cherished for her, embraced her with such transports of joy, that the Queen herself was surprised at them.

The Fairy, her sister, could not imagine to what fortunate miracle she was indebted for her liberty; but the royal Fairy informed her that she owed her happiness solely to her own courage, which had impelled her to hazard her own existence to preserve another's. "You are aware," said she to the Fairy, "that the daughter of our Queen was received into the order at her birth; that her father was not a sublunary being, but the sage Amadabak, whose alliance is an honour to the fairy race, and whose sublime knowledge invests him with much higher powers. Notwithstanding this, however, it was imperative for his daughter to become a serpent at the end of her first hundred years. The fatal period arrived, and our Queen, as tender a mother, and as anxious respecting the fate of this dear infant as any ordinary parent could be, could not resolve to expose her to the many chances of destruction in that shape, the misfortunes of those who had perished being but too notorious for her not to feel the greatest alarm. My wretched situation depriving me of all hope of again beholding my affectionate husband and my lovely daughter, I had conceived a perfect disgust for a life which I was doomed to pass apart from them. Without the least hesitation, therefore, I offered to become a crawling reptile in the place of the young Fairy. I saw with delight a certain, prompt, and honourable mode of delivering myself from all the miseries with which I was overwhelmed, by death or by a glorious emancipation, which would render me mistress of my own actions, and thereby enable me to rejoin my husband.

"Our Queen hesitated as little to accept this offer, so gratifying to her maternal affection, as I did to make it. She embraced me a hundred times, and promised to restore me to liberty unconditionally, and re-establish me in all my privileges, if I was fortunate enough to pass unharmed through that perilous enterprise. I did do so, and the fruit of my labours was enjoyed by the young Fairy, for whom I had been the substitute. The success of my first trial encouraged me to make a second for my own benefit. I underwent the transformation anew, and was equally fortunate. This last act made me an Elder, and, consequently, independent. I was not long in profiting by my liberty, and flying hither to rejoin a family so dear to me."

As soon as the Fairy had finished her narrative, the embraces were renewed by her affectionate auditors. It was a charming confusion, in which each caressed the other almost without knowing what they were about: beauty, particularly, enchanted at appertaining to such an illustrious family, and no longer fearing to degrade the Prince, her cousin, by causing him to form an alliance beneath him.

But although transported by the excess of her happiness, she did not forget the worthy man whom she had formerly believed to be her father. She recalled to her fairy aunt the promise she had made to her, that he and his children should have the honour of being present at her marriage. She was still speaking to her on this subject when they saw from the window sixteen persons on horseback, most of whom had hunting-horns, and appeared in considerable confusion. Their disorder evidently arose from their horses having ran away with them. Beauty instantly recognised them as the six sons of the worthy merchant, the five daughters, and their five lovers.

Everybody but the Fairy was surprised at this abrupt entrance. Those who made it were not less so, at finding themselves carried by the speed of their unmanageable horses into a palace totally unknown to them.

This is the way it happened. They were all out hunting, when their horses, suddenly uniting themselves as in one squadron, galloped off with them at such speed to the Palace that all their efforts to stop them were perfectly useless.

Beauty, thoughtless of her present dignity, hastened to receive and re-assure them. She embraced them all kindly. The good man himself next appeared, but not in the same disorder. A horse had neighed and scratched at his door. He had no doubt that it came to seek him by order of his dear daughter. He mounted him without fear, and, perfectly satisfied as to whither the steed would bear him, he was not at all surprised to find himself in the court-yard of a Palace which he now saw for the third time, and to which he felt convinced he had been conducted to witness the marriage of Beauty and the Beast.

The moment he perceived her he ran to her with open arms, blessing the happy moment that presented her again to his sight, and heaping benedictions on the generous Beast who had permitted him to return; he looked about for him in every direction, to offer him his most humble thanks for all the favours he had heaped on his family, and particularly on his youngest daughter. He was vexed at not seeing him, and began to apprehend that his conjectures were erroneous. Still, the presence of all his children seemed to support the idea he had formed, as they would scarcely have been all assembled in that spot if some solemn ceremony, such as that marriage, were not to be celebrated.

These reflections, which the good man made to himself, did not prevent him from pressing Beauty fondly in his arms, and bathing her cheek with tears of joy. After allowing due time for this first expression of his feelings, "Enough, good man," said the Fairy. "You have sufficiently caressed this Princess. It is time that, ceasing to regard her as a father, you should learn that that title does not appertain to you, and that you must now do her homage as your sovereign. She is the Princess of the Happy Island, daughter of the King and Queen whom you see before you. She is about to become the wife of this Prince. Here stands the Prince's mother, sister of the King. I am a Fairy, her friend, and the aunt of Beauty. As to the Prince," added the Fairy, observing the expression of the good man's face, "he is better known to you than you imagine; but he is much altered since you last saw him. In a word, he was the Beast himself."

The father and his sons were enchanted at these wonderful tidings, while the sisters felt a painful jealousy, but they endeavoured to conceal it under the mask of a gratification which deceived no one. The others, however, feigned to believe them sincere. As to the lovers, who had been rendered inconstant by the hope of possessing Beauty, and who had only returned to their first attachments on their despairing to obtain her, they knew not what to think.

The merchant could not help weeping, without being able to tell whether his tears were caused by the pleasure of seeing the happiness of Beauty, or by the sorrow of losing so perfect a daughter. His sons were agitated by similar feelings. Beauty, extremely affected by this evidence of their love, entreated those on whom she now depended, as well as the Prince, her future husband, to permit her to reward such tender attachment. Her entreaty testified the goodness of her heart too sincerely not to be listened to. They were laden with bounties, and by permission of the King, the Prince, and the Queen, Beauty continued to call them by the tender names of father, brothers, and even sisters, though she was not ignorant that the latter were as little so in heart as they were in blood. She desired they would all, in return, call her by the name they were wont to do when they believed her to be a member of their family. The old man and his children were appointed to offices in the Court of Beauty, and enjoyed the pleasure of living continually near her, in a station sufficiently exalted to be generally respected. The lovers of her sisters, whose passion for Beauty might easily have been revived, if they had not known it would be useless, thought themselves too happy in being united to the good man's daughters, and becoming allied to persons for whom Beauty retained so much goodwill.

All those she desired to be present at her wedding having arrived, the celebration of it was no longer delayed. The festivities lasted many days, and ended at length only because the fairy aunt of the young bride pointed out to them the propriety of leaving that beautiful retreat, and returning to their dominions, to show themselves to their subjects.

It was quite time she should recall their kingdom to their recollection and the indispensable duties which demanded their presence. Enraptured with the scenes around them, entranced by the pleasure of loving and expressing their love to each other, they had entirely forgotten their royal state and the cares that attend it.

The newly-married pair, indeed, proposed to the Fairy that they should abdicate, and resign their power into the hands of any one she should select; but that wise being represented to them clearly that they were under as great an obligation to fulfil the destiny which had confided to them the government of a nation as that nation was to preserve for them an unshaken loyalty.

They yielded to these just remonstrances, but the Prince and Beauty stipulated that they should be allowed occasionally to visit that spot, and cast aside for a while the cares inseparable from their station, and that they should be waited on by the invisible Genii or the animals who had attended them during the preceding years. They availed themselves as often as possible of this liberty. Their presence seemed to embellish the spot. All were eager to please them. The Genii awaited their visits with impatience, and received them with joy, testifying in a hundred ways the delight their return afforded them.

The Fairy, whose foresight neglected nothing, gave them a chariot, drawn by twelve white stags with golden horns and hoofs, like those she drove herself. The speed of these animals was almost greater than that of thought; and, drawn by them, you could easily make the tour of the world in two hours. By this means they lost no time in travelling. They profited by every moment of leisure, and went frequently in this elegant equipage to visit their father, the King of the Happy Island, who had grown so young again through the return of his Fairy Queen, that he equalled in face and form the Prince, his son-in-law. He felt also equally happy, being neither less enamoured nor less eager to prove to his wife his unceasing affection, while she, on her part, responded to his love with all that tenderness which had previously been the cause of so much misfortune to her.

She had been received by her subjects with transports of joy as great as those of grief which her loss had occasioned them. She had always loved them dearly, and her will being now unfettered, she proved as much, by showering upon them for many centuries all the benefits they could desire. Her power, assisted by the friendship of the Queen of the Fairies, preserved the life, health, and youth of the King, her husband, for ages. He only ceased to exist because no mortal can live for ever.

The Queen and the Fairy, her sister, were equally attentive to Beauty, her husband, the Queen, his mother, the old man, and all his family, so that there never was known people who lived so long. The Queen, mother of the Prince, caused this marvellous history to be recorded in the archives of her kingdom and in those of the Happy Island, that it might be handed down to posterity. They also disseminated copies of it throughout the Universe, so that the world at large might never cease to talk of the wonderful adventures of Beauty and the Beast.

BEAUTY AND THE BEAST

BY
ANDREW LANG

FROM *THE BLUE FAIRY BOOK* (1889)

ONCE upon a time, in a very far-off country, there lived a merchant who had been so fortunate in all his undertakings that he was enormously rich. As he had, however, six sons and six daughters he found that his money was not too much to let them all have everything they fancied, as they were accustomed to do.

But one day a most unexpected misfortune befell them. Their house caught fire and was speedily burnt to the ground, with all the splendid furniture, the books, pictures, gold, silver, and precious goods it contained; and this was only the beginning of their troubles. Their father, who had until this moment prospered in all ways, suddenly lost every ship he had upon the sea, either by dint of pirates, shipwreck, or fire. Then he heard that his clerks in distant countries, whom he trusted entirely, had proved unfaithful; and at last from great wealth he fell into the direst poverty.

All that he had left was a little house in a desolate place at least a hundred leagues from the town in which he had lived, and to this he was forced to retreat with his children, who were in despair at the idea of leading such a different life. Indeed, the daughters at first hoped that their friends, who had been so numerous while they were rich, would insist on their staying in their houses now they no longer possessed one. But they soon found that they were left alone, and that their former friends even attributed their misfortunes to their own extravagance, and showed no intention of offering them any help. So nothing was left for them but to take their departure to the cottage, which stood in the midst of a dark forest and seemed to be the most dismal place upon the face of the earth.

As they were too poor to have any servants, the girls had to work hard, like peasants, and the sons, for their part, cultivated the fields to earn their living. Roughly clothed, and living in the simplest way, the girls regretted unceasingly the luxuries and amusements of their former life;only the youngest tried to be brave and cheerful. She had been as sad as anyone when misfortune overtook her father, but, soon recovering her natural gaiety, she set to work to make the best of things, to amuse her father and brothers as well as she could, and to try to persuade her sisters to join her in dancing and singing. But they would do nothing of the sort, and, because she was not as doleful as themselves, they declared that this miserable life was all she was fit for. But she was really far prettier and cleverer than they were; indeed, she was so lovely that she was always called Beauty.

After two years, when they were all beginning to get used to their new life, something happened to disturb their tranquillity. Their father received the news that one of his ships, which he had believed to be lost, had come safely into port with a rich cargo. All the sons and daughters at once thought that their poverty was at an end, and wanted to set out directly for the town; but their father, who was more prudent, begged them to wait a little, and, though it was harvest time, and he could ill be spared, determined to go himself first, to make inquiries. Only the youngest daughter had any doubt but that they would soon again be as rich as they were before, or at least rich enough to live comfortably in some town where they would find amusement and gay companions once more. So they all loaded their father with commissions for jewels and dresses which it would have taken a fortune to buy; only Beauty, feeling sure that it was of no use, did not ask for anything. Her father, noticing her silence, said: "And what shall I bring for you, Beauty?"

"The only thing I wish for is to see you come home safely," she answered.

But this only vexed her sisters, who fancied she was blaming them for having asked for such costly things. Her father, however, was pleased, but as he thought that at her age she certainly ought to like pretty presents, he told her to choose something.

"Well, dear father," she said, "as you insist upon it, I beg that you will bring me a rose. I have not seen one since we came here, and I love them so much."

So the merchant set out and reached the town as quickly as possible, but only to find that his former companions, believing him to be dead, had divided between them the goods which the ship had brought; and after six months of trouble and expense he found himself as poor as when he started, having been able to recover only just enough to pay the cost of his journey. To make matters worse, he was obliged to leave the town in the most terrible weather, so that by the time he was within a few leagues of his home he was almost exhausted with cold and fatigue. Though he knew it would take some hours to get through the forest, he was so anxious to be at his journey's end that he resolved to go on; but night overtook him, and the deep snow and bitter frost made it impossible for his horse to carry him any further. Not a house was to be seen; the only shelter he could get was the hollow trunk of a great tree, and there he crouched all the night which seemed to him the longest he had ever known. In spite of his weariness the howling of the wolves kept him awake, and even when at last the day broke he was not much better off, for the falling snow had covered up every path, and he did not know which way to turn.

At length he made out some sort of track, and though at the beginning it was so rough and slippery that he fell down more than once, it presently became easier, and led him into an avenue of trees which ended in a splendid castle. It seemed to the merchant very strange that no snow had fallen in the avenue, which was entirely composed of orange trees, covered with flowers and fruit. When he reached the first court of the castle he saw before him a flight of agate steps, and went up them, and passed through several splendidly furnished rooms. The pleasant warmth of the air revived him, and he felt very hungry; but there seemed to be nobody in all this vast and splendid palace whom he could ask to give him something to eat. Deep silence reigned everywhere, and at last, tired of roaming through empty rooms and galleries, he stopped in a room smaller than the rest, where a clear fire was burning and a couch was drawn up closely to it. Thinking that this must be prepared for someone who was expected, he sat down to wait till he should come, and very soon fell into a sweet sleep.

When his extreme hunger wakened him after several hours, he was still alone;

but a little table, upon which was a good dinner, had been drawn up close to him, and, as he had eaten nothing for twenty-four hours, he lost no time in beginning his meal, hoping that he might soon have an opportunity of thanking his considerate entertainer, whoever it might be. But no one appeared, and even after another long sleep, from which he awoke completely refreshed, there was no sign of anybody, though a fresh meal of dainty cakes and fruit was prepared upon the little table at his elbow. Being naturally timid, the silence began to terrify him, and he resolved to search once more through all the rooms; but it was of no use. Not even a servant was to be seen; there was no sign of life in the palace! He began to wonder what he should do, and to amuse himself by pretending that all the treasures he saw were his own, and considering how he would divide them among his children. Then he went down into the garden, and though it was winter everywhere else, here the sun shone, and the birds sang, and the flowers bloomed, and the air was soft and sweet. The merchant, in ecstacies with all he saw and heard, said to himself:

"All this must be meant for me. I will go this minute and bring my children to share all these delights."

In spite of being so cold and weary when he reached the castle, he had taken his horse to the stable and fed it. Now he thought he would saddle it for his homeward journey, and he turned down the path which led to the stable. This path had a hedge of roses on each side of it, and the merchant thought he had never seen or smelt such exquisite flowers. They reminded him of his promise to Beauty, and he stopped and had just gathered one to take to her when he was startled by a strange noise behind him. Turning round, he saw a frightful Beast, which seemed to be very angry and said, in a terrible voice:

"Who told you that you might gather my roses? Was it not enough that I allowed you to be in my palace and was kind to you? This is the way you show your gratitude, by stealing my flowers! But your insolence shall not go unpunished." The merchant, terrified by these furious words, dropped the fatal rose, and, throwing himself on his knees, cried: "Pardon me, noble sir. I am truly grateful to you for your hospitality, which was so magnificent that I could not imagine that you would be offended by my taking such a little thing as a rose." But the Beast's anger was not lessened by this speech.

"You are very ready with excuses and flattery," he cried; "but that will not save you from the death you deserve."

"Alas!" thought the merchant, "if my daughter could only know what danger her rose has brought me into!"

And in despair he began to tell the Beast all his misfortunes, and the reason of his journey, not forgetting to mention Beauty's request.

"A king's ransom would hardly have procured all that my other daughters asked." he said: "but I thought that I might at least take Beauty her rose. I beg you to forgive me, for you see I meant no harm."

The Beast considered for a moment, and then he said, in a less furious tone:

"I will forgive you on one condition -- that is, that you will give me one of your daughters."

"Ah!" cried the merchant, "if I were cruel enough to buy my own life at the expense of one of my children's, what excuse could I invent to bring her here?"

"No excuse would be necessary," answered the Beast. "If she comes at all she must come willingly. On no other condition will I have her. See if any one of them is courageous enough, and loves you well enough to come and save your life. You seem to be an honest man, so I will trust you to go home. I give you a month to see if either of your daughters will come back with you and stay here, to let you go free. If neither of them is willing, you must come alone, after bidding them good-by for ever, for then you will belong to me. And do not imagine that you can hide from me, for if you fail to keep your word I will come and fetch you!" added the Beast grimly.

The merchant accepted this proposal, though he did not really think any of his daughters could be persuaded to come. He promised to return at the time appointed, and then, anxious to escape from the presence of the Beast, he asked permission to set off at once. But the Beast answered that he could not go until next day.

"Then you will find a horse ready for you," he said. "Now go and eat your supper, and await my orders."

The poor merchant, more dead than alive, went back to his room, where the most delicious supper was already served on the little table which was drawn up before a blazing fire. But he was too terrified to eat, and only tasted a few of the dishes, for fear the Beast should be angry if he did not obey his orders. When he had finished he heard a great noise in the next room, which he knew meant that the Beast was coming. As he could do nothing to escape his visit, the only thing that remained was to seem as little afraid as possible; so when the Beast appeared and asked roughly if he had supped well, the merchant answered humbly that he had, thanks to his host's kindness. Then the Beast warned him to remember their agreement, and to prepare his daughter exactly for what she had to expect.

"Do not get up to-morrow," he added, "until you see the sun and hear a golden bell ring. Then you will find your breakfast waiting for you here, and the horse you are to ride will be ready in the courtyard. He will also bring you back again when you come with your daughter a month hence. Farewell. Take a rose to Beauty, and remember your promise!"

The merchant was only too glad when the Beast went away, and though he could not sleep for sadness, he lay down until the sun rose. Then, after a hasty breakfast, he went to gather Beauty's rose, and mounted his horse, which carried him off so swiftly that in an instant he had lost sight of the palace, and he was still wrapped in gloomy thoughts when it stopped before the door of the cottage.

His sons and daughters, who had been very uneasy at his long absence, rushed to meet him, eager to know the result of his journey, which, seeing him mounted upon a splendid horse and wrapped in a rich mantle, they supposed to be favorable. He hid the truth from them at first, only saying sadly to Beauty as he gave her the rose:

"Here is what you asked me to bring you; you little know what it has cost."

But this excited their curiosity so greatly that presently he told them his adventures from beginning to end, and then they were all very unhappy. The girls lamented loudly over their lost hopes, and the sons declared that their father should not return to this terrible castle, and began to make plans for killing the Beast if it should come to fetch him. But he reminded them that he had promised to go back.

Then the girls were very angry with Beauty, and said it was all her fault, and that if she had asked for something sensible this would never have happened, and complained bitterly that they should have to suffer for her folly.

Poor Beauty, much distressed, said to them:

"I have, indeed, caused this misfortune, but I assure you I did it innocently. Who could have guessed that to ask for a rose in the middle of summer would cause so much misery? But as I did the mischief it is only just that I should suffer for it. I will therefore go back with my father to keep his promise."

At first nobody would hear of this arrangement, and her father and brothers, who loved her dearly, declared that nothing should make them let her go; but Beauty was firm. As the time drew near she divided all her little possessions between her sisters, and said good-by to everything she loved, and when the fatal day came she encouraged and cheered her father as they mounted together the horse which had brought him back. It seemed to fly rather than gallop, but so smoothly that Beauty was not frightened; indeed, she would have enjoyed the journey if she had not feared what might happen to her at the end of it. Her father still tried to persuade her to go back, but in vain. While they were talking the night fell, and then, to their great surprise, wonderful colored lights began to shine in all directions, and splendid fireworks blazed out before them; all the forest was illuminated by them, and even felt pleasantly warm, though it had been bitterly cold before. This lasted until they reached the avenue of orange trees, where were statues holding flaming torches, and when they got nearer to the palace they saw that it was illuminated from the roof to the ground, and music sounded softly from the courtyard.

"The Beast must be very hungry," said Beauty, trying to laugh, "if he makes all this rejoicing over the arrival of his prey." But, in spite of her anxiety, she could not help admiring all the wonderful things she saw.

The horse stopped at the foot of the flight of steps leading to the terrace, and when they had dismounted her father led her to the little room he had been in before, where they found a splendid fire burning, and the table daintily spread with a delicious supper.

The merchant knew that this was meant for them, and Beauty, who was rather less frightened now that she had passed through so many rooms and seen nothing of the Beast, was quite willing to begin, for her long ride had made her very hungry. But they had hardly finished their meal when the noise of the Beast's footsteps was heard approaching, and Beauty clung to her father in terror, which became all the greater when she saw how frightened he was. But when the Beast really appeared, though she trembled at the sight of him, she made a great effort to hide her terror, and saluted him respectfully.

This evidently pleased the Beast. After looking at her he said, in a tone that might have struck terror into the boldest heart, though he did not seem to be angry:

"Good-evening, old man. Good-evening, Beauty."

The merchant was too terrified to reply, but Beauty answered sweetly: "Good-evening, Beast."

"Have you come willingly?" asked the Beast. "Will you be content to stay here when your father goes away?"

Beauty answered bravely that she was quite prepared to stay.

"I am pleased with you," said the Beast. "As you have come of your own accord, you may stay. As for you, old man," he added, turning to the merchant, "at sunrise tomorrow you will take your departure. When the bell rings get up quickly and eat your breakfast, and you will find the same horse waiting to take you home; but remember that you must never expect to see my palace again."

Then turning to Beauty, he said:

"Take your father into the next room, and help him to choose everything you think your brothers and sisters would like to have. You will find two traveling-trunks there; fill them as full as you can. It is only just that you should send them something very precious as a remembrance of yourself."

Then he went away, after saying, "Good-by, Beauty; good-by, old man"; and though Beauty was beginning to think with great dismay of her father's departure, she was afraid to disobey the Beast's orders; and they went into the next room, which had shelves and cupboards all round it. They were greatly surprised at the riches it contained. There were splendid dresses fit for a queen, with all the ornaments that were to be worn with them; and when Beauty opened the cupboards she was quite dazzled by the gorgeous jewels that lay in heaps upon every shelf. After choosing a vast quantity, which she divided between her sisters -- for she had made a heap of the wonderful dresses for each of them -- she opened the last chest, which was full of gold.

"I think, father," she said, "that, as the gold will be more useful to you, we had better take out the other things again, and fill the trunks with it." So they did this; but the more they put in the more room there seemed to be, and at last they put back all the jewels and dresses they had taken out, and Beauty even added as many more of the jewels as she could carry at once; and then the trunks were not too full, but they were so heavy that an elephant could not have carried them!

"The Beast was mocking us," cried the merchant; "he must have pretended to give us all these things, knowing that I could not carry them away."

"Let us wait and see," answered Beauty. "I cannot believe that he meant to deceive us. All we can do is to fasten them up and leave them ready."

So they did this and returned to the little room, where, to their astonishment, they found breakfast ready. The merchant ate his with a good appetite, as the Beast's generosity made him believe that he might perhaps venture to come back soon and see Beauty. But she felt sure that her father was leaving her for ever, so she was very sad when the bell rang sharply for the second time, and warned them that the time had come for them to part. They went down into the courtyard, where two horses were waiting, one loaded with the two trunks, the other for him to ride. They were pawing the ground in their impatience to start, and the merchant was forced to bid Beauty a hasty farewell; and as soon as he was mounted he went off at such a pace that she lost sight of him in an instant.

Then Beauty began to cry, and wandered sadly back to her own room. But she soon found that she was very sleepy, and as she had nothing better to do she lay down and instantly fell asleep. And then she dreamed that she was walking by a brook bordered with trees, and lamenting her sad fate, when a young prince, handsomer than anyone she had ever seen, and with a voice that went straight to her heart, came and said to her, "Ah, Beauty! you are not so unfortunate as you suppose. Here you will be rewarded for all you have suffered elsewhere. Your every wish shall be gratified. Only try to find me out, no matter how I may be disguised, as I love you dearly, and in making me happy you will find your own happiness. Be as true-hearted as you are beautiful, and we shall have nothing left to wish for."

"What can I do, Prince, to make you happy?" said Beauty.

"Only be grateful," he answered, "and do not trust too much to your eyes. And above all, do not desert me until you have saved me from my cruel misery."

After this she thought she found herself in a room with a stately and beautiful lady, who said to her:

"Dear Beauty, try not to regret all you have left behind you, for you are destined to a better fate. Only do not let yourself be deceived by appearances."

Beauty found her dreams so interesting that she was in no hurry to awake, but presently the clock roused her by calling her name softly twelve times, and then she got up and found her dressing-table set out with everything she could possibly want; and when her toilet was finished she found dinner was waiting in the room next to hers. But dinner does not take very long when you are all by yourself, and very soon she sat down cosily in the corner of a sofa, and began to think about the charming Prince she had seen in her dream.

"He said I could make him happy," said Beauty to herself.

"It seems, then, that this horrible Beast keeps him a prisoner. How can I set him free? I wonder why they both told me not to trust to appearances? I don't understand it. But, after all, it was only a dream, so why should I trouble myself about it? I had better go and find something to do to amuse myself."

So she got up and began to explore some of the many rooms of the palace.

The first she entered was lined with mirrors, and Beauty saw herself reflected on every side, and thought she had never seen such a charming room. Then a bracelet which was hanging from a chandelier caught her eye, and on taking it down she was greatly surprised to find that it held a portrait of her unknown admirer, just she had seen him in her dream. With great delight she slipped the bracelet on her arm, and went on into a gallery of pictures, where she soon found a portrait of the same handsome Prince, as large as life, and so well painted that as she studied it he seemed to smile kindly at her. Tearing herself away from the portrait at last, she passed through into a room which contained every musical instrument under the sun, and here she amused herself for a long while in trying some of them, and singing until she was tired. The next room was a library, and she saw everything she had ever wanted to read, as well as everything she had read, and it seemed to her that a whole lifetime would not be enough to even read the names of the books, there were so many. By this time it was growing dusk, and wax candles in diamond and ruby candlesticks were beginning to light themselves in every room.

Beauty found her supper served just at the time she preferred to have it, but she did not see anyone or hear a sound, and, though her father had warned her that she would be alone, she began to find it rather dull.

But presently she heard the Beast coming, and wondered tremblingly if he meant to eat her up now.

However, as he did not seem at all ferocious, and only said gruffly:

"Good-evening, Beauty," she answered cheerfully and managed to conceal her terror. Then the Beast asked her how she had been amusing herself, and she told him all the rooms she had seen.

Then he asked if she thought she could be happy in his palace; and Beauty answered that everything was so beautiful that she would be very hard to please if she could not be happy. And after about an hour's talk Beauty began to think that the Beast was not nearly so terrible as she had supposed at first. Then he got up to leave her, and said in his gruff voice:

"Do you love me, Beauty? Will you marry me?"

"Oh! what shall I say?" cried Beauty, for she was afraid to make the Beast angry by refusing.

"Say 'yes' or 'no' without fear," he replied.

"Oh! no, Beast," said Beauty hastily.

"Since you will not, good-night, Beauty," he said.

And she answered, "Good-night, Beast," very glad to find that her refusal had not provoked him. And after he was gone she was very soon in bed and asleep, and dreaming of her unknown Prince. She thought he came and said to her:

"Ah, Beauty! why are you so unkind to me? I fear I am fated to be unhappy for many a long day still."

And then her dreams changed, but the charming Prince figured in them all; and when morning came her first thought was to look at the portrait, and see if it was really like him, and she found that it certainly was.

This morning she decided to amuse herself in the garden, for the sun shone, and all the fountains were playing; but she was astonished to find that every place was familiar to her, and presently she came to the brook where the myrtle trees were growing where she had first met the Prince in her dream, and that made her think more than ever that he must be kept a prisoner by the Beast. When she was tired she went back to the palace, and found a new room full of materials for every kind of work -- ribbons to make into bows, and silks to work into flowers. Then there was an aviary full of rare birds, which were so tame that they flew to Beauty as soon as they saw her, and perched upon her shoulders and her head.

"Pretty little creatures," she said, "how I wish that your cage was nearer to my room, that I might often hear you sing!"

So saying she opened a door, and found, to her delight, that it led into her own room, though she had thought it was quite the other side of the palace.

There were more birds in a room farther on, parrots and cockatoos that could talk, and they greeted Beauty by name; indeed, she found them so entertaining that she took one or two back to her room, and they talked to her while she was at supper; after which the Beast paid her his usual visit, and asked her the same questions as before, and then with a gruff "good-night" he took his departure, and Beauty went to bed to dream of her mysterious Prince.

The days passed swiftly in different amusements, and after a while Beauty found out another strange thing in the palace, which often pleased her when she was tired of being alone. There was one room which she had not noticed particularly; it was empty, except that under each of the windows stood a very comfortable chair; and the first time she had looked out of the window it had seemed to her that a black curtain prevented her from seeing anything outside. But the second time she went into the room, happening to be tired, she sat down in one of the chairs, when instantly the curtain was rolled aside, and a most amusing pantomime was acted before her; there were dances, and colored lights, and music, and pretty dresses, and it was all so gay that Beauty was in ecstacies. After that she tried the other seven windows in turn, and there was some new and surprising entertainment to be seen from each of them, so that Beauty never could feel lonely any more. Every evening after supper the Beast came to see her, and always before saying good-night asked her in his terrible voice:

"Beauty, will you marry me?"

And it seemed to Beauty, now she understood him better, that when she said, "No, Beast," he went away quite sad. But her happy dreams of the handsome young Prince soon made her forget the poor Beast, and the only thing that at all disturbed her was to be constantly told to distrust appearances, to let her heart guide her, and not her eyes, and many other equally perplexing things, which, consider as she would, she could not understand.

So everything went on for a long time, until at last, happy as she was, Beauty began to long for the sight of her father and her brothers and sisters; and one night, seeing her look very sad, the Beast asked her what was the matter. Beauty had quite ceased to be afraid of him. Now she knew that he was really gentle in spite of his ferocious looks and his dreadful voice. So she answered that she was longing to see her home once more. Upon hearing this the Beast seemed sadly distressed, and cried miserably.

"Ah! Beauty, have you the heart to desert an unhappy Beast like this? What more do you want to make you happy? Is it because you hate me that you want to escape?"

"No, dear Beast," answered Beauty softly, "I do not hate you, and I should be very sorry never to see you any more, but I long to see my father again. Only let me go for two months, and I promise to come back to you and stay for the rest of my life."

The Beast, who had been sighing dolefully while she spoke, now replied:

"I cannot refuse you anything you ask, even though it should cost me my life. Take the four boxes you will find in the room next to your own, and fill them with everything you wish to take with you. But remember your promise and come back when the two months are over, or you may have cause to repent it, for if you do not come in good time you will find your faithful Beast dead. You will not need any chariot to bring you back. Only say good-by to all your brothers and sisters the night before you come away, and when you have gone to bed turn this ring round upon your finger and say firmly: 'I wish to go back to my palace and see my Beast again.' Good-night, Beauty. Fear nothing, sleep peacefully, and before long you shall see your father once more."

As soon as Beauty was alone she hastened to fill the boxes with all the rare and precious things she saw about her, and only when she was tired of heaping things into them did they seem to be full.

Then she went to bed, but could hardly sleep for joy. And when at last she did begin to dream of her beloved Prince she was grieved to see him stretched upon a grassy bank, sad and weary, and hardly like himself.

"What is the matter?" she cried.

He looked at her reproachfully, and said:

"How can you ask me, cruel one? Are you not leaving me to my death perhaps?"

"Ah! don't be so sorrowful," cried Beauty; "I am only going to assure my father that I am safe and happy. I have promised the Beast faithfully that I will come back, and he would die of grief if I did not keep my word!"

"What would that matter to you?" said the Prince "Surely you would not care?"

"Indeed, I should be ungrateful if I did not care for such a kind Beast," cried Beauty indignantly. "I would die to save him from pain. I assure you it is not his fault that he is so ugly."

Just then a strange sound woke her -- someone was speaking not very far away; and opening her eyes she found herself in a room she had never seen before, which was certainly not nearly so splendid as those she was used to in the Beast's palace. Where could she be? She got up and dressed hastily, and then saw that the boxes she had packed the night before were all in the room.

While she was wondering by what magic the Beast had transported them and herself to this strange place she suddenly heard her father's voice, and rushed out and greeted him joyfully. Her brothers and sisters were all astonished at her appearance, as they had never expected to see her again, and there was no end to the questions they asked her. She had also much to hear about what had happened to them while she was away, and of her father's journey home. But when they heard that she had only come to be with them for a short time, and then must go back to the Beast's palace for ever, they lamented loudly. Then Beauty asked her father what he thought could be the meaning of her strange dreams, and why the Prince constantly begged her not to trust to appearances. After much consideration, he answered: "You tell me yourself that the Beast, frightful as he is, loves you dearly, and deserves your love and gratitude for his gentleness and kindness; I think the Prince must mean you to understand that you ought to reward him by doing as he wishes you to, in spite of his ugliness."

Beauty could not help seeing that this seemed very probable; still, when she thought of her dear Prince who was so handsome, she did not feel at all inclined to marry the Beast. At any rate, for two months she need not decide, but could enjoy herself with her sisters. But though they were rich now, and lived in town again, and had plenty of acquaintances, Beauty found that nothing amused her very much; and she often thought of the palace, where she was so happy, especially as at home she never once dreamed of her dear Prince, and she felt quite sad without him.

Then her sisters seemed to have got quite used to being without her, and even found her rather in the way, so she would not have been sorry when the two months were over but for her father and brothers, who begged her to stay, and seemed so grieved at the thought of her departure that she had not the courage to say good-by to them. Every day when she got up she meant to say it at night, and when night came she put it off again, until at last she had a dismal dream which helped her to make up her mind. She thought she was wandering in a lonely path in the palace gardens, when she heard groans which seemed to come from some bushes hiding the entrance of a cave, and running quickly to see what could be the matter, she found the Beast stretched out upon his side, apparently dying. He reproached her faintly with being the cause of his distress, and at the same moment a stately lady appeared, and said very gravely:

"Ah! Beauty, you are only just in time to save his life. See what happens when people do not keep their promises! If you had delayed one day more, you would have found him dead."

Beauty was so terrified by this dream that the next morning she announced her intention of going back at once, and that very night she said good-by to her father and all her brothers and sisters, and as soon as she was in bed she turned her ring round upon her finger, and said firmly, "I wish to go back to my palace and see my Beast again," as she had been told to do.

Then she fell asleep instantly, and only woke up to hear the clock saying "Beauty, Beauty" twelve times in its musical voice, which told her at once that she was really in the palace once more. Everything was just as before, and her birds were so glad to see her! But Beauty thought she had never known such a long day, for she was so anxious to see the Beast again that she felt as if suppertime would never come.

But when it did come and no Beast appeared she was really frightened; so, after listening and waiting for a long time, she ran down into the garden to search for him. Up and down the paths and avenues ran poor Beauty, calling him in vain, for no one answered, and not a trace of him could she find; until at last, quite tired, she stopped for a minute's rest, and saw that she was standing opposite the shady path she had seen in her dream. She rushed down it, and, sure enough, there was the cave, and in it lay the Beast -- asleep, as Beauty thought. Quite glad to have found him, she ran up and stroked his head, but, to her horror, he did not move or open his eyes.

"Oh! he is dead; and it is all my fault," said Beauty, crying bitterly.

But then, looking at him again, she fancied he still breathed, and, hastily fetching some water from the nearest fountain, she sprinkled it over his face, and, to her great delight, he began to revive.

"Oh! Beast, how you frightened me!" she cried. "I never knew how much I loved you until just now, when I feared I was too late to save your life."

"Can you really love such an ugly creature as I am?" said the Beast faintly. "Ah! Beauty, you only came just in time. I was dying because I thought you had forgotten your promise. But go back now and rest, I shall see you again by and by."

Beauty, who had half expected that he would be angry with her, was reassured by his gentle voice, and went back to the palace, where supper was awaiting her; and afterward the Beast came in as usual, and talked about the time she had spent with her father, asking if she had enjoyed herself, and if they had all been very glad to see her.

Beauty answered politely, and quite enjoyed telling him all that had happened to her. And when at last the time came for him to go, and he asked, as he had so often asked before, "Beauty, will you marry me?"

She answered softly, "Yes, dear Beast."

As she spoke a blaze of light sprang up before the windows of the palace; fireworks crackled and guns banged, and across the avenue of orange trees, in letters all made of fire-flies, was written: "Long live the Prince and his Bride."

Turning to ask the Beast what it could all mean, Beauty found that he had disappeared, and in his place stood her long-loved Prince! At the same moment the wheels of a chariot were heard upon the terrace, and two ladies entered the room.

One of them Beauty recognized as the stately lady she had seen in her dreams; the other was also so grand and queenly that Beauty hardly knew which to greet first.

But the one she already knew said to her companion:

"Well, Queen, this is Beauty, who has had the courage to rescue your son from the terrible enchantment. They love one another, and only your consent to their marriage is wanting to make them perfectly happy."

"I consent with all my heart," cried the Queen. "How can I ever thank you enough, charming girl, for having restored my dear son to his natural form?"

And then she tenderly embraced Beauty and the Prince, who had meanwhile been greeting the Fairy and receiving her congratulations.

"Now," said the Fairy to Beauty, "I suppose you would like me to send for all your brothers and sisters to dance at your wedding?"

And so she did, and the marriage was celebrated the very next day with the utmost splendor, and Beauty and the Prince lived happily ever after.

THE ENCHANTED FROG

BY
CARL AND THEODOR COLSHORN

GERMANY, 1854

Once upon a time there was a merchant who had three daughters, but his wife was with God. Once he planned a journey across the ocean to a foreign land in order to bring back gold and other valuable things. He consoled his weeping children, saying, "I will bring back something beautiful for you. What do you want?"

The oldest asked for a silk dress, "and it must be made of three kinds of silk."

The second desired a feathered hat, "and it must have three kinds of feathers."

The youngest finally said, "Bring me a rose, dear father, and it must be fresh and have three colors."

The merchant promised to do this, kissed his daughters, and departed.

After arriving in the foreign land, he ordered the dress of three kinds of silk for his oldest daughter and the hat with three kinds of feathers for the second one. Both were soon finished, and of seldom splendor. Then he sent messengers throughout the entire country to seek a three-colored rose for his youngest and dearest daughter, but they all returned empty handed, even though the merchant had promised a high price, and even though there were more roses there than there are daisies here.

Sadly he set off for home and was downhearted the entire voyage. This side of the ocean he came to a large garden in which there was nothing but roses and roses. He went inside and looked, and behold, on a slender bush in the middle of the garden there was a three-colored rose. Filled with joy, he plucked it, and was about to leave, when he was magically frozen in place.

A voice behind him cried out, "What do you want in my garden?" He looked up. A large frog was sitting there on the bank of a clear pond staring at him with its goggle-eyes. It said, "You have broken my dear rose. This will cost you your life unless you give me your youngest daughter to wife."

The merchant was terrified. He begged and he pleaded, but all to no avail, and in the end he had to agree to marry his dearest daughter to the ugly frog. He could now move his feet, and he freely walked out of the garden. The frog called out after him, "In seven days I shall come for my wife!"

With great sorrow the merchant gave his youngest daughter the fresh rose and told her what had happened. When the terrible day arrived, she crept under her bed, for she did not at all want to go. At the hour of noon a stately carriage drove up. The frog sent his servants into the house, and they immediately went to the bedroom and dragged the screaming maiden from beneath her bed, then carried her to the carriage. The horses leaped forward, and a short time later they were in the blossoming rose garden. In the middle of the garden, immediately behind the clear pond, there stood a small house. They took the bride into the house and laid her on a soft bed. The frog, however, sprang into the water.

Darkness fell, and after the maiden had awakened from her unconsciousness, she heard the frog outside singing wonderfully sweet melodies. As midnight approached, he sang ever more sweetly, and came closer and closer to her. At midnight the bedroom door opened, and the frog jumped onto her bed. However, he had touched her with his sweet songs, and she took him into bed with her and warmly covered him up.

The next morning when she opened her eyes, behold, the ugly frog was now the handsomest prince in the world. He thanked her with all his heart, saying, "You have redeemed me and are now my wife!" And they lived long and happily together.

THE FAIRY SERPENT (A CHINESE TALE)

BY
A.M. FIELDE

FROM *CHINESE FAIRY STORIES* (1893)

ONCE there was a man who had three daughters, of whom he was devotedly fond. They were skillful in embroidery, and every day on his way home from work he gathered some flowers for them to use as patterns. One day when he found no flowers along his route homeward he went into the woods to look for wild blossoms, and he unwittingly invaded the domain of a fairy serpent that coiled around him, held him tightly, and railed at him for having entered his garden. The man excused himself, saying that he came merely to get a few flowers for his daughters, who would be sorely disappointed were he to go home without his usual gift to them. The snake asked him the number, the names, and the ages of his daughters and then refused to let him go unless he promised one of them in marriage to him. The poor man tried every argument he could think of to induce the snake to release him upon easier terms, but the reptile would accept no other ransom. At last the father, dreading greater evil for his daughters should they be deprived of his protection, gave the required promise and went home. He could eat no supper, however, for he knew the power of fairies to afflict those who offend them, and he was full of anxiety concerning the misfortunes that would overwhelm his whole family should the contract be disregarded.

Some days passed; his daughters carefully prepared his meals and affectionately besought him to eat, but he would not come to the table. He was always plunged in sorrowful meditation. They conferred among themselves as to the cause of his uncommon behavior, and, having decided that one of them must have displeased him, they agreed to try to find out which one it might be by going separately to urge him to eat. The eldest went, expressed her distress at his loss of appetite, and urged him to partake of food. He replied that he would do so if she would for his sake marry the snake to whom he had promised a wife. She bluntly refused to carry out her father's contract and left him in deeper trouble than before.

The second daughter then went to beg him to take food, received the same reply, and likewise declined to fulfill the engagement he had made. The youngest daughter then went and entreated him to eat, heard his story, and at once declared that if he would care for his own health properly, she would become the bride of the serpent. The father therefore took his meals again, the days sped without bringing calamity, and the welfare of the family for a time seemed secure.

But one morning as the girls were sitting at their embroidery, a wasp flew into the room and sang:

Buzz! I buzz and come the faster;
Who will wed the snake, my master?

143

Whenever the wasp alighted the girls prodded him with their needles and followed him up so closely that he had to flee for his life. The next morning two wasps came, singing the same refrain; the third morning three wasps came; and the number of wasps increased day by day, until the girls could no longer put them to rout, nor endure their stings.

Then the youngest said that in order to relieve the family of the buzzing plague, she would go to her uncanny bridegroom. The wasps accompanied her on the road and guided her into the woods where the fairy serpent awaited her in a palace that he had built for her reception. There were spacious rooms with carved furniture inlaid with precious stones, chests full of silken fabrics, caskets of jade, and jewels of gold. The snake had beautiful eyes and a musical voice, but his skin was warty and the girl shuddered at the thought of daily seeing him about.

After the wedding supper, at which the two sat alone, the girl told her spouse that she appreciated the excellence of all that he had provided for her and that she should perform all her domestic duties exactly. For many days she kept the house neat, cooked the food, and made all things pleasant for her repulsive bridegroom. He doted upon her and pined whenever she was out of his sight. So heedful was he of her wishes and her welfare that she grew to like his companionship and to feel a great lonesomeness when ever he was absent.

Having no help in her household work, she was, one day, on finding the well dried up, obliged to go into the forest in search of water, which she finally discovered and toilsomely brought back from a distant spring. On returning she found the snake dying of thirst, and in her eagerness to save his life she grasped and plunged him into the water, from which he rose transformed, a strong and handsome man. He had been the subject of wicked enchantment, from which her dutiful quest and gracious pity set him free. Thereafter she often with her admirable husband visited her old home and carried gifts to those who were less happy than she.

THE MAIDEN AND THE BEAST

BY
CONSIGLIERI PEDROSO

TRANSLATED FROM *PORTUGUESE FOLK-TALES* BY MISS HENRIETTA
MONTEIRO, 1882

THERE was once a man who had three daughters; he loved them all, but there was one he loved more than the others. As he was going to the fair one day he inquired what they would like him to bring them. One said she would like to have a hat and some boots, the other one asked for a dress and a shawl, but the one he loved most did not ask for anything. The man, in surprise, said, "Oh! my child, do you not want anything?" "No, I want nothing; I only wish that my dear father may enjoy health." "You must ask for something, it matters not what it is, I shall bring it to you," replied the father. But, in order that the father should not continue to importune her, she said, "I wish my father to bring me a slice of roach off a green meadow." The good man set off to the fair, bought all the things that his daughters had asked him, and searched every where for the "slice of roach off a green meadow," but could not find it, for it was something that was not to be had. He there fore came home in great distress of mind, because she was the daughter he loved most and wished most to please. As he was walking along he happened to see a light shining on the road, and, as it was already night, he walked on and on until he reached the light. The light came from a hut in which lived a shepherd; the man went in and inquired of him, "Can you tell me what palace is that yonder, and do you think they would give me shelter there?" The shepherd replied, in great astonishment, "Oh! sir, but in that palace no one resides, some thing is seen there which terrifies people from living in it." "What does it matter, it will not eat me up; and, as there is no one living in it, I shall go and sleep there to-night." He went up to the building, found it all lit up very splendidly, and, on entering into the palace, he found a table ready laid. As he approached the table, he heard a voice which said, "Eat and lie down on the bed which you see there, and in the morning rise and take with you what you will find on that table, which is what your daughter asked you for; but at the end of three days you must bring her here." The man was very pleased to be able to take home what his daughter had asked him for, but at the same time was distressed at what the voice had said it required him to do. He threw himself on the bed, and on the following morning he arose, went straight to the table, and found upon it the slice of roach off a green meadow. He took it up and went home; the moment he arrived his daughters surrounded him: "Father, what have you brought us? let us see what it is;" the father gave them what he had brought them. The third daughter, the one he loved most, did not ask him for anything, but simply if he was The father answered her, "My daughter, I come back both happy and sad! Here you have what you asked me for." "Oh! father, I asked you for this because it was a thing which did not exist; but why do you come back sad?" "Because I must take you at the end of three days to the place where this was given to me." He recounted all that had occurred to him in the place, and what the voice had told him to do. When the daughter heard all she replied, "Do not distress yourself, father, for I shall go, and whatever God wills, will happen." And so it happened that at the end of three days the father took her to the enchanted palace. It was all illuminated and in a blaze of light; the table was laid, and two beds had been prepared. As they entered they heard a voice saying, "Eat and remain with your daughter three days that she may not feel frightened." The man remained the three days in the palace, and at the end went away leaving the daughter alone! The voice spoke to her every day but no form was seen. At the end of a few days the girl heard a bird singing in the garden. The voice said to her, "Do you hear that bird sing?" "Yes, I hear him," replied the girl, "Does it bring any news?" "It is your eldest sister who is going to be married, would you like to be present?" asked the voice. The girl in great delight said, "Yes, I should like to go very much,-will you let me go?" "I will allow you," rejoined the voice, "but you will not return!" "Yes, I shall come back," said the girl. The voice gave her then a ring so that she should not forget her promise, saying, "Now mind that at the end of three days a white horse will go for you; it will give three knocks,-the first is for you to dress, and get ready, -the second for you to take leave of your family,-and the third for you to mount it. If at the third knock you are not on the horse, it will go away and leave you there." The girl went home. A great feast had been prepared and the sister was married. At the end of three days the white horse came to give the three knocks.

At the first the girl commenced to get ready, at the second knock she took leave of her family, and at the third she mounted on the horse. The voice had given the girl a box with money to take to her father and her sisters; on that account they did not wish her to return to the enchanted palace, because she was now very rich. But the girl remembered what she had promised, and the moment she found herself on the horse she darted off. After a certain time the bird returned and began to sing very contentedly in the garden. The voice said to her, "Do you hear the bird sing?" "Yes I hear it," replied the girl, "Does it bring any news?" "It is that another of your sisters is about to marry [1]; and do you wish to go?" "Yes, I wish to go; and would you allow me to go?" "I will let you go," replied the voice; "but you will not return!" "Yes, I shall return," said the girl. The voice then said, "Remember that if at the end of three days you do not come back you shall remain there, and you will be the most hapless girl there is in the world!" The girl started off. A great feast was given and the sister was married. At the end of three days the white horse came-it gave the first knock, and the girl dressed herself to go; it gave the second knock, and the girl took leave of her friends; it gave the third knock, and the girl mounted the horse and returned to the palace. After some time the bird again sang in the garden, but in melancholy tones,--very dull tones indeed. The voice said to her, "Do you hear the bird sing?" "Yes, I hear it," replied the girl: "is there any news?" "Yes, there are; it is that your father is dying, and does not wish to die without taking leave of you." "And will you allow me to go and see him?" asked the girl, indeed much distressed. "Yes, I will let you go; but I know you will not return this time." "Oh yes, I shall come back," replied the girl. The voice then said to her, "No, you will not return--you will not! for your sisters will not let you come; you and they will be the most unhappy girls in this world if you do not come back at the end of three days." The .girl went home, the father was very ill, yet he could not die until he saw her, and he had hardly taken leave of his daughter when he died. The sisters gave the girl a sleeping draught as she had requested them, and left her to sleep. The girl had begged them most particularly to awaken her before the white horse should come. What did the sisters do? They did not awaken her, and they took off the ring she wore. At the end of three days the horse came--it gave the first knock; it knocked the second time; it knocked the third time, and went away and the girl remained at home. As the sisters had taken away the ring, she forgot everything of the past and lived very happily with her sisters. A few days after this fortune began to leave her and her sisters, until one day the two said to her, "Sister, do you remember the white horse?" The girl then recollected everything and began to cry, saying, "Oh I what misfortune is mine, oh! you have made me very wretched what has become of my ring?" The sisters gave her the ring, and the girl took her departure in great affliction. She reached the enchanted palace and found everything about it looking very dull, very dark, and the palace shut up. She went straight into the garden and she there found a huge beast lying on the ground. The beast had barely seen her when he cried out, "Go away, you tyrant, for you have broken my spell! Now you will be the most wretched girl in the world, you and your sisters." As the beast finished saying this it died. The girl returned to her sisters in great distress, weeping very bitterly, and she remained in the house without eating or drinking, and after a few days died also. The sisters became poorer by degrees for having been the cause of all this trouble.

1: There are different variations of this story, viz.: "It is that your sister has given birth to a girl; I would like you to be her godmother. And do you wish to go?"

BEAUTY AND THE BEAST

BY
CHARLES LAMB

FROM *THE WORKS OF CHARLES AND MARY LAMB*, 1903. CHARLES
LAMB WAS A BRITISH POET WHO LIVED FROM 1775-1834. HE WROTE
BEAUTY AND THE BEAST IN 1811.

A merchant, who by generous pains
Prospered in honourable gains,
Could boast, his wealth and fame to share,
Three manly SONS, three DAUGHTERS fair;
With these he felt supremely blest.--
His latest-born surpass'd the rest:
She was so gentle, good and kind,
So fair in feature, form and mind,
So constant too in filial duty,
The neighbours call'd her LITTLE BEAUTY!
And when fair childhood's days were run,
That title still she wore and won;
Lovelier as older still she grew,
Improv'd in grace and goodness too.--
Her elder Sisters, gay and vain,
View'd her with envy and disdain,
Toss'd up their heads with haughty air;
Dress, Fashion, Pleasure, all their care.

'Twas thus, improving and improv'd;
Loving, and worthy to be lov'd,
Sprightly, yet grave, each circling day
Saw BEAUTY innocently gay.
Thus smooth the May-like moments past;
Blest times! but soon by clouds o'ercast!

Sudden as winds that madd'ning sweep
The foaming surface of the deep,
Vast treasures, trusted to the wave,
Were buried in the billowy grave!
Our Merchant, late of boundless store,
Saw Famine hasting to his door.

With willing hand and ready grace,
Mild BEAUTY takes the Servant's place;
Rose with the sun to household cares,
And morn's repast with zeal prepares,
The wholesome meal, the cheerful fire:
What cannot filial love inspire?
And when the task of day was done,
Suspended till the rising sun,
Music and song the hours employ'd,
As more deserv'd, the more enjoy'd;
Till Industry, with Pastime join'd,
Refresh'd the body and the mind;
And when the group retir'd to rest,
Father and Brothers BEAUTY blest.

Not so the Sisters; as before
'Twas rich and idle, now 'twas poor.
In shabby finery array'd,
They still affected a parade:
While both insulted gentle BEAUTY,
Unwearied in the housewife's duty;
They mock'd her robe of modest brown,
And view'd her with a taunting frown;
Yet scarce could hold their rage to see
The blithe effects of Industry.

In this retreat a year had past,
When happier tidings came at last,
And in the Merchant's smile appear'd
Prospects that all the Cotters cheer'd:
A letter came; its purport good:
Part of his ventures brav'd the flood:
"With speed," said he, "I must to town,
"And what, my girls, must I bring down?"
The envious Sisters, all confusion,
Commissions gave in wild profusion;
Caps, hats, and bonnets, bracelets, broaches,
To cram the pockets of the coaches,
With laces, linens, to complete
The order, and to fill the seat.

Such wants and wishes now appear'd,
To make them larger BEAUTY fear'd;
Yet lest her silence might produce
From jealous Sisters more abuse,
Considerately good, she chose,
The emblem of herself, --a ROSE.

The good Man on his journey went,
His thoughts on generous BEAUTY bent.
"If Heav'n," he said, and breath'd a prayer,
"If Heav'n that tender child should spare,
"Whate'er my lot, I must be bless'd,
"I must be rich:"--he wept the rest.
Timely such feeling!--Fortune still,
Unkind and niggard, crost his will;
Of all his hopes, alas, the gains
Were far o'erbalanc'd by the pains;
For after a long tedious round,
He had to measure back his ground.

A short day's travel from his Cot,
New misadventures were his lot;
Dark grew the air, the wind blew high,
And spoke the gathering tempest nigh;
Hail, snow, and night-fog join'd their force,
Bewildering rider and his horse.
Dismay'd, perplext, the road they crost,
And in the dubious maze were lost.

When glimmering through the vapours drear,
A taper shew'd a dwelling near.
And guess our Merchant's glad surprise,
When a rich palace seem'd to rise
As on he mov'd! The knee he bent,
Thankful to Heaven; then nearer went.
But, O! how much his wonder grew,
When nothing living met his view!--
Entering a splendid hall, he found,
With every luxury around,
A blazing fire, a plentous board,
A costly cellaret, well stor'd,
All open'd wide as if to say,
"Stranger, refresh thee on thy way!"

The Merchant to the fire drew near,
Deeming the owner would appear,
And pardon one who, drench'd in rain,
Unask'd, had ventur'd to remain.
The court-yard clock had number'd seven,
When first he came; when eleven
Struck on his ear as mute he sate,
It sounded like the knell of Fate.
And yet so hungry was he grown,

He pick'd a capon to the bone;
And as choice wines before him stood,
He needs must taste if they were good:
So much he felt his spirits cheer'd--
The more he drank, the less he fear'd.

Now bolder grown, he pac'd along,
(Still hoping he might do no wrong),
When, entering at a gilded door,
High-rais'd upon a sumptuous floor,
A sofa shew'd all Persia's pride,
And each magnificence beside:
So down at once the Merchant lay,
Tir'd with the wonders of the day.
But had it been a rushy bed,
Tuck'd in the corner of a shed,
With no less joy had it been press'd:
The good man pray'd, and sank to rest.

Nor woke he till the noon of day;
And as he thus enchanted lay,
"Now for my storm-sopp'd clothes," he cries;
When lo! a suit complete he spies;
"Yes, 'tis all fairy-work, no doubt,
"By gentle Pity brought about!"
Tenfold, when risen, amazement grew;
For bursting on his gazing view,
Instead of snow, he saw fair bowers
In all the pride of summer flowers.
Entering again the hall, behold,
Serv'd up in silver, pearl, and gold,
A breakfast, form'd of all things rare,
As if Queen Mab herself were there.

As now he past, with spirits gay,
A shower of ROSES strew'd the way,
E'en to his hand the branches bent:
"One of those boughs--I go content!
"BEAUTY, dear BEAUTY--thy request
"If I may bear away, I'm blest."
The Merchant pull'd--the branches broke!--
A hideous growling while he spoke,
Assail'd his startled ears; and then
A frightful BEAST, as from a den,
Rushing to view, exclaim'd, "Ingrate!
"All that my castle own'd was thine,
"My food, my fire, my bed, my wine:

"Thou robb'st my Rose-tress in return,
"For this, base Plunderer, thou shalt mourn!"

"My Lord, I swear upon my knees,
"I did not mean to harm your trees;
"But a lov'd Daughter, fair as spring,
"Intreated me a ROSE to bring;
"O didst thou know, my Lord, the Maid!"

"I am no Lord," BEAST angry said,
"And so no flattery!--but know,
"If, on your oath before you go,
"Within three wasted Moons, you here
"Cause that lov'd Daughter to appear,
"And visit BEAST a volunteer
"To suffer for thee, thou mayest live:--
"Speak not!--do this!--and I forgive."
Mute and deprest the Merchant fled,
Unhappy traveller, evil sped!

BEAUTY was first her sire to meet,
Springing impatient from her seat;
Her Brothers next assembled round;
Her straying Sisters soon were found.
While yet the Father fondly press'd
The Child of Duty to his Breast,--
"Accept these Roses, ill starr'd Maid!
"For thee thy Father's life is paid."

The merchant told the tale of BEAST;
And loud lamentings, when he ceas'd,
From both the jealous Sisters broke,
As thus with taunting rage they spoke:
"And so thou kill'st thy Father, Miss,
"Proud, sinful creature, heard'st thou this?
"We only wish'd a few new clothes;
"BEAUTY, forsooth, must have her ROSE!
"Yet, harden'd Wretch, her eyes are dry,
"Tho' for her Pride our Sire must die."

"Die! not for worlds!" exclaim'd the Maid;
"BEAST kindly will take me instead:
"And O, a thousand deaths I'd prove
"To show my father how I love!"

The Brothers cried, "Let us away,
"We'll perish, or the Monster slay."

"Vain hope, my gen'rous Sons, his power
"Can troops of men and horse devour;
"Your offer, BEAUTY, moves my soul;
"But no man can his fate control:
"Mine was the fault; you, Love, are free;
"And mine the punishment shall be."
BEAUTY was firm! the Sire caress'd
Again his Darling to his breast;
With blended love and awe survey'd,
And each good Brother blest the Maid!

Three months elaps'd, her Father's heart
Heav'd high, as she prepar'd to part,
The Sisters try'd a tear to force,
While BEAUTY smil'd as she took horse;
Yet smil'd thro' many a generous tear,
To find the parting moment near!
And just as evening shades came on,
The splendid Palace court they won.
BEAUTY, now lost in wonder all,
Gain'd with her sire the spacious hall;
Where, of the costliest viands made,
Behold, a sumptuous table laid!
The Merchant, sickening at the sight,
Sat down with looks of dire affright,
But nothing touch'd; tho' BEAUTY prest,
And strove to lull his fears to rest.

Just as she spoke, a hideous noise
Announc'd the growling monster's voice.
And now BEAST suddenly stalk'd forth,
While BEAUTY wellnigh sank to earth:
Scarce could she conquer her alarms,
Tho' folded in a father's arms.
Grim BEAST first question'd fierce, if she
Had hither journeyed WILLINGLY?
"Yes," BEAUTY cried--in trembling tone:
"That's kind," said BEAST, and thus went on--
"Good Merchant, at to-morrow's dawn,
"I charge and warn you to BE GONE!
"And further, on life's penalty,
"Dare not again to visit me.
"BEAUTY, farewell!" He now withdrew,
As she return'd the dread adieu.

Each then their separate pillow prest,
And slumber clos'd their eyes in rest.

As zephyr light, from magic sleep,
Soon as the sun began to peep,
Sprang BEAUTY; and now took her way
To where her anguish'd father lay.--
But envious time stole swiftly on;

"Begone, lov'd Father! ah! begone!
"The early dew now gems the thorn,
"The sun-beams gain upon the morn.
"Haste, Father, haste! Heaven guards the good!"
In wonder rapt the Merchant stood;
And while dread fears his thoughts employ,
A child so generous still was joy.
"My father's safe!" she cried, "blest heaven!
"The rest is light, this bounty given."

She now survey'd th' enchanting scene,
Sweet gardens of eternal green;
Mirrors, and chandeliers of glass,
And diamonds bright which those surpass;
All these her admiration gain'd;
But how was her attention chain'd,
When she in GOLDEN LETTERS trac'd,
High o'er an arch of emeralds plac'd,
"BEAUTY'S APARTMENT! Enter blest!
"This, but an earnest of the rest!"

The fair one was rejoic'd to find,
BEAST studied less her eye, than mind.
But, wishing still a nearer view,
Forth from the shelves a book she drew,
In whose first page, in lines of gold,
She might heart-easing words behold:
"Welcome, BEAUTY, banish fear!
"You are Queen, and Mistress here:
"Speak your wishes, speak your will,
"Swift obedience meets them still."

"Alas!" said she, with heartfelt sighs,
The daughter rushing to her eyes,
"There's nothing I so much desire,
"As to behold my tender sire."

BEAUTY had scarce her wish express'd,
When it was granted by the BEAST:
A wond'rous mirror to her eye,
Brought all her cottage family.
Here her good Brothers at their toil,
For still they dress'd the grateful soil;
And there with pity she perceiv'd,
How much for her the Merchant griev'd;
How much her Sisters felt delight
To know her banish'd from their sight,
Altho' with voice and looks of guile,
Their bosoms full of joy the while,
The labour'd hard to force a tear,
And imitate a grief sincere.

At noon's repast, she heard a sound
Breathing unseen sweet music round;
But when the evening board was spread,
The voice of BEAST recall'd her dread:
"May I observe you sup?" he said;

"Ah! tremble not; your will is law;
"One question answer'd, I withdraw--
"Am I not hideous to your eyes?"
"Your temper's sweet," she mild replies.
"Yes, but I'm ugly, have no sense:"--
"That's better far, than vain pretence"--
"Try to be happy, and at ease,"
Sigh'd BEAST,"as I will try to please."--
"Your outward form is scarcely seen
"Since I arriv'd, so kind you've been."

One quarter of the rolling year,
No other living creature near,
BEAUTY with BEAST had past serene,
Save some sad hours that stole between.
That she her Father's life had sav'd,
Upon her heart of hearts was grav'd:
While yet she view'd the BEAST with dread,
This was the balm that conscience shed.
But now a second solace grew,
Whose cause e'en conscience scarcely knew.
Here on a Monster's mercy cast,--
Yet, when her first dire fears were past,
She found that Monster, timid, mild,
Led like the lion by the child.
Custom and kindness banish'd fear;

BEAUTY oft wish'd that BEAST were near.

Nine was the chosen hour that BEAST
Constant attended BEAUTY's feast,
Yet ne'er presum'd to touch the food,
Sat humble, or submissive stood,
Or, audience crav'd, respectful spoke,
Nor aim'd at wit, or ribald joke,
But oftner bent the raptur'd ear
Or ravish'd eye, to see or hear.
And if th' appointed hour past by.
'Twas mark'd by BEAUTY with a sigh.
"Swear not to leave me!" sigh'd the BEAST:
"I swear"--for now her fears were ceas'd,
"And willingly swear,--so now and then
"I might my Father see again--
"One little WEEK--he's now alone."
"Granted!" quoth BEAST: "your will be done!"
"Your RING upon the table lay
"At night,--you're there at peep of day:
"But, oh--remember, or I die!
He gaz'd, and went without reply.

At early morn, she rang to rise;
The Maid beholds with glad surprise,
Summons her Father to her side,
Who, kneeling and embracing, cried,
With rapture and devotion wild,
"O bless'd be Heaven, and blest my Child!"

BEAUTY the Father now address'd,
And strait to see her Sisters press'd.
They both were married, and both prov'd
Neither was happy or belov'd.
And when she told them she was blest
With days of ease, and nights of rest;
To hide the malice of the soul,
Into the garden sly they stole,
And there in floods of tears they vent
Their hate, and feel its punishment.
"If," said the eldest, "you agree
"We'll make that wench more curs'd than we!
"I have a plot, my sister dear:
"More than her WEEK let's keep her here.
"No more with MONSTER shall she sup,
"Who, in his rage, shall eat her up."

And now such art they both employ'd
While BEAUTY wept, yet was o'erjoy'd;
And when the stated hour was come,
"Ah! can you quit so soon your home?"
Eager they question'd--tore their hair--
And look'd the Pictures of Despair.
BEAUTY, tho' blushing at delay,
Promis'd another week to stay.

Meantime, altho' she err'd from love,
Her conscious heart could ill approve--
"Thy vow was giv'n, thy vow was broke!"
Thus Conscience to her bosom spoke.

Thoughts such as these assail'd her breast,
And a sad vision broke her rest!
The palace-garden was the place,
Which her imaginations trace:
There, on the lawn, as if to die,
She saw poor BEAST extended lie,
Reproaching with his latest breath
BEAUTY's ingratitude in death.

Rous'd from her sleep, the contrite Maid
The RING upon her toilette laid,
And Conscience gave a sound repose.
Balmy her rest; and when she rose,
The palace of poor BEAST she found,
Groves, gardens, arbours, blooming round:
The morning shone in summer's pride,
BEAUTY for fairer evening sigh'd--
Sigh'd for the object once so fear'd,
By worth, by kindness now endear'd.
But when had past the wonted hour,
And no wish'd footstep pass'd the door;--
When yet another hour lagg'd on,--
Then to the wide canal she ran:
"For there in vision," said the fair,
"Was stretched the object of my care!"

And there, alas! he now was found
Extended on the flowery ground.
"Ah! fond and faithful BEAST," she cried,
"Hast thou for me perfidious died!
"O! could'st thou hear my fervid prayer,
"'Twould ease the anguish of despair."

157

BEAST open'd now his long clos'd eyes,
And saw the fair with glad surprise.
"In my last moments you are sent;
"You pity, and I die content."
"Thou shalt not die," rejoin'd the Maid;
"O rather live to hate, upbraid--
"But no! my grievous fault forgive!
"I feel I can't without thee live."

BEAUTY had scarce pronounc'd the word,
When magic sounds of sweet accord,
The music of celestial spheres,
As if from seraph harps she hears!
Amaz'd she stood,--new wonders grew;
For BEAST now vanish'd from her view;
And, lo! a PRINCE, with every grace
Of figure, fashion, feature, face,
In whom all charms of Nature meet,
Was kneeling at fair BEAUTY's feet.
"But where is BEAST?" still BEAUTY cried:
"Behold him here," the PRINCE replied.

"Orasmyn, lady, is my name,
"In Persia not unknown to fame;
"Till this re-humanising hour,
"The victim of a Fairy's pow'r;--
"Till a deliverer could be found,
"Who, while the accursed spell still bound,
"Could first endure, tho' with alarm,
"And break at last by love the charm!"

BEAUTY delighted gave her hand,
And bade the PRINCE her fate command;
The PRINCE now led through rooms of state,
Where BEAUTY's family await,
In bridal vestments all array'd,
By some superior power convey'd.

"BEAUTY," pronounc'd a heavenly voice,
"Now take from me your princely choice.
"VIRTUE, to every good beside
"While wit and beauty were denied,
"Fix'd your pure heart; for which, unseen,
"I led your steps, and now a QUEEN,
"Seated on Persia's glittering throne,
"'Tis mine and Virtue's task to crown!

"But as for you, ye Sister's vain,
"Still first and last in Envy's train,
"Before fair BEAUTY's Palace-gate,
"Such Justice has decreed your fate,
"Transform'd to statues you must dwell,
"Curs'd with the single power, to feel--
"Unless by penitance and prayer--
"But this will ask long years of care,
"Of promise and performance too,
"A change of mind from false to true--
"A change I scarce can hope from you."

Instant the Power stretch'd forth her wand,
Her sceptre of supreme command,
When lo! at her resistless call,
Gay crouds came thronging through the hall,
The blissful hour to celebrate
When Persia's Prince resum'd his state:
At once the dome with music rang,
And virgins danc'd, and minstrels sang;
It was the Jubilee of YOUTH,
Led on by Virtue and by Truth;
The pride of Persia fill'd the scene,
To hail ORASMYN and his QUEEN!

THE PRINCE WHO WAS CHANGED INTO A SNAKE

BY

LUCY MARY JANE GARNETT

From *New Folklore Researches: Greek Folk Poesy*, Volume II: Folk-Prose, 1896

Scarlet thread, spun with the wheel,
Wound on twirling, giddy reel,
Like the dancers turn and spin,
And let me my tale begin;
But first, my worthy Company,
I wish you all good e'en!

This is the beginning of the story — good-evening to your Honours!

Once upon a time there was a merchant, and he traded all the way to Pagtdtin, as the saying is. He had twelve ships in which he sailed about, and he had three daughters. When this merchant's wife died, and his daughters were left orphans, year by year he grew poorer and poorer; he lost his ships, and the unfortunate man fell so low that he had hardly bread to eat, and was so needy that he was obliged to sell all his property, and nothing remained to him but his big farm.

Then the poor merchant made up his mind to tell his daughters that they must live on the farm and look after it. Two of his daughters, the eldest and the second one, refused to go; but the youngest, who was good-natured and would not displease him, said, 'Papa mine, I will go and live there!'

So the youngest daughter bestirred herself, and dug and raked like a gardener, and got up early in the morning, and gathered the produce, and her father took it every morning to the market to sell it. (This is a story, so I will be brief.) Thus they continued every morning to gather the produce and sell it until twelve years had passed away.

In the twelfth year there returned three of his ships. Then his daughters, the eldest and the middle one, begged their father to bring them a gown each. The father, pleased with the youngest, asked her what she would like. She answered her father, 'I want nothing, papa, but to see you released from your poverty. '

When her father pressed her to say what she would like, she replied, 'I want nothing, papa, but a rose. They sell them now in sievesful, and I want you to bring me a choice rose.'

Well, at last the merchant mounted his horse, and went and landed his goods. In twelve days, from the time his poverty had come to an end, he had finished; but he had found no rose. Again he mounted his horse and set off to his farm. As he

160

went, God commanded such a rain to fall as had never been known before. What was the poor man to do? He pulled his cape up over his head and crouched down on his horse's saddle; and presently the beast came to a door-way and stood out of the rain. The man raised his cape, saw the doorway, and praised God that he had found a shelter from the downpour. Then he went and found a manger, to which he tied his beast, and afterwards he went in and found a chamber and sat down on the divan, and coffee came, and sweets, and a chibouk, without his seeing anyone. Then the rain stopped, and the merchant arose, and went from chamber to chamber to seek the host, and thank him.

When he could find no one, he was going to fetch his beast to go home, when he saw a rose-bush which had three blossoms on one branch, and he stretched out his hand and plucked them. Immediately there appeared before him a Snake, who said to him, 'Ah! thankless man, after the kindness I have shown thee in saving thee from death! Canst thou not see a rose or two without desiring and plucking them?'

The merchant answered and said, 'I looked through the chambers to find the host, and say a "Thank you" to him, but could not find him.'

'Listen to me,' said the Snake. 'Thou hast three daughters, thou must bring me the youngest. Think not to thyself that I am only a Snake, and shall not come and find thee.'

The merchant asked how long he would wait — what could the poor man say? — and he gave him forty days.

The merchant mounted his horse and went about his business. When at last he got to his house, his daughters gathered around him and got their gowns, but his youngest daughter stood sadly by. Her father said to her, 'Come here, my girl, here are the roses thou didst ask of me,' and he began to weep.

When his daughter saw him weep, she asked, 'What is the matter, papa, that thou weepest?'

Then her father began and told her all about it. Her sisters began to reproach her and to point their fingers at her, 'Wretch, thou must have a rose, thou wantedst no gowns, so that the Snake might come and eat us!'

Then the maiden, who was sensible, went to her father, and asked how many days' grace had been given.

Her father replied, 'He said forty days, my girl.' Then she went to her chamber and took paper and ink, and wrote down the day; but the maiden troubled herself nothing at all about it, though her sisters reproached her night and day. Afterwards she went and opened the paper, and saw that there were but two days left. So she said to her father, 'Go and saddle the horse that we may go where I have been invited.'

'Shall I take thee, my daughter, to thy Charon, where the Snake will eat thee?'

'Arise,' she said, 'and let us go, for the Snake will not eat me if I do his bidding; what ill-will has he against me?'

Then the maiden arose and said 'Farewell' to her sisters, and went away. They came to the house; her father tied up his beast at the manger; they went into the chamber and sat on the divan; their coffee came and their sweets, without anyone being seen. In a very little while the Snake appeared before them, and asked, 'Hast thou done my bidding, and brought her?'

Then the merchant answered and said, 'I have brought her.'

Then the merchant arose and mounted, and went home, and the maiden stayed behind with the Snake.

Her father fell ill with regret and grief, and took to his bed.

It became the Snake's custom, when the girl was eating bread, to lie down in her lap and ask her,

'Wilt thou take me for thy husband?'

The maiden said to him, 'I am afraid of thee!' And she was very sad because her father was long in coming to see her. When she was sitting with the table before her, the table opened, and she saw a mirror, in which all the world was reflected, and she saw her father ill, and began to weep and to tear her hair. Then the Snake, who was in the garden, heard her cries and her breast-beatings, and he rushed to her and asked, 'What ails thee, my Rose?'

'See in the mirror,' she said to the Snake, 'how my father lies nigh unto death!'

Then the Snake said, 'Open the drawer of the table, and thou wilt find a ring. Put it on thy finger, and tell me,' he said, 'how many days thou wilt be absent.'

She replied, 'I will come as soon as my father recovers.'

'I give thee thirty-one days' leave. If thou comest one day later, thou wilt find me dead upon some mound.'

The girl replied, 'Do thyself no harm — when my leave has expired, I will come to thee.'

Then the Snake said, 'Let supper be served, and do thou sup and I will counsel thee.' When the girl had eaten her supper, he said to her, 'Put the ring on thy tongue and thou wilt find thyself on the bed in thy chamber.'

The girl lay down on the mattress, and put the ring on her tongue, and she was in her own chamber. Her servants, in passing, heard her breathing, and went and told her sisters, 'Our mistress is in her chamber.'

The sisters hastened in and found her asleep, and they awoke her, and she got up. Then the maiden praised God when she found that she had come home to her father. When her father saw her, he began to ask her how it had happened, and what had become of the Snake. And she began to tell him what the Snake had said to her when she was eating bread, how he had sat on her knees and said, 'Wilt thou take me for thy husband?' and how she had said, 'I am afraid of thee!'

Then her father answered and said to her, 'My daughter, tell him that thou wilt take him, and we shall see.' Then the maiden resolved that she would say that. But her sisters advised her not to go back, so that he might die. The girl replied, 'How could I leave my Beast to die, who have received such help from him?'

She remained with her father for as many days as she had leave, and then she rose, saluted her sisters and her father, laid down on her bed, put the ring in her mouth, and went back to the Snake. When the Snake saw her, he said, 'Hast thou come, my Rose?'

When the coffee came for her to drink, the Snake lay down in her lap, and when he said, 'Wilt thou take me for thy husband?' the girl replied, 'I will take thee.'

His skin fell off, and he became a Prince, and the earth opened, and the whole world was seen within.

Then the maiden began to ask him what manner of man he was, and how he had become a Snake. Then the Prince told her that he had loved an orphan, and she had laid him under a curse to become a Snake and never cast his skin until he should find a woman who would consent to marry him. Then he wrote a letter to tell his father-in-law and her sisters that she was going to be married. So her father came with her two sisters. But, as they dismounted in the porch, he turned them into two pillars. When their father and their sister saw it, they wept. But the Prince bade them not to weep, for, as they had deserved, so it had befallen them.

Then they were married, and he made his father-in-law his Vizier. And we will leave them well, and return and find them better — God be praised!

THE THREE DAUGHTERS OF KING O'HARA

BY

JEREMIAH CURTIN

FROM *MYTHS AND FOLK-LORE OF IRELAND*, 1890

THERE was a king in Desmond whose name was Coluath O'Hara, and he had three daughters. On a time when the king was away from home, the eldest daughter took a thought that she 'd like to be married. So she went up in the castle, put on the cloak of darkness which her father had, and wished for the most beautiful man under the sun as a husband for herself.

She got her wish; for scarcely had she put off the cloak of darkness, when there came, in a golden coach with four horses, two black and two white, the finest man she had ever laid eyes on, and took her away.

When the second daughter saw what had happened to her sister, she put on the cloak of darkness, and wished for the next best man in the world as a husband.

She put off the cloak; and straightway there came, in a golden coach with four black horses, a man nearly as good as the first, and took her away.

The third sister put on the cloak, and wished for the best white dog in the world.

Presently he came, with one man attending, in a golden coach and four snow-white horses, and took the youngest sister away.

When the king came home, the stable-boy told him what had happened while he was gone. He was enraged beyond measure when he heard that his youngest daughter had wished for a white dog, and gone off with him.

When the first man brought his wife home he asked: "In what form will you have me in the daytime, - as I am now in the daytime, or as I am now at night?"

"As you are now in the daytime."

So the first sister had her husband as a man in the daytime; but at night he was a seal.

The second man put the same question to the middle sister, and got the same answer; so the second sister had her husband in the same form as the first.

When the third sister came to where the white dog lived, he asked her: " How will you have me to be in the daytime, as I am now in the day, or as I am now at night?"

"As you are now in the day."

So the white dog was a dog in the daytime, but the most beautiful of men at night.

After a time the third sister had a son; and one day, when her husband was going out to hunt, he warned her that if anything should happen the child, not to shed a tear on that account.

While he was gone, a great gray crow that used to haunt the place came and carried the child away when it was a week old.

Remembering the warning, she shed not a tear for the loss.

All went on as before till another son was born. The husband used to go hunting every day, and again he said she must not shed a tear if anything happened.

When the child was a week old a great gray crow came and bore him away; but the mother did not cry or drop a tear.

All went well till a daughter was born. When she was a week old a great gray crow came and swept her away. This time the mother dropped one tear on a handkerchief, which she took out of her pocket, and then put back again.

When the husband came home from hunting and heard what the crow had done, he asked the wife, " Have you shed tears this time?"

"I have dropped one tear," said she.

Then he was very angry; for he knew what harm she had done by dropping that one tear.

Soon after their father invited the three sisters to visit him and be present at a great feast in their honor. They sent messages, each from her own place, that they would come.

The king was very glad at the prospect of seeing his children; but the queen was grieved, and thought it a great disgrace that her youngest daughter had no one to come home with her but a white dog.

The white dog was in dread that the king wouldn't leave him inside with the company, but would drive him from the castle to the yard, and that the dogs outside wouldn't leave a patch of skin on his back, but would tear the life out of him.

The youngest daughter comforted him. "There is no danger to you," said she, "for wherever I am, you'll be, and wherever you go, I'll follow and take care of you."

When all was ready for the feast at the castle, and the company were assembled, the king was for banishing the white dog; but the youngest daughter would not listen to her father, - would not let the white dog out of her sight, but kept him near her at the feast, and divided with him the food that came to herself.

When the feast was over, and all the guests had gone, the three sisters went to their own rooms in the castle.

Late in the evening the queen took the cook with her, and stole in to see what was in her daughters' rooms. They were all asleep at the time. What should she see by the side of her youngest daughter but the most beautiful man she had ever laid eyes on.

Then she went to where the other two daughters were sleeping; and there, instead of the two men who brought them to the feast, were two seals, fast asleep.

The queen was greatly troubled at the sight of the seals. When she and the cook were returning, they came upon the skin of the white dog. She caught it up as she went, and threw it into the kitchen fire.

The skin was not five minutes in the fire when it gave a crack that woke not only all in the castle, but all in the country for miles around.

The husband of the youngest daughter sprang up. He was very angry and very sorry, and said:

"If I had been able to spend three nights with you under your father's roof, I should have got back my own form again for good, and could have been a man both in the day and the night; but now I must go."

He rose from the bed, ran out of the castle, and away he went as fast as ever his two legs could carry him, overtaking the one before him, and leaving the one behind. He was this way all that night and the next day; but he couldn't leave the wife, for she followed from the castle, was after him in the night and the day too, and never lost sight of him.

In the afternoon he turned, and told her to go back to her father; but she would not listen to him. At nightfall they came to the first house they had seen since leaving the castle. He turned and said:

"Do you go inside and stay in this house till morning; I'll pass the night outside where I am."

The wife went in. The woman of the house rose up, gave her a pleasant welcome, and put a good supper before her. She was not long in the house when a little boy came to her knee and called her "mother."

The woman of the house told the child to go back to his place, and not to come out again.

Here are a pair of scissors," said the woman of the house to the king's daughter, " and they will serve you well. Whatever ragged people you see, if you cut a piece off their rags, that moment they will have new clothes of cloth of gold."

She stayed that night, for she had good welcome. Next morning when she went out, her husband said: " You 'd better go home now to your father."

"I'll not go to my father if I have to leave you," said she.

So he went on, and she followed. It was that way all the day till night came; and at nightfall they saw another house at the foot of a hill, and again the husband stopped and said: "You go in; I'll stop outside till morning."

The woman of the house gave her a good welcome. After she had eaten and drunk, a little boy came out of another room, ran to her knee, and said," Mother." The woman of the house sent the boy back to where he had come from, and told him to stay there.

Next morning, when the princess was going out to her husband, the woman of the house gave her a comb, and said: "If you meet any person with a diseased and a sore head, and draw this comb over it three times, the head will be well, and covered with the most beautiful golden hair ever seen."

She took the comb, and went out to her husband.

"Leave me now," said he, "and go back to your own father."

"I will not," said she, " but I will follow you while I have the power." So they went forward that day, as on the other two.

At nightfall they came to a third house, at the foot of a hill, where the princess received a good welcome. After she had eaten supper, a little girl with only one eye came to her knee and said, "Mother."

The princess began to cry at sight of the child, thinking that she herself was the cause that it had but one eye. Then she put her hand into her pocket where she kept the handkerchief on which she had dropped the tear when the gray crow carried her infant away. She had never used the handkerchief since that day, for

166

there was an eye on it.

She opened the handkerchief, and put the eye in the girl's head. It grew into the socket that minute, and the child saw out of it as well as out of the other eye; and then the woman of the house sent the little one to bed.

Next morning, as the king's daughter was going out, the woman of the house gave her a whistle, and said: "Whenever you put this whistle to your mouth and blow on it, all the birds of the air will come to you from every quarter under the sun. Be careful of the whistle, as it may serve you greatly."

Go back to your father's castle," said the husband when she came to him, "for I must leave you to-day."

They went on together a few hundred yards, and then sat on a green hillock, and he told the wife:

"Your mother has come between us; but for her we might have lived together all our days. If I had been allowed to pass three nights with you in your father's house, I should have got back my form of a man both in the daytime and the night. The Queen of Tir na n-Og [the land of youth] enchanted and put on me a spell, that unless I could spend three nights with a wife under her father's roof in Erin, I should bear the form of a white dog one half of my time; but if the skin of the dog should be burned before the three nights were over, I must go down to her kingdom and marry the queen herself. And 't is to her I am going to-day. I have no power to stay, and I must leave you; so farewell, you'll never see me again on the upper earth."

He left her sitting on the mound, went a few steps forward to some bulrushes, pulled up one, and disappeared in the opening where the rush had been.

She stopped there, sitting on the mound lamenting, till evening, not knowing what to do. At last she bethought herself, and going to the rushes, pulled up a stalk, went down, followed her husband, and never stopped till she came to the lower land.

After a while she reached a small house near a splendid castle. She went into the house and asked, could she stay there till morning. "You can," said the woman of the house, " and welcome."

Next day the woman of the house was washing clothes, for that was how she made a living. The princess fell to and helped her with the work. In the course of that day the Queen of Tir na n-Og and the husband of the princess were married.

Near the castle, and not far from the washer-woman's, lived a henwife with two ragged little daughters. One of them came around the washer-woman's house to play. The child looked so poor and her clothes were so torn and dirty that the princess took pity on her, and cut the clothes with the scissors which she had.

That moment the most beautiful dress of cloth of gold ever seen on woman or child in that kingdom was on the henwife's daughter.

When she saw what she had on, the child ran home to her mother as fast as ever she could go.

"Who gave you that dress?" asked the henwife.

"A strange woman that is in that house beyond," said the little girl, pointing to the washer-woman's house.

The henwife went straight to the Queen of Tir na n-Og and said: " There is a strange woman in the place, who will be likely to take your husband from you, unless you banish her away or do something to her; for she has a pair of scissors different from anything ever seen or heard of in this country."

When the queen heard this she sent word to the princess that, unless the scissors were given up to her without delay, she would have the head off her.

The princess said she would give up the scissors if the queen would let her pass one night with her husband.

The queen answered that she was willing to give her the one night. The princess came and gave up the scissors, and went to her own husband; but the queen had given him a drink, and he fell asleep, and never woke till after the princess had gone in the morning.

Next day another daughter of the henwife went to the washer-woman's house to play. She was wretched-looking, her head being covered with scabs and sores.

The princess drew the comb three times over the child's head, cured it, and covered it with beautiful golden hair. The little girl ran home and told her mother how the strange woman had drawn the comb over her head, cured it, and given her beautiful golden hair.

The henwife hurried off to the queen and said: "That strange woman has a comb with wonderful power to cure, and give golden hair; and she'll take your husband from you unless you banish her or take her life."

The queen sent word to the princess that unless she gave up the comb, she would have her life.

The princess returned as answer that she would give up the comb if she might pass one night with the queen's husband.

The queen was willing, and gave her husband a draught as before. When the princess came, he was fast asleep, and did not waken till after she had gone in the morning.

On the third day the washerwoman and the princess went out to walk, and the first daughter of the henwife with them. When they were outside the town, the princess put the whistle to her mouth and blew. That moment the birds of the air flew to her from every direction in flocks. Among them was a bird of song and new tales.

The princess went to one side with the bird. " What means can I take," asked she, " against the queen to get back my husband? Is it best to kill her, and can I do it?

"It is very hard," said the bird, "to kill her. There is no one in all Tir na n-Og who is able to take her life but her own husband. Inside a holly-tree in front of the castle is a wether, in the wether a duck, in the duck an egg. and in that egg is her heart and life. No man in Tir na n-Og can cut that holly-tree but her husband."

The princess blew the whistle again. A fox and a hawk came to her. She caught and put them into two boxes, which the washerwoman had with her, and took them to her new home.

When the henwife's daughter went home, she told her mother about the whistle. Away ran the henwife to the queen, and said: "That strange woman has a whistle that brings together all the birds of the air, and she'll have your husband yet, unless you take her head."

"I'll take the whistle from her, anyhow," said the queen. So she sent for the whistle.

The princess gave answer that she would give up the whistle if she might pass one night with the queen's husband.

The queen agreed, and gave him a draught as on the other nights. He was asleep when the princess came and when she went away.

Before going, the princess left a letter with his servant for the queen's husband, in which she told how she had followed him to Tir na n-Og, and had given the scissors, the comb, and the whistle, to pass three nights in his company, but had not spoken to him because the queen had given him sleeping draughts; that the life of the queen was in an egg, the egg in a duck, the duck in a wether, the wether in a holly-tree in front of the castle, and that no man could split the tree but himself

As soon as he got the letter the husband took an axe, and went to the holly-tree. When he came to the tree he found the princess there before him, having the two boxes with the fox and the hawk in them.

He struck the tree a few blows; it split open, and out sprang the wether. He ran scarce twenty perches before the fox caught him. The fox tore him open; then the duck flew out. The duck had not flown fifteen perches when the hawk caught and killed her, smashing the egg. That instant the Queen of Tir na n-Og died.

The husband kissed and embraced his faithful wife. He gave a great feast; and when the feast was over, he burned the henwife with her house, built a palace for the washerwoman, and made his servant secretary.

They never left Tir na n-Og, and are living there happily now; and so may we live here.

THE KING OF ERIN AND THE QUEEN OF THE LONESOME ISLAND BY JEREMIAH CURTIN

FROM MYTHS AND FOLK-LORE OF IRELAND

THERE was a king in Erin long ago, and this I king went out hunting one day, but saw nothing till near sunset, when what should come across him but a black pig.

"Since I've seen nothing all day but this black pig, I'll be at her now," said the king; so he put spurs to his horse and raced after the pig.

When the pig was on a hill he was in the valley behind her; when he was on a hill, the pig was in the valley before him. At last they came to the sea-side, and the pig rushed out into the deep water straight from the shore. The king spurred on his horse and followed the black pig through the sea till his horse failed under him and was drowned.

Then the king swam on himself till he was growing weak, and said: "It was for the death of me that the black pig came in my way."

But he swam on some distance yet, till at last he saw land. The pig went up on an island; the king too went on shore, and said to himself: "Oh! it is for no good that I came here; there is neither house nor shelter to be seen." But he cheered up after a while, walked around, and said: "I'm a useless man if I can't find shelter in some place."

After going on a short space he saw a great castle in a valley before him. When he came to the front of the castle he saw that it had a low door with a broad threshold all covered with sharp-edged razors, and a low lintel of long-pointed needles. The path to the castle was covered with gravel of gold. The king came up, and went in with a jump over the razors and under the needles. When inside he saw a great fire on a broad hearth, and said to himself, "I'll sit down here, dry my clothes, and warm my body at this fire."

As he sat and warmed himself, a table came out before him with every sort of food and drink, without his seeing any one bring it.

"Upon my honor and power," said the king of Erin, "there is nothing bad in this! I'll eat and drink my fill."

Then he fell to, and ate and drank his fill. When he had grown tired, he looked behind him, and if he did he saw a fine room, and in it a bed covered with gold. "Well," said he, "I'll go back and sleep in that bed a while, I 'm so tired."

He stretched himself on the bed and fell asleep. In the night he woke up, and felt the presence of a woman in the room. He reached out his hand towards her and spoke, but got no answer; she was silent.

When morning came, and he made his way out of the castle, she spread a beautiful garden with her Druidic spells over the island, - so great that though he travelled through it all day he could not escape from it. At sunset he was back at the door of the castle; and in he went over the razors and under the needles, sat at the fire, and the table came out before him as on the previous evening. He ate, drank, and slept on the bed; and when he woke in the night, there was the woman

170

in the room but she was silent and unseen as before.

When he went out on the second morning the king of Erin saw a garden three times more beautiful than the one of the day before. He travelled all day, but could not escape, - could not get out of the garden. At sunset he was back at the door of the castle; in he went over the razors and under the needles, ate, drank, and slept, as before.

In the middle of the night he woke tip, and felt the presence of the woman in the room. "Well," said he, "it is a wonderful thing for me to pass three nights in a room with a woman, and not see her nor know who she is!"

"You won't have that to say again, king of Erin," answered a voice. And that moment the room was filled with a bright light, and the king looked upon the finest woman he had ever seen.

Well, king of Erin, you are on Lonesome Island. I am the black pig that enticed you over the land and through the sea to this place, and I am queen of Lonesome Island. My two sisters and I are under a Druidic spell, and we cannot escape from this spell till your son and mine shall free us. Now, king of Erin, I will give you a boat to-morrow morning, and do you sail away to your own kingdom."

In the morning she went with him to the sea-shore to the boat. The king gave the prow of the boat to the sea, and its stern to the land; then he raised the sails, and went his way. The music he had was the roaring of the wind with the whistling of eels, and he broke neither oar nor mast till he landed under his own castle in Erin.

Three quarters of a year after, the queen of Lonesome Island gave birth to a son. She reared him with care from day to day and year to year till he was a splendid youth. She taught him the learning of wise men one half of the day, and warlike exercises with Druidic spells the other half.

One time the young man, the prince of Lonesome Island, came in from hunting, and found his mother sobbing and crying.

"Oh! what has happened to you, mother?" he asked.

"My son, great grief has come on me. A friend of mine is going to be killed to-morrow."

"Who is he?

"The king of Erin. The king of Spain has come against him with a great army. He wishes to sweep him and his men from the face of the earth, and take the kingdom himself."

"Well, what can we do? If I were there, I'd help the king of Erin."

Since you say that, my son, I'll send you this very evening. With the power of my Druidic spells, you'll be in Erin in the morning."

The prince of Lonesome Island went away that night, and next morning at the rising of the sun he drew up his boat under the king's castle in Erin. He went ashore, and saw the whole land black with the forces of the king of Spain, who was getting ready to attack the king of Erin and sweep him and his men from the face of the earth.

The prince went straight to the king of Spain, and said, "I ask one day's truce."

"You shall have it, my champion," answered the king of Spain.

The prince then went to the castle of the king of Erin, and stayed there that day as a guest. Next morning early he dressed himself in his champion's array, and, taking his nine-edged sword, he went down alone to the king of Spain, and, standing before him, bade him guard himself.

They closed in conflict, the king of Spain with all his forces on one side, and the prince of Lonesome Island on the other, They fought an awful battle that day from sunrise till sunset. They made soft places hard, and hard places soft; they made high places low, and low places high; they brought water out of the centre of hard gray rocks, and made dry rushes soft in the most distant parts of Erin till sunset; and when the sun went down, the king of Spain and his last man were dead on the field.

Neither the king of Erin nor his forces took part in the battle. They had no need, and they had no chance.

Now the king of Erin had two sons, who were such cowards that they hid themselves from fright during the battle; but their mother told the king of Erin that her elder son was the man who had destroyed the king of Spain and all his men.

There was great rejoicing and a feast at the castle of the king of Erin. At the end of the feast the queen said: "I wish to give the last cup to this stranger who is here as a guest;" and taking him to an adjoining chamber which had a window right over the sea, she seated him in the open window and gave him a cup of drowsiness to drink. When he had emptied the cup and closed his eyes, she pushed him out into the darkness.

The prince of Lonesome Island swam on the water for four days and nights, till he came to a rock in the ocean, and there he lived for three months, eating the seaweeds of the rock, till one foggy day a vessel came near and the captain cried out: "We shall be wrecked on this rock!" Then he said, "There is some one on the rock; go and see who it is."

They landed, and found the prince, his clothes all gone, his body black from the seaweed, which was growing all over it.

"Who are you?" asked the captain.

"Give me first to eat and drink, and then I'll talk," said he.

They brought him food and drink; and when he had eaten and drunk, the prince said to the captain: "What part of the world have you come from?

"I have just sailed from Lonesome Island," said the captain. "I was obliged to sail away, for fire was coming from every side to burn my ship."

"Would you like to go back?"

"I should indeed."

"Well, turn around; you'll have no trouble if I am with you."

The captain returned. The queen of Lone-some Island was standing on the shore as the ship came in.

"Oh, my child!" cried she, "why have you been away so long?"

The queen of Erin threw me into the sea after I had kept the head of the king of Erin on him, and saved her life too.

"Well, my son, that will come up against the queen of Erin on another day."

Now, the prince lived on Lonesome Island three years longer, till one time he came home from hunting, and found his mother wringing her hands and shedding bitter tears.

"Oh! what has happened?" asked he.

"I am weeping because the king of Spain has gone to take vengeance on the king of Erin for the death of his father, whom you killed."

"Well, mother, I'll go to help the king of Erin, if you give me leave."

"Since you have said it, you shall go this very night."

He went to the shore. Putting the prow of his bark to the sea and her stern to land, he raised high the sails, and heard no sound as he went but the pleasant wind and the whistling of eels, till he pulled up his boat next morning under the castle of the king of Erin and went on shore.

The whole country was black with the troops of the king of Spain, who was just ready to attack, when the prince stood before him, and asked a truce till next morning.

"That you shall have, my champion," answered the king. So there was peace for that day.

Next morning at sunrise, the prince faced the king of Spain and his army, and there followed a struggle more terrible than that with his father; but at sunset neither the king of Spain nor one of his men was left alive.

The two sons of the king of Erin were frightened almost to death, and hid during the battle, so that no one saw them or knew where they were. But when the king of Spain and his army were destroyed, the queen said to the king: "My elder son has saved us." Then she went to bed, and taking the blood of a chicken in her mouth, spat it out, saying: "This is my heart's blood; and nothing can cure me now but three bottles of water from Tubber Tintye, the flaming well."

When the prince was told of the sickness of the queen of Erin, he came to her and said: "I'll go for the water if your two sons will go with me."

"They shall go," said the queen; and away went the three young men towards the East, in search of the flaming well.

In the morning they came to a house on the roadside; and going in, they saw a woman who had washed herself in a golden basin which stood before her. She was then wetting her head with the water in the basin, and combing her hair with a golden comb. She threw back her hair, and looking at the prince, said: " You are welcome, sister's son. What is on you? Is it the misfortune of the world that has brought you here?"

"It is not; I am going to Tubber Tintye for three bottles of water."

"That is what you'll never do; no man can cross the fiery river or go through the enchantments around Tubber Tintye. Stay here with me, and I'll give you all I have."

"No, I cannot stay, I must go on."

"Well, you'll be in your other aunt's house tomorrow night, and she will tell you all."

Next morning, when they were getting ready to take the road, the elder son of the queen of Erin was frightened at what he had heard, and said:

"I am sick; I cannot go farther."

"Stop here where you are till I come back," said the prince. Then he went on with the younger brother, till at sunset they came to a house where they saw a woman wetting her head from a golden basin, and combing her hair with a golden comb. She threw back her hair, looked at the prince, and said: "You are welcome, sister's son! What brought you to this place? Was it the misfortune of the world that brought you to live under Druidic spells like me and my sisters?" This was the elder sister of the queen of the Lonesome Island.

"No," said the prince; "I am going to Tubber Tintye for three bottles of water from the flaming well."

"Oh, sister's son, it's a hard journey you're on! But stay here to-night; to-morrow morning I'll tell you all."

In the morning the prince's aunt said: "The queen of the Island of Tubber Tintye has an enormous castle, in which she lives. She has a countless army of giants, beasts, and monsters to guard the castle and the flaming well. There are thousands upon thousands of them, of every form and size. When they get drowsy, and sleep comes on them, they sleep for seven years without waking. The queen has twelve attendant maidens, who live in twelve chambers. She is in the thirteenth and innermost chamber herself. The queen and the maidens sleep during the same seven years as the giants and beasts. When the seven years are over, they all wake up, and none of them sleep again for seven other years. If any man could enter the castle during the seven years of sleep, he could do what he liked. But the island on which the castle stands is girt by a river of fire and surrounded by a belt of poison-trees."

The aunt now blew on a horn, and all the birds of the air gathered around her from every place under the heavens, and she asked each in turn where it dwelt, and each told her; but none knew of the flaming well, till an old eagle said: "I left Tubber Tintye to-day."

"How are all the people there?" asked the aunt.

"They are all asleep since yesterday morning," answered the old eagle.

The aunt dismissed the birds; and turning to the prince, said, "Here is a bridle for you. Go to the stables, shake the bridle, and put it on whatever horse runs out to meet you."

Now the second son of the queen of Erin said:

"I am too sick to go farther."

"Well, stay here till I come back," said the prince, who took the bridle and went out.

The prince of the Lonesome Island stood in front of his aunt's stables, shook the bridle, and out came a dirty, lean little shaggy horse.

"Sit on my back, son of the king of Erin and the queen of Lonesome Island," said the little shaggy horse.

This was the first the prince had heard of his father. He had often wondered who he might be, but had never heard who he was before.

He mounted the horse, which said: "Keep a firm grip now, for I shall clear the river of fire at a single bound, and pass the poison-trees; but if you touch any part of the trees, even with a thread of the clothing that's on you, you'll never eat another bite; and as I rush by the end of the castle of Tubber Tintye with the speed of the wind, you must spring from my back through an open window that is there; and if you don't get in at the window, you 're done for. I'll wait for you outside till you are ready to go back to Erin."

The prince did as the little horse told him. They crossed the river of fire, escaped the touch of the poison-trees, and as the horse shot past the castle, the prince sprang through the open window, and came down safe and sound inside.

The whole place, enormous in extent, was filled with sleeping giants and monsters of sea and land, - great whales, long slippery eels, bears, and beasts of every form and kind. The prince passed through them and over them till he came to a great stairway. At the head of the stairway he went into a chamber, where he found the most beautiful woman he had ever seen, stretched on a couch asleep. " I'll have nothing to say to you," thought he, and went on to the next; and so he looked into twelve chambers. In each was a woman more beautiful than the one before. But when he reached the thirteenth chamber and opened the door, the flash of gold took the sight from his eyes. He stood a while till the sight came back, and then entered. In the great bright chamber was a golden couch, resting on wheels of gold. The wheels turned continually; the couch went round and round, never stopping night or day. On the couch lay the queen of Tubber Tintye; and if her twelve maidens were beautiful, they would not be beautiful if seen near her. At the foot of the couch was Tubber Tintye itself, - the well of fire. There was a golden cover upon the well, and it went around continually with the couch of the queen.

"Upon my word," said the prince, "I'll rest here a while." And he went up on the couch, and never left it for six days and nights.

On the seventh morning he said, " It is time for me now to leave this place." So he came down and filled the three bottles with water from the flaming well. In the golden chamber was a table of gold, and on the table a leg of mutton with a loaf of bread; and if all the men in Erin were to eat for a twelvemonth from the table, the mutton and the bread would be in the same form after the eating as before.

The prince sat down, ate his fill of the loaf and the leg of mutton, and left them as he had found them. Then he rose up, took his three bottles, put them in his wallet, and was leaving the chamber, when he said to himself: "It would be a shame to go away without leaving something by which the queen may know who was here while she slept." So he wrote a letter, saying that the son of the king of Erin and the queen of the Lonesome Island had spent six days and nights in the golden chamber of Tubber Tintye, had taken away three bottles of water from the flaming well, and had eaten from the table of gold. Putting this letter under the pillow of the queen, he went out, stood in the open window, sprang on the back of the lean and shaggy little horse, and passed the trees and the river unharmed.

When they were near his aunt's house, the horse stopped, and said: " Put your hand into my ear, and draw out of it a Druidic rod; then cut me into four quarters, and strike each quarter with the rod. Each one of them will become the son of a king, for four princes were enchanted and turned into the lean little shaggy horse that carried you to Tubber Tintye. When you have freed the four princes from this form you can free your two aunts from the spell that is on them, and take them with you to Lonesome Island."

The prince did as the horse desired; and straightway four princes stood before him, and thanking him for what he had done, they departed at once, each to his own kingdom.

The prince removed the spell from his aunts, and, travelling with them and the two sons of the queen of Erin, all soon appeared at the castle of the king.

When they were near the door of their mother's chamber, the elder of the two sons of the queen of Erin stepped up to the prince of Lonesome Island, snatched the three bottles from the wallet that he had at his side, and running up to his mother's bed, said:

"Here, mother, are the three bottles of water which I brought you from Tubber Tintye."

"Thank you, my son; you have saved my life," said she.

The prince went on his bark and sailed away with his aunts to Lonesome Island, where he lived with his mother seven years.

When seven years were over, the queen of Tubber Tintye awoke from her sleep in the golden chamber; and with her the twelve maidens and all the giants, beasts, and monsters that slept in the great castle.

When the queen opened her eyes, she saw a boy about six years old playing by himself on the floor. He was very beautiful and bright, and he had gold on his forehead and silver on his poll. When she saw the child, she began to cry and wring her hands, and said: " Some man has been here while I slept."

Straightway she sent for her Seandallglic (old blind sage), told him about the child, and asked:

"What am I to do now?"

The old blind sage thought a while, and then said: "Whoever was here must be a hero; for the child has gold on his forehead and silver on his poll, and he never went from this place without leaving his name behind him. Let search be made, and we shall know who he was."

Search was made, and at last they found the letter of the prince under the pillow of the couch. The queen was now glad, and proud of the child.

Next day she assembled all her forces, her giants and guards; and when she had them drawn up in line, the army was seven miles long from van to rear. The queen opened through the river of fire a safe way for the host, and led it on till she came to the castle of the king of Erin. She held all the land near the castle, so the king had the sea on one side, and the army of the queen of Tubber Tintye on the other, ready to destroy him and all that he had. The queen sent a herald for the king to come down.

"What are you going to do?" asked the king when he came to her tent. "I have had trouble enough in my life already, without having more of it now."

"Find for me," said the queen, "the man who came to my castle and entered the golden chamber of Tubber Tintye while I slept, or I'll sweep you and all you have from the face of the earth.

The king of Erin called down his elder son, and asked: "Did you enter the chamber of the queen of Tubber Tintye?"

"I did."

"Go, then, and tell her so, and save us."

He went; and when he told the queen, she said:

"If you entered my chamber, then mount my gray steed."

He mounted the steed; and if he did, the steed rose in the air with a bound, hurled him off his back, in a moment, threw him on a rock, and dashed the brains out of his head.

The king called down his second son, who said that he had been in the golden chamber. Then he mounted the gray steed, which killed him as it had his brother.

Now the queen called the king again, and said:

"Unless you bring the man who entered my golden chamber while I slept, I 'll not leave a sign of you or anything you have upon the face of the earth."

Straightway the king sent a message to the queen of Lonesome Island, saying: "Come to me with your son and your two sisters!"

The queen set out next morning, and at sunset she drew up her boat under the castle of the king of Erin. Glad were they to see her at the castle, for great dread was on all.

Next morning the king went down to the queen of Tubber Tintye, who said: "Bring me the man who entered my castle, or I'll destroy you and all you have in Erin this day."

The king went up to the castle; immediately the prince of Lonesome Island went to the queen.

"Are you the man who entered my castle?" asked she.

"I don't know," said the prince.

"Go up now on my gray steed! " said the queen.

He sat on the gray steed, which rose under him into the sky. The prince stood on the back of the horse, and cut three times with his sword as he went up under the sun. When he came to the earth again, the queen of Tubber Tintye ran over to him, put his head on her bosom, and said:

"You are the man."

Now she called the queen of Erin to her tent, and drawing from her own pocket a belt of silk, slender as a cord, she said: " Put this on."

The queen of Erin put it on, and then the queen of Tubber Tintye said: "Tighten, belt! " The belt tightened till the queen of Erin screamed with pain. "Now tell me," said the queen of Tubber Tintye, "who was the father of your elder son."

"The gardener," said the queen of Erin.

Again the queen of Tubber Tintye said:

"Tighten, belt!" The queen of Erin screamed worse than before; and she had good reason, for she was cut nearly in two. " Now tell me who was the father of your second son."

"The big brewer," said the queen of Erin.

Said the queen of Tubber Tintye to the king of Erin: "Get this woman dead."

The king put down a big fire then, and when it was blazing high, he threw the wife in, and she was destroyed at once.

Now do you marry the queen of Lonesome Island, and my child will be grandchild to you and to her," said the queen of Tubber Tintye.

This was done, and the queen of Lonesome Island became queen of Erin and lived in the castle by the sea. And the queen of Tubber Tintye married the prince of Lonesome Island, the champion who entered the golden chamber while she slept.

Now the king of Erin sent ten ships with messages to all the kings of the world, inviting them to come to the wedding of the queen of Tubber Tintye and his son, and to his own wedding with the queen of Lonesome Island.

The queen removed the Druidic spells from her giants, beasts, and monsters; then went home, and made the prince of Lonesome Island king of Tubber Tintye and lord of the golden chamber.

THE BROWN BULL OF RINGLEWOOD

BY

PETER BUCHAN

FROM *ANCIENT SCOTTISH TALES*, 1908

WHEN old king Coil lived, he had three pretty daughters, on whom he doted much, and his chief enjoyment was in seeing them happy. It so happened one day while he was awalking for his recreation, that he met with an old man in apparently decayed circumstances, who asked charity of him, the king being well known for his benevolence to all those in need.   On receiving an alms, the poor man said, that as he was not an earthly person, but merely assumed such an appearance to try his generosity, and having found him liberal and kind, he would reward him with any three wishes he could think of; or as he had three beautiful daughters, it might be more agreeable to him to give each of them a wish, which he promised to see accomplished. Having parted with this stranger, wondering as he went home, if what he had promised would ever come to pass. On arriving at his palace, in a jocular manner, he told his oldest daughter to wish for her heart's desire, and she should have it, be what it would. He went to the other two daughters and told them the same.

The oldest daughter having no sooner been informed of this, than she wished the king of Westmoreland would come and marry her; which was no sooner wished for than done, as he carried her off to his kingdom. The second daughter having seen the efficacy of her sister's wish, immediately wished that the king of Southland would come and marry her; this also having been done to the satisfaction of all concerned. The king now asked his youngest daughter what she wished for; when, in a jesting manner, she wished that the Brown Bull of Ringlewood would come and carry her off.

She had   scarcely uttered the words when the Bull appeared, and having mounted her on his horns, immediately   carried her off to his castle, when he disappeared, but at night returned to the castle, being metamorphosed into the figure and shape of a man, he lay down beside her, and continued going from in the morning, and returning in the evening to the castle, during the space of three years, when the young princess bore unto him three beautiful sons.

Having wearied with this way of living, she at length ventured to ask an old woman who frequented the castle, why her husband assumed the appearance of a Brown Bull through the day, but came home a handsome young man at night. The old woman having instructed her to burn the Bull's hide which lay above his bed, some morning before he got out of his bed. Having done as directed, the skin went out of the chimney with a noise like thunder. The young prince, for so he was, immediately awoke from his slumber; rose from his bed, and told the princess that it was time for him to depart unto a far country. She asked him to what place he belonged, and he told her his father was king of a country far beyond the sea, to which he intended going immediate!, for he had been kept by some magical power in the shape and likeness which she had seen him for many years, but now the charm was broken. The princess wished much to accompany him hither, which he agreed to, but desired her never to look behind, or she would forget all that had past. At length they arrived at a most beautiful hill, pure as crystal, and as transparent as air, which was called the hill of forgetfulness. On arriving at this hill the princess could not by any means contrive to ascend it. He therefore requested her to look between her and the sky, And there she would a castle spy.

Into this castle he desired her to put one of his boys, where he would be well educated, clothed and fed. In the same manner he requested of her to look east and west, and she would see other castles, into which she would put her other two sons. The prince having ascended the hill himself, entirely forgot her, so that she was obliged to go and serve seven years as a cook to a nobleman that lived hard by the hill of forgetfulness, before he would give her any assistance to mount the hill. Her task having been accomplished, the people of the castle whom she had served, provided her with everything necessary for her journey, which on receiving, she went away rejoicing, and ascended the hill with ease. On reaching the top, she met with an old woman who requested her to pull for her three of the pears that hung on a tree in the midst of a garden through which she had to pass, and she would reward her with three eggs which would be of the utmost consequence to her in her after life, if well managed. She was not, however, to open them upon every emergency, upon any consideration whatever, but to wait patiently till she was very hard beset, and saw no other way of accomplishing her designed purpose. Having thus obtained the three wonderful eggs, she went in pursuit of a lodging and applying for the same at the king's palace, she was told, as the young prince was to be married soon, she could not be accommodated there, as all were bustle and confusion.

On hearing this, she was greatly cast down; but recollecting herself, she broke one of her eggs, when out sprung a little wheel spinning gold yarn. At this instant, the queen passing by, requested to have the wheel; but upon no other terms would the young princess part with it than for a night of the young prince. This she was denied; but as no other thing could purchase the wheel, she at last consented, but gave him such a powder, and enchanted bed clothes, that during the right he never wakened; so that her labour was lost. The second night came, when she broke the second egg, and out there came a reel, reeling gold yarn. The queen spied it also, and got it on the same terms. The third egg was broken, when out of it came a singing bird. The queen must needs be the purchaser of it with the other two, when the princess consented on the former terms. At length a bird requested her to take the bed clothes and throw them all to the foot of the bed, and the prince would immediately thereafter awaken. This having been done, the prince awaked from his drowsy slumber, and on recognising his former consort, he renewed his former love and obligations to her, and promised her his hand in a public manner. He then caused a large chair to be placed in the midst of the palace, intimating at the time, that whoever filled it best, was to be his wife. This caused many to try it but all in vain, till his former prialcess made the same attempt, when she sat down in it with ease, and graced it. Immediately after the prince set her sons beside her, one on each side, and the youngest on her knee. They were then publicly married, and lived happy ever after.

THE STORY OF FIVE HEADS (SOUTH AFRICA)

BY

GEORGE MCCALL THEAL

FROM *KAFFIR (XHOSA) FOLK-LORE*, 1886

HERE was once a man living in a certain place, who had two daughters big enough to be married.

One day the man went over the river to another village, which was the residence of a great chief The people asked him to tell them the news. He replied, that there was no news in the place that he came from. Then the man inquired about the news of their place. They said the news of their place was that the chief wanted a wife.

The man went home and said to his two daughters: "Which of you wishes to be the wife of a chief?"

The eldest replied: "I wish to be the wife of a chief, my father." The name of that girl was Mpunzikazi.

The man said: "At that village which I visited, the chief wishes for a wife; you, my daughter, shall go."

The man called all his friends, and assembled a large company to go with his daughter to the village of the chief. But the girl would not consent that those people should go with her.

She said: "I will go alone to be the wife of the chief."

Her father replied: "How can you, my daughter, say such a thing? Is it not so that when a girl goes to present herself to her husband she should be accompanied by others? Be not foolish, my daughter."

The girl still said: "I will go alone to be the wife of the chief."

Then the man allowed his daughter to do as she chose. She went alone, no bridal party accompanying her, to present herself at the village of the chief who wanted a wife.

As Mpunzikazi was in the path, she met a mouse.

The mouse said: "Shall I show you the way?"

The girl replied: "Just get away from before my eyes."

The mouse answered If you do like this, you will not succeed."

Then she met a frog.

The frog said: "Shall I show you the way?"

Mpunzikazi replied: "You are not worthy to speak to me, as I am to be the wife of a chief."

The frog said: "Go on then; you will see afterwards what will happen."

When the girl got tired, she sat down under a tree to rest. A boy who was herding goats in that place came to her, he being very hungry.

The boy said: "Where are you going to, my eldest sister? "

Mpunzikazi replied in an angry voice: "Who are you that you should speak to me? just get away from before me."

The boy said: "I am very hungry; will you not give me of your food? "

She answered "Get away quickly."

The boy said: "You will not return if you do this."

She went on her way again, and met with an old woman sitting by a big stone.

The old woman said: "I will give you advice. You will meet with trees that will laugh at you: you must not laugh in return. You will see a bag of thick milk: you must not eat of it. You will meet a man whose head is under his arm: you must not take water from him."

Mpunzikazi answered: "You ugly thing! who are you that you should advise me?"

The old woman continued in saying those words.

The girl went on. She came to a place where were many trees. The trees laughed at her, and she laughed at them in return. She saw a bag of thick milk, and she ate of it. She met a man carrying his head under his arm, and she took water to drink from him.

She came to the river of the village of the chief. She saw a girl there dipping water from the river. The girl said: "Where are you going to, my sister? "

Mpunzikazi replied: "Who are you that you should call me sister? I am going to be the wife of a chief."

The girl drawing water was the sister of the chief. She said: "Wait, I will give you advice. Do not enter the village by this side."

Mpunzikazi did not stand to listen, but just went on.

She reached the village of the chief. The people asked her where she came from and what she wanted.

She answered: "I have come to be the wife of the chief."

They said: "Who ever saw a girl go without a retinue to be a bride? "

They said also: "The chief is not at home; you must prepare food for him, that when he comes in the evening he may eat."

They gave her millet to grind. She ground it very coarse, and made bread that was not nice to eat.

In the evening she heard the sound of a great wind. That wind was the coming of the chief. He was a big snake with five heads and large eyes. Mpunzikazi was very much frightened when she saw him. He sat down before the door and told her to bring his food. She brought the bread which she had made. Makanda Mahlanu (Five Heads) was not satisfied with that bread. He said: "You shall not be my wife," and he struck her with his tail and killed her.

Afterwards the sister of Mpunzikazi said to her father: "I also wish to be the wife of a chief."

Her father replied: "It is well, my daughter; it is right that you should wish to be a bride."

The man called all his friends, and a great retinue prepared to accompany the bride. The name of the girl was Mpunzanyana.

In the way they met a mouse.

The mouse said: "Shall I show you the road?"

Mpunzanyana replied: "If you will show me the way I shall be glad."

Then the mouse pointed out the way.

She came into a valley, where she saw an old woman standing by a tree.

The old woman said to her: "You will come to a place where two paths branch off. You must take the little one, because if you take the big one you will not be fortunate."

Mpunzanyana replied: "I will take the little path, my mother." She went on.

Afterwards she met a cony.

The cony said: "The village of the chief is close by. You will meet a by the river: you must speak nicely to her. They will give you millet to grind: you must grind it well. When you see your husband, you must not be afraid."

She said: "I will do as you say, cony."

In the river she met the chief's sister carrying water.

The chief's sister said: "Where are you going to?"

Mpunzanyana replied: "This is the end of my journey."

The chief's sister said: "What is the object of your coming to this place?"

Mpunzanyana replied: "I am with a bridal party. "

The chief's, sister said: "That is right, but will you not be afraid when you see your husband?"

Mpunzanyana answered: "I will not be afraid."

The chief's sister pointed out the hut in which she should stay. Food was given to the bridal party. The mother of the chief took millet and gave to the bride, saying, "You must prepare food for your husband. He is not here now, but he will come in the evening."

In the evening she heard a very strong wind, which made the hut shake. The poles fell, but she did not run out. Then she saw the chief Makanda Mahlanu coming. He asked for food. Mpunzanyana took the bread which she had made, and gave it to him. He was very much pleased with that food, and said:

"You shall be my wife." He gave her very many ornaments.

Afterwards Makanda Mahlanu became a man, and Mpunzanyana continued to be the wife he loved best.